Whispers from the Shadows

Books in The Culper Ring Series
BY ROSEANNA M. WHITE

BOOK 1—*Ring of Secrets*

▶ *To Watch Book Trailer*
http://bit.ly/RingofSecrets

Fairchild's Lady
(free e-novella)

BOOK 2—*Whispers from the Shadows*

A Hero's Promise
(free e-novella)

BOOK 3—*Circle of Spies*

ROSEANNA
M. WHITE

HARVEST HOUSE PUBLISHERS
EUGENE, OREGON

Scripture quotations are from the King James Version of the Bible.

Cover by Garborg Design Works, Savage, Minnesota

Cover photos © Chris Garborg; Bigstock/avdbrandt, Chris Marion

Some of the prayers are taken from *The Valley of Vision: A Collection of Puritan Prayers and Devotions*, published by Banner of Truth, www.banneroftruth.org.

This is a work of fiction. Names, characters, places, and incidents are products of the author's imagination or are used fictitiously. Any resemblance to actual persons, living or dead, is entirely coincidental.

WHISPERS FROM THE SHADOWS
Copyright © 2013 by Roseanna M. White
Published by Harvest House Publishers
Eugene, Oregon 97402
www.harvesthousepublishers.com

Library of Congress Cataloging-in-Publication Data
    White, Roseanna M.
    Whispers from the shadows / Roseanna M. White.
    pages cm. — (Culper Ring series ; book 2)
    ISBN 978-0-7369-5101-2 (pbk.)
    ISBN 978-0-7369-5102-9 (eBook)
    1. Women spies—Fiction. 2. United States—History—War of 1812—Fiction. 3. Maryland—History—War of 1812—Fiction. I. Title.
    PS3623.H578785W48 2013
    813'.6—dc23

                                                    2013000624

Printed in the United States of America

       13 14 15 16 17 18 19 20 21 /LB-JH/ 10 9 8 7 6 5 4 3 2 1

To my sister, Jennifer.
Whenever I write a heroine with a knack for art—
or a hero more than a foot taller than said heroine—
I think of you (and that towering brother-in-law of mine).
You bring beauty to my life,
and I'm proud to be your Pooky.

Acknowledgments

With every book I write, it seems the list of people who help me grows longer. As always, I have to start with my awesome-beyond-imagining family. My husband, David, who gets excited over minute historical details with me. My adorable kids, Xoë and Rowyn, who look at me every day and ask, "Aren't you done writing that one yet?" My mother-in-law, who saves my sanity with a weekly babysitting time. My parents, for their never-ending encouragement and faith. My grandparents, for their pride in me. And my sister and brother-in-law, both artists and art teachers, for inspiring me.

I have an amazing collection of friends who form my support group. Stephanie, who is subjected to every random thought to flutter through my head—the price of being my best friend. Amanda, who is always so quick to read my chapters and offer her fabulous historical eye. Dina, with her outstanding instinct for plot. Thanks to Naomi for being a brainstorming buddy, and to "Louisiana Rachel" for reading all my manuscripts to check the fashion details for me. I have to deliver my gratitude to Laurie Alice, who sent me a list of research books to read before attempting to write this era, and all the ladies in my prayer group—I know I can go to you with hopes and fears big and small, and that you'll stand with me before our Father.

And, finally, the team at Harvest House. I'm pretty sure I have the most fantastic publishing family in the world, and the more we work together, the more I appreciate each and every one of you who toil to make these books a success. Special thanks to Kim, for listening and laughing with me over all my random questions, for being my champion and friend—I couldn't ask for a better editor. And, of course, my agent, Karen Ball, who wows me with her expertise and never fails to make me laugh. I couldn't possibly write this series without you all.

Ye were sometimes darkness, but
now are ye light in the Lord:
walk as children of light...
See then that ye walk circumspectly,
not as fools, but as wise,
redeeming the time, because the days are evil.

EPHESIANS 5:8,15-16

❧

"We have the greatest opportunity the world has ever seen,
as long as we remain honest—which will be as long as
we can keep the attention of our people alive.
If they once become inattentive to public affairs,
you and I, and Congress and Assemblies, judges and governors,
would all become wolves."

THOMAS JEFFERSON

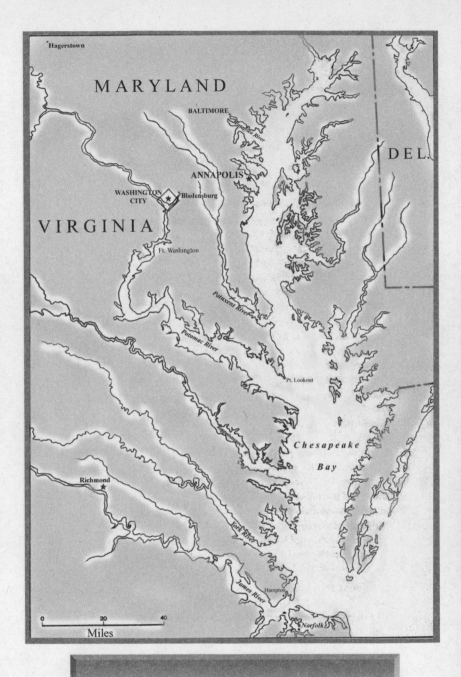

THE CHESAPEAKE BAY REGION

One

The servants hefting her trunks onto the carriage might as well have been loading her coffin. Gwyneth Fairchild pulled her pelisse close and gazed across Hanover Square with a sick feeling in her stomach. Surely she would awaken from this nightmare and walk down to the breakfast room to find Papa smiling at her. He would speak and say something that actually made sense.

Not like yesterday.

She shut her eyes against the image of all that was familiar, all that she might never see again. What if the *Scribe* went down? Was attacked by a renegade French ship or those dreadful American pirates? What if, assuming she made it to Annapolis, they killed her the moment she stepped ashore?

Annapolis. Had Papa not looked so sorrowful, so determined when he said that word yesterday, she would have thought he had gone mad.

His hand settled on her shoulder now, warm and large. Those hands had steadied her all her life. Capable, that was what General Isaac Fairchild had always been. Capable and steady and so very noble.

All that was worthy of love and respect. So surely she could trust him now when logic and reason said she couldn't.

"I know it makes little sense to you, dear heart." He touched her chin, a silent bid for her to look at him. She found his eyes gleaming with moisture he would never shed. Not when anyone could see him, though she had heard his heartrending sobs when Mama died last fall. "I wish there were another way, but there is not."

Another way *for what?* He hadn't said, wouldn't say. Gwyneth drew in a tremulous breath and tried to stand tall and proud, the way Mama had taught her, the way Papa himself had instilled. To convey with her posture that she was the great-granddaughter of a duke, the grand-daughter of two earls, the daughter of a general.

A daughter sent into exile for no apparent reason. Separated from all those she loved, the only people left in the world who mattered. "Papa—"

"I know." He leaned in and pressed a kiss to her forehead. "I do. But I cannot entrust you to anyone but the Lanes."

A light mist descended, heavier than fog but too tame to be called rain. At this moment, a thunderstorm would have better matched her confusion. "Please tell me what is happening. Why must you entrust me to anyone? And if you must, why not Aunt Poole or Aunt Gates?"

His jaw moved for a moment but no words came. Nay, he simply looked past her, his eyes searching for something unseen. Then he sighed. "The Lanes will welcome you and take care of you, Gwyn. I will follow as quickly as I can. A month at the outside. No more."

Exactly what he said yesterday too. He would give no explanation as to why he was sending her to a nation with whom they were at war, across the Atlantic to a family she had met only once, when she was but a tot.

"Papa, your words hint at danger, but what could threaten me here more than the sea and its pirates? The French, the Americans?"

"The French ought to pose no threat now that we've subdued them." He reached inside his coat of blazing red and pulled out an envelope. "In all likelihood your ship will reach harbor safely, but if by chance you do encounter American privateers, offer them this."

She frowned as she took the envelope. It was too thin to contain anything but a single sheet of paper. "What—"

"Trust me. 'Twill suffice." Chatter from the house grew louder, and Papa looked away again, to the nearing housekeeper and gardener. "There are the Wesleys. Time to go."

A million arguments sprang to her tongue. She didn't want to leave. Not her home, not him, not all she held dear. Not her first Season, the one that had been put off because of Mama's illness last year. Not her friends.

And what about Sir Arthur? She hadn't even spoken to him to tell him she was leaving, hadn't dared send a note. "Papa, Sir Arthur…"

"It isn't to be, Gwyn, not now. Perhaps when this has passed, when it is safe for you to return."

Tears burned, begging to be set loose, but she clenched her teeth and blinked. How had it come to this? Promise had finally shone its light again. Shopping with Aunt Gates had made it feel as though Mama were with her still. Making the rounds with her friends had finally distracted her from the loss. Getting vouchers for Almack's, and then Sir Arthur's court—she had, at long last, looked forward to the future.

"Please don't cry, dear heart." Papa thumbed away a wily tear that escaped her blockade and kissed her forehead again. "Up with you, now. You must be at the docks soon."

Instead, she surged forward and wrapped her arms around him. "I don't want to leave you, Papa. I can't. Don't make me go. Or come with me."

He held her close. "Would that I could. Would that I didn't have to bid goodbye, yet again, to the one who matters most." He gave her another squeeze, another kiss, and then he set her back. His eyes were rimmed with red. "I love you, Gwyneth. Go with God."

He let her go and pivoted on his heel, all but charging back into the house. She almost wished she could resent him, but how could she, seeing his struggle? Whatever his reasons, they must be valid.

And whatever his reasons, they must be dire. A shiver coursed up her spine and made the mist seem colder. Isaac Fairchild was a respected general, a man loved by all. A man of considerable sway in London and beyond. If there were something frightening enough that he must send her away, was planning on leaving himself—

And for America, no less. Would he be going there to take

command of troops? Possibly. Though why would he be secretive about it? But then, there was much about Papa's work he could not discuss. Secrets, always secrets.

"All's secure, Miss Fairchild," the driver called down from the bench.

She slipped the envelope into her reticule and took a step toward the Wesleys. They, at least, would provide familiar faces for the journey. They would be an anchor on the foreign seas.

Quick hoofbeats snagged her attention. "Miss Fairchild!"

Her eyes went wide when she saw the dashing figure astride the horse. Sir Arthur reined to a halt beside the carriage and leaped down, fervor ablaze in his eyes.

"Miss Fairchild." He gripped her hands as he searched her face with his gaze. He had the loveliest brown eyes, so warm and beckoning, the perfect fit to his straight nose and sculpted mouth. "Is it true, then? Broffield just told me that Miss Gregory said you were leaving Town."

"I…" He was holding her hands. Sir Arthur Hart, Knight of the Order of Saint Patrick, presumed heir to a viscountcy, the most sought-after bachelor in England, grasped her fingers as if he never intended to let go. The mass of confusion inside twisted. "Yes, it is true. My father…"

He eased closer, his gaze so compelling she feared she might drown in it. "Something to do with military business, then? You will return soon?"

"I don't know. I don't think Papa knows."

"Dear Miss Fairchild. Gwyneth." His fingers tightened around hers, much like the band around her chest. Never before had he spoken her given name. Hearing it in his rich tenor, spoken with such affection, made her fear her tears would overcome her after all. "Why must you go with him? Can you not stay here with your aunt?"

Her attempt at swallowing got stuck in her throat. "I am all Papa has now since my mother passed away, and he is loath to be separated." True, so true. Why, then, was he sending her an ocean away to a hostile land?

"But surely there is a way to convince him. What if…" He paused and then swallowed before using their joined hands to pull her closer. "What if you were betrothed?"

Her heart quickened inside her, beating a desperate tattoo against her ribs. *Would* that change anything? Could it? "I…don't know."

"Gwyneth." Oh, he made her name into music. The breeze toyed with his honey-colored hair under the brim of his hat, making her itch to touch the curls. "My darling, I have such a love and admiration for you. If you would feel inclined toward accepting my hand, I will speak with your father this very moment."

At first all she could think was *He proposed!* Then she drew in a quick breath and nodded with too much enthusiasm. "Of course I am inclined if he agrees. Only…" She drew away when he moved closer still, recalling Papa's discomposure mere minutes before. "Let me speak with him first, as he was out of countenance."

"Certainly. Yes. Anything." He laughed and raised her hands to kiss her knuckles. As if surprised she had said yes. "I will take a turn through your garden to try to calm myself."

"Perfect." If only she could be sure Papa would agree. If only she could be sure that, if not, Sir Arthur would wait for her. She pulled away, but he snagged her hand again.

"Gwyneth. Darling." He smiled, so bright and handsome it made her doubt trouble could exist. "I will make you very happy."

A smile stole onto her lips. It melted away again in a moment, but he had turned toward the garden by then.

Mrs. Wesley snagged her attention with a shooing motion toward the door. "You had better hurry, love. If the general does not change his mind, we must hasten on our way."

Gwyneth flew through the mist up the steps to the door and back into the house. For a moment she paused to breathe in home, but she hadn't time to savor it. If her mission went well, she needn't say good-bye to it at all.

Please, Lord. Please let him relent.

She sped down the hallway and around the corner toward Papa's study. He always ended up there, either busy at work or staring at the picture of Mama she'd painted for him. A professional portrait hung in the drawing room, but he said she had done the better job. Praise which always made her heart expand.

The study door was before her by the time she realized voices spilled out. Two of them—though when had anyone else arrived? Surely no servant would dare speak over Papa like this.

"Isaac, listen to yourself!"

Gwyneth froze a step from the door. It was open a crack, letting her look in, though only the corner of the desk was visible, and just behind it, where Papa stood. But she recognized Uncle Gates's voice.

"'Isaac' now, is it?" Papa's laugh sounded dry. "Odd how you only remember our familial ties when we disagree. Otherwise it is always my rank to which you appeal."

A loud bang made Gwyneth jump. Uncle's fist connecting with wood, perhaps? "Blast it, Fairchild, it's your rank you are abusing!"

"No! 'Tis my rank I honor. Someone, Gates, must do what is right. Someone must stand for justice rather than—"

"Hang all that noble rot." A nasty curse spilled from Uncle Gates's lips as glass shattered. Gwyneth recoiled, staring in horror at the sliver of room. What keepsake had he destroyed? The vase Mama had chosen two years ago? The small porcelain figure Gwyneth had given Papa for his birthday when she was fifteen? Something precious, for only the most special pieces gained a place of honor on Papa's shelves.

And why? Why would Mama's own brother do such a thing?

He sent something else toppling. "You are undermining *years* of careful work! The Home Office—"

"The Home Office, you say?" Papa leaned forward onto his desk, a look of deathly calm upon his face. "Nay. The Home Office has decent men in it yet. A few, at least, though you are not one of them. This evil must be stopped, Gates. *You* must be stopped."

There came a shuffling sound, one Gwyneth couldn't comprehend but which made Papa snap upright. Made him lift his hands, palms out, and make a placating motion. "Gates—"

"I am through reasoning with you, Fairchild. Tell me where they are. *Now.*"

One of Papa's hands lowered toward his desk drawer, but another shuffle made him pause. "I am only—"

"You think me so great a fool? I already removed *that*, dear brother." More curses exploded from Uncle Gates. Closer now, as though he were rounding the desk, just out of her view. "Tell me where they are!"

Papa's sharp inhalation was clearly audible. "Gone."

"Gone? *Gone?* What do you mean, *gone?*"

"Just that. Out of my hands and on their way to those who can put a stop to this before you destroy two nations in the name of avarice."

A cry tore through the room, guttural and animalistic. Light flashed on something metallic as her uncle charged into view, the gleaming length held before him. Still, she had no idea what he wielded until she saw the silver stained red.

She pressed her hands to her mouth to hold back the scream, hold back the horror, but it didn't help. Uncle still hissed words of hatred. Papa still staggered back, away from the blade. Then he crumpled and fell.

Gates followed him down, muttering, "You couldn't have, not yet. You must have it." His hands shoved into Papa's jacket and searched.

Papa, fight back! But he didn't. He gasped, seemed to struggle for a moment, and then went lax. *No. No, no, no, no, no!*

Did she bleed too? She must. She couldn't move, couldn't make a sound, couldn't *be*. Not anymore.

When Papa's head lolled to the side, he blinked and his gaze focused on her. There was life yet in those familiar depths, but it flickered. Sputtered. "Gwyneth."

She didn't hear it. She just saw the movement of his lips. But her uncle, tossing Papa's case of calling cards into the wall, snarled. "*Now* you worry about your darling daughter? Oh, have no fear, Fairchild. Dear Uncle Gates will take care of our precious girl."

Bile burned her throat.

Papa blinked again as he tried to pull in a breath that choked him. Again his gaze sharpened, caught hers. This time when his lips moved, he made no sound whatsoever. *Run!*

Then it was gone, all the light in his eyes. Extinguished like a flame left before an open window.

And she ran. She turned on silent slippers and fled back around the corner and down the hall. Out the doors and straight into the waiting carriage.

"Gwyneth? Miss Fairchild?"

All she noted of the voice was that it wasn't Uncle Gates's. Nothing else mattered. Seeing that the Wesleys were already seated, their eyes now wide, Gwyneth pulled the door shut herself. "Go!"

An eternal second later, the driver's "Yah!" reached her ears, and the carriage jolted forward.

When she closed her eyes, all she could see was darkness yawning before her.

Two

Baltimore, Maryland
10 May 1814

A h, bah."

Thaddeus Lane watched as the teetering Johnson stood, sending a snarl at Smitty, seated across from him. Thad was glad he stood well out of range of the sure-to-be-foul exhalation of breath.

"Them British won't waste their time in the Chesapeake."

Smitty's face mottled red. "They won't, eh? What of the atrocity at Hampton?"

Johnson hiccupped. "Years ago. I say that…that…I say if Mr. President don't care, why should we?" He turned in a slow, wobbling circle, confusion on his brow. "Where'd I put me hat?"

Thad pushed off from the wall and scooped up from the floor a filthy bit of felt. With a grin, he jammed it onto the man's head. "There you are, Johnson."

The inebriated sailor gave him a gap-toothed smile. "Bless you, young Lane. You're a good one, you are."

Smitty scowled and thunked his mug onto the table, sloshing ale. "Lane, tell him. Tell him we ought to take the threat seriously."

"Yeah, Laney, tell him it's nothin'."

Thad grinned at one sot and the other. Sometimes he picked up a few gems of information from these ale-soaked tongues, and sometimes he just got caught in their foxed arguments.

The door swung open, and relief surged through him when his oldest friend stepped into the dank tavern. With brows raised, Thad moved his hand down in front of his torso, thumb up, then away from his body, palm out. *Anything?*

Alain Arnaud shook his head. Ah, well. Thad smiled and refocused on Smitty's question. "I think if Arnaud's dear Napoleon had taken care of the Redcoats as he ought to have, we wouldn't have to worry about it at all."

Arnaud scowled in that way that made it obvious, even more than his dark Bourbon looks, that he'd been born an aristocrat. "My Napoleon? I have not stepped foot in France since I was five, but he is *my* Napoleon?"

"See?" Smitty wiped a grubby sleeve over his mouth. "He be worried. And if Thaddeus Lane be worried…"

"He ain't worried. And if Thaddeus Lane ain't worried…"

Thad chuckled and clapped a hand to Arnaud's shoulder to push him back out the door. "Let us leave them to their quarrel, shall we?"

Arnaud grunted, but his frown didn't ease as Thad propelled him into the warm sunshine. "No one made it into port today. Did you learn anything?"

"Nothing we did not already know, though I had hoped news of Napoleon's defeat would loosen a few tongues." He glanced down the street, at the bay with its ships too long at anchor. His was there, the masts barely visible beyond his warehouse. Other than a few scouting trips up the Patapsco River, the *Masquerade* had scarcely pulled anchor since he slipped past the British blockade a year ago. It was enough to bring a man to tears. "We need to get back to the Caribbean to rendezvous with the privateers. Napoleon's defeat will surely mean more British forces sent here."

"I have already made the arrangements. The *Demain* will be easier to get to open waters than the *Masquerade*."

His tone was matter-of-fact, unaffected—but the words pulled Thad to a halt and made his brows knit. "*You* cannot go."

Arnaud had long ago perfected that look, the one that labeled

Thad a dunce. "Of course I can. I gather my crew, we make our way to the estuary, meander back out to the bay, and *voilà*. Open water."

Thad crossed his arms over his chest and glared. "And what of Jack? No. I will go and you will stay with your son."

A string of low, blistering French slipped out. Arnaud shook his head and took off again, heading away from the bay's gray waters.

Sometimes the man could be downright pigheaded. "Alain, you know I am right."

"I know you think yourself the only man in America capable of doing what needs done, but you are wrong, *mon ami*." Pivoting at the corner, Arnaud spared him a scathing glance. "Delegate."

"But—"

"But what? The *Demain* is the faster."

And it never ceased to irritate him. "But—"

"You have the better contacts on land."

Unfortunately, some did still view Arnaud with suspicion simply because he was born a European noble. "But—"

"But?" Quick as a flash, Arnaud went from scowling to laughing. "But you are jealous and want to get back to the sea."

The mere mention was enough to make Thad yearn for salty wind and a pitching deck. He loosed an exaggerated sigh. "Oh, to take a few prizes. Sink a few British ships. Swash a few bucklers."

"And if Congressman Tallmadge were not relying on you…but for now, you know well it is I who must go."

Blast. He hated it when Arnaud was right. But he put on a smile and tipped his hat when a few pretty young ladies exited a shop. "Mrs. Caldwell, Miss Raines."

"Captain Lane." Miss Raines fluttered her fan and dimpled. "Are you still planning on attending my parents' ball this Saturday?"

Unless he could find a way to make Arnaud keep his next appointment with Tallmadge and escape to the sea… "Certainly. Will you save me a dance?"

"Of course I will!"

Mrs. Caldwell offered her own smile, a bit flirtatious given her new marriage. "We look forward to seeing you there."

Arnaud's hands moved in a series of quick, muted motions. *Too much, if you ask me.* Thad had to work to keep his own smile neutral.

Leave it to his friend to use the family's language of signs, developed by his grandfather for the sake of the deaf Great-Grandmother Reeves, to be droll.

The young ladies, oblivious, giggled their way down the street and disappeared into another shop.

Arnaud rolled his eyes. "I am afraid I will have to miss the event, Miss Raines. My apologies. But thank you so much for inquiring."

Chuckling, Thad gave him a friendly shove to get them moving again. "According to Philly, you are the most handsome man in Maryland—after her own husband, of course."

His friend's gaze went suspicious. "There is never any arguing with your sister. But I assume you have some less-flattering point?"

He tilted his head toward the shop into which the ladies had disappeared. "To get their attention, a little charm is more useful than a pretty face."

"*Pardonnez-moi?*" Were it not for the outrage on his face, Thad might have thought Arnaud had lost his command of the English language. "I am not *pretty*."

Taking in his friend's slight, lithe frame, the dark curls tossed by the wind, and the chiseled features, Thad had to laugh. "Pretty as a picture, ye are," he said, borrowing Johnson's salt-laden speech. "All ye be needin' is a ribbon for those bonny curls."

"I ought to…" Arnaud pulled back his hand, but a grin bullied its way onto his mouth. "And though I prefer not to be ignored, I have no desire to charm anyone."

Thad sighed and, after waiting for a wagon to rumble past, crossed the cobbled street. He had bitten his tongue for a good while now, but… "Alain, it is time. Jack needs a mother, and you—"

"Jacques does not need some silly young female. And why would I need another wife?" The look he sent Thad was as dark as a storm over the Atlantic and every bit as deadly. "So you can steal her if I am a week late to port?"

He would not engage. Not here, not now. Thad stomped onto the sidewalk. "What will you do with Jack when you leave? Mrs. George cannot keep him indefinitely, not with her rheumatism."

Mischief eased back onto Arnaud's countenance. "True. That is why I took him to your mother."

Though he still had a list of errands he needed to run, Thad came to a stop again. "You could not have possibly made it to Annapolis and back since I saw you this morning."

"And *you* have obviously not made it home."

Not knowing whether to laugh with joy or shout with alarm, Thad bolted for the alleyway before him—the quickest way back to his house. "Is this a visit, or did they evacuate Annapolis?" he called over his shoulder.

Arnaud's answer was a French something-or-another in which Thad caught only "questions" and "slow down." Ignoring that, he concentrated on darting around the children playing tag, sidestepping the dubious stream of liquid being poured from a window, and skidding around the next corner.

Home lay one more block down, where shops and town houses gave way to the more stately Federal-style edifices. He had invested in one of those solely for times like these—when his family arrived unannounced.

"Ah, Thaddeus."

He drew up when the wispy voice reached his ears. Though he hadn't known old Mr. Matthews as a child, the gentleman had only to frown to make him feel like a recalcitrant schoolboy. "Good day, Mr. Matthews."

His neighbor tottered a few steps, leaning heavily on his cane. "Your parents have arrived, I see."

A blessing, yes, but what of Father's classes? Had the college shut down? "So it would seem."

As the old man drew nearer, his expression came into focus. Worry deepened each well-earned crease. "They plan on a long stay, from the looks of it. Has Annapolis been evacuated?"

Thad made sure his smile shone with confidence. "I will ask them if they know how your granddaughter fares."

A measure of peace softened the man's brow. "I do appreciate it, Thaddeus. And tell your father I would be delighted to share a pot of tea with him later."

"I imagine he will be along as soon as they are settled." Thad looked up when Arnaud huffed up to them. "Ah, you decided to join me."

His friend, wheezing, punched him in the arm.

Mr. Matthews chuckled and turned back toward his house. "You had best go greet Mrs. Lane. She is no doubt wondering where you are."

Ever curious, Winter Reeves Lane would indeed wonder and be eager for any tidbits of intelligence he had learned since they last spoke. Which was precious little of import. At least until he laid hands on that elusive key.

None of which was relevant to his neighbor, so Thad gave a quick bow, a warm, "Good day to you, Mr. Matthews," and turned back down the street.

Arnaud sucked in a lungful of air. "How do you move so quickly at our age?"

He had little choice but to return the punch to the arm. "*Your* age, perhaps, old man, but I am a mere eight-and-twenty and in the prime of my youth."

Arnaud snorted a laugh—he was, after all, only a few months older. "I feel eighty some days, trying to keep up with Jacques." He dragged in another deep breath and then squinted, his gaze also on the corner. "Thunder, man, did your parents bring their whole house? When I came by earlier, only your mother in the carriage had arrived. Your father had not yet come with the wagon."

Thad focused on one of the larger objects in the wagon and let out a groan. His long legs stretched, closing the distance between him and the tall figure supervising the line of men going to and from his house. "No, no, no! Father, you *didn't*."

Bennet Lane spun around, a smile of greeting blooming full and bright as his arms spread wide. "Thaddeus! We were wondering when you might be home."

Even as he embraced his father, Thad kept his gaze upon the loaded-down wagon. "What did you do, bring your entire laboratory?"

"Well, of course. 'Tis impossible to conduct any worthwhile experiment without one's equipment."

Thad winced when Henry, his housekeeper's son-in-law, nearly bobbled a large metal something or another. Who knew what might blow up if anything were dropped? He leveled a finger at his father's chin. "There will be no experiments in my house."

His eyes seeking the heavens, Father shook his head. "One minor accident fifteen years ago, and you never let me live it down."

"It was an explosion."

"Only a small one. A trifle, really."

Thad folded his arms over his chest. "The repercussion destroyed half of Mother's china—"

"Which was a dreadful pattern inherited from her grandmother and no great loss. Ah, good day, Alain." Father reached out and clasped Arnaud's wrist. "Have you been keeping this rapscallion in line?"

"If only it were possible." Arnaud smiled, though his usual frown overtook his features a moment later when two neighborhood boys maneuvered a large wooden box off the wagon.

Father lunged forward. "Careful, boys! Those are beakers—glass, very fragile. They go to the library."

His library? Thad scrubbed a hand over his face. "If so much as a thread of my favorite rug is bleached, burned, or otherwise irritated by your chemicals—"

"If you would prefer we stay with your sister, I can crate it all back up." Father shot him an innocent smile.

Thad narrowed his eyes. "By all means. Stay with Philly."

The innocence gave way to mischief. "We would, but then I would be fighting her for space in my own laboratory. Besides, your—Jack, careful!"

Thad and Arnaud turned in time to see the four-year-old barrel through the front door. He ran directly between the two young men and under the box of beakers and didn't stop until he had tossed himself at Father, screaming all the while, "Grandpapa, Grandpapa!"

Father scooped him up with a laugh and set him atop his shoulders. "Jack, my boy, one of these days you will give me such a fright I shall simply keel over."

Jack laughed with all the maniacal glee of any boy of four and slapped his hands to his would-be grandfather's cheeks. "I missed you."

"And I you, you little imp. Your grandmama tells me you will be staying with us while your papa goes to sea."

"Yea!" Jack threw his arms up. And apparently tightened his legs around Father's neck to compensate, given the shade of red his face turned. "We all get to stay at Uncle Thad's house!"

"It will be a veritable holiday." Thad tugged on the boy's foot, well remembering how it felt to be atop Father's shoulders. Now he had to climb a mast to get that same sensation.

If only he had an excuse to do so. He nudged Arnaud with his elbow. "You can stay and visit. I can take the *Demain* out for you."

His friend shot him a glare.

Father laughed. "Your mother would…" His voice trailed off, his gaze on the street. A look of awkwardness took over his face, so that it was no surprise when he muttered out a low, "Ladies. Good day."

Thad pivoted as the *clip-clop* of hooves penetrated his consciousness, and then he tipped his hat to the four ladies within the phaeton that rolled past. "Good day, Miss Rhodes, Miss Margaret, Miss Georgiana." The stair-step sisters smiled at him, but his gaze went to their mother. When he had bought the house on this street, Mrs. Rhodes had been a bright woman, full of laughter and plots to pair him with one of her daughters, but in recent weeks her face had taken on lines of worry that deepened every time he saw her.

With a few long strides he matched pace with the slow-moving carriage. "Mrs. Rhodes, have you heard the latest stories from the sea? A British frigate was engaged in a most remarkable chase a fortnight ago and lost to one of Baltimore's own privateers."

The woman's eyes lit up, and a few years fell from her face. "The *Dragon*, Captain Lane?"

"Without question. My friends do not use names lest the British intercept the missives, but the description was sure. Your husband and son are proving an invaluable menace."

Mrs. Rhodes pressed a hand to her lips as her daughters erupted into a symphony of excited babbling. He kept his gaze on the matron, however, and lifted his hand to wave them beyond his lawn.

She lowered her hand enough to call out, "Bless you, Captain! Come by tomorrow. I shall have a pie for you!"

Arnaud snorted. "As I brought you that news, 'tis I who should get the pie."

"Very well. You lay claim to the pie, and I shall lay claim to the sea." He turned back around, his brows arched.

Arnaud made a show of debating and then grinned. "Enjoy your pastry, *mon ami*."

They started back for the walkway, where Father stood shaking his head. Thad could hardly resist sending him a crooked smirk. "You can join me for the pie, Father. Enjoy an afternoon with Mrs. Rhodes and her daughters."

Father narrowed his eyes. "How can you speak so easily to those baffling creatures? Sometimes I wonder from whence you came, Thaddeus."

Laughter filled his throat and spilled out. "If you had not figured that out by the third child…"

"Thaddeus!"

His mother's voice tugged him toward the door and made the smile stretch wider on his face. He jogged her way, arms wide.

Father followed, muttering, "Perhaps you are a changeling. Stolen at birth and replaced with an identical child, but one with a confounding bent toward society."

Mother chuckled as she came into his arms. The scent of lavender and violets drifted to his nose. Why was it that his own house never made him feel as at home as did that one whiff of her perfume? She gave him a squeeze and then, as always, pulled back enough to study him. "As handsome as ever, just like your father. Who," she added with a pointed look past Thad, "knows well from where that streak of charm came."

"Knowledge which would be even more frightening than the idea of a changeling, had our boy not inherited our sense along with my brother's affability." Father winked and rubbed at his neck.

The gesture made Thad wonder when he had put Jack down and where the boy had gone. A happy squeal from the back of the house answered that question, so he focused on his parents again. "Mother, did he *have* to bring his entire laboratory?"

Her smile seemed never to change. Ever since he could remember, it had been that lovely, that faithful. "It seemed the wisest course, Thaddeus. One never knows when he might need to mix up a new batch of elixir." By which, of course, she meant the invisible ink and the counter liquor to develop it. "And we certainly could not risk all his compounds falling into British hands, should they come to Annapolis."

All inclination to jest dissolved on his tongue. He glanced over at Arnaud and then back to Mother. "Have you reason to think they will?"

"Nothing new." Father urged them off the walk a step as Henry emerged again, set to grab the last of the wagon's load. "But normal operations have all but ground to a halt. My students have either taken up arms or gone to protect their homes, so there was no reason to stay."

Mother nodded. "Amelia and the children are safely ensconced on their plantation, so we thought we would come here, nearer to you and Philly."

"Put us to work, son."

Exchanging a look with Arnaud, Thad gave a slow nod. With Father's arsenal of chemical agents and Mother's history with codes, they could prove invaluable indeed. Perhaps between them, they could make sense of the missive that had been bewildering him for the last week. The one from too important a source to be as benign as it appeared.

He turned to the door and crooked a finger. "Come inside. I have a letter you may want to see from an old friend of yours. One Isaac Fairchild."

Three

The cabin blurred, doubled, yawned. Darkness oozed toward her, though Gwyneth knew the ferocious teeth of the sea waited beyond. She pressed herself to the corner of the floor and clenched her jaw. If she slid into that open mouth…

She squeezed her eyes shut, and when she opened them again, the cabin looked like it had when she first stepped foot in it some six weeks ago. Wooden planks for floor, walls, and ceiling, the few pieces of furniture nailed into place. The bed to which she'd lashed herself in rough seas.

The bed that had provided no rest, nothing but nightmare upon nightmare.

A rattle came from the door, and a moment later Mrs. Wesley slid in, her face a web of concern. She scanned the room with alarm before finally spotting Gwyneth in her place between the small desk and the wall. "Ah, love, what are you doing on the floor?"

She hadn't the energy to resist Mrs. Wesley's gentle hands. Dizziness washed over her and made her sway, but when it cleared she was on her feet, standing in the middle of the tiny room and staring at the wall that had been a mouth.

Mrs. Wesley clicked her tongue. "Still in yesterday's dress I see,

27

though you promised me you would change into your nightgown. Did you sleep at all?"

Gwyneth couldn't convince her gaze to leave the wall, lest it open again. "Sleep?" She took a step away from the monster of a bed. "I do not know. Perhaps for an hour or two."

Before the nightmare had snapped its fangs around her, before the scream had battled for a place on her lips and, when denied, tried to choke the life from her.

Mrs. Wesley's worried frown was yet another arrow through her heart. "Dear girl." She laid a soft hand against the Gwyneth's cheek and swept a thumb under her eye, where circles had deepened to hollows. "You cannot survive on so little rest. Why, if the general finds you in such a state, he will think me a sorry guardian indeed."

Her voice had been light, straining for a jest, but it struck like one of the rogue waves of which the sailors had spoken, the kind that hit without warning and swept all life into the depths. Gwyneth squeezed shut her eyes and opened her lips. She must tell her, must tell the Wesleys that their master was no more. She must…she ought to…

Her lips pressed together as tightly as her eyes. She couldn't speak, couldn't scream. He would hear her, and he would come after her. Come and…what?

Have no fear, Fairchild. Dear Uncle Gates will take care of our precious girl.

Her stomach pitched and rolled, sending her to the floor in search of the chamber pot. She pulled it out in time to heave into it, though there was nothing in her stomach to come up again.

"'Tis the strangest case of seasickness I have ever seen."

Gwyneth nearly shrieked at the voice, too deep, too masculine. Then she sat up and saw the captain and Mr. Wesley. When had they come in?

"Has she slept at all this week?"

Gwyneth rested her head against the side of the desk. The captain never bothered speaking directly to her anymore, only about her. Perhaps because she could never wrap her tongue around coherent answers.

Her eyes slid shut. She was tired. So very tired.

"Not to speak of." Mourning filled Mrs. Wesley's tone. As if Gwyneth had already been lost. As if she somehow knew Papa had been too. "How long until we reach port, Captain? She cannot survive this much longer."

"Not long now. If the winds remain with us, it should be but another few days. We—"

"Sail ho! Captain Stokes, she flies an American flag!"

Gwyneth opened her eyes in time to see the gray-haired captain lurch for the door. "Stay in here together."

Mr. Wesley stopped him with an outstretched hand. "You will not engage, will you, Captain?"

The man tugged his coat down and straightened his spine. "I swore to the general I would see his daughter safely to Annapolis. I will do nothing that would endanger her. We will outrun this vessel."

As he strode from the cabin, the world tipped again and doubled. Gwyneth had little choice but to wrap her arms around the leg of the desk and shut her eyes.

Now blurred into forever, with nothing but the ever-increasing ache in her muscles telling her time passed. At some point shouts rang out and echoed, turning to a deafening roar from which she could pluck no single word. Hands touched, urged, but when she felt the prickly tick of the bed under her, she choked on a scream, lunged away, and fell yet again to the floor.

Tomorrow. The whisper came from within her but made little sense. She tried to focus on the promise of reaching port, as if that would make the nightmares cease. As if that would make sleep come peacefully. As if land would steady the roiling of her world.

But it wouldn't. She knew that. Seasickness was not her malady. Could one die of heartsickness? Of fear? Of insomnia?

Tomorrow.

The shouting changed in timbre, and thunder split the world in two. A scream rent the air. Fog overtook her vision; cursing blistered her ears. Papa would be furious if he heard such words uttered in her presence. He would…

He would do nothing. Because he was gone.

The door crashed open, and its collision with the wall made her vision snap back into alignment and the echoes cease. When two unfamiliar men charged into the room, Gwyneth pushed herself to her feet, though she had to put a hand upon the surface of the desk to keep herself steady.

Mrs. Wesley slid an arm around her waist. Mr. Wesley stood in the center of the cabin, a pistol leveled at the intruders.

One of them smirked. "Put that away, old man. The captain has surrendered."

"No." Voice quavering, Mr. Wesley lifted the gun another inch.

Gwyneth took a step forward, though her knees wobbled. "Mr. Wesley, please. Do nothing foolish."

The pirate's eyes softened. "You've nothing to worry about, sir. We are Americans, not monsters. Our interest is in the ship. We will deliver everyone safely to Barbados, and you can write home or arrange new transport."

Write. Her brow furrowed, her thoughts pounded against one another. *Papa*. The letter! Where had she put the letter, the one he had given her just before…the one she was to present if taken by American privateers? It was…no, she had put it in her reticule. It must be still in her reticule. Which was…

She turned, slowly lest the dizziness strike again, her gaze moving about the cabin in search of the small bag. Mrs. Wesley said something, but she could not spare the attention to discern what. All her concentration was needed to stagger over to the trunk wedged between the bed and the wall.

She lifted the lid, her ears buzzing at a sudden loud noise. There, right on top, lay her reticule. She grabbed it and turned back too quickly, and then wished she hadn't when the world kept spinning after her feet had come to a stop. When her eyes refocused, she saw the muzzle of a gun inches from her face.

Her throat went tight, paralysis seized her limbs. All she could do was clutch the bag to her chest and stare at the man before her.

Oddly, he looked more exasperated than angry. "What in blazes are you doing, miss? I told you to stop."

"I did not hear you."

Frustration twisted his countenance, but Mrs. Wesley slid to her side again. "Please, sir. She has scarcely slept since we left England due to seasickness. Her perception has been...dubious."

Dubious. Her whole life, it seemed, was dubious. Her fingers tightened around her reticule, her gaze going to the doorway when another unfamiliar figure filled it. This one strode in with the confidence that bespoke authority and tossed out a casual, "What is going on here?"

The man before her lowered his gun and stepped away. "A misunderstanding, Captain. The girl went for her trunk, and I..."

"Hmm." The captain halted in the middle of the room and regarded her steadily. "Are you unwell, miss?"

No doubt she looked like something left for dead. She hardly cared, though even her sleep-deprived eyes had no trouble seeing this captain was handsome enough to set female hearts pounding. The way his hair curled brought Sir Arthur to mind, though he was dark where Sir Arthur was fair.

Thoughts of him caused only a numb little thump in her chest. There was no room, it seemed, to mourn the loss of a suitor.

Mrs. Wesley gave her waist a squeeze. "Insomnia, sir. You are the captain?"

He swept his hat from his head and bowed with far too much grace for some American pirate. "Alain Arnaud of the *Demain*, at your service."

Demain—the French word for "tomorrow." She must have heard them shouting it. But it only lit another burning question, and her vision blurred again. "Are you French or American, sir?"

His grin flashed bright as lightning and just as fleeting. "Both. Born in France, but when the Revolution descended, my family fled to America."

Gwyneth's fingers tangled in the strap of her reticule. "Mama was French nobility as well. Papa helped her escape Versailles the very day they stormed the Bastille in Paris."

Captain Arnaud held out a hand. "It would seem we have common ground then, Miss...?"

Her fingers stumbled over the latch of her reticule. "Fairchild."

His face froze. All but his eyes, which snapped with questions. Did he know of her father? Quite possibly—a privateer preying on British ships would stay abreast of British military.

"Fairchild? Any relation to the general by that name?"

She pulled out the letter Papa had given her, crumpled now from so many weeks stuffed carelessly into her bag. Rather than putting her fingers in his for a greeting, she set the sealed envelope upon his outstretched palm. "He is—" if only *is* were still the proper word— "my father."

Captain Arnaud frowned at the letter. "And this is…?"

"For you. He said if we were set upon by American privateers, to give it to them." She shrugged, her shoulders heavy.

Curiosity evident, the captain broke the wax seal and unfolded the paper. His eyes darted across the page. And went wide.

"Captain." The other sailor edged forward, the one who had thus far said nothing and remained at the door. "A general's daughter. We could ransom her. Use her for leverage, at the least."

Fear hadn't even time to beat its wings before the captain lowered the paper. "No."

"But, Captain—"

"Unless you would like to explain to Thad why we chose to hold his ward prisoner when he was expecting her delivered safely to Baltimore?"

Gwyneth had to grip the desk again. Who in the world was Thad? And why Baltimore? Papa had said she was to go to Annapolis. To the Lanes. Bennet and Winter. She should have been *their* ward.

Yet both of the sailors relaxed, and the one the captain addressed even looked amused. "How in thunder does Thaddeus Lane know General Fairchild's daughter?"

Thaddeus *Lane*? She blinked rapidly, trying to clear the haze from her eyes. Trying to remember the stories to which she had scarcely paid attention. Their son, he must be. "May I see the letter, Captain?"

"Of course." His amusement now matched that of his man as he handed it to her, and then he planted his hands on his hips. "I always said he knows everybody the world over."

Gwyneth looked to the page, but her hand shook too badly for her to read it. She set it upon the desk and felt the burn of tears when her eyes drank in the familiar, precious script.

Dear Sir,

If you are reading this, then it is because you have intercepted the Scribe and, along with it, my daughter and her chaperones. But before you start planning how to make use of this capture, I must enlighten you. Thaddeus Lane is expecting my daughter and has sworn his protection over her and the Wesleys. I implore you to honor the promise of he who I know is held in your greatest esteem. I trust you to deliver her safely to him.

Respectfully,
General Isaac Fairchild

Gwyneth lifted a hand to her temple. Had the throbbing been there all along, or was it new? "You know Mr. Lane?"

"It's Captain Lane, and I should think so. He is all but a brother to me." Indeed, his voice rang with warmth.

Mrs. Wesley emitted a sound of relief. "Oh, praise the Lord, then, that you are the ones to have taken the *Scribe*."

Captain Arnaud loosed a low breath of a laugh. "It would not have mattered, madam, had it been any other American privateer. Thad is equally esteemed by all."

How had her father known that? As a sudden stab of pain behind her eyes forced Gwyneth's head down, her eyes closed. She pressed her fingers to the spot and heard Papa's voice in her mind. *I cannot entrust you to anyone but the Lanes.*

Ben and Winter, not this Thaddeus.

"Come." The captain's voice reverberated, distant and muted. "Gather your things and join me on the *Demain*. I will escort you directly to Baltimore."

To Baltimore, not Annapolis. To Thaddeus Lane, not his parents. That wasn't right, was it?

A touch upon her arm, so soft she nearly missed it. "His parents have gone to Baltimore too, Miss Fairchild."

She jerked back, wondering how he had heard her thoughts…and then realized she must have spoken aloud. Her gaze tangled with Captain Arnaud's.

He gave her a small, gentle smile. "Your father obviously knew which name to call upon with the privateer fleet. There is no man more trusted in America than Thad."

She didn't give a fig whom the Americans trusted, but she nodded and followed the captain's outstretched arm. Because one other truth blazed across her mind.

Papa trusted Thaddeus Lane. Trusted him with her life, with her well-being. And if Papa trusted him, then so would she.

Four

Sir Arthur Hart paced the parlor of the elegant home he had visited too many times these past six weeks. This call would yield a different result though, surely. This time the butler had shown him in rather than taking his card. This time Mr. Gates was, from all accounts, at home.

This time he would make his plea.

His hands clasped behind his back, he pivoted on his heel and headed across the room once more. He came nose-to-nose with a painting, its gilt frame gleaming, its subject of absolutely no import until he saw the signature in the corner. *Gwyneth Fairchild*.

"Gwyneth." Her name tasted like honey, yet it did not soothe. Not so long as he knew not where she had gone. Not so long as he feared the worst.

He shuffled back a step and tilted his head. Her hands had put brush to this canvas, had brought to life this garden scene with the fanciful woman touching a finger to a rose. Her mother, most likely, though he could let himself imagine it Gwyneth herself in the painting.

His Gwyneth. He had not known she painted, much less with such skill. What else had he not yet discovered? All he knew of her was that she was the most beautiful young woman in England, that she had a sweetness about her far different from most of her friends, that she could make his heart stop with one soft smile.

He knew he wanted—nay, needed—to know more of her.

Measured footsteps sounded from the hall, providing Arthur warning enough to face the door, straighten his waistcoat, and school his features. He even managed a tight smile when Mr. Gates stepped into the room.

"Sir Arthur, good day." The few times they had crossed paths, the thing that had struck him the most about Gates was neither the man's elegant clothing nor stately bearing, but rather that look in his eyes that said he was focused, always, on something beyond a mere social exchange. "I saw that you called several times while I was on the Continent. My apologies for missing you."

Arthur nodded. "Had I realized you were on an extended trip, sir, I would not have cluttered your tray with my cards."

"'Twasn't cluttered." He offered a smile as measured as his gait had been and held out a hand to the sofa. "Would you sit, sir? You must have a topic of some import on your mind."

With another nod, Arthur moved to the sofa and took a seat on its edge. "I saw you at the funeral, of course, but it hardly seemed the time for a conversation."

Gates' face went tight as he lowered himself to a high-backed chair. "Indeed. I have wanted to speak with you too. The chaps on Bow Street told me you were the one who discovered my brother-in-law's body."

Arthur's nostrils flared at the memories. The horror, the stupefaction of walking into the man's study ready to argue about his daughter and instead finding him slain. "Forgive me, Mr. Gates, but I must get directly to my purpose. Do you know where Miss Fairchild has gone?"

A slow blink was Gates's only hint at emotion. "May I ask why my niece's whereabouts are your concern?"

Arthur's fingers dug into the cushion beneath him. "Because she is my betrothed."

"I beg your pardon." If possible, Gates went even more stoic. "Betrothed?"

His throat tight and dry, Arthur could only nod. Heat crept up his neck at the man's steady regard. "I asked her to marry me that morning.

She accepted, and I wanted to speak immediately with the general, but she said she would talk to him first. Then…" He shifted his gaze to the window, though the passersby did nothing to soften the memory. "He must have refused to change his mind, for she came flying out the door, leaped into the carriage, and ordered it away before I could catch her."

A muscle ticked in the man's jaw. "Did you follow?"

"Nay. Not right then. I was…" He let his eyes slide shut as the disappointment and incredulity flooded him again. "I was heartbroken, Mr. Gates. I went for a ride and tried to convince myself that all would be well. That she would only be gone a short time and would then return to me. But the more I told myself that story, the more I had the feeling that if she left, I would lose her forever. So I returned to Hanover Square to speak with the general. That was when I found him."

Found him, eyes empty and focused on the door, hand outstretched. His study ransacked, with anything of value stolen. A robbery gone awry, Bow Street had determined.

But why, then, had the thief only bothered with that one room, one unlikely to have many costly items? Why had the drawing room, the parlor, or the bedchambers with their jewel safes been left untouched?

Questions Gates must have asked as well. He was too astute to let such obvious inquiries go unmade.

Rumors flew through London, of course. That it had been some agent of the French who had killed General Fairchild. Or an American one, which was even less likely.

A veil of sympathy clouded the older man's eyes. "I am sorry you were the one to find him, Sir Arthur. It must have been troubling."

Assistance he needed—sympathy he did not. Arthur lifted his chin and rested an elbow on the arm of the couch. "I would invite you to remember that I earned my knighthood through my service in France, Mr. Gates. I am no stranger to death and cruelty. My finding the body was a far better alternative than one of the servants or, may the Lord forbid it, Gwyneth."

Sharp respect replaced the veil over his gaze. "My apologies. It is easy to forget your service in the face of your geniality. As for my niece…" He reached over to the table beside his chair and flipped open the lid on a wooden box. After withdrawing a cigar, he tested its fragrance and then picked up the cutter. "I am afraid I am as unaware as you of her whereabouts. I know only what she told her friends—that her father was sending her away for several months."

"But what if it is not so simple?" Arthur leaned forward and pitched his voice low. "You would have seen what I did, Mr. Gates, that General Fairchild's murder was not a random act. Someone targeted him, and the timing of the attack leads me to believe he suspected the danger. That is why he sent Gwyneth away. What if she is in danger too?"

For a long moment Gates studied him, immobile. Then with a quick *snap,* he sliced the end off his cigar. "I had the same thought, I confess. Which is why I have been out of the country these past weeks, searching likely places the general would have sent his daughter. No one has heard from our missing sparrow."

No surprise, yet Arthur's chest squeezed tight. What if she were even now hunted by her father's murderer? What if it *was* some agent of espionage, and he was on her trail, hidden in the shadows? "We must not give up, sir. You have invaluable resources, but I have a few you do not as a knight of the realm and a friend of the prince. I propose we join forces for Gwyneth's sake."

Gates rolled the cigar between his fingers as he kept his gaze on Arthur. Perhaps weighing whether he would be help or nuisance. Perhaps judging whether Arthur was a good match for the niece he loved like a daughter. Perhaps wondering what General Fairchild would have wanted him to do.

At long last he lowered the cigar and held out a hand. "You have a deal, Sir Arthur. Consider us allies."

Thad shuffled the paper onto the stack to his right, the one with the other correspondence from the privateers in the Caribbean and Atlantic. He read each one several times to pick up any subtleties, and then he encoded the news of import and sent it to Congressman Tallmadge.

Simple, compared with trying to uncover the meaning in General Fairchild's letter. He unlocked his desk drawer, pulled it out, and stared at it for what felt like the millionth time. Tight, elegant script covered the page, but the words meant nothing to him. Prattle about family plans, as if nothing but a missive sent to update someone in regular communication with him.

But Thad had never received a letter from the general before. His parents did, to be sure, but when they had read this, both had shaken their heads and insisted the facts were all wrong. There must be more to it.

Mother had tested a few codes, but she couldn't decipher anything without knowing what book he had used as a key. Father had tried the counter liquors to known invisible inks, but all that had gotten him was burnt edges and a few blurred words.

Please, Father. Open my eyes. Help me discern what secrets this letter holds, for I feel in my spirit it is critical. I need Your wisdom.

He shut his eyes and waited, waited for that quiet whisper, that gentle prod. The one that so often steered him toward the tavern whose gossip was useful, or toward the docks when a privateer had just run the blockade.

He heard instead a rap upon the door. Raising his head, he smiled when he saw his mother in the doorway with Jack nestled against her shoulder. "Up from his nap already?"

The boy whimpered and stretched out an arm for Thad. He accepted the burden with a chuckle, happy to wrap his arms about the little one and ignore work for a while. 'Twas beyond his power, it seemed, to rein in his affection for the boy after he had started loving him as his own.

Mother peeked at the pile of correspondence with a frown. "I still cannot fathom that you send intelligence to and from the sea without either codes or a sympathetic stain."

A point she had made time and again. Thad rubbed a hand over Jack's back and reclined in his chair. "I cannot equip every privateer with a code book and stain. 'Twould be too dangerous with so many of them losing their ships to the British. Besides which, we fight a different war now than you did during the Revolution. The greatest danger is not that our neighbors will turn against us; rather, it is that our neighbors will do nothing at all."

She probably would have argued the point had the front door not banged open with suspicious enthusiasm. Thad stood, supporting Jack with an arm under his bottom. The only one to ever disturb him so gleefully ought not be back on land yet.

Why, then, did the "Hallo!" that filled the house sound so very much like Arnaud's?

"Thad!"

"Alain?" He strode down the hall, smiling at the way Jack perked up at the beloved voice. "Why are you back already?"

His friend stood just inside the door, a crooked grin upon his mouth and his arms folded across his chest. "Is that any way to greet a returning hero?"

"Allow me to rephrase." He handed over Jack when the boy lunged toward Arnaud. "Did you bring me a present?"

His friend laughed and pulled his son tight to his chest. "As a matter of fact, I did. Come outside and see."

"Outside?" Thad exchanged a glance with his mother, who had followed him through the hall. "Let me guess. You brought another letter from Fairchild with instructions on what to do with his first."

Arnaud pressed a kiss to the top of Jack's head and led the way out the door. "Better."

"What could be better? Fairchild himself?"

"Close." Arnaud motioned to a carriage pulling up to the curb.

Thad halted on the lawn, noting the three silhouettes within the coach. "Who is that?"

"Fairchild's daughter."

"What?" He turned his back to the new arrivals lest they see his frown. "Why in blazes is she here?"

Arnaud shifted Jack to a new position and blinked in that way of his. "Were you not expecting her?"

"Would you not have known if I were?"

He granted that with a tilt of his head. "I did wonder. But she had this." He pulled a sheet of paper from his pocket and handed it over. "We took the ship on which her father had bought her passage."

Thad unfolded it and held it out so Mother could read along with him. *Dear Sir…*

By the time he read the signature, he had to bite back a choice word. If he had needed more proof that something was amiss with the British general, here it was. "And you brought her here?"

"Of course he did." Mother turned back to face the carriage, her eyes lighting with a smile. "The last time we saw Gwyneth she was no bigger than Jack."

"Mother." Was she not usually the suspicious one? The one who worried about traitors hiding among them? "You cannot even be sure it is her."

She swatted at his arm, a smile blooming. "Nonsense, Thaddeus. 'Tis Isaac's hand, and look—she is the image of Julienne."

He had only the vaguest memory of Mrs. Fairchild from one week-long visit with them in London fifteen years ago, but he remembered her as lovely. When he pivoted back to the street and saw the young lady descend, however, his eyes went wide. And his heart twisted.

No doubt she was as lovely as her mother under normal circumstances. She had the bones of beauty in her face, which were protruding too prominently, with hollows in her cheeks and bruises under her eyes. Her hair glinted in the sun, with shades from gold to red, yet it lacked a natural luster. And the fine dress she wore, no doubt in the height of London fashion, looked as if it had been made for a larger woman. "Seasickness?"

"Hmm." Arnaud stepped up beside him. "Resulting in insomnia. Her guardians say she has scarcely had two hours sleep together since they left England. She keeps going utterly still and then lashes out as if a monster is after her."

He had heard tales before of hallucinations chasing those whose minds were overtired. Such things happened too often at sea when weather or illness forced a crew beyond its limits.

"Poor darling." Mother pressed a hand to his arm and then swept across the yard, her arms extended toward Miss Fairchild. "Gwyneth dear."

Thad edged closer, his gaze not leaving the haunted face of his supposed guest. The way she blinked made him wonder if it took her a few seconds to process the greeting, or if perhaps her vision were unclear. When she attempted a curtsy, her knees buckled, and the woman behind her had to steady her.

"Mrs. Lane?" Her tremulous voice was as wispy as a cloud.

"Yes." Mother took the girl's hands and squeezed them. Though Thad could not see her face, he knew the smile she would give Miss Fairchild, all warm welcome and limitless compassion. "I daresay you do not remember me, but I fondly recall our last visit. Welcome to Maryland."

"I thank you. Papa...Papa sent me to you. He said there was no one else he could..." The trail of her voice sounded not as though she was unsure of what to say next, but rather as if she forgot she had been speaking. Her gaze wandered past Mother and locked upon him.

Where manners said he should take his cue to step forward and welcome her to his home, those eyes held him riveted. A blue-green to put the Caribbean waters to shame, just as light and clear, just as fathomless.

And just as troubled as the sea when a tempest tossed it.

His fingers curled into his palm. Why had Fairchild sent his daughter here, now, to him? Clearly she had something more than seasickness stalking her, something born of the storms within herself. And, blast it all, Thad hadn't the time to put her pieces back together.

As if reading his thoughts, Mother sent him a pointed look and moved one palm across the other. *Be nice*.

As if he needed to be told that.

His mother tucked her arm securely around Miss Fairchild's waist and led her forward. "Allow me to make introductions, as no doubt you two do not recall each other. This is my son, Thaddeus. 'Tis his house in which we will all be staying for the duration of the war."

The nearer his mother brought her, the more intense her gaze seemed. When they halted, she tilted her head back to look up at him. Searching, it seemed, for something to latch onto. After a moment she drew in a sharp breath and let it slowly out. "You gave me a doll."

He nearly chalked it up to meaningless prattle—until the memory descended and brought a smile to his lips. "The one I had been whittling for my cousin. But she was a fright and you were far more charming." He remembered her now, small and dainty, with a riot of red-gold curls and mischief sparkling in those oceanic eyes.

Eyes that now went damp, though surely not over that ugly little doll. "My father trusts you."

So it would seem. Or else he intended to use him for some complex scheme. Though that, somehow, did not fit with the image he had of General Isaac Fairchild.

He held out a hand and, when she settled her fingers upon his, bowed. "Your father is one of the best men in my acquaintance, Miss Fairchild, no matter that politics has once again deemed us enemies."

For a moment he feared she would burst into tears, the way her face contorted, but then it relaxed and she swayed. Mother steadied her, but perhaps she overcompensated, for the girl then teetered forward. Thad had little choice but to release her hand so he could catch her when her knees buckled again.

He pulled her against him when she went lax. The older woman who must be her servant fluttered up, her countenance cloaked in worry. "Did she faint? Oh, my poor love."

He looked down at the young woman, but her face was not the empty mask of one who had fainted, nor did she hang limp in his arms. Her arm had curled against his chest, her cheek pressed to it. Her breath came in and out, slowly and steadily.

"Nay." He bent enough to scoop her up, and she didn't so much as stir. "She is sleeping."

Five

Gwyneth jerked upright, her chest heaving and arms raised to fight off the darkness. But the phantasms fled, their flashing fangs and dripping claws evaporating into mist. "Only a nightmare." How many times had she whispered the same thing in the past weeks?

Perhaps she would better believe it if the monsters didn't take Papa with them every time they disappeared.

She rubbed a hand over her face and then froze. The walls around her neither dipped nor swayed. The mattress felt feather stuffed, and no salt tinged the air. Obviously she was no longer aboard a ship, but in the shadows of the room, she could not place where she was.

Scrambling to her feet, she headed to the strip of golden light glowing between the heavy drapes. Perspiration dripped from her forehead and made her dress cling, and the air felt heavy and wet. Where was she? Some outer ring of Dante's inferno?

A tug upon the curtains brought sunlight flooding in, saturated in shades of pink and violet. Sunset—of what day? And over what land?

The street brought a tickle of memory and the crawl of heat up her neck. Her eyelids slid shut. Baltimore, at the home of the Lanes. And given that she had no memory between staring up at the towering son of the family and waking up a moment ago, she could only assume that she had made a cake of herself in some fashion or another.

"Perfect." She loosed the fabric in her fingers and turned to examine the room in the fading light. Smaller than her room at home, but comfortable. The furniture looked relatively new, absent the flourish of decoration Mama had always favored but lovely in its simplicity.

Her trunk sat in a corner, an island of familiarity. She opened it and pulled out a white muslin day gown not too terribly wrinkled or so complicated she would require assistance to get into it. After making use of the pitcher and basin and fantasizing about a bath—perhaps she would order one later—she changed, pinned up her hair, and felt marginally better.

In the hall outside her room, shadows cloaked the windowless walls and made night feel closer. From behind the door nearest hers she heard familiar snoring in two tones. The Wesleys. She touched a hand to their door and drew in a long breath. No doubt they were nearly as exhausted as she from having to tend her. Try as she might, she could make out no other sounds from anywhere in the house. Were the Lanes all out? Gwyneth headed for the stairs and made her way down, though silence permeated the air.

From the front rooms came only the *tick-tock* of the case clock in the parlor. She paused at the base of the stairs and turned in a circle. She had no idea where she ought to go, but it was cooler down here, so she intended to discover some corner in which to huddle.

Or perhaps a table. She could draw, something the pitching of the ship had prohibited. And perhaps tomorrow she could get out her paints. Any table with a lamp would do for work with a pencil, but she would need a sunny spot if she were to dabble in oils. Did Captain Lane have any kind of a garden? Somewhere with flowers in bloom, a riot of color. Pinks and purples and yellows, oranges and greens of every shade. The play of light upon darkness.

Darkness that oozed and yawned.

No. She pressed a hand to her eyes to force that image away. Flowers, she would think about flowers. Roses and orchids and lilacs and lilies and…and…

"Miss Fairchild, are you all right?"

The intrusion of the voice made her jump and spin, but the start gave way to calm when she spotted Thaddeus Lane leaning into the doorway to the dining room.

He was so tall his head would have hit the frame had he been stand-ing straight, taller even than Papa. Slender, but the fit of his frock coat hinted at hard muscles. He had a pleasing face, not quite so handsome as his captain friend but with a more open expression in his eyes that drew her a step toward him before she remembered she did not know this man a whit.

"I am…" She could not claim to be well. That was too obvious a falsehood. But the truth was hardly polite conversation. She twisted her fingers together and said no more. The fact that she *was* would have to do for now.

Something sparked in his eyes, putting her in mind of the dark yel-low topazes Mama had favored on autumn days. He stepped from the doorway and straightened. "You must be famished. Come, sit." He motioned toward the room behind him. "I will ask Rosie to prepare you a plate. We expected you to sleep the night through."

"It is still today, then?"

Only when he breathed a laugh did she realize how ridiculous a question that was. Heat kissed her cheeks, but the smile he sent her bespoke understanding.

"Still today. You slept only four hours." He ushered her into the brightly lit dining room, where the scent of beef lingered.

"Four! I have not slept so much at once since I left."

She half expected him to echo Captain Arnaud and the Wesleys, to say that now that her feet were firmly upon the land, she would soon return to normal. Instead he only acknowledged her statement with a hum low in his throat.

Gwyneth drifted to a stop, her gaze fastened on the cup at the head of the table. At home that was where Papa would have sat, steaming coffee before him.

Captain Lane touched a hand to her elbow and pulled out the chair adjacent to the one that must be his. "Would you like some cof-fee, Miss Fairchild?"

She had never cared for the stuff, but her father had always said a good cup of it could wake him like nothing else. At this point, it was worth a try. "Yes, please."

He set another white cup on the table and poured. "Cream and sugar are there if you take them. I will be back in a moment."

Pulling the mug closer, Gwyneth stared into the inky liquid. Then she had to close her eyes at a sudden assault of images. The grin on Papa's face when she had begged him for a taste of his favorite brew. Mama's laughter when she had wrinkled her nose at the first touch of bitterness on her tongue. The joy of realizing Papa must have returned from campaign when the scent filled the house again in the mornings.

A clink brought her eyes open. A plate of food had appeared before her, and her host was taking his chair. "There you are. Your guardians retired and my parents took a stroll, but we only just finished. It was still warm."

"Thank you." She lifted her fork but then paused to regard him. "You were not expecting us, were you. Despite what that letter from Papa said."

He cleared his throat and poured more coffee into his cup. "Correspondence from England has been rather undependable, but my home is always open to my friends."

"I am hardly that, Mr. Lane. I am only the daughter of your parents' friend."

"Close enough." He took a sip. "And it is 'Captain.' Or 'Thad'— with my father in residence, it may otherwise be confusing."

Her fingers tightened around her fork. She couldn't possibly.

He leaned back in his chair and studied her. "What are your plans? Will you stay with us a while, or are you en route to somewhere else?"

"I…" The muggy air seemed to converge upon her, weighing her arm down until she had to rest it upon the table. "Papa said to come here, and that he would be no more than a month behind me."

Except that he would never come, would never give her instruction on what she should do next. She was trapped in this land that wasn't home, among a people who considered her the enemy.

Why hide the truth? The London papers would report his murder, and they would not be far behind her.

Her stomach cramped, and the world doubled again. Uncle Gates would come. He might already be on his way. What if he thought she knew about whatever he had been looking for? He would come, and he would kill her too, and the Wesleys, and perhaps even the Lanes.

Through the fog over her eyes she saw the flash of a blade, wicked and sharp and aimed at her heart. Her throat ached with the scream she could not release. She didn't dare. He would hear her, would turn on her.

"Miss Fairchild?"

Who was he, that man she called uncle? He was no soldier like Papa, to be trained to kill. He was only…what was it he had said, when she asked how he spent his days? *I deal in words, Gwyn.*

Words. At the time she had thought he must be a writer, one working under a *nom de plume*. But was it so innocuous? Words could be such dangerous things. A few cruel or untrue ones, and a reputation could be ruined. One whisper from her uncle's lips, and all of England could blame her for her father's murder.

She could even now be hunted by the law. Her only hope was to keep pretending ignorance. Then when they came after her, she could claim with some believability not to have known until the papers reached her.

"Gwyneth." Warm fingers covered her icy hand and bade her look up. His gaze parted the fog like the beam from a lighthouse. She ought to pull her hand away, tried to, but her fingers would not obey. "You are safe here. There is no need to fear. I promise you, I do not take lightly the trust your father puts in me."

A breeze blew in from the open window and soothed the fire of panic from her neck. She managed a nod.

Thad smiled and withdrew his hand. "Eat. I know well what the fare is like on board a vessel crossing the Atlantic, and I promise this will be the best meal you have had in weeks."

It did smell good. She pulled off a piece of tender beef with her fork and put it in her mouth. Only after she'd taken several bites did she look at him again. "Did I see a child here earlier?"

He had been studying her, but with a gaze so concerned she couldn't mind it. And now he grinned as if a child himself. "Jack Arnaud. I imagine you will see a good deal of him, as my mother is the closest thing he has to a grandmother."

The captain's son. "Captain Arnaud said you were like a brother to him, but I am afraid I cannot remember anything else he may have told me. Has he a wife I will meet soon? Have you?"

All light left his smile. "Widowers. Both of us."

The bite of creamy potatoes turned to sand. "I am so sorry." If they had loved their wives even half as much as Papa had Mama, then she could well imagine their grief.

"Thank you. And I am sorry for the loss of your mother. We received that sad news some six months ago."

Gwyneth nodded and set her fork back down. "Forgive me, sir. Delicious as it is, I haven't much appetite after all. I think I ought to rest again."

"Of course." He was quick to stand and pull her chair out for her, to offer his arm. "Once the sun goes down the air will begin to cool. Though if it is too stifling in your room, you are welcome to find your repose down here."

Tucking her hand into the crook of his arm, she let him lead her into the hall, finding some small amusement in the way he ducked his head under the threshold. "Thank you, Thad."

She hadn't meant to use his name, regardless of his invitation. But it slipped from her tongue as if she had been saying it for years. When she glanced up, and up still more, her gaze collided with his.

The force of it knocked the breath from her lungs. "Why do you look at me like that?"

Did her voice sound as tremulous to his ears as it did to her own? He shook his head and frowned, eyes still locked on hers. "I have never seen such shadows."

Of all the—she lifted her hand to touch the bruises under her eyes. Obvious as they might be, what sort of gentleman drew attention to them?

The same sort, apparently, who dared to take her hand and lower it, and to offer a crooked, sorrowful smile. "I was not referring to the ones under your eyes, Gwyneth."

The same sort to use her given name without permission. But there was no one else left to use it, was there? She knew not what to do other than look away and drag in a shaky breath. "I think perhaps I will read or draw down here somewhere."

He pulled her forward, away from the stairs. "The drawing room, then. Usually I would recommend the library, but who knows what noxious fumes might be emanating from there these days?"

"I beg your pardon?"

His chuckle seemed to chase away twilight's encroaching fingers. "My father has laid claim to it for his chemistry laboratory."

"Oh, how interesting. I recall that Mr. Lane teaches chemistry and philosophy, now that you have reminded me."

"My library is a far cry from the laboratory he created at their home in Annapolis, I assure you. He and my..." Turning a corner, he scowled at a partially opened door from which light spilled.

She looked from him to it, wondering what garnered his attention. When he put a finger to his lips, a frisson of fear slid up her spine.

Silent as a cat, he leapt forward and pushed open the door. Gwyneth, her hand still tucked in his arm, had no choice but to move with him.

The two figures within spun at the bang of wood on wall, the female shrieking and tossing a glass container, the man slapping a hand to his heart and scowling much like Thad had a moment before.

Gwyneth could scarcely make sense of the tumult of voices. From Thad came an exasperated, "What in thunder are you two doing in here? I thought you went out, Father."

The older man, the elder Mr. Lane apparently, tossed the book he'd been holding onto a table. "Blast it, Thad, you have ruined the experiment. We were at the most sensitive juncture."

"Oh, no. No, no, no." The young lady wiped at her dress with a rag. Even with the expression of dismay etched onto her face, she was quite possibly the most beautiful woman Gwyneth could recall seeing. Hair a rich auburn, features chiseled to perfection, flawless complexion, and a figure set off just so by a burgundy silk dress.

Thad moaned, his gaze riveted to the floor. "What in blazes was that stuff, Philly? Look what it has done to my rug!"

"Your rug?" The woman—Philly—turned large, outraged eyes on him. "Of what matter is your rug? When Reginald sees that I have ruined yet another gown—"

"I bought that rug in Turkey!"

Mr. Lane sighed and handed Philly another cloth. "Darling, what are you doing wearing such a fine dress in the laboratory anyway?"

Her dismay gave way to a grin. "I was at a dinner party when the epiphany struck. You know how it is, Papa."

The last talon of fear released Gwyneth. This, then, was the middle Lane child, Phillippa. Philly. Of course.

Thad loosed an exaggerated whimper. "I was overtaken by Barbary pirates. I nearly gave my life for that rug."

Mr. Lane came from behind the table, amusement crinkling his eyes. "And you fought your way out with admirable skill and unmatched bravery, coming home with, I believe, *three* nearly identical rugs. The second of which is in Annapolis, and the third…?"

"In my attic with the fourth, but that is hardly the point. If you go through them at this rate, I shall have bare floors by August."

Mr. Lane's gaze shifted to her, and he held out a hand. "Gwyneth dear. You will not remember me, but we were good friends fifteen years ago. I could scarcely pry you from my knee."

Gwyneth took her hand from Thad's arm so she might place it in Mr. Lane's. No memory filtered into her mind, but she smiled simply to realize that this was one of Papa's dearest friends. "It is so nice to meet you again, sir."

"Papa." Philly's voice carried enough urgency to steal everyone's attention. A mass of bubbles rose from one of the glass containers.

Mr. Lane rushed back to the table. "I look forward to visiting with you later, Gwyneth."

Tucking her hand in his arm again, Thad pulled her back toward the door. "Welcome to life with the Lanes." He cast one more frowning glance at his father, though it was colored with amusement. "He is not usually so articulate among unrelated females. Perhaps…"

Gwyneth waited for him to finish his thought, but he said no more. He merely delivered her into another softly lit room and indicated the simple but pleasant appointments.

"Make yourself at home. I have moved a fair selection of books in here in the last few weeks, and there is paper and whatnot in the *secretaire*."

"Thank you." She released his arm and took a few steps inside before her feet refused to budge anymore. Looking over at him, she found he had retreated to the doorway and leaned into it in what must be his habitual way—the only way to keep from knocking his head against the lintel.

Her throat tightened, and swallowing did nothing to ease it. She had to curl her fingers into her palm and force a smile.

Thad studied her a moment more and then nodded. "If you have need of anything, you can risk interrupting my father again or else find my housekeeper, Rosie."

The weakness started in her knees. He was leaving, leaving her to fend for herself. "Where are you going?" Gwyneth slapped a hand to her mouth, her cheeks burning at the sharp look he sent her. Around her fingers she muttered, "I beg your pardon."

Of course he was leaving. She had arrived unannounced and was a veritable stranger besides. He could not be expected to interrupt his plans. And it didn't matter. She was safe here. The Wesleys slept just up the stairs, and Mr. Lane and his daughter were right across the hall.

She slid closer to the circle of lamplight and locked her knees to keep them from buckling.

His gaze went from questioning to fierce. "Why did your father send you to us, Miss Fairchild?"

"Miss Fairchild" again—had his manners returned, or had his friendly feelings simply fled? Gwyneth shrugged, not trusting herself to open her mouth lest more mortifying nonsense spill out.

Thad folded his arms over his chest. "Forgive me for asking, but you can surely understand my curiosity."

Her fingers slipped from her mouth as her arm fell to her side, heavy and useless. "I…I do not know."

He pushed off from the door and took a few slow steps toward her. Towering above her so much that craning her head seemed insufficient, and she had to back up. Her legs bumped into some sort of cushion.

"Do not know, Miss Fairchild, or will not say?"

Her legs gave out, and she sank to the cushion of the sofa. "Do not know. Truly."

He narrowed his eyes and leaned down, boxing her in. "Did he send you here to observe our goings-on and report back to him?"

The words pierced and lit a fire that exploded within her. She shot to her feet again, shoving him away and surely spewing flame from her eyes, it consumed her so. "How *dare* you! You accuse me of spying? Do I strike you as so baseborn a creature, sir? So vile? I am a gentlewoman, the great-granddaughter of a duke and granddaughter of two earls! To even *think* that— I say it again, sir. How *dare* you!"

The fierceness left his eyes, but no apology filled them. Nor did any good humor touch the half smile he sent her way. "How innocent you are." He shook his head and turned to the door. "Good evening, Miss Fairchild. I will see you at breakfast."

Whatever had pulled her taut released her when he strode away. She sank to the couch once more.

Innocent, he said. She was innocent.

So why did her hands feel stained with blood?

Six

That had let himself in through the back door, humming an old maritime ballad as dawn kissed the horizon. Given the brilliant shades of crimson and fuchsia and the heat still weighting the air, a thunderstorm would likely roll through before day's end.

Smells of coffee and bread greeted him when he stepped into the kitchen. He met Rosie's arched gaze with a grin. "Good morning, Rosie Posy."

His housekeeper may have been a speck of a woman, but she knew how to pack a wallop into her every look. "Were you out all night again, Thaddeus?"

'Twas like having two mothers, except the other one understood why he must be out at all hours seeking information to pass along to Tallmadge. "Only half of it. The other half I spent helping Alain with Jack." He slid over to the stove to peek in a pot.

She swatted him away with a dish towel. "Did he have trouble settling home?"

Thad indicated the coffeepot, brows raised. When Rosie handed him a mug, he took that as permission to pour himself a cup. "He awoke when we went back there to exchange news and would not be consoled."

"Poor mite." Rosie poured something into the pot, and the sweet smell of maple came drifting upward.

"They will get through it, as they always do. Have you heard from Emmy?"

Her face lit up at the mention of her daughter. "Henry said she can't leave his sister alone yet, but Emmy is well." Rosie set the spoon upon the rest and held up a hand. "I just remembered. A letter came from Uncle Freeman yesterday, and it had a page for you."

He waited while Rosie disappeared into her room off the kitchen, wondering what Free might have to share from the Canadian front. He took a sip of his coffee and let his gaze go to the window. Yes, storm clouds knuckled on the horizon, purplish gray where the crimson had seeped out.

"Here you are." Rosie bustled back again with a folded piece of paper outstretched and worry in her eyes. "About that Miss Fairchild…"

He waited a moment as he tucked the page into his breast pocket, but she didn't continue. "What about her?"

She sighed. "She be sore troubled, Thaddeus. Far as I can tell, the girl stayed in the drawing room all night. She was still up when I came out this morning, hunched over the desk."

"Hmm. I will look in on her." He nodded his thanks and strode from the kitchen, coffee in hand.

Comfortable dimness cloaked the hallway, no lamps lit nor daylight finding foothold. Thad traversed the space with sure, silent steps and ducked into the drawing room. He spotted the young lady exactly where Rosie had said she would be, hunched over the writing desk with papers scattered all about. An oil lamp burned next to her, and the sound of a pencil's steady stroke filled the air.

"Miss Fairchild?" He spoke softly, wary of startling her. But needlessly, since yet again she seemed not to hear him. Thad edged closer, trying to make a bit of noise as he went, though still she didn't look up or give any indication of sensing his presence.

He ended up beside her, torn at which picture to look at—the one beneath her fingers or the one upon her face. Both begged for attention, but for now he ignored the detailed drawing and focused on her.

The lamplight caught her hair and spun it a fiery gold. Though she had worn it up when she came downstairs last night, the pins had loosed their hold, and curls tumbled all about her shoulders and down her back. Chaos—of the most alluring variety.

Dark circles still stained the fair skin beneath her eyes, but still it was the shadows within them that struck up an ache in his chest. Shadows that looked all the deeper because of the feverish light in them as she drew. "Gwyneth?"

She blinked, once, twice, thrice. Her pencil slowed.

Was she ill? He reached out cautiously to touch a hand to her forehead, expecting her to jump or scream. Expecting to find heat radiating. But her skin was cool to the touch, and she merely drew in a long breath and finally focused her gaze upon him with a small smile.

"Thad. I thought you were going out."

What was he to do with this girl? He removed his fingers from her forehead, though he couldn't stop them from then brushing a tangled curl away from her cheek. "I did."

"Oh." She jerked her head toward the window. "Oh. I am sorry. I...I always get lost in my art. Mama used to say my muse was a cruel task-master."

"I would have thought you too exhausted to succumb to your muse last night." He took a step back so as not to crowd her and leaned onto the edge of the *secretaire*. So that, he admitted, he could better study her face.

Such an interesting face it was, with its broken beauty and emotion flitting on and off it like sunlight through the clouds. What did those troubled eyes seek? What could he do to ease the torment within her?

She touched a hand to her tousled hair, alarm sparking in her gaze. Resignation followed a second later, and her hand dropped back to the desk. "I had a snack at some point to sustain me. Your servant brought it—what is her name?"

"Rosie."

"That is right." Her brow knit. "I confess I found it startling to see so many Negroes along the streets. My family has never owned slaves."

"Nor has mine." At her wide eyes he aimed a smile. "Rosie's uncle is my grandfather's closest friend. She had been a house slave in Virginia, but he purchased her and her daughter's freedom when I was a child, and my parents gave her employment so she might support herself and Emmy. When I offered her the position of housekeeper if she moved to Baltimore with me, she agreed. Emmy is married to another free black, a ship's pilot. Henry has been serving as a handyman for me now that there is little piloting to be done."

"Is Maryland not a slave state, then? I know there is some division."

At that he sighed and shifted his gaze to the drawings on the desk. "The northern states all outlawed slavery back in eighty-three. Maryland was not among them, though. It and Virginia are now the leaders in the slave trade, sending slaves south and west since the international trade was banned five years ago."

He frowned at the picture she had been working on when he entered. A library, from the looks of it, or perhaps a study. The detail was exquisite, each tome looking as though he could reach out and pull it from the shelf, each title legible, but why had she drawn such a scene? One with intricacy but no real subject. There, in the center, at the desk, where one would think a figure would repose, was naught but gaping, empty space.

"You sound bothered. By the state of the states and the trade." She leaned an elbow on the desk and rested her head in her hand, sending a river of red-gold curls onto the paper.

Thad noted the genuine concern on her face but went back to the drawing. Something about a shadow on the floor felt off. One looked almost like a…sword?

"Well, for starters, my family comes from New England, Miss Fairchild, where slavery is banned. I was raised with corresponding sensibilities, and I despise how it continues to drive a wedge into the heart of my nation."

She made no response. He looked down and loosed a soft laugh. Her eyes were closed, her respiration deep and even.

"And you accuse *me* of putting people to sleep with my conversation." Father eased into the room, his voice a quiet whisper and a smile upon his face. A smile that faded to a concerned frown as he studied her. "The poor girl. What do you think is haunting her so?"

The better question might be why whatever it was made Thad yearn to reach out and smooth back her hair, to promise her all would be well.

He shook his head and clasped his hands behind his back to keep them in order. "Something more than the pitching of a ship, that is certain. Perhaps it is tied to whatever inspired Fairchild to send her here."

"That itself is certainly odd, given the circumstances." Father moved his regard to Thad, that steady, probing gaze he knew so well. The one that saw well below the surface. "You wonder as to his motives. And, hence, hers. But I know him, Thad. He would never exploit the bonds of friendship for a political purpose."

Mother came quietly into the room. "He is better than the rest of us in that regard." She stopped in her usual place at Father's side, and his arm went around her.

They had always been this way. They shared a love he had assumed was comfortable and normal until he grew up and realized it was so very rare. His sisters had found the same strong bond with their husbands, and he was grateful for that. But Thad...perhaps he wasn't built quite like the rest of them. He had been fond of Peggy, to be sure, but he hadn't loved her the way his parents loved each other.

He shook off that thought and looked again to Gwyneth. "Why, then, Mother? Why would he send her here? It is hardly an appropriate time for a holiday."

And why did Mother's lips seem to itch at a grin? "I know not, Thaddeus, but given how much like your father you are, I daresay you shan't rest until you figure it out. You Lane men never can let a mystery go unsolved."

He snorted a laugh. "Especially since *this* Lane man is half Reeves, and you are every bit as bad about it as Father."

"Precisely." She leaned into Father for another moment and then pulled away to crouch at Gwyneth's side and smooth her hair. "Gwyneth darling. Wake up. I shall take you to your room."

Though it took a minute of repeatedly speaking her name and gently shaking her, Mother managed to get the girl to her feet and leaning against her for support. They made it halfway across the room before Gwyneth stopped. Expecting her to have succumbed more fully to unconsciousness, Thad shifted when she pulled away from Mother and spun around, her gaze flying about the room in a panic.

"Gwyneth? What is the matter?" He started forward but halted when the fear evaporated from her turquoise eyes.

Perhaps she had only forgotten where she was in her stupor, and peace returned with realization. That must be why her gaze settled on him with such relief, and why a smile touched her lips. She said nothing, but she let Mother slide an arm around her again and lead her out the door.

Thad waited until he heard their footsteps on the stairs. "Tell me it's not a mistake, Father. Having her here."

"Logic says it may be." Father clapped a hand to his shoulder and squeezed. "But something tells me this is not a matter for logic."

An odd enough statement coming from him that Thad couldn't argue. Instead, he went back to the desk. "Take a look at this, will you? What do you see?"

Father joined him, humming low in his throat in that way that said he was impressed with what he beheld. "Astounding. Her attention to detail…"

Precisely. Which was why those shadows bothered him. The one that looked like a sword, yes, but also the pattern that stretched across the whole picture. Perhaps from a scalloped curtain?

Father leaned down, frowning. "This is her father's study, Thad. I recognize the books."

"You recognize the *books*?"

"You have the things you notice, I have mine." He straightened again, but his frown didn't lessen. "Not all of them, of course, but most. Especially this one." He indicated a tome upon the second shelf, though his finger didn't touch the paper, no doubt to keep from smudging her careful work. "I gave it to him. Look, see that crease? 'Tis where Philly dropped it upon the corner of his desk. How on earth did she remember that crease, Thaddeus?"

He could only shake his head. "Remarkable." He shuffled the papers and pulled another forward. A garden, this one, with buds holding tight their petals and a mist seeming to slither throughout it. And there, in the far corner, barely visible behind a tree, was a figure with his back to the viewer.

Father squinted. "It almost looks like Alain."

"The hair is too fair." An invisible hand squeezed his chest. "Does it feel desperate to you?"

At Father's silence, Thad looked over to find his brow raised. A corner of his sire's lips tugged up to match. "I can examine the technical aspect of the drawing, Thad, but you know well I have never been an expert on how a piece of art makes one feel."

Thad sent his gaze toward the ceiling and then back to the paper. "Were it a Greek epic, you could pinpoint tone and emotion in every conjugation."

"But it is instead pictures. Pictures are not my forte. But I presume it feels desperate to you?"

"In a strange way." He sank into the chair. "As if that figure is out of reach."

"Lost to the mist, perhaps?"

Though he sounded proud of himself, Thad had to chuckle. "That is not what struck me, no. More that he is...too far away. And with his back to her, as if denying her somehow."

The case clock ticked. Father sucked in a deep breath. "'Tis a depiction of a spring garden, that I can tell you. You see how this bush here has yet to bloom, how small the leaves are? And these buds are still a good week from opening. I would say sometime in April, depending upon the year. If it were a warm one, possibly late March, if a cool one, as late as the first of May."

And horticulture wasn't even his specialty. Thad grinned. "Her garden?"

"Possibly. The architecture of the building to the side there is correct, though I don't recall the layout."

"Yet you recall the crease in a book's spine."

"Priorities, man. I have mine in order."

A laugh spilled out as Thad looked around to remember where and when he had put down his coffee. Apparently on the corner of the desk at some point. He picked it up, let the warmth seep into his palm, and took a sip. "At any rate, the detail is again confounding. Though the shadows feel wrong in this one too."

"Do they?" Father picked up the paper and tilted it this way and that. "The dappled shade of a tree, I should think. That would account for the odd shape of it."

"Perhaps." He had no better explanation.

Father patted Thad's shoulder and set the garden drawing down. "Try not to worry overmuch about the purpose in Fairchild sending his daughter here."

He could only snort at that and send his father an arched glance. "It is too confounding. Nearly as confounding as how you seemed perfectly at ease in her company, despite the fact she is female."

Father grinned. "Let it confound you, then. We shall see how long it takes you to see what I did at first glance yesterday. For now, I believe I shall go peek in on Rosie and the breakfast preparations. You stare at those drawings until you have unraveled a few mysteries of the universe, hmm?"

As Father went out, Thad relaxed into the chair, content to brood into his coffee. His gaze wandered to the window.

Father was a master at spotting hidden patterns, be they in the elements or the written word. But people—they had to be unique indeed to capture his attention. What had he spotted within Gwyneth Fairchild to make him forget she was one of "those baffling creatures"?

Thad knew what *he* had seen. Mysteries. Questions that had no answers. Shadows too fleet of foot for him to examine.

Trouble. The intriguing kind.

He scrubbed a hand over his face and then opened a drawer in the base of the *secretaire*. He withdrew a scrap of paper onto which he'd written in bold ink a verse from his grandfather's book of prayers. The one he needed reminding of most often.

> *Give me a deeper trust, O Lord,*
> *that I may lose myself*
> *to find myself*
> *in Thee.*

Seven

As Arthur followed Gates through the doorway, he felt as though he were treading upon a grave. His companion headed for a shelf on the far wall, but Arthur drew in a long breath and clenched his teeth.

Emotions had their place, to be sure, but war had taught him well that sometimes, in order to stand tall, one must stand hollow. Let everything drain away and simply focus on facts. Mere, simple facts.

One—the room smelled musty after being shut up for eight weeks. It begged for the heavy drapes to be pulled back, the window opened.

Two—the floor was empty where the rug had lain.

Three—blood must have soaked through it, for the wood by the massive desk was stained.

Arthur turned on his heel and put his back to that particular fact. Better to face the man who was peeking behind picture frames. "How may I assist you, Mr. Gates?"

Gates didn't so much as glance over his shoulder. "Anywhere you think a strongbox might be hidden, Sir Arthur, look. I cannot believe I forgot so long that my brother-in-law had one fabricated."

The younger man cleared his throat and cast his gaze around the room. The chair was no longer overturned and glass fragments were no longer scattered about the floor, but the chamber still felt the way it had when he stepped into it two months prior. The same way *he* felt now to be poking about it. *Wrong.*

"Are you certain this is necessary?"

Gates lowered a frame back into place and sent him a patronizing look. "I suppose we could shrug our shoulders and admit Gwyneth has been lost to us."

A year ago, when this feeling came upon him, his hand would have settled of its own will upon the hilt of his sword. Now, his belt empty of both blade and pistol, he had to merely clench his hand and wait for the pulse of insult to fade.

Once it had, Arthur headed toward the opposite side of the room. The desk and the bookcase behind it. Though he refused to look down, his feet nonetheless took the liberty of avoiding that telltale stain.

Blood had become a common sight in war, one they had all learned to ignore. On the battlefield it was expected. Accepted. But in a man's own study? What was the purpose of fighting if not to ensure that one could come home and live without fear?

He crouched beside the desk and ran his hands down the sides, comparing the dimensions from the outside with the space available in the drawers. No unexpected compartments, so far as he could tell. He leaned into the space underneath and checked the floorboards. Tight and varnished.

Giving up on that idea, he faced the shelves and began moving the books out a few inches to look behind them. Pull three out, check, push them back. Pull three out, check, push them back.

On the bottom shelf, he found a piece of paper crumpled behind a volume of Montesquieu. There was nothing upon it but a few notes on the text. On the second shelf, a letter from some chap from the Colonies was tucked within the pages of Lavoisier's *Méthode de Nomenclature Chimique*. He found nothing else until he moved over to the next bookcase. On the third shelf down, in a collection of French poetry, rested another letter. The scent of rose water still clung to it, the elegant script on the outside matching the fragrance.

Mon amour.

French? He glanced over his shoulder to be sure Gates was still occupied with his own shelves, and then he unfolded the paper. General Fairchild certainly wouldn't be the first army officer to find a *paramour* from among the French while on campaign, but he had to admit that the thought shocked him. Though he hadn't served directly under him, Arthur knew Fairchild's reputation.

But if he had secrets like this, it could be tied to his murder. Arthur studied out the French text.

> *My dearest Isaac, how I yearn for you. How much longer until you return to me? This dreadful weakness is seeping more and more through my limbs. I fear, my love. I fear I will not live to see your homecoming. I fear leaving Gwyneth alone.*

Gwyneth. Arthur's gaze went to the end of the letter, where *Julienne* was written. Mrs. Fairchild, not some secret mistress. He had forgotten she was half French. This would not help him determine who could have killed the man or why. It could not lead him to Gwyneth. He set the letter on top of the row of books.

"Ah!"

Gates's exclamation brought Arthur around. The older man knelt by the window seat, the lower paneling of which had been removed. He maneuvered a strongbox from within the hidden cubbyhole.

Though a skitter of unease swept up his spine, as Arthur hurried to his companion he told himself that if it would save Gwyneth it was not prying. "How will we open it?"

From within a pocket Gates produced a large metal key. "I procured it from the Bow Street runners. 'Twas in the general's boot." He set it at the lock but then paused to shoot Arthur one of his serious looks. "Do be aware, sir, that you are not to poke into any military-related articles that may be within."

Again his hand flexed, craving the surety that came with his trusted sidearms. "Mr. Gates, I was a military man for a decade, sent home because of injury and for no other reason. You need not lecture *me* on such things."

This time Gates offered no apology. He turned back to the box, inserted the key, and gave it a hard quarter turn.

Clank.

Another quarter turn.

Clank.

Once more.

Clank.

And a final twist, a final release, a final metal-on-metal *clank*. Arthur strained forward, leaned in, and frowned.

Gates withdrew the single sheet of paper and held it so they could both read it.

You are too late. The game, as they say, is up. You have lost.

Pushing to his feet, Gates tossed the paper to the window seat. "It seems our hunch was correct, Sir Arthur. Fairchild's death could not be a result of a random burglary, given this."

"Indeed." Still frowning, he looked from the safe to the page. Speculation flew through his mind, but he focused again upon the facts.

One—Fairchild had expected someone to look in this strongbox.

Two—he therefore knew he had an enemy closing in upon him.

Three—if Fairchild expected someone to look in here, then he expected them to have the key. The key which he wore in his boot. It therefore stood to reason that he suspected his enemy capable of murder.

He had taken steps to counteract this enemy, though, clearly. Likely with the removal of whatever *had* been in the safe at one point. Just as likely with the removal of his daughter from harm's way.

"Where does that leave us?"

A muscle in Gates's jaw pulsed, as if he clenched his teeth too tightly. "I know not. I have already canvassed every stop along the post roads from London, the shipyard, everything. No one recalled seeing her, and if they did not recall it two months ago, they will not now."

"She can't have disappeared." Yet she seemed to have. Arthur walked over to the window, pushed aside the drapes, and looked out into the garden. Heavy with blooms and lustrous with life, but empty. So very empty. "I asked after her in all the likely places too during that first week. I even followed several false leads. The only one I could not track down was at the shipping office."

"What?" Gates had been turning away but halted. "I checked there. No one saw any young ladies the days in question."

"None of the officials, but a young lad searching for odd jobs thought he'd seen her."

"Interesting."

Arthur shook his head. "It could not have been Gwyneth. She would not have been boarding a ship bound for America."

"America." A spark ignited in Gates's eyes, blazed, and then went cool. Controlled. "What ship? To where was it headed?"

Did he really think any potential chance of finding her lay in that direction? "Somewhere in Maryland, I believe. I cannot recall its name."

A smile curled the corners of Gates's mouth, though his eyes remained devoid of feeling. "I thought to check my sister's distant relatives on the Continent, the friends we have abroad. That is where most of the general's contacts still are."

"Which would make sense, especially given that Napoleon has been defeated. But General Fairchild would never have sent his daughter into the escalating war in America."

Something snapped to life in Gates's eyes, quickly rising and quickly gone. "Exactly. No one would expect it, which would make it safe."

For lack of anything useful to do with his hands, Arthur clasped them behind his back. He shook his head again. "Safe? Nay. Not with those blasted American privateers on the loose, even in British waters—and he would not send his daughter into a war without a protector."

Gates's face was stoic once more. "Ah, but what if he was sending her *to* a protector? To trusted friends?"

"Trusted friends in *America?*"

"He was stationed in the City of New York during much of the Revolution. He made friends among the Colonists, who have since moved to Maryland, if I recall correctly."

"But that is..." Realization sent Arthur back to the bookcase behind the desk. He lifted out the tome of Lavoisier, extracted the letter, and looked at the address. "Bennet Lane of Annapolis?"

Gates snapped his fingers. "That is he. I know they were in regular correspondence."

"Perhaps. But still, I cannot fathom the general sending her there."

The laugh that shuffled its way past Gates's lips sounded more resigned than amused. "You did not know him."

Arthur's shoulders snapped back, his spine in perfect alignment.

"I know he was a noble man, sir, and an admirable one. I know he achieved his rank through honor and bravery. And I know that he loved his country. He would not send his daughter to England's enemy."

"He defined that last word differently than we do, Sir Arthur." He bent over and lifted the strongbox enough to wiggle it back into place. "Perhaps it is this friendship that blinded him, I cannot say. But he failed to see that America is our enemy. And I fear—I truly fear—that his inability to identify them as such may have been what allowed one close enough to kill him."

Arthur's throat tightened, wanted to close off, but he swallowed and lifted his chin a notch. Was Gates seriously implying that General Fairchild was the victim of espionage?

His fingers fisted around the letter from the American. His uncle, Viscount Hart, was a difficult man to please, one who had given only begrudging approval of Arthur's choice of bride. Gwyneth's blood was beyond reproach, but the viscount had wanted his nephew to choose a nobleman's daughter. Or at least a gentlewoman of resounding wealth that could be added to the viscountcy when Arthur inherited. If he got a whiff of anything as unsavory as espionage surrounding the Fairchilds…

There was only one thing to do. He must find Gwyneth and marry her as soon as he did before anything could besmirch the Fairchild name.

He smoothed out the missive, tucked it into his pocket in case it contained any information that would aid him in his search, and then reached for the one from Mrs. Fairchild too. When he found his lady, she would appreciate the connection to her parents.

He pivoted to face Gates, who was raising the paneling back into its place under the seat. "It seems we have a voyage for which to pack. I trust with your connections that you can attain us passage to Maryland?"

The older man straightened and smoothed his great coat back into place. "There is a supply ship sailing to the Chesapeake with tomorrow's tide. Meet me at the Black Cauldron Inn at dawn."

Eight

Gwyneth stood immobile upon the step, shielding her eyes against the merciless sun overhead. Midday. But *which* day? The same one she had seen briefly at the *secretaire* after her night of drawing? The next? The next week? She could remember only snatches after Thad smoothed back her hair. Voices echoing, a gentle touch that felt like Mama. The familiar clucking of Mrs. Wesley.

The nightmares. Cruel and dark, with vicious teeth and hurtful words.

She shuddered, wishing for a shawl to wrap around herself in spite of the heat that hung heavy and damp.

A bath had done wonders for Gwyneth's mental clarity, but she hadn't wanted to ask Rosie what day it was. Not when the woman already looked at her as if she might shatter with one wrong move. No, better to find those answers herself without alarming anyone.

Hanging from one of the tree's limbs was a swing, no doubt there for Captain Arnaud's little boy. What was his name? She strolled along the path toward the large maple. Jack, that was it.

Jack surely wouldn't mind if she borrowed his toy for a few minutes since he was nowhere in sight. She brushed a few stray twigs and leaves from the wooden seat, mindful of the fact that her dress was her usual white muslin, easily soiled. Sitting down, she squeezed her eyes shut.

She ought to be in black. These last weeks ought to have been spent agonizing over whether to expend the cost on a specially made mourning gown or to dye an old one and broaden the hem. She ought to have been surrounded by the uncles and aunts who would be grieving her father, perhaps disappearing to Fairmonte for a respite with Papa's brother and his family.

But thoughts of uncles sent a shiver up her spine and made her throat close off. She had thought them so close, her father and Uncle Gates. He was the one who most often visited, whose wife had seemed the most affected by Mama's passing. And with no children of his own...

A sob heaved up and was caught. She swallowed it down. He did not care for them as she had thought. Not her, perhaps not even Mama. Certainly not Papa...

"Papa. Oh, Papa. I love you so."

The wind snatched her whisper and took it over the roof, over the city. Perhaps all the way up to heaven.

With one toe on the ground, her hands wrapped around the rough rope, she gave herself a little push. She closed her eyes as the air caressed her hot cheeks and pretended she was a child again at Grandpapa's country house. That the whiff of roses was Mama strolling her way.

"Oh, good. You are awake."

The voice, feminine and melodic, brought her eyes open. Only when she spotted the strikingly beautiful woman coming through the back gate did she recognize it as belonging to Philly. Though dressed more casually than when in the library, she looked no less lovely now in simple pale yellow. And absent that panic in her eyes that came from a bubbling beaker.

Gwyneth offered a smile and put her foot down to stop herself so she might stand to greet the newcomer properly.

Philly waved her on. "No need to halt for my sake. I often sneak back here myself." She leaned against the maple, not seeming the slightest bit concerned for how the rough bark might affect her fine dress. "Have you settled in?"

The very word seemed foreign. Her world had begun rocking long before she stepped foot on the *Scribe*, and she didn't anticipate it settling any time soon. How could it, when her anchors were gone? Her smile no doubt went feeble. "Everyone has been very welcoming."

"Ah." The way the woman blinked gave Gwyneth the impression that she heard far more than her answer. She raised her arm and took a book from the basket dangling from it. "I brought you something."

Gwyneth reached for it. From the wear on the binding, it seemed to be a well-loved tome. "*Charlotte Temple*. Why was I expecting some scientific treatise?"

Philly laughed. And no dainty society laugh for her, nay. She tossed her head back and let it come from deep within. "I learned long ago not to foist those on unsuspecting guests. Have you read Mrs. Rowson's work?"

"I have not. A cautionary tale, correct?"

Philly laughed again. "If you ask those who enjoy it, yes. If you ask its critics, it is naught but a seduction novel."

Chuckling, Gwyneth flipped open the cover and then drew in a startled breath at the familiar script on the endpaper. Mama's hand, wishing Philly a felicitous birthday. "I did not realize…"

"Mmm." Philly moved behind her and gripped the ropes of the swing. She pulled Gwyneth back and let her go. "Strange, is it not, to consider how people from such different places can be connected? Both my parents came from largely Loyalist families, and my uncle inherited an estate in England after serving in the British army during the Revolution. We have been working to reconcile the rift all my life, yet here we are at war again."

Gwyneth traced a finger over the inscription, its ink faded to brown. She scarcely noticed the gentle forward-and-back motion of the swing. "I had forgotten that. But it is how my father came to know your parents, is it not? In New York."

"Indeed. Mama and your father…" Philly cleared her throat.

Half a smile found its way onto her lips. "I know the story. He was courting her until your father won her away, but they remained friends, all of them, even when it came out that your parents were Patriots."

"They say it is a testament to your father's noble heart."

Gwyneth's eyes shut again as she felt the earth sway. "I miss him."

"I imagine." Soft hands settled on her back when she swung back and pushed her forward again. "I miss my parents when I do not see them often, and Annapolis is near enough that I can visit them whenever I please. It must be much worse for you, being an ocean away."

An eternity away. Gwyneth gripped the book until her knuckles ached. "And you have your brother here. That is surely a comfort."

Philly chuckled. "For most of the last decade he was at sea far more than he was home. A regular swashbuckler was our Thad, able to find adventure where a sane person would see none."

An image took shape behind her eyes of Thaddeus Lane with his boots planted on a ship's deck, his hands gripping the wheel, an adventurous smile upon his lips. Strange how quickly the picture formed, and how it made her fingers itch for a pencil.

She flexed them, and the cloth cover of the book stole her attention again, reminding her of her mother. Papa had not been a sailor, but he too had been gone frequently on campaign. The separations had never been easy. "How long was he married?"

Perhaps it was too personal a question, but she would rather ask it of his sister than of him.

Philly sighed and gave her another soft push. "Only eight months, and he did not leave her side during it except for a week now and then on a quick run up the coast. Peggy was dying already when they wed. It was, in fact, largely *why* they wed, so he could care for her. She had no one else and no income."

A noble act...and yet so very sad. "They obviously had no children, then."

Philly cleared her throat. "She was with child when she died. 'Tis a topic still quite sore, so we avoid mentioning it."

"Did it happen recently?"

"Two years ago." A blustery sigh sounded from behind her. "It was a difficult time all round. Alain was thought to be dead, we lost Peggy, one of Reggie's cousins was impressed, stolen right from the Virginia shore, I lost another babe...and then the war."

Gwyneth nodded. Two years ago had been difficult for them too, what with Mama's sickness coming upon her and Papa still in France.

"But there was good too. Grandmama Caro finally agreed to come live with me and Reggie."

The smile was so bright in Philly's voice that Gwyneth felt her lips tug upward in response. "You are close with your grandmother?"

"Very. I ought to have been named after her, but when Papa told her their intentions, she insisted they name me after my mother's grandmother instead, in an attempt to heal the relationship there." Something in her voice as she said it...

"Did it work?"

Philly emitted an unamused laugh. "Not a whit. Grandmother Phillippa never would have anything to do with us. But we tried."

A hum filled Gwyneth's throat. Her family had had its breaks too, but the biggest rifts had already been healed by the time she was born.

Her eyes became unfocused, her vision doubled, and she had to clutch at the rope to keep from toppling off the swing. Perhaps her grandparents' separation *hadn't* been the biggest rift. There was obviously hidden strife between Papa and Uncle Gates. Hidden, vicious strife. Devouring hatred.

"Speaking of Grandmama Caro, she mentioned a craving for an apple pie, and I have already used the last of my apples. I thought perhaps Thad has some stashed in the cellar."

Gwyneth drew in a long breath and blinked until her vision returned to normal. Apples. Pie. Normal, everyday life. Strange how it could continue on an upside-down world. "Your brother is out, and Rosie mentioned needing to run a few errands as well. I am not certain if she has left yet."

Philly chuckled. "That man is never at home when I come by."

Gwyneth frowned and fastened her gaze upon the swaying house, searching her mind for more information on where Thad had gone. All she came up with was the question of how she even knew he was out. To be sure, she hadn't seen him since she rose an hour ago, but she had come straight from her room to the garden. She hadn't searched for him. Still, she was certain he was away. As certain as she was of anything else these days.

"Well, I will see if I can catch Rosie. Or else I shall check the cellar myself."

Philly stepped away from the swing, and Gwyneth let her toes drag until she slowed to a halt. Perhaps she would read *Charlotte Temple* for a while. Or, better still, get out her paints. She had wanted to paint, hadn't she? Something niggled in the back of her mind. Something particular. Something…perhaps a more complete version of something she had already sketched?

She stood, her brows pulled down. What had she even sketched? And what was wrong with her, that she could not remember something so basic? She recalled the pencil in her hands and that intense concentration Mama had called her muse. The crick in her neck from being too long hunched over the desk. That burning need to join line to curve and shade to light. And the startling realization that night had passed and morning had come along with Thad.

His fingers on her forehead, brushing through her hair.

Her cheeks burned. His image filled her mind's eye. Those yellow-topaz eyes, looking at her with the same focus she gave her art.

Did he really distrust her? Think her so ignoble that she could be here to spy?

"Are you all right, Gwyneth?" Opening her eyes, she saw that Philly had walked to the door but stood in the threshold, waiting. "You look flushed. Perhaps you ought to avoid the midday sun until you have acclimated to the heat."

The mere mention of it made her realize how heavy and humid the air hung. Yet the thought of going back inside… She had scarcely seen the sun for two months, being always closeted below deck on the *Scribe* under the fearful watch of the Wesleys.

But she needed a bite to eat, or at least something to drink. She could take it by an open window, perhaps, and enjoy both sunshine and breeze. She smiled at Philly and followed her in.

Mrs. Lane emerged from the library when she heard them enter. She embraced her daughter and then grasped Gwyneth's hand. "Up already? I had hoped you would rest more than a few hours."

No lost day, then. Gwyneth smiled and realized it must have been Mrs. Lane who helped her up to bed that morning. Hers was the touch that felt like Mama's. "I suspect it will take some time to adjust. But I feel better than I did on the ships. Clearer." Mostly.

"Good." Mrs. Lane looked as though she would say more, but the sound of the front door interrupted her.

Thad charged around the corner, so fast that they surely would have collided had Mrs. Lane not pulled them to the side. "Thaddeus! Did I not teach you against running in the house?"

He grinned and doffed his hat. "You always said no running in *your* house. This one is mine."

Laughter sparkled in her eyes, though her lips remained straight. "But I am in its halls and in danger of being bowled over. Have a care."

"Yes, Mother. Sorry, Mother." Looking as though he would rather laugh than play the part of meek son, he nevertheless leaned over to plant a kiss on his mother's cheek. Then he turned his probing gaze on Gwyneth and frowned. "Shouldn't you be sleeping?"

"She is not an owl, Thad." Philly turned toward the kitchen. "Have you any apples for Grandmama Caro?"

Thad pursed his lips, his gaze still on Gwyneth. "You were asleep when I left an hour ago, at least. You had to have gotten five hours."

He had left only an hour ago? That was when she had awoken. Perhaps she had heard him leave and that was what roused her. It would account for that insistence in the back of her mind that he was not at home.

"Perhaps if the air cools this evening, we will all go for a promenade. A bit of exercise would no doubt help." Mrs. Lane turned Gwyneth around with her.

Philly was already halfway down the hall. "The apples, Thad?"

"It depends on how many Jack pilfered while he was here." Amusement wove through the words. "That little imp will devour them by the half dozen if he isn't checked."

Mrs. Lane chuckled. "I tried to limit him. Go look, Philly. There ought to be plenty left."

His gaze was still upon Gwyneth. She felt it like a hand upon her cheek, but she couldn't be sure whether it meant to slap or caress.

She darted a glance up at him. No hatred spewed from his eyes, no suspicion. But then, even when he had narrowed his eyes at her last night—was it just last night?—it had been only intensity in his gaze. Contemplation perhaps, or calculation. But no dislike.

Thankfully Mrs. Lane kept a hand upon her arm as she guided her toward the kitchen, for her vision blurred again. She kept moving, but with each step the floor wobbled more.

Fire balled in her stomach. When would this stop, this infuriating weakness? They would all think her a burden, an invalid, a spoiled child incapable of standing on her own feet.

Mrs. Lane's voice echoed in her ears, but she could make out no particular words. A chaotic din filled her mind.

Or, no, it was just that the entire household had converged upon the kitchen. The fog lifted from her eyes enough as they stepped into the room that she could see the Wesleys had both appeared, along with Mr. Lane, his arms laden with baskets from which Rosie unloaded vegetables and fruits. A Negro man leaned against the wall—he must be Henry, Rosie's son-in-law. Philly was telling her father about something that required sweeping gestures of her hands, and little Jack had even returned. He bounced about like a marble in a ring, chanting, "Apples? Apples? I want apples!" until Mr. Lane stopped his ricocheting with a hand atop his head. The chant dissolved into giggles.

Mrs. Lane headed for her husband—or perhaps the boy—and Gwyneth feared her knees would buckle, traitorous things.

But then new hands braced her, cradling her elbows from behind. Thad. Obviously, as everyone else was in front of her. A glance down merely confirmed it. His long fingers, yes, curling around her arm. With that jagged nail on his left pointer finger, and the scar upon his opposite knuckle. Rough enough to declare he was a man of trade, yet smooth enough to prove he had done well at it and paid others, now, to take on the heavy burdens.

And strong. Strong enough to all but lift her from her feet and set her gently upon a chair at the wide, thick table. When he then pressed a cool tin mug into her hands, she lifted it to her lips.

Lemonade. Sweet and tart and blessedly cold. Gwyneth let her eyes slide shut and sipped again.

"The market was all abuzz." The elder Mr. Lane? It must be. "I trust you heard the same news I did, Thad."

"About the action along the Patuxent?" His voice flowed steady and smooth over her.

"Aye."

"Battles? That close to us?" Who was that? A female, but who would be talking of war? Aunt Gates perhaps. "Who won?"

"There was no tactical advantage to it, but Barney's men won the day."

Barney. She had heard that name. One of the American leaders. Gwyneth sighed and leaned onto the arm she propped on the table. "That is a shame."

The silence pounded, scattering the lovely haze that had overtaken her. Her eyes flew open, and her pulse raced when she saw that every single person in the room stared at her, even little Jack.

Oh, heavens. What had she said? Had she…? No, surely she had not replied to their news as she would have had Papa been the one sharing it. She was not so stupid, nor so insensitive.

The fire seemed to leap from the stove directly onto her face. "Forgive me. I am so sorry. I was not thinking— Of course, you would…it is just that my father and his friends…forgive me. Please."

They all moved again, their gazes shifted, but she felt no relief. Not until Mrs. Lane knelt at her side and pressed a cool hand to her hot cheek. Gwyneth blinked burning tears away and focused on the warm green eyes of her hostess.

"We understand, Gwyneth," she said. Softly, calmly. "You are accustomed to giving the opposite reactions of ours to such news. We do not hold that against you. And never, never feel you must feign anything in our company. You may disagree all you like with us, with our positions, with our loyalties. Do you understand?"

How could she, when she had just shouted with that careless murmur that she was their enemy? Gwyneth shook her head.

Mrs. Lane smiled and smoothed the damp tendrils from Gwyneth's cheek. "For years during the Revolution, I had to pretend to be what I was not. I had to deny everything I held dear. You will *not* be asked to do the same. Think what you will, believe what you will, sweet one. Our only requirement is that you take no action that could endanger us."

She covered the woman's hand with her own and held on lest the tide snatch her away from this oasis and out to the ravaging sea. "I could not. Would not. I swear to you that."

A plate slid onto the table, a yellow square covered in melting butter. She sent a questioning look up, and up still more into Thad's face.

He nodded toward the plate. "Corn bread. Sweet but hearty. You need to eat."

"Thad." What did she intend to say? She could hardly expect her feeble words to convince these people that she could be trusted, that though she wished her homeland victory always, that did not mean she wished theirs defeat. She let her gaze drop. "Thank you."

He nodded and then turned back to his father. "That is not all I heard. They are raiding again."

Raiding...again. The words made something clang in the back of her mind, some memory from home. Words drifting down a hallway, out of Papa's study. His precious voice, raised in frustration. Insisting that this was not how England waged war.

Mr. Lane sighed. "Provisions?"

"If only that, it would be nothing beyond the expected."

Another, deeper sigh. "We have friends along the Patuxent."

"I know. Let us pray they abandoned their farm before the British arrived. The reports I heard were of savage attacks on innocents. Houses burned, churches destroyed."

"Much like Hampton."

"But at Hampton 'twas the Independent Foreigners that committed the atrocities." Thad's tone was hard, cool. "Now the British ranks all seem to have adopted the tactics that outraged them at the start."

Though her stomach churned, she picked up the crumbly bread and told herself it was hunger that made her hands shake so. Not fear, not dread, not revulsion. Only hunger.

Nine

Thad shoved his fingers through his hair and concentrated on the document before him. He blew on the final word, still darkening from the layer of counter liquid he had applied, and watched it turn from pale green to blue to nearly black. The news from Freeman was, in a way, exactly what he had expected.

The northern front of the war was an entirely different enterprise from what they faced in the Chesapeake. On the Canadian border, the British weren't the aggressors, they were the ones defending their territory—territory the politicians in Washington City had decided to try to annex since war had handed them a shiny excuse.

For a good while little effect had been felt here, given that the British didn't know the waterways well enough to either stop the American privateers from escaping the blockade or to navigate their fleet away from the coast. But they had fallen back on proven tactics—luring slaves away from their masters with the promise of freedom in exchange for their help. And given Maryland and Virginia's large slave population, more effort had been put into stemming revolts than in fending off the British.

Freeman had taken too great a risk, posing as a runaway himself, to get Thad names, and no doubt it would have proven fruitless had the man, now seventy, not looked fifteen years younger than he was.

But now they knew. Now they knew which parts of the British navy had native pilots to lead them through the estuaries. No wonder the raids along the Patuxent, the aggression, the confidence.

Thad drew his letter forward, the one he would send with Arnaud to Washington City tomorrow to be delivered directly into Congressman Tallmadge's hand. He uncorked the vial of sympathetic stain.

The formula was similar to the one the Culper Ring had used during the Revolution. But when the brothers Jay had ceased its production after the war, Father had taken it over and made a few small changes.

Thad drew out his code book as well, though he only occasionally needed to refer to it. Mother and Father had set to work on this too after peace settled over the land some thirty years ago. They had used Tallmadge's original code as a base but had studied other examples of cryptography and had made improvements accordingly. No longer, for instance, did they encode the shortest words—such as "a," "an," "I," and "the"—for doing so would all but guarantee that anyone who got their hands on a developed message could crack it. He had been rather surprised to look at both new and old versions and see that Tallmadge hadn't considered that from the start.

But then, they had been novices, all of them. Trained only in love for their country, not in espionage.

Thad flipped open the book. He had found it in a hidden drawer of Mother's *secretaire* when he was thirteen and had set about memorizing it so that he and Arnaud could pass messages between them in school. It had earned him a knuckle rapping from Mr. Taylor, but still the memory made him grin. When his parents realized what he'd done, they had been far too impressed with him to dole out any extra punishment.

And a ruler across his hands was not so great a penalty, not when one considered that his mother had risked her life every time she wrote a message. Had she been caught, she would have been hung. Thad had no such danger facing him. Though the British would no doubt be happy to see him dead, they were hardly within reach.

He and Tallmadge had political enemies aplenty, though.

As Mother would say, better to spend an hour encoding and decoding than a lifetime wishing one had.

He dipped his quill into the vial of stain. Careful not to let the straw-colored ink cross over the iron gall and leave telltale smudges, he penned the pertinent information into the blank space between the visible lines. Even as he wrote, the pale stain faded and dried, disappearing entirely.

Magic. Two centuries earlier, Father would have been called a sorcerer for creating such a potion and likely burned at the stake. Praise the Lord they lived in a more enlightened age.

Once the message was dry, Thad folded the sheet, let a few drops of melted wax fall onto the edge, and pressed to seal it. He slid the code book and vials back into their drawer, cleaned and mended his quill to be ready for its next use, and then pushed away from his desk. Arnaud had said he would be over to collect Jack before dinner, which meant anytime.

As if summoned by his thoughts, Jack came flying into his study, leaping upon his legs and trying to climb him like a ratline. Thad laughed and hauled him up into his arms.

But the boy stuck out his lip. "Not funny."

No? Odd, he had heard him laughing like a loon not five minutes earlier. "What is not funny?"

"Papa said it is time to go home, but I don't *want* to go home. 'Tis no fun there."

Thad lifted his brows and met the boy's scowling brown eyes. "Is that not where all your toys are? Your carved horse, your tin soldiers? Your wagon?"

For some reason, that reminder only served to bring the lip out farther. "Papa is mean."

"Oh?"

"I asked if he would bring them all back here, and he said no. But I bringded them all before."

"Brought." Thad tapped Jack's nose and gave him his best wise-uncle look. "And that was because you were staying with us for a month, my little mate, not for an afternoon."

"But—"

"Jacques?" Arnaud appeared in the doorway, his smile edged in frustration. "Are you ready?"

The boy squirmed so that Thad had no choice but to put him down lest he fall and then went tearing from the room shouting something to the effect of "No!"

Rather than chase after him, Arnaud fell into one of the leather chairs with a long sigh and rubbed a hand over his face. "I am a monster, you know, for expecting my son to live at his own home with me."

Thad sat on the edge of his desk. "Hmm. That is because you have no Grandmama Winnie there. Though if you wish to transfer Father's laboratory to *your* house and have them stay with you..."

The look Arnaud shot him was far too pained to play along with the jest. "Am I doing wrong by him, Thad?"

Sorrow pulsated from his friend's hunched shoulders. Thad sent a silent prayer heavenward. "He is still so young, Alain. He hasn't the reason yet to sort through his conflicting emotions—his love for you and his fear for you."

Arnaud seemed not to hear him. His gaze remained fastened on a tassel of the rug, his shoulders now slumped. "I still miss her so. I still think, every time I feel at a loss with him, that Marguerite would know exactly what to do."

Thad sighed and gripped the edge of wood under his hands. "She would be proud of you. Proud of you for taking charge of him when it would have been so easy to entrust him to someone else."

The way Arnaud winced, eyes closed, made Thad wonder if the pain would ever dull for this friend of his. "If only I had not missed so much of his life, perhaps then it would be better. Perhaps I would not feel so helpless had I been here when he was born, before Marguerite died."

"'Tisn't your fault you were not. Those pirates all but killed you—"

"But I ought not have gone." Arnaud surged to his feet and paced to the window. "Had I but listened to that blasted feeling of yours..."

How different it all would be. So many years of questions and grief that never would have been. So many fewer nightmares. So many shadows that would have no place.

But still, there was light anew. "We must simply thank the Almighty yet again for the miracle of your escape, of your return to Jack, and trust that He is leading you still. Just as He led you out of that infested pit in Istanbul."

Arnaud braced himself against the window frame. "I know. And I have no trouble crediting Him with the miracles, but seeing Him in the hours of tedium is…" He squinted out the window as he cocked his head to the side. "That looks like— But it cannot be."

Thad gained the window with two quick strides, his eyes going wide at the figure riding down the street who looked to barely be keeping his saddle. "Whittier?"

"It cannot be. Last I heard, he joined up with Barney's flotilla after the British sealed the harbor. He ought to be well up the Patuxent."

The river's name, along with the way the man in the saddle listed to the side, lit a spark of urgency within Thad in the same place that warned him against Arnaud's disastrous trip to the Mediterranean. He ducked his head through the open window, his left leg following.

Arnaud loosed a questioning grunt. "What in blazes are you doing?"

"That man needs help." His left leg on the ground, he swung his right over the windowsill. "And will likely be a heap on the road before I could find a door."

Though he muttered something under his breath, Arnaud was pulling himself through the frame as Thad sprinted across his lawn toward the now-halted horse.

By the time he reached the lathered beast, all question of the man's identity had been answered. 'Twas Joseph Whittier all right. Though with a face white as sea foam, and tinged with green. "Witty? Are you ill?"

His old friend turned unfocused eyes his way. One hand held the limp reins while the other arm remained folded across his unfastened uniform jacket. "Lane. I made it, then."

Thad made sure his smile was calm and reassuring, even though the wisp-thin voice sounded so little like the robust man he knew. "Aye, you did. Come, Witty. Let us help you down."

"I…" Whittier clutched the arm more tightly to his stomach and blinked too heavily. "Hurts."

Arnaud came to a halt beside the horse, his frown well justified this time. "Your arm?"

Witty listed further to the side, his arm shifting along with him, and Thad got a glimpse of the filthy shirt under the jacket—the shirt stained a dark, rusty red. "Nay, 'tis his stomach. Look at all the blood. Inside with him. Hurry."

Their friend moaned as they pulled him off the horse as gently as they could. Because he couldn't support himself, Thad lifted him with a shake of his head. "Will you get the door? And have Rosie clear the table?"

Arnaud ran ahead as Henry appeared beside him, brows drawn. "What can I do?"

"Would you see to his horse?"

His friend nodded and headed for the street while Thad continued toward the house. Whittier let out a low grunt of pain, but his eyes opened again, and they were fired with panic. "You must warn them."

Thad's throat went tight. "We will, Witty, but first we must see to this wound. What happened?"

He shook his head, nearly thwacking it against the door frame. "Shot. Not important. Cockburn is...Cochrane coming from Bermuda."

Clenching his teeth until the muscles in his jaw twitched, Thad drew in a long breath and aimed for the kitchen. Tantalizing as any information on those two British admirals was, he must first tend his friend. "Save your strength, please. You can tell me about it afterward."

"Nay. Now. Before—" A cry of agony interrupted the words, and Whittier's face contorted.

Thad lengthened his stride. "Rosie! Are you ready for us?"

"Get him on in here, Thaddeus." Rosie had spread a length of old canvas on the table, onto which he lowered Whittier. His housekeeper hissed out a breath when she saw the stained shirt. "Lawd o' mercy, help us now."

"Amen." Thad pushed the jacket away and gently rolled up the ruined cotton shirt. His own stomach cramped when he saw the wound seeping deadly, nearly black blood. Though his medical expertise was limited, he had seen enough to know that this was bad. Over his shoulder, toward the sound of footsteps, he said, "We're going to need Dr. Miller. Fast."

Whittier seized Thad's shirtfront, strong enough at first to bring his head whipping back around, though then his hands loosened and fell away. His chest rose slowly, as if the effort to fill his lungs required all his strength. "No time." His voice was even thinner than a minute earlier. "Cockburn, Lane. He...soon as Cochrane arrives...attack. Awaiting...orders on where. Annapolis or...or Washington."

The knot in his stomach twisted. "Are you certain?"

"Heard them." Whittier's eyes went shut again. "Thought I...dead. Talking. Crawled away and...took a horse. You must...warn..."

Calm descended, loosening the twist in Thad's gut and bringing him down into the chair by the table. Purpose took the place of urgency, though it was sorrow stained. He gripped his friend's forearm. "I will take care of it."

"I know." Another quavering breath, another raising of his eyelids. "My parents. Jill. My love."

"I will go to them myself. I will tell them."

Whittier's other arm lifted slightly and then fell again. "Samuel. Proud of him. And of little Jilly."

"I know. And so do they."

With a minuscule nod Witty closed his eyes again. Drawing in another wheezing breath, he let it out. And then...he wasn't.

Rosie's sniff sounded, and her familiar hand rested on his shoulder. "I'll see if I can catch Alain. No call for bringing the doctor now."

"Thank you, Rosie." He gave her hand a pat and then stood. He turned, expecting to find his mother hovering in the doorway.

But it was Gwyneth who leaned into the post, gripping it with white knuckles. Her eyes were as wide and damp as the sea, looking toward the table but glazed in a way that made him think she saw Whittier no longer.

Had he known it was she in the doorway, he would have ordered her away before she could have caught a glimpse of the horrific wound. Thad slowly eased forward, afraid she would yet again go weak-kneed. "Gwyneth?"

"Who was he?" Her voice emerged like a spring breeze, nothing more than a soft stirring.

"An old friend." He took another step, this one to put himself between her and the table. To block her view, to force her to focus on him instead.

She did, with a blink and a lift of her head. "I am sorry. I never... Papa always said war was an ugly thing."

"'Tis that." Thad lifted his chin, motioning behind her. "You ought not be in here. It will only unsettle you."

What thoughts were those that flashed through her eyes like lightning? They were too swift for him to make out, too much cloaked in those shadows that marred the depths of her gaze, but at least she seemed to hear him. She nodded, loosed the door frame, and half turned.

And then she had to grip the other side. 'Twas more convulsion than tremor that swept up her figure, and she squeezed shut her eyes as if to hold back tears.

"Gwyneth." He went to her side, ready to catch her should she fall, ready to rescue her should she be overcome.

But the moment he touched a hand to her shoulder, she lifted her chin and swallowed, fighting back whatever demons chased her. And then she strode away.

Thad could only lean into the post and shake his head. It was as though she were a pane of glass, shattered yet still in its frame. What tragedy had struck to destroy her so?

And what strength must she have within to still hold herself upright?

He turned back toward the table and the prone body upon it. He had a family to notify.

And a message to the congressman to revise.

Ten

Gwyneth stared into her mirror, willing the image to change. Willing the circles under her eyes to disappear, her skin to regain its color, her hair its luster. She looked like a beggar who had stolen fine clothes.

Mrs. Wesley tugged on a lock of Gwyneth's hair and then jabbed her scalp with a pin.

"Ow!" She jerked away, pressing a hand to the sore spot. "Take care!"

The woman's face appeared beside hers in the mirror, consternation etched upon it. "My apologies. I am so poor at doing another's hair."

Heat bubbled and churned, moving from her stomach to her throat until it erupted from her lips. "Then perhaps Papa should have sent me with my lady's maid instead of you."

She slapped a hand over her mouth, but it did nothing to stop the hurt from settling on Mrs. Wesley's face. Dear, sweet Mrs. Wesley, who had stayed faithfully by her side. Always there, waiting to be needed. Hovering. Chiding. Suffocating.

No. Gwyneth squeezed her eyes shut and tried to push down the bilious thoughts. Where did they even come from? "Please forgive me. I am so very grateful you are here with me. Truly I am."

"You are not yourself yet." Though it looked as though it took effort, Mrs. Wesley smiled at her reflection. "'Tis the exhaustion, love, not you. I only wish I knew why the sickness still plagues you. We have been on land over a week now."

And had it been the sea that caused it... Gwyneth shrugged and focused her gaze on the curling tongs Mrs. Wesley removed from the small built-to-purpose fire. "Could we forego the curling? It is so dreadfully hot already." She wanted to add that if the woman could not be trusted with pins, she certainly didn't want to put her head near scorching metal, but she bit her tongue.

She would *not* be a slave to exhaustion and its moods. She would *not*.

Mrs. Wesley sighed. "But this will be the first you have gone out since you arrived, love, and it was so kind of Captain Lane to offer to take you to the shops. Ought you not look your best?"

She had no "best." Not anymore. Only varying degrees of awful. Where on the scale could she hope to land today, after seven straight nights of terror that combined that poor felled soldier with Papa?

Another man dying before her eyes, the life extinguished like a candle too soon snuffed out. Leaving what? Vapors. Tendrils of smoke. Worse, the shifting shadows of smoke, the kind that one could only see in one's periphery, that fled when one tried to focus upon it.

Was life any more than that? Did what one accomplished before death matter at all, or would it all be blown away like smoke?

She squeezed her eyes shut, blocking out the image of her hollow face. Papa's life mattered. He did great things, fought battles, won wars for his country. Stood, always, as a shining example for those around him. Mama had brought grace and faith wherever went. But Gwyneth? No one would miss her if she were to fade away like a whisper. London would have forgotten her. Her friends would have turned against her when she failed to keep in touch. Sir Arthur would have found another young lady to woo, one more to the taste of his uncle.

And the Lanes—she was naught but a burden to them.

A light tug on the tendrils, and the familiar sound of hair being wrapped around the curling tongs filled her ears. "There now, it will only take a moment."

She mustered a close-lipped smile and clasped her fingers together, digging nails into palms. She must focus. Must shake off melancholy as well as bile. Must determine what she was to do with herself.

She could not impose on the Lanes forever. As soon as word reached them of her father's death, she must leave and find some safe place. Somewhere to hide away. Someplace she could…could… A sob tried to rise, but she minimized it to a gasp.

"Heavens, child, whatever is the matter?" Mrs. Wesley patted her cheek and loosed the now-perfect curl. "Perhaps you ought to nap rather than go out."

"No." She swallowed against the rising tide and reached up to her hair. She selected the next curl to tighten and extended it toward Mrs. Wesley. "I want to see some of the city." She had already missed church, being too exhausted after a sleepless night following Mr. Whittier's demise to join the rest of them. She would not miss out on this opportunity. Who knew when Thad would have the time for such leisure again?

Though she couldn't determine what kept him so busy. He was out at all hours, usually her wakeful ones, and home at odd times. If Rosie or Mrs. Lane inquired as to his whereabouts, he would inevitably name some public house—yet he never carried even the slightest whiff of alcohol.

But if he were not there to drink, why would he be?

While Mrs. Wesley finished up on her left side and moved around to her right, Gwyneth reached for the pencil and paper on the vanity. The scene under her fingers would be better in oil on canvas so she could properly capture the glint of sun on water, the green cast that would edge the clouds on the horizon, but she dared not take this particular picture out of her room. Not when the master of the house was the subject, his feet braced on the pitching deck of the ship and spyglass in hand.

She set her pencil upon his face. He would have straight brows, eyes slightly narrowed to show concentration, yet sparkling with… not quite amusement. More…fascination with the world around him.

Mrs. Wesley hummed an old hymn as she twirled another lock of hair around the tongs, leaning over to watch Gwyneth shape his eyes. Her hymn turned to a hum of approval. "Never does your skill cease amazing me, love." She chuckled. "Had I even half your ability, I would be a rich woman indeed from selling my work in London."

Gwyneth's pencil moved quickly. The line of his nose, leading to the peculiar quirk of his lips, one side raised and the other steady. Not quite laughing in the face of the encroaching storm, but showing clearly that his respect for it gave no way to fear.

Her hand stilled. No, this one could not leave her chamber. Not when every time she left a work in some other part of the house, she found Thad studying it later. Who knew what he would think if he saw this. "I have never considered selling them."

"Of course not. You have no need of that."

Gwyneth frowned and gripped the pencil harder. What if she did have need? She had no idea how much sterling Papa had sent with her. No idea how she would ever access what had been in the banks at home. Everything must be hers now, the London house, the small country cottage Mama had so loved—unless Uncle Gates's treachery had somehow stolen that from her—but what good did any of it do her? When could she ever return?

Nay. She was trapped here in America, trapped not by the war but by her own family. And what if she hadn't funds enough to support herself for long? Perhaps she *could* sell her art. Did the Americans spend money on such frivolities? She had heard scathing whispers about them in the drawing rooms when hostilities were renewed, about how uncultured and barbaric they all were, prideful but with nothing deserving of pride. Far from what she had seen thus far.

Though she also had not seen any artwork on Thad's walls.

"There." Mrs. Wesley smiled and moved behind her, urged her chin up with a soft finger until she met her own reflected gaze. "There is my beautiful girl."

Gwyneth forced a smile for Mrs. Wesley's sake but did not long study the sallow face in the mirror. Instead, she gathered up her pencil and paper and headed to her trunk to stash them. "I had best hurry. He will be waiting."

She tossed open the lid to her trunk, set the page upon the other she had sketched of Thad three days prior, and paused. "Mrs. Wesley, do you know how much coin Papa sent with us?"

The woman made a dismissive noise. "More than enough to hold us all over until he joins us, love. Not to worry. You can well afford to buy yourself a little trinket while you are out today."

"But…" She squeezed her eyes shut and rested her hand on her velvet purse. "But what if he is delayed? With the war worsening…"

"And you think your wise father did not take that into account?" Matronly hands urged her up. "You've enough in your trunk alone to see you through several months. He sent more in mine, and more still in Mr. Wesley's. In case one of us were robbed, he said, and our trunks have a hidden drawer for to keep it. You've no worries, love. Here."

Gwyneth took the reticule Mrs. Wesley held out and watched her drop a few coins into it. Her mind still reeled even as she nodded and snapped shut the top of the pineapple-shaped bag. Papa had sent plenty indeed, but she could not use it all on herself. The Wesleys must be cared for too, as the family they were. Would they stay with her? Or at war's end would they want to return to England? They had a son in London, after all.

"You look as though you carry the world on your shoulders." Mrs. Wesley gave her a nudge toward the door. "Go and enjoy a morning out with our handsome host. And you had best return with some color in your cheeks."

"With this insufferable heat, that ought not be a difficult order to obey." Bonnet in hand, Gwyneth paused at the threshold. "Thank you, Mrs. Wesley. For your assistance and for being patient with me."

The woman clucked and waved it off, but her smile looked pleased. "Go on with you."

She put her bonnet on as she descended the stairs. Though it was still morning, already the pleasant night air had begun to sizzle. And already the exhaustion crept up on her.

Mrs. Wesley was not the only one worrying. This past week, she had kept stranger hours than ever before. Up and reading or drawing or painting until she all but fell over. Sleeping until the red-saturated nightmares chased her from the sanctuary of slumber. Then up again. Rarely did she give any thought to whether sun or moon shone in the heavens but to evaluate how the light would dictate her pursuit.

And inevitably, at some point in the hours of waking, she would shake off concentration or distraction or daze and see a Lane studying her. Concern pulling their smiles into contemplative frowns.

They must all think her an eccentric. Or, worse, unhinged.

Gwyneth gripped her reticule tighter and paused at the base of the stairs. Thad had not said where he would be waiting, but her feet headed down the hall toward his study, so she let them take her where they willed. Perhaps they knew more than her head.

He ducked through the door as soon as she turned the corner, proving her feet right. And though they ought to have paused at his appearance and waited for him to come her way, they yet again took on life of their own when he smiled at her. Drew nearer until she could tuck her hand into the crook of his proffered elbow.

Thad covered her fingers with his. "You look lovely, Gwyneth."

She had forgotten her gloves. His warm hand made a strange little pull-and-tug flutter in her chest. How long had it been since someone had complimented her? "Thank you."

"Shall we?" He removed his hand and led her toward the front door, off the porch, out into the intensifying sunlight.

Gwyneth turned her head so that the brim of her bonnet shielded her eyes and saw that his gaze was focused upon her in that studious way of his. Today, for whatever reason, it made her throat go dry. "Is something the matter?"

"I hope not." The thoughtful tone of his voice made his regard even heavier. "The Wesleys are troubled over you. They cannot fathom why your seasickness has followed you onto land."

What could she do but lower her head and study the bricks paving the walk?

His hand covered hers again. "Seeing Whittier made it worse, did it not?"

The mere name brought the image back, that gaping wound in the same place Papa had been run through. That same agony on his face, that same desperation to convey one last message.

Run!

It had taken all her will to keep from obeying that silent command again, from running pell-mell into the street and not stopping until her legs gave out, until she outran the monsters behind her.

"Gwyn?"

But no command to flee had been on Mr. Whittier's lips. She drew in a breath, measuring it out into a careful inhale–exhale. Nay, the fallen sailor had spoken far different words. Which made far less sense. "How is his family?"

"They are grieving, of course. And they are proud of his service. Otherwise, they are maintaining a very stoic facade."

She risked a blinding from the sun in order to look up into his face. He appeared stoic himself but for his eyes. Those churned with contemplation. "Have they need of any aid? Will they be able to get on?"

A blink, and his eyes cleared and brightened as he smiled down at her. "They are well enough situated, what with his father's shop supporting them."

Her nod did little to quell the questions that had been niggling at the corners of her mind for the past week. Still they pushed their way forward, following the route the bilious words had earlier. "Why did he not go home in his final moments? Why did he come to you?"

Thad's only response was a delayed, unamused breath of a laugh.

They turned at the corner, the same one she had watched Thad round last evening, and headed down the same street on which Rosie had told her the Whittiers resided. The street the man had ridden directly past, though home had been no farther away than Thad's house, so far as she could discern.

"He obviously knew he hadn't much time left. And he obviously loved his family. Why, then, would he choose to give you that message of affection for them rather than see them a final time and leave with them the message for you about the pending attack?"

Something shifted in the man beside her. Subtle, but with an undeniable effect. 'Twas as if he stood even taller, broader, just by tilting his chin.

Confound it, she would have to do another sketch.

"Perhaps," he said so quietly she could scarcely hear him over the rumble of a passing carriage, "his thinking was muddled with pain. Perhaps he thought he had time enough to see us both."

"He did not." She had heard him insisting his time was short.

His gaze tugged until hers met it, and then he held her captive. "Perhaps it was because he knew I could be trusted to give them his message, but was not so certain they would remember to give me mine."

"But—"

"Is it so beyond reckoning that a family struck by sudden loss would forget to relay something to a mere acquaintance?"

Gwyneth struggled for a breath and tore her gaze away. If she let him look any longer into her eyes, surely he would see within her the answer to that rhetorical question. That so many clouds obscured parts of her mind, so many holes gaped. So many simple answers escaped her, while some details stood out in stark relief.

Had she forgotten anything important from her father's last moments? She didn't know. Couldn't know. And she hated it.

So then, she would focus on those details still so clear. "Are you in the military, Thad?"

His gait hitched. "Pardon?"

"You certainly do not seem to be, and that is something about which I can boast a bit of knowledge. So why, then, did he come to *you* to pass along this information about the target of the fleet's next attack?" She did her best to look at him as Mama would have, with an arched brow and pursed lips that said *I know something is amiss*.

Except he was not supposed to smile in the face of it. "I am a member of one of the local militias."

"A militia."

Now he turned the look around on her. "You needn't say it with such disdain. It was our militias as well as our general army that sent you Redcoats packing once before."

Of all the... "But a mere 'member of one of the local militias' is by no means the authority one runs to when one overhears sensitive information, Thaddeus."

He came to a halt, forcing her to one as well. He regarded her for a long moment in utter stillness before sighing and pulling her onward again, past a line of elegant town houses. "Alain likes to say I know everyone in these United States. An obvious exaggeration, but he says it because I *do* know most of the leading families. Between my parents' connections with them and the ones I have made myself...I make friends, Miss Fairchild, 'tis my best gift. And so when one friend has a need to let some other friend with whom he is *not* acquainted know something, he comes to me. There is no mystery. I simply have friends in Washington City that Whittier did not."

Did he really take her for such a simpleton? There was more to Thaddeus Lane than a friendly demeanor. A plethora of acquaintances alone did not give one's chin that angle. Though she couldn't think what did.

"Paper."

"Pardon?"

Thad motioned toward a shop at the next corner. "We shall need more for you at the rate you have been drawing. I would have already purchased some, but I thought you may like to select it yourself."

Gwyneth tried her hand at lifting her chin, though she suspected it would lend her no air of mysterious authority. "Are you trying to distract me?"

The gleam of amusement in his eyes rivaled the sun. "Is it working?"

What, row upon row of creamy, decadent paper, all blank and pure and waiting for the whisper of her muse? "All too well."

He laughed, a sound she had heard often enough in his house. Still, it tickled out a smile to think that *she* was the one bringing joy. A feat far too rare these past months.

For a moment she breathed it in, holding all other thoughts at bay. And then she let the smile bloom. "I have noticed a sad lack of art upon your walls, Thad."

"Have you now?" He pulled her closer to his side to lead her around a sunken spot in the sidewalk. "Well, I suppose that is because until now I hadn't an artist friend to fill them."

"Are you unacquainted with the practice of *purchasing* art? Much as you did those rugs you so love?"

He made a dismissive sound. "Why would I do that? 'Twas inevitable that eventually I would make friends with an artist to give me a picture or two. But now, rugs—what were the chances I could charm a Turk into gifting me one?"

A light laugh surprised its way from her throat. "So that is where your powers of friend making end?"

"Of course not." He pronounced it with exaggerated bluster and then ruined it with a boyish grin. "But I did not dare assume anything with them."

"Oh, but you will with me?" Her nose in the air, Gwyneth sniffed much like her friend Eliza Gregory was wont to do. "And who is to say

I will not charge you a fee? Perhaps I have been inspired by this capitalist land of yours."

He chuckled and held out a hand to indicate they ought to cross the street before the stationer's. "And who is to say *you* are the artist whose work I would like?"

How long had it been since someone had jested with her? Emitting a huff of exaggerated offense felt like pure bliss. "You would be lucky to have one of my pieces, Captain Lane."

His sigh was long, the roll of his eyes slow, his gesture indulgent. "Fine, fine. Give me one, then. I will suffer it." The grin winked out again. "Make it of the sea, will you? Something with frothing waves and glistening sun and a storm on the horizon."

Were she not dodging the unsavory leavings of a horse in the middle of the road, she would have closed her eyes in delectation. 'Twas as if he looked into her very soul and saw the image she had already imagined. "And your ship. What is her name?"

"*Masquerade.*" His tone was the very one Papa had used when speaking of Mama. Pure, selfless love. "She is a brig."

Gwyneth had never pretended to be an expert on things naval, to know the difference between a brig and any other type of ship, but the name she could appreciate. "My parents first met at a masquerade."

"Did they?" Thad led the way onto the opposite sidewalk and reached for the door of the shop. "I suppose you thought that terribly romantic."

"It was, by their telling." She stepped inside, her breath catching in delight at the shelves of heaven. "Though I confess the one I attended did not live up to my expectations."

"Ah, Captain Lane! Good day!"

He relaxed his arm, freeing her hand. "Mr. Hatcher, good day to you too. How is Susan this week?"

The proprietor made some reply, but Gwyneth took a step in the opposite direction. Her gaze had already latched onto a stack of creamy stock.

Thad caught her fingers and gave them a squeeze as he grinned down at her. "Look your fill and select whatever you please. I have some canvas at home we can stretch whenever you need."

The kindness made her eyes sting. "Thank you." After a smile at him, she headed toward the shelves and trailed her fingers over the different weights and shades. The parchments and vellums and linen-cotton blends.

Within a few minutes she had put together a fair pile of paper in various sizes and thicknesses and textures, fingers twitching already. She would need new pencils too. And perhaps some charcoal sticks. And—

A shadow crossed her path when she turned toward the writing implements, one that nearly made her lose her grip on the paper. One that sent a bolt through her, fear so brilliant she could not move an inch.

Uncle Gates.

No, it couldn't be! Not here in some random shop in a random neighborhood in a city she had never intended to visit.

But yet... Her stomach twisting, she turned her eyes to follow the man who had just entered the store. He strode toward Thad and Mr. Hatcher, calling out a greeting.

Not her uncle's voice. Just similar to his build, his way of moving. But dark hair instead of gray. Too young. Too American an accent. Too extravagant in his clothing.

Not her uncle. But still his image overtook her, that sneering voice ringing in her ears. The flash of a blade, the stain of blood, a dying sailor on the table before her, a stranger who stood in that coiled way of her uncle, ready to pounce.

A monster's mouth stretched wide before her, teeth sharp as blades. And the darkness, the too-familiar darkness yawned wide as it swallowed her whole.

Eleven

Blast!" Thad shoved Nathaniel Mercer out of the way and leaped forward, managing to catch Gwyneth the moment her knees buckled and before the ream of mismatched paper could spill onto the floor. He had looked over at her in time to see her pupils dilate just before her face went blank.

When he had uttered a silent prayer for an escape from Mercer, this had not been the one he had in mind. Mother always said he ought to be careful what he prayed for.

Her head landed against his shoulder as he knelt, and her fingers knotted in his shirt. She must be struggling her way back to consciousness, but thus far there was no flutter of her lashes. So he loosened her bonnet and cradled her against him, the sweet scent of lilac teasing his nose.

A grating whistle sounded, and a moment later Mercer's shadow fell over them. "How did I walk past that tempting armful without noticing her?"

Thad gritted his teeth for only a moment. Surely he received some divine credit for dredging up a smile before he turned toward the man. "She is unwell. Hatch, will you see what we have here and put it on my account?" He eased the paper from between him and Gwyneth and handed it over.

"Of course, of course." Hatcher patted his considerable girth with one hand as he flipped through the sheets with the other.

Mercer clasped his hands behind his back in that too-still way of his, but, as always, calculation clicked away in his cold blue eyes. "Do you know her?"

"I ought to, as she is staying with my family." Not that he was yet sure he did, but he had enjoyed the glimpse he had gotten on the walk here. She was a keen one, observant. Sharp, witty. With a quicker tongue than her exhaustion had thus far let her prove.

Even if that did mean she saw more than she ought and had no qualms about calling him on it.

"What is her name?"

He shot a glance at Mercer, who still studied Gwyneth with too much interest. In public he got on with the man as well as anyone, but always he was left with a skin-crawling distaste when they parted. Before, he had chalked it up to his hatred for the man's chosen living, but now he might have to add his way of perusing Gwyneth to his list. As if *she* were naught to him but another slave to be traded.

No matter what Mother had promised her, he wasn't about to declare who she was for all of Baltimore to learn by sundown, not with that whisper in his mind that advised caution. "Gwyn Hampton. A distant relation on my mother's side, apparently."

"Lucky you. Would that I could boast such lovely relations. Will she be in town for the summer, then?"

Her fingers twisted his shirt and her jaw went tight, as if she clenched her teeth. Thad held her closer. "Her plans are not firm. Hatch, could I take her into your back room until she recovers?"

The proprietor looked up from his tallying with a gentle smile. "You know you may, Captain Lane. I shall get this wrapped up for you in the meantime, hmm?"

Thad stood with her, frowning. When he turned toward the storeroom, he found Mercer blocking his way. "I could fetch her something to drink."

"There is a pot of fresh tea in the back," Hatcher said without looking up again. "And a plate of cookies. Help yourself."

"Thank you." Though his baser man wanted to sneer at Mercer,

Thad instead smiled and nodded. "Do give your mother my regards when next you see her, Mr. Mercer."

"I will." If reluctantly, he nevertheless stepped aside. "I hope to see you and your lovely guest again soon."

Of course he did, at least when it came to said lovely guest. With another nod, Thad carried her past the shelves and through the partially open door at the rear of the shop, easing it closed with a toe.

Gwyneth's breath caught, and her eyes fluttered open. Thad used a foot to pull a chair away from the table and sat upon it with her in his lap. Not exactly what a London miss would deem a proper arrangement, but he doubted she would be able to stay upright in one of the armless chairs. "Gwyn, sweetheart, you must choose more appropriate times to take your naps."

He caught only a glimpse of a small smile before she turned her face into his chest. "I am sorry for being so weak." The words came out quiet and muffled against him.

"No need for that." His gaze fastened on the careful styling of her hair. How long would it take her in front of that new paper or a canvas before she would pull out every pin and set it tumbling again? And why did he have to battle the urge to assist her with that? By thunder, he would scare her off to parts unknown.

Inhaling, she shook her head. "I hate that I have become this way. It is not who I am, not *how* I am."

"You cannot help being ill."

She turned her eyes to his, revealing those sparkling, churning, tempestuous blue-green depths. Yes, every bit as alluring as the fathomless ocean. "'Tis not seasickness, Thad."

He couldn't help but smile. "I have known that from the start, Gwyn. And when you are ready to share what *is* plaguing you, I am happy to listen."

Though she didn't greet his invitation with an immediate confidence, he read acknowledgment in her eyes. Perhaps one day she would share her burden.

In the meantime she glanced down as if just realizing she was perched upon his lap and shot upward. A wise move on her part. Indelicate as the phrase might be, Mercer had been right when he called her a tempting armful.

She pulled out the second chair and sat before he could rise to assist her. But when she reached for the china teapot with shaking hands, he stayed her with an upheld palm. "Please, allow me. You are not quite steady yet." He took up one of Mrs. Hatcher's famed cinnamon cookies and handed it to her. "This will restore you in a blink."

Her fingers closed around the treat, but her eyes strayed to the door. "That man out there. Who was he?"

Thad poured her a cup of tea and added a generous dollop of honey. "Mercer?"

"I suppose." She picked up the lone spoon and stirred.

He poured himself a cup and let the scent fill his nose. "He is too far beneath you for you to worry about."

When she sipped, he was reminded of a hummingbird, so delicate yet with a mysterious strength. "I thought you Americans had risen above the trappings of rank or some such nonsense."

Thad snorted a laugh and took a small drink from his unsweetened cup. "Perhaps we have risen above titles, but there are still lines not to be crossed. And you, my friend, will have nothing to do with the likes of him."

"Is he in trade?" The twitch of her lips indicated she knew well that was an objection that applied to him as well as Mercer. The imp.

He narrowed his eyes and put another cookie before her. "It is his particular trade. Slaves."

"Oh." Her cup clattered against its saucer. "That is…"

"Exactly." Though he knew a few gentlemen with interests in the slave trade, they never dirtied their hands with it directly. The fact that Mercer did… He had made a fortune, but to Thad's mind, 'twas no better than blood money. And Mercer no better than the Barbary pirates who had left Arnaud for dead and then, when they discovered he still lived, sold him in Istanbul as though he were nothing more than a rug.

Only when small fingers touched his hand did he realize he gripped his cup so tightly it was in danger of fracturing. He looked up and saw Gwyneth's frown. "Are you all right?"

His face must have worn a dark cloud indeed for her to ask such a thing in her own upset state. "Well enough. There are just few things in this world I detest as much as slavery."

Her frown went from concerned to perplexed. "Yet you are friends with Mr. Mercer?"

"Not friends. I try to make an enemy of none, but some I simply cannot like."

"Hear, hear." She lifted her cup in salute, though the hint of revelry faded from her eyes as quickly as it had sprung up. "Have you ever? Made an enemy?"

"Hmm." He took another sip and noted the new tremor to her hands. "None of a personal nature, so far as I know. And you?"

Her eyes snapped for only a moment before her lips curved up. "A few, perhaps. I did, after all, steal the attention of Sir Arthur Hart from the other young ladies vying for it."

Sir Arthur Hart? A namby-pamby name if ever he'd heard one. No doubt belonging to some English dandy who had earned a knighthood by lending the Prince Regent a handkerchief on a day he had a runny nose.

Thad selected a cookie and bit into it, figuring he needed the dose of sugar. "Your beau?"

"No. Papa did not give his approval." She turned sorrowful eyes upon him. "Could we go home?"

His gaze fell from her eyes to the twitching fingers of her right hand. "Of course. You want to draw."

"Close. I need to paint."

He nodded, helped her up, and then wove his fingers through those of her right hand to see if they would still. For a moment he thought she would pull away. He expected her to. But then her palm relaxed against his, and her eyes reflected calm.

'Twould have been a comfort, had he not been so busy wondering what shadows would appear in this soon-to-be painting of hers.

Arthur gripped the rail of the ship and told himself the whipping wind was invigorating. That the constant damp was refreshing. That the incessant rocking and pitching was soothing.

But there was a reason he had joined the army rather than the navy.

The sickness had eased, at least. Praise be to heaven for that. Gates had begun to look at him as though he were nothing but a green-gilled nuisance. In the day since he had resumed somewhat-normal activities, he liked to think he had acquired decent sea legs. Well enough to see him through the next five to seven weeks, anyway.

"Did the ginger water help the seasickness, sir?"

Arthur let go of the rail with one hand and turned in the direction of the semi-familiar voice. The boy, called Scrubs by the crew, stood with a mop in hand, as he often did. So far as Arthur could figure, the lad could be no more than seventeen, with a shuttered face that made him seem older and a drawl to his speech that begged the question of from where he hailed. "Quite an improvement, yes. Thank you."

Scrubs nodded, though nothing changed in his expression. "The captain gave me leave to bring you some morning and eve."

"I daresay that would be wise."

"Very well, then." The boy turned away.

"Scrubs?" Arthur lifted a hand without quite knowing why he wanted to detain him.

He turned back around with not so much as a spark of curiosity in his deep brown eyes. "Sir?"

Arthur sighed. Perhaps it wasn't Scrubs he wished to distract so much as himself. "Where do you call home, boy?"

He blinked. "The *Falcon*, sir."

At that Arthur shook his head. "And before you joined her crew?"

Did Scrubs's fingers tighten around the mop handle, or was it only Arthur's imagination? He couldn't be sure, but the lad's chin lifted half a degree. Some indication, at least, of feeling. "Virginia, sir. Born and raised."

Virginia. Arthur pressed his lips together, but only for a moment. Some questions demanded answers, no matter how insensitive. "You were impressed?"

"Three years ago, from my uncle's fishing boat. Captain Yorrick claimed I was a runaway cabin boy from some British ship."

"Were you?"

Scrubs turned again. "The only truth that counts on the *Falcon* is the captain's."

Arthur let the boy stride away. Sad as it was to see someone forced into service, 'twas a necessity. The fleet was dangerously low on manpower, with desertion a rampant if risky business. What choice did captains have but to stop and search other vessels for their missing men?

Yet he also knew they used that right as an excuse to take whatever men they needed, be they deserters or not, and who was to prove they were wrong? Scrubs was right about a captain's word. It was more important than truth. It was law.

He turned back to the rail and the vast, open nothingness of water beyond it. Nasty business, this naval one.

"There you are, Sir Arthur." Gates's voice beckoned from the direction opposite Scrubs's, and he looked that way to see the man approaching with the captain.

Yorrick nodded toward Scrubs's retreating back. "Is he bothering you?"

"Nay. He only asked if the ginger water had helped." He glanced from the captain to Gates, whose quirked brow questioned the truth of his claim. "And I asked him where he was from, as I could not quite place his speech."

"Ah. I found him in the waters of Virginia, with a deserter of an uncle." The captain clasped his hands behind his back and directed his face toward Gates. "He claimed he had never stepped foot off Virginia soil, but the uncle was a Scot, no question."

Gates waved a hand in dismissal. "I would not question your tactics, Captain. The Americans may claim they are no longer under our rule, but they are naught but recalcitrant children left too long without the guiding hand of their parent."

Arthur leaned against the rail until he remembered nothing lay on the other side to catch him. Straightening his spine, he said, "I daresay they disagree, Mr. Gates, having won a war for their independence."

The man looked amused. "Just as a child of seven will insist he is able to care for himself after a scuffle in the schoolyard, but that does not mean he has the wisdom to do so. The American government is too young, too idealistic, too untried. It will fracture and fail, and then they will beg us to come set them to rights again, like a tot running for its mama."

Captain Yorrick chuckled. "Just so. Why, they think because

they claim a thing, it must *be*. That regardless of the laws that have been governing British citizens for centuries, they can grant someone exemption from them after a man spends a few years' tenure on their soil. They have no respect for us, yet expect us to have respect for them."

"As I say, they are children."

"And so they need the rod taken to them." Yorrick gave a decisive nod and motioned them toward the companionway. "Have you children yourself, Gates?"

The man gave a sigh that sounded soul weary. "I am afraid that blessing has been withheld from my wife and me."

"I am sorry for that. My sons are among my greatest joys."

Gates nodded. "It has been an eternal sorrow to Mrs. Gates. Fortunately, my niece Gwyneth has long been like a daughter to us. I am most eager to be reunited with her now that she is parentless, to make her a part of our home." Over his shoulder he sent the closest thing to a smile Arthur had seen from him. "At least for the short time we shall have her before she makes her own."

A day that could not come soon enough. Arthur could only hope they would find her in time to keep her safe from whatever danger stalked her.

Twelve

If there were such a thing as a muse, she had taken over the house with a fury. Thad leaned against the trunk of the tree and watched the same basic activity he had been viewing for the past five days. Father dashing in and out on the quest for a new variation of a pigment he had concocted in his laboratory. Mother reading aloud to keep their guest soothed. Rosie emerging every hour to refresh drinks and all but force-feed the artist. Henry raising makeshift canopies to soften the glaring light.

And Gwyneth. Thad could scarcely take his eyes off her and counted it a blessing she was too absorbed to notice.

"She is a pretty thing, isn't she?" Arnaud leaned into the bark beside him, his eyes on her too. "Jacques cannot cease talking about how she let him use some of her paints."

Pretty? Nay. Pretty was too tame a word for the way she looked as she stood before the easel Thad had made her, eyes focused on the canvas with unwavering intensity. They fairly glowed with concentration, like the water of the Caribbean when the sun shot through it. Her hair, gold spun with fire, had tumbled down again and, again, been tied into a knot and secured with a brush. Which he now knew would last until she needed said brush, at which point she would pull it out and send the curls down her back again, until one had the audacity to fall into her face. Then out would come another brush to play the part of a pin.

Thad drew in a breath, watching as she made a broad, sweeping stroke in saffron. Then his friend's words fully penetrated and he frowned. "You like her."

Arnaud's lips twitched. "Certainly. Who would not? She is sweet and kind, and lovely besides."

Sweet, kind, and lovely? Those were the best words Arnaud could come up with to describe her? Thad shook his head and let his gaze drift her way again. She was more than those, so much more. She was heady honeysuckle, a wide open azure sky, pure sunshine gleaming through snow-white clouds. She was tossing waves and frothing white-caps, churning tempests and searing lightning.

And if Arnaud was smitten…the thought pierced. But if his interest was kindled by this nymph before them, then Thad would have to put aside his own intrigue.

He had no choice. Not with all he owed him. With all the pain he had already caused. "Will you…come to call on her?"

The twitch gave way to a grin. "Do I look daft? *Non*, admiration here is stayed by practicality. Something our charming Miss Fairchild is sorely lacking."

Thad's straight spine stiffened. "She is not impractical."

Arnaud snorted a laugh. "You said yourself you keep coming home to find her near collapse, with that blasted brush still in her hands. That thrice this week you have had to carry her up to her room when she fell asleep on her feet. She hasn't so much as a dash of temperance. Which is fine and well in a friend but not at all what one needs in a wife. The house would go to ruins in a week."

Thad's house seemed to be ticking along just fine, but he saw no reason to talk his friend into paying her court if he weren't so inclined.

Arnaud's snort turned to a full-bred chuckle. "She baffles you, *n'est-ce pas*? Unlike with every other man, woman, and child in these United States, you cannot look at her and divine exactly what she needs because she is far too scattered."

Yes, that was it. That was why he had found so many occasions this week to simply stand here and watch her. He was trying to determine what she needed and not just memorize the way her eyes narrowed or her teeth caught her lower lip, that curve of her shoulder when she made the smallest of motions with brush on canvas. "I will figure it out eventually."

"Hmm. Well, *mon ami*, you keep up the study. I need to get home. Find me when you return from Washington City tomorrow." Arnaud clapped a hand to his shoulder and disappeared.

Father emerged from the house yet again, stirring a pot of something or another. "Try this one, Gwyneth. Ground cochineal as one would expect, but I tried a different method of heating it with the linseed oil."

Gwyneth took a step back from her canvas and smiled as she lifted the stick from the pot and saw the crimson within. "It looks perfect, Mr. Lane, thank you. Let us hope it dries correctly."

"If not, let me know and I shall try a different ratio." Father gave her a warm smile, full of contentment at getting to put his love for chemistry to use, and motioned to Mother. "Are you ready, my love? We don't want to be late to Mr. Matthews's."

Mother put a slip of paper in her volume of Shakespeare. "Of course. Gwyneth, do you need anything before we go?"

A moment later, after the shake of Gwyneth's head, his parents took their leave and silence descended upon the garden. Thad let it settle and wrap its arms around them. Let the birdsong filter into his consciousness. Breathed in the scent of the herbs Rosie had planted. Felt the bite of bark against his back. And watched her.

Watched as she turned fully back to the painting. Watched as she dipped that brush into blood-red paint.

Watched as tears welled in her eyes and her face pulled into a mask of taut agony.

He pushed off from the tree. For the last five days, he had looked only at her. Her as she wielded paint and brush, not the canvas onto which she put it. But something whispered that it was time. Time to see the painting.

Finally, after an eternity of working and mixing and glazing and drying, the world on the canvas began to pulse. Only then did she know a piece was nearing completion. When she felt the thud of blood through veins and timed each stroke accordingly. When light and shadow joined together and danced. When the elusive vision she had been chasing stayed, solidified, and *became*.

When the critical shade waited, trial after trial of this hue and that finally giving way to the right color. The right preparation. The right use of sublimers and levigating mills and mullars, the right consistency of oil and pigment and turpentine.

All for red. Crimson red, pure and bright, tending neither toward orange nor purple. No vermilion, no cinnabar. No rose nor carmine. *Red.* Red that gleamed like a ruby. Red that bespoke England and the army. Red that meant life and its loss.

Her vision blurred, forcing her hand to pause. *No.* No, not now. She could not let the world double and waver. This moment, of all the moments of the past months, she needed clarity.

Swallowing, blinking, and sucking in a long draft of air, she waited. *There.* No more haze. Just the canvas, every inch covered with paint. The garden outside Papa's window, misty with greens and yellow. Verdigris, sap green, and the terra verte Mr. Lane had helped her perfect. King's yellow, oker, and sienna unburnt.

The desk, the shelves, Papa's hair in shades of brown. Extract of liquorice, asphaltum, and umber.

The play of light with white lead and crushed pearl. The score of shadow in lampblack and Indian ink.

Scalloped edges and intricate curves. A window to a world forever lost.

And now red. Brighter than the jacket that painted-Papa wore, underscoring, overcoming. There, here, dripping, staying. Hidden, always hidden.

Always there. Taunting. Haunting.

Shaking.

She jerked her arm away before she could ruin it all, and the brush fell from her fingers and rolled down her dress. White turned crimson, with slashes and gashes on the swath moments ago still pure. Just like that, ruination and destruction.

"Gwyneth."

Thad. When had he moved? Gwyneth lifted her head to find him beside her and realized his hand rested on her back. But he didn't look at her. His gaze remained latched on the canvas, moving over it as if following a path. Reading a line. Darting and jumping, tracing the exact journey her brush had taken, the trail of colors in the order she had applied them.

His face went tight. The hand on her back slid down to her waist and anchored there. When finally he looked to her, his eyes burned like a candle's flame. "What happened to him?"

Trembling, quaking that she couldn't still. She looked to the painting. How did he see? There was no blade, no pool of blood. Just Papa, standing as he had been before the shelves she had practiced with pencil, behind the desk with its familiar scratches and dings. Papa, tall and strong.

Papa, pierced through. But Thad wasn't to see that. He wasn't to see the slight variation in shade between jacket and blood, so easily attributed to light and shadow. He wasn't to realize the look upon his face was that one moment between fear and pain.

"Gwyneth." He tightened his grip on her, demanding that her gaze return to his, making the tremors quicken. He searched her eyes until she felt sure he saw every thought, every fear, every monster hiding within. And he looked as though it rent him to pieces as it had done her. "He is dead?"

The word bit like a sword, made her knees buckle and her stomach heave. Like Papa, she crumpled. Like Papa, she fell. But rather than a hard floor catching her, strong arms held tight, and her fingers found Thad's lapels. A keening welled up, but her throat closed off to trap it.

"Tell me." Too quiet to be called speech, naught but a murmur in her ear. A bid more than a command, a begging. "You need to tell me."

"I...can't." Even those two words made her tongue twist. Made the black monster gnash its teeth. "He will hear me."

"He will not. Gwyn, look at me." He pulled her head back and tilted her chin up. Gently but insistently, until those yellow-topaz eyes burned her anew. "You are safe. You can tell me. Tell me what you saw."

"Nothing." She loosed his coat, but only with one hand. Only so she could grip his wrist and hold on. Hold it there, where it cradled and steadied. "I saw nothing. I can't have. If he thinks I did, he will kill me next."

"He will not." His words burned like his eyes.

"He is coming, I know he is. He mustn't hear me. He mustn't know I know, or he will…he will…"

"I'll not let him. I swear to you." His thumb swept over her jaw and lit a new quake that shivered through her. "Tell me, sweet. Tell me who killed your father."

The cry ripped out, savage and fierce. So long held at bay, but rising now like a tidal wave, pounding at the walls of her being until it forced her to the ground.

Thad went down with her, never letting go. *Tell me.*

Did he speak it again or just think it so loudly it echoed along with the sobs in her mind? She tried to shake it away, close it back up, and knit it tight, but tears rushed down her cheeks and surged through her throat. Through the hole they made came the gasp. "Un–un–cle."

"Oh, Gwyn." He must have pulled her closer, for she felt his chin rest on the top of her head, his fingers tangle in her hair. Arms tight around her, keeping the demons away. "One of his brothers?"

"M–mama's. G–g—"

"Gates." Certain dread made the word fall like lead. "Do you know why?"

The river of tears hit a bank of rocks within her, making rapids. Gasps. She could only shake her head and bury her face in his chest, letting the floodwaters empty her. Letting them spill out until there was nothing left within. Not a torrent, not a trickle, not a tear. No horror, no hope. Nothing.

Nothing but the soothing brush of fingertips through her hair and the drifting scent of sandalwood. "You are safe now, sweet. I'll not let him harm you, so help me God. You can start anew here."

But there was nothing new to start.

The tan of his frock coat faded to the black of her eyelids, and she held tight to whatever fabric was under her fingers now. "Don't let go."

"I won't. Not ever."

Not ever. *Never.* The only hope she had left…and it was a promise for nothing.

Thirteen

T had lowered Gwyneth's still form to the divan in the drawing room, where the breeze could whisper its way over her from the nearby window. Though her head rested on the pillow, her fingers still gripped his jacket. Perhaps another day, it would have made him smile.

Today, his breath shook as he dragged it in. He pried her fingers loose but then held them tightly.

"Thaddeus." Rosie bustled in, setting a pitcher down on the end table with an angry thump, her scowl directed at his chest. "She got paint all over you both."

"Don't fuss, Rosie. Not now." His voice felt strained, a perfect match to the tension pulling his insides tight. With his free hand, he brushed the burnished curls from Gwyneth's cheek.

Rosie stepped close and went still. "Something wrong?"

"Very wrong." The curls wrapped themselves around his hand. Of their own will, surely. No fault of his. "She saw her father murdered. That is what has been haunting her so."

Rosie's breath hissed out through her teeth. "Lord, bless her. No wonder, then. So she has no one? No one left in England?"

No one she could trust, it seemed. He let the hair weave itself through his fingers. A tapestry of flame and gold. "She thinks his killer will follow her here."

Rosie pressed a hand to her damp forehead and adjusted the turban holding back her midnight hair. "As if a war ain't enough to worry about. You promise to keep her safe?"

"Of course."

"Good. She trusts you. Guess that's why she can only sleep when you're home."

"What?" His head jerked up, and he frowned into Rosie's exasperated sigh.

"You haven't noticed that?" She clucked her tongue and planted her hands on her slight hips. "She's even worse than Emmy when Henry's gone a-piloting. Soon as the door closes on you, she wakes up. Never until you get home that she can rest sound again."

"I..." What was he to do? Nights were when the soldiers and sailors gathered and talked. But if he could actually help Gwyneth recover simply by staying home a few days...

Rosie shook her head and held out her hand. "Give me that jacket and let me see if I can get the paint out before it sets. We should get her up to her room so Mrs. Wesley can help her out of her dress."

"Let her rest a few minutes first." He pulled his hands away from Gwyneth's just long enough to shrug out of his frock coat and pass it to Rosie. He marveled out how cold his fingers seemed without Gwyneth's laced through them, how right it felt to slide his palm under hers again a moment later as Rosie left the room.

God of my end, show me what I am to do. How I can help her. Please, help me understand why You sent her to me, to comprehend the wheels of Your orchestration so I do not foul them up by jumping in the way. Show me, my Providence and Guide. Please, show me.

Sometimes the Lord answered with an image in his mind. A place he ought to go or a person for whom he ought to watch. Sometimes He gave him a peace that meant *be still and wait.*

Never before had He sent a crushing wave over Thad's spirit, so forceful it pushed him to his knees on the wide-planked floor. Never before had he felt a hand press like this on his head, warm and welcoming, yet without compromise.

Never before had he felt his soul be bound to another's. But when his fingers tightened around Gwyneth's, fire touched his heart. Branded him. So bright it eclipsed all else, so fast it was gone before he could lay hold of it.

Yet in its wake a few simple words echoed in his mind. *I called you beloved.*

The statement resonated, crystalline. And he understood. He must love as he was loved. Whatever she needed, that was what he must be. Brother, friend, champion, guardian. Confidant and confider. Trustworthy and trusting. *Beloved.*

A caress on his cheek brought his eyes open. His face was mere inches from hers, their noses nearly touching, and her fingers had found him. He could see the faint smudge of ultramarine at her temple, a few swipes of blue caught in the roots of her hair. The fan of red-gold lashes that swept up and then down onto the cream of her cheek again.

And in that brief, half-second glimpse into her sleep-filled eyes, the silken ropes pulled taut. Only three weeks ago had she entered his life, but he knew in that moment she would not leave it again. Must not. She was his, and loving her would be the easiest thing the Lord had ever asked of him.

But that was not all He asked, was it? He also demanded Thad be hers. That he trust her and lean upon her, even though she looked too fragile to survive it. Even though she could not possibly believe in his cause. Even though it made no sense. He must need her. Let her love him.

Beloved.

"Thad." His name was a sigh upon her lips, her fingers a sigh upon his face. She opened her eyes again, though they were clouded. "Stay."

"I will." Unable to resist, he traced the contour of her cheek too. So soft, like the petal of a rose.

"Do you promise?"

His smile felt strange—slow and secret. "I promise. So long as you do too."

Her brows drew down into a delicate V. "Do what too?"

"Stay."

"Oh." If her cheek felt like a rose, the curve of her lips looked like one unfurling in the first light of morning. "I promise."

"Good." Were he a rake, he would lean over now, close that breath of a gap between them, and claim her lips as she had claimed his heart. But he knew he mustn't. Not when tragedy still tormented her so.

So he pressed his lips only to her forehead and caught her fingers in his once more. "I am sorry, sweet. So sorry about your father."

She squeezed his fingers tight and didn't loose them again. "I am glad you know. I think…I think he would have wanted you to. He trusted you."

And so she, because she trusted her father, trusted him too. Thad closed his eyes and rested his head on their joined hands. *Why* did the man trust him, when they hadn't met but once fifteen years ago? "I am glad he sent you here."

"Are you?" Her eyelids fluttered down again. "I did not understand why he would."

Nor, truth be told, did Thad. "Perhaps he knew something we do not."

"He often did." She drew in a long breath and eased it back out. "I wish I knew…knew why…what it was. Uncle Gates was looking for something. Papa said he had sent it away."

Could it be? He closed his eyes too and called to mind the image of that letter. *Gates.* The name was in it, just past the middle of the first page, but Mother had declared it a nonsensical line. He had said something about Gates being like a son to him. But they were brothers-in-law, of an age. Friends.

Was this murderous uncle of Gwyneth's the same Gates rumored to be set on the destruction of America? Who, through his position in the Home Office, had been gathering information on U.S. soil ever since the Revolution ended? What, exactly, would that mean?

A chill raced down his spine. If he *was* that man…then for what, as Gwyneth said, had he been looking?

All Thad knew was there were two things Fairchild had "sent away" that had come to *him*. A letter, mysterious and full of blatantly wrong facts.

And the sleeping woman before him.

For the first time since she fled Hanover Square, Gwyneth opened her eyes lazily. She yawned, stretched, and relaxed against the pillow.

Morning light touched the pane of glass, inched over the floor, and reflected off the mirror. It made her sigh in wonder.

Light. No horrific monsters, no creeping puddles of darkness. No terror stalking her. She had simply slept. Slept and dreamed of idyllic things. Thad had been in them, smiling and laughing. Swinging little Jack high above his head. Teasing Philly and her husband.

Taking Gwyneth's hand, touching her cheek, toying with her hair.

She settled a hand over her thudding heart and felt the soft cotton of her nightdress under her fingers. Part of that had been no dream. At least she *thought* she remembered opening her eyes down on the divan and seeing his face so close, feeling his touch. Glimpsing that light in his eyes that had made her feel…safe. Treasured.

Her fingers twirled through the ribbon at her neckline. She knew she had stirred long enough to eat with Thad last night, but that was only a hazy recollection. Perhaps her mind had blurred it deliberately, as dinner conversation had been her reliving those horrific moments— hurrying into the house, hearing the argument, seeing the blade, and watching the life extinguished from Papa's eyes.

Then came Thad's promise not to leave again until after breakfast, and he had called Mrs. Wesley to help her up to bed. Darkness had been falling by then.

She had slept the night through. The whole, entire night. Without any nightmares.

More memories filtered in from the night before. Her begging Thad not to tell anyone else about her father, him insisting that the household needed to know. His tone had been soft but unyielding, and he had sworn she would not have to be the one to recount it again.

Her hand fell to the mattress, and she pushed herself up. Had he told them after she retired? His parents, who counted Papa one of their dearest friends? The Wesleys?

Mrs. Wesley entered with only a cursory knock on the door. Her feet shuffled rather than bustled as usual. Her shoulders were hunched, her eyes red and puffy.

Gwyneth had her answer. "Good morning, Mrs. Wesley."

The woman trudged over to the window and pulled back the drapes.

"You should have told us. You should have let us share the grief and heartache."

It wasn't the words that pierced. It was the tone, dull and full of censure. Gwyneth slid to the edge of the bed and put her feet upon the floor. "I am sorry. I was too frightened."

"Frightened?" Mrs. Wesley faced her, the wrinkles made all the deeper and fiercer by the sunshine behind her. "How could you be too frightened to have the sense to run for the authorities rather than across the ocean? He was your *father*, and you let his murderer go free."

Though Gwyneth tried to stand, her knees buckled, and she sank back onto the mattress. "You are right." Why had she not considered that? She squeezed her eyes shut, but the accusation still wagged its gruesome finger at her, shouting that she was an idiot, had made a mull of everything. "They would have caught him. Then Uncle Gates would be in Newgate and I—"

"Mr. Gates?" Claws dug into her shoulders and shook until she opened her eyes, looking straight into Mrs. Wesley's blazing ones. "What do you mean by such slanderous rubbish? Your uncle is a good, God-fearing man, and I'll not suffer you speaking so of him."

Gwyneth recoiled and shoved her hands into the mattress to keep them from shaking. "I saw him, Mrs. Wesley. I saw him run Papa through with a sword."

"I am to trust what *you've* seen? Like the monsters on the ship, the teeth you cried out where gnashing at you?" A derisive snort fouled the air. "More ravings of a madwoman."

"It isn't." Her voice emerged as naught but a squeak. If Mrs. Wesley, who had known her all her life, did not believe her, then perhaps she had been wise not to go to the authorities after all. "They were arguing, Papa accused him of greed, Uncle demanded something, and when Papa refused, he…he—"

She was cut off by the connection of Mrs. Wesley's bony hand with her face. The slap was not hard; it scarcely stung her flush. But the shock of it stole her breath, her words, her will to recover from it.

The woman's brown eyes threw sparks. "Your sainted father deserves justice that you have denied him. And your uncle—he is a man of heart and purpose. He is the one who recommended us to your father when he and your precious mother set up house. He always, always took the time to speak with us, to ask after John as well as your family. But *you*."

Gwyneth drew her knees to her chest and buried her face in them, but could not stop her ears against the words. Nor insulate her mind from the new pounding of fear. What had he asked the Wesleys about them? What had they told him, never suspecting him to be an enemy? What did he know from their lips that could be her undoing?

"You are a stranger. Not the child I knew all these years, and I don't much like the creature I see in her place. Selfish and cruel and...and unhinged." A sob interrupted, though Gwyneth daren't look up. "To think of how I've served you these months, with you lying about everything. Snapping and biting at me—and now this? You have betrayed your family. Your country."

She wrapped her arms tighter around her knees, squeezed her eyes shut.

A slight breeze moved over her exposed wrists and toes, and footfalls moved to the door. No longer shuffling, nay. Now heavy and brisk. Furious. The door whooshed as it opened, but the expected slam didn't immediately follow.

"Mr. Wesley has a cousin in Canada. We will make our way to him, and from there go home whenever we may. Rest assured we will take no more coin than is rightfully ours. We want nothing of yours."

She winced as if the door *had* slammed—directly onto her fingers. She had thought yesterday's bout would be all she could possibly cry in the span of a few hours, but no. The tears rolled down her cheeks, scalding and sticky. Filled her throat so that it was all she could do to keep them silent.

They were the only link she had to home, and they were abandoning her.

Of course they were. Why would they stay when they realized she had lied to them for months? About something as important as her father's murder? They wouldn't trust her anymore, couldn't. They *ought* to leave. Go home and see their son, their friends, find employment elsewhere and...and...

And they would likely go straight to Uncle Gates and tell him what she had said. Where she was. Everything. He would laugh with them, shake his head, call her a madwoman, and promise to look into an asylum for her.

Then he would come.

Fire licked at her nerves and sent her scrabbling for the edge of the bed, her brine-filled eyes focused upon her trunk. She must leave, must escape before he could find her. Before he could kill the Lanes for harboring her.

Her feet tangled in the hem of her nightgown, and rather than leap to the floor, she fell to it. Pain bit at the rap of her knees, but what did it matter? She rolled onto them and fought her nightgown into place. And then she swallowed another sob when a brown skirt filled her vision and a brown hand reached to wipe away her tears.

"Don't you fret none about the Wesleys." Rosie put a finger under her chin, bidding her to look up. Where Mrs. Wesley's eyes had shown a dark eruption, Rosie's were as calm and gray as a morning fog. "Folks deal with loss in their own way. Hers is getting angry, with you the only one she has to blame. You just let her go. Let them go home, or at least make a start for it before they come to their senses. We'll take care of you."

Perhaps that advice edged out the panic. Yet when emptied of that, 'twas just a return to yawning nothingness. She pulled her chin away. "They will tell my uncle, the man who killed my father, where I am. He will come for me."

"Not today he won't." Rosie lifted her apron and used the material, worn soft and thin, to clean Gwyneth's face. "I have been helping Thaddeus long enough to know how long it takes to cross the Atlantic and come back again. We got four months at the least before he could get here. More likely six or seven, taking into account that they won't have an easy time of finding a ship home, 'specially if they mean to go to Canada first."

Six months. Half a year. Gwyneth's shoulders sagged. Far better, then, to let them get well on their way before she devised any plans. Plans they couldn't be privy to. Time to prepare. Time to pray they would change their minds and not go to England yet. Stay in Canada. Return to Baltimore.

Forgive her.

Fourteen

T had let his horse have her head over the last open stretch between Washington and Baltimore and wished he were the one pounding the ground until he made thunder rumble beneath him. Happy as Electra may have been with the gallop, it did nothing to relieve the frustration boiling up inside him.

Nothing new upon a return from Washington. But worse than usual.

"Whoa." He reined her to a halt when his city appeared over the rise. So many familiar streets and well-known buildings. All the avenues and alleys he had prowled with Arnaud, hunting up any tidbit of information that could prove useful. The Chesapeake's harbor glistening in the sun, Fort McHenry looming in the distance.

Exposed. Ill-prepared. All because the blasted politicians would take no action. Thunder and turf, a more pigheaded lot he had never encountered. He had thought for sure the news from the ambassador in Belgium would have convinced them, but no. The cabinet had all dismissed the president's concerns this morning when he demanded action.

The British care only for Canada, they had said. *There's no tactical reason for them to attack us*.

"You are all a bunch of dunderheads," Thad muttered under his breath, hoping the wind would carry the sentiment back to the capital. Had they a lick of sense, they would realize this was neither about military tactics nor logic. This was about revenge for the Revolution. It was about men now admirals whose fathers had been killed here a generation before. It was about hatred.

Thad twisted the reins around his hands and clicked Electra up into an easy trot. At least the president had been alarmed by the news from Europe, but to launch an effective campaign against the British, secretaries Jones and Armstrong had to take action.

And from what he had seen, that was unlikely.

Heat welled up inside. 'Twas like April 1810 all over again. That dread expectation. That *knowing* he had been right but without the power to change anything. And then looking into the hollow eyes of a weary sailor and hearing the words that sealed his future. *Arnaud is dead. Barbary pirates took his ship and killed everyone but me.*

Now the harried script of the ambassador in Ghent. *There is an outcry for vengeance. With France surrendered, the populace of England is now demanding they teach America a lesson. That they burn our cities and punish us for our audacity. Our shores will soon be covered in Redcoats again.*

Four years ago, there was nothing he had been able to do. He could not go back in time and tie Arnaud to a chair to keep him from taking that voyage. He had been able only to go to his widow, hat in hand, and tell her his premonition had been right. Watch as the pain shattered her gaze and then bent her back, sending her into labor with Jack. Swear to her he would keep them safe.

He clenched his teeth together as Electra clopped her way from dusty road to cobbled street. He would not sit idly now and be ignored. He would not merely utter a prayer and then dismiss that tug in his spirit that cried *Do something!*

He would act.

Mother's face filled his mind, her emerald eyes sober and gleaming with purpose. He could see her once again handing over the crate filled with their legacy. The codes she and Father had rewritten. The invisible ink they had perfected.

The mantle.

"Welcome to the Culper Ring," she had said that day in 1811, when

war was still but a whisper on the lips of sailors enraged by the impress-
ment. "You will answer to Congressman Tallmadge, code-named John
Bolton. He will refer to you as Samuel Culper III. Whenever you bring
someone into the Ring, assign them a designation, either a name or
numeral. But Thaddeus."

She had gripped the crate tighter rather than releasing it. "This
is no game. Only those you trust most implicitly can know about the
Culpers. Anonymity is the best tool in this box."

With that advice he had never wanted to argue. It was her next
directive that had grated.

"We do not take direct action. We merely put information into the
hands of those who need it."

We do not take direct action. Thad had known that was one tenant he
could not obey. It had proven itself right for Mother and Father, when
action had nearly undone them, but he had learned his own lessons
about what one could lose when one did not act.

The key, in either case, was to obey that Voice in the spirit, of the
Spirit. That whisper that said *go* or *stay. Act* or *wait.* That murmur that
told him now the fate of his nation could not be left solely to the politicians.

He turned down the road that was the most direct route home—
and pulled Electra to a halt when he spotted the Wesleys rolling his
direction in an unfamiliar wagon. "Mr. Wesley?"

Though his wife merely folded her arms and averted her face, Mr.
Wesley regarded him wearily. "We are going to Canada, Captain Lane.
If we can without passes. And from there, home."

Thad's horse shifted. "You are abandoning her?"

"'Tis hardly abandonment." Mrs. Wesley huffed and lifted her chin.
"She is safe enough, though cold-hearted and cracked in the nob."

"Now, Georgetta—"

"The girl left her father to die, Marcus, and now she is trying to
blame it on her uncle." The woman's sniff seemed to be holding back
tears. "Next you know, it'll be us she turns on and leaves slain somewhere."

Mr. Wesley sighed. "I admit she ain't been right since we got on
that ship. But—"

"I'll not stay with her, Marcus. When I think of how she ran out of that house and never once hinted at what she left behind her—" Mrs. Wesley pressed a hand to her lips, but it did nothing to contain the sob. "The poor general."

Thad drew in a long breath as the rope within him went taut. One side pulled him to help, to calm them, to offer them whatever support he could. To convince them Gwyneth had not hurt *them*; she had been hurt herself. But he saw no crack in their armor. Getting through to them would take more time than they would grant him.

And he must hurry home. Gwyneth was no doubt hurting anew too.

"Here." He reached into a saddlebag, drew out a piece of paper, and handed it to Mr. Wesley.

The man didn't so much as unfold it. "What is this?" Suspicion saturated his tone.

"A pass to get you into British-held territory in the north. You shouldn't encounter any problems until you near the Canadian border."

The suspicion traveled from voice to eyes. "Why do you have one of these?"

"Apparently for such a time as this." He urged his horse forward until he was just past the wagon's bench. "She is not the one to blame for this, my friends. Her father was already dead. There was nothing she could have done. Nothing but obey the last words he spoke to her."

The woman stared straight ahead. "Let us away, Mr. Wesley, before we lose any more daylight."

Mr. Wesley tucked the pass into his pocket and picked up the reins again. Snapped them. But he at least met Thad's eyes again and nodded.

Not enough, not nearly enough to compensate for what they were doing by leaving.

Electra snorted as he clicked her up again. "I agree, girl." He patted her neck and let her head toward home. "It was a mite crowded anyway."

Once he reached his house, he entrusted Electra to a grim-faced Henry, grabbed his saddlebags, and ran toward the kitchen door.

Rosie met him, a spoon in her hand and her mouth in a thin line. "You see them leaving?"

"I did." He patted her arm and eased past her so he could put his things away before she scolded. "I gave them my pass."

She tossed the spoon into the sink. "You should have let them get stopped. Serves them right, taking their grief out on that poor girl like they done."

With a sigh he put a hand on Rosie's shoulder and gave it an encouraging squeeze. "I did it not for them, Rosie Posy, but for Gwyneth. She needs nothing more to cause her worry."

"True enough." She stood still long enough to pat his hand and then retrieved her spoon. "You think her uncle is gonna come like she fears?"

"Hard to say without knowing why he did it." But his gut said yes. "She isn't alone, is she? She must be upset."

Rosie waved the spoon in the direction of the doorway. "Your mama spent the morning with her, the two of them crying and reminiscing about General Fairchild. Your father's with her now, reading to her, I think."

"Oh, saints above. She may not survive it." He ducked under the lintel and managed two strides.

"Thaddeus." Rosie poked her head out after him. "The day had some good in it too. She slept the night through. She woke when you left, but not until. No nightmares."

"Praise God." It nearly soothed the fray and frustration. Nearly. He nodded his thanks and headed down the hall.

His first thought was to deposit his bags in his study before searching them out, but that whisper inside stayed him. *Show her.*

Thad sucked in a quick breath. *Really, Lord? Now?*

Nothing. If the Lord had eyebrows, he imagined He was arching them, giving Thad the look his parents had both perfected. The one that said, "If I did not mean *now*, would I have told you to do it?"

He lifted his hands, saddlebags and all, in silent surrender and then turned toward the sound of Father's reading voice in the library.

"'...I shall waive giving any process for it here; especially as every book which treats of the chemical pharmacy contains one.'"

Thad stepped into the makeshift laboratory, his gaze moving from his father, who sat in his usual chair with a book before his nose, to Gwyneth, perched at the table with pencil and unmarked paper. He let his saddlebags fall by means of announcing himself. "What are you doing, Father, trying to put her to sleep? From what Rosie tells me, this is the one day she ought not need such assistance."

Father flashed him a grin over the tome. "'Tis *The Handmaid to the Arts*, Thad. Our dear Gwyneth was regretting not bringing her copy, so I found one. We are now reminding ourselves of the use of mercury in creating a fine enamel paint."

"Riveting."

Gwyneth put her pencil down and pushed herself up. Her lips bowed, and for once the circles under her eyes were faint. But those eyes were bloodshot, and fine posture could not overcome the stoop to her shoulders. She stepped around the table in his direction, but then drifted to a halt as if unsure she had taken the wise course. Still, her smile brightened for a second. "How was your day, Thad?"

"Frustrating, but probably better than yours. I brought you something." He reached into his breast pocket and pulled out a long, thin leather pouch.

A question punctuated her expression as she came a few steps nearer. "You thought to get me a present during your frustration?"

"Technically, it was before the frustration. But, yes." For the first time in hours, he felt like smiling. "You seemed to be in need."

She was finally close enough to take the pouch, and when she sent him a quick glance of curiosity and thanks as she opened it, he felt it all the way down in his stomach. By Neptune, she had the loveliest eyes. And they got all the more beautiful when she unwrapped the set of paintbrushes and joy lit them. "Thad—how did you know I needed these exact ones?"

"They seemed the scraggliest of your set. Did I get the sizes and shapes right?"

"Exactly so." For a moment he thought she might embrace him, the way she leaned onto her toes and strained forward, but proper breeding apparently won out—blast it to pieces—and she merely clutched the brushes to her chest. "You cannot know what this means to me today. Or perhaps you can, as you always seem to divine what people most need."

A snort slipped out, and Thad paced to the open window. "If only everyone agreed. Sometimes trying to convince them feels akin to bashing one's head against a rock."

"He is always like this after a trip to Washington City," Father said. Normal, everyday words. But Thad heard the note of warning hidden beneath the syllables. And certainly didn't miss the sign he made. *Careful*.

Thad leaned into the windowsill and folded his arms. "A letter arrived yesterday from Belgium. The ambassador in Ghent reported that the British people have been crying against us, demanding retribution for our perceived audacity. Tallmadge said—"

"Ah, good ol' Ben." Father all but leaped to the edge of his seat, his hard-glinting eyes belying the bright smile on his face. He brushed his right hand twice over his left fist. *Enough*. "An old friend of ours, Gwyneth."

Thad sighed and rubbed a hand over his face, half wishing he could obey the silent commands. "Madison called a cabinet meeting this morning. They all dismissed his concerns."

"And already it is the subject of gossip?" Father chuckled.

A question that deserved ignoring. "We must take action. An attack is coming, and we are grossly unprepared."

Father's false mirth faded to sobriety, but still Thad could see the protective wall shuttering his eyes. "There is only so much we can do, son. You can talk with the leader of your regiment—"

"There is much we can do, Father, but it is going to require creativity and something I know will make you and Mother uncomfortable— the Culpers need to *act*."

"Culpers?" Though she could have no familiarity with the name, Gwyneth had obviously noted the tension pulsing in the room and had backed herself into the edge of the table. "Who are they?"

Father stood, a tic in his jaw. "Thaddeus Lane, you are not—"

"—a child," he finished for him. "Nor am I alone in my feelings. Tallmadge agrees. It is not enough anymore to ferry information from one location to another, not when those who should be acting on it continue to twirl their thumbs!"

The clatter of wood on wood interrupted, and one of the paintbrushes rolled to his boot. Gwyneth went deathly pale, her eyes round, her lips quivering.

And she was looking at him as though he were a masked highway-man waiting to relieve her of her jewels. "You...you are a...*spy?*"

Father muttered a choice word—in Latin, which was all Mother ever let slide—and tossed *The Handmaid to the Arts* onto his chair. "Thad!"

"Spy is hardly the best word." He couldn't quite restrain his smile. "I am no cloaked fiend out to steal secrets and pass them to the high-est bidder, sweet. Merely someone in a position to help my country by keeping its leaders abreast of the goings-on."

"Someone who will have a tanned hide once his mother gets ahold of him."

His father's mumble stole his attention for only a beat. Far more concerning was the way Gwyneth shook her head as if in a trance. "Why are you telling me this?"

Father folded his arms. "Yes, Thaddeus, why are you telling her this?"

He looked from sire to guest, the answer more a certainty in his gut than a fact he could put upon paper. And all the more trustworthy for that as facts were so easily twisted. "Because," he said, silently bidding her to meet his gaze and waiting until she did, "she is already involved."

Fifteen

Gwyneth wished, prayed she would wake up and prove this scene nothing more than another nightmare. But despite the table corner biting into her palm, the image wouldn't waver. Instead, Thad's words kept echoing through her head.

How could it be true? She tried to draw in a breath deep enough to soothe, but an invisible hand pressed on her chest.

Thad was a spy. Whatever he wanted to call it, that was what it came down to. That was why he heard so often from all his sailor friends. That was why Mr. Whittier had sought him out in his last moments. That was why he disappeared at odd hours. Because he was involved in espionage. Perhaps not the filthy kind, perhaps not for gain. But still he went slinking around in the dark, still he passed along information to those for whom it was not intended. Still he sought to undermine the British cause. Not openly, honorably, on a field of battle, but underhandedly.

Why, then, did her feet still want to pull her his way?

She gripped the edge of the table until her knuckles ached. "I most certainly am *not* involved."

"Not willingly." Thad pushed off the windowsill, and for half a pulse she feared he would come to her.

He walked past, to the door, and her heart sighed in disappointment. Fickle thing.

A moment later she heard him opening one of his saddlebags, though she didn't turn to watch. Couldn't. What did it matter what he was pulling out? *Culpers*. The name still reverberated, though she had no notion why it would or what it mattered.

"This arrived on the same ship as the news from Belgium." His voice drew nearer again, but then his steps halted. "Mother, there you are."

Gwyneth finally convinced her head to move, though the rest of her frame remained rigid. Mrs. Lane entered the room with caution in her step, her gaze wary. Her eyes were still red rimmed, her lovely face swollen with grief.

Tears threatened Gwyneth's eyes yet again at the sight. It had been a solace to grieve with someone who mourned Papa as well. She had felt, sitting beside Mrs. Lane on the couch, as if she had a real friend again, someone who could be there when she so desperately needed Mama.

Now she wished she could spare her this truth about her son.

"What is it?" Despite the evidence of her sorrow, Mrs. Lane's gaze was sharp as she glanced around the room. "Tell me there is no more bad news."

Thad merely cleared his throat and motioned for her to move toward his father. "I was about to explain to Gwyneth and Father how, whether she wished to be or not, Gwyneth is irrevocably involved in our Culper business."

Our? Gwyneth sagged against the table. They could not possibly all…

"Thaddeus." Mrs. Lane's outrage rang differently than Gwyneth had expected. "This had better be an exceptional explanation."

Thad lifted the folded paper in his hand. "Like this, perhaps? 'When we captured the ship, one rather smirking sailor told us there would be no stopping the British now that their forces were free from Europe, especially after the murder. I asked him what in thunder he meant by that, and he made mention of a beloved general, slain in his home. Said he heard from the lips of the general's brother-in-law, who holds a government office, that an American spy was most likely responsible, and that he planned to personally see to retribution.'" He lowered the page and captured Gwyneth's gaze, though she tried to look away before he could. "Sound familiar, sweet?"

She shook her head, sending a loose curl to irritate her cheek. "I have no uncle in the government. Two are in the House of Lords, but that is not exactly an *office*." Although a beloved general, slain in his home…who else could it possibly mean? There was no other general so beloved in England.

"I believe you do, in fact." He folded the page, his every move slow and quiet, as if she were a rabbit he feared startling away. "There is a Gates in the Home Office. I was not sure at first it was *your* Gates, but I have been convinced."

"The Home…" Her head would not shake quickly enough to show how completely she rejected that idea. "Nay. My uncle is a…a writer." Was he not? *I deal in words*, he had said. What if…? What if those words were not written in some Gothic novel, but in…*this*?

Images flashed, lightning-fast portraits, frozen in time. And then Papa's accusation came back to her. *The Home Office has decent men in it yet. A few at least, though you are not one of them.*

How, why had she forgotten that so long? Her knees wanted to give way, but she held fast to the table. If she let herself fall, Thad would be at her side in a heartbeat. He would lift her and carry her to the couch. Touch her face and smooth her hair.

And she would enjoy it far too much. "No. Papa would have nothing to do with espionage."

A snort of a laugh spilled from Thad's lips. "He was a general, Gwyneth. Generals rely on intelligence to plot their campaigns."

"Scouting is different."

His lips twitched again into an infuriating grin. "Good to know you think so, as that is a more accurate description of what we do. Though I daresay he used intelligence from other sources too."

"You do not understand. He lost his dearest friend to espionage. He hated the entire practice." Though she felt the elder Lanes shift, she kept her gaze on Thad. "I heard him many times speak of the devastation of losing Major André."

"It was quite a blow to us all." Mrs. Lane's voice slipped into the conversation quietly, gently. "André was a fine man, yet had he succeeded in his task, Benedict Arnold would have handed West Point over to the British. There would be no United States of America today."

Something in her tone drew Gwyneth's gaze to her face, where she read regret mixed with determination.

Mrs. Lane shook her head. "It can be a sad business indeed, and a dangerous one. Yet sometimes, my dear, it must be done for the greater good, for the greater calling. Much as he detested it, your father knew that. It is, in fact, how he met your mother."

"No." She couldn't explain why the denial came so fast and hot, except that it grated against all she knew.

Thad eased a step closer. Had she any room to do so, she would have backed up a step in response. He held out a hand, imploring. "Think about it, sweet. What was a British officer doing in France on the eve of revolution?"

Why must they do this? Why must they make her question what had always just *been*? "France and England were not at war yet. He was…on holiday." Yet the claim sounded so weak now, where it had always been undeserving of examination before.

"On holiday," Thad echoed softly. "At Versailles? Paris, perhaps, I would believe, but the palace itself?"

A tremor swept through her. He must have been scouting, then. That was all. Scouting out the situation that everyone the world over knew was tense. Seeing…evaluating…oh, mercy. He had already reached the rank of brigadier general. Such mundane tasks would never fall to him, not unless there were a specific purpose that only he could fulfill. "You think my father went to France on covert business?"

Mrs. Lane released her husband's arm and glided over to take Gwyneth's hand. "I know he did. We came to London for the wedding, and he confided in us. He was sent in under the guise of a comte to whom he bore an especial resemblance, and who had been in British custody for many years. First he went to get a gauge of how things stood in the fracturing political system. And then he returned to help your mother and grandmother escape before the Revolution erupted, upon your grandfather's request."

A convulsion pulsed through her, made a cry try to rip from her throat, but she reined it in. "So you know, then, that it was my uncle."

Mrs. Lane's fingers squeezed hers. "He never said who sent him. But at this point it seems clear. Which I find terrifying. Because the one thing I remember about Mr. Gates from the two times I met him was that, under his polite smile, he hated us simply for being American."

Mr. Lane followed his wife to Gwyneth's side. No merriment sparked now in his eyes, only calculating sobriety. "Let us pray Isaac never confided in Gates, or it would be more than an ambiguous hatred he feels for us."

Before she could wrap her lips around the question of why that would be so, Mrs. Lane sighed and tightened her grasp on Gwyneth's fingers. "Your father knew of our part in the Revolution—that through a chain of well-trusted intelligencers I was feeding General Washington information. He cannot have known we revived the Culpers three years ago—"

"Give the man credit, Mother. 'Tis logical." Thad drummed the fingers of one hand against the opposite arm. "And I suspect he also knew I had taken over its primary function, given that letter he sent with you, Gwyneth. Not to mention the one two months earlier."

She twitched to alert like a hound who had caught the fox's scent. "My father wrote you before he sent me here? What did he say?"

"Nothing intelligible, but I will fetch it."

A moment later he was out the door, leaving Gwyneth to stare at his parents. They looked, standing there with their quick-witted gazes, like any well-settled couple. Bound by love, comfortably situated, well but simply dressed. Handsome and pleasant.

Why could it not be so easy? "What am I to do with this information?" The question whispered out before she could stop it.

Mr. Lane's mouth pulled into a half smile. "The same thing your father did, my dear. Accept us for who we are and follow the leading of the heavenly Father. You must do what He tells you, above all."

Her gaze fell to the floor. "What if He tells me to turn you over to the British authorities?"

A gentle touch on her chin drew her gaze up again. Mrs. Lane's eyes glistened. "I believe that would be to your uncle, Gwyneth. Which means Thaddeus is right. You are involved because your family is involved, and because you are fleeing that family."

Thad ducked back under the door frame, a piece of paper in hand.

"There is a reason your father entrusted you to us, sweet. He must have thought that, together, we could best Gates."

Together. Together with a family that had more secrets than London had soirees. Together with this man who made her insides a jumble of trust and frustration, fascination and fear.

A man who would be the target of each and every British rifle if they knew who he was and what he did.

He held out the paper. "Any light you can shed on this would be welcome."

Ought she? But this was from Papa, and he would have sent nothing to compromise England. She took the page, ignoring the trill of awareness when her fingers brushed Thad's. Her head began to shake only a line or two in. 'Twas Papa's hand, sure enough, but the message made no sense. All the right names were mentioned—Mama, Uncle Gates, even Gwyneth—and the sentences made sense as mere arrangements of words. Just not as facts. "This is all wrong. Every bit of it."

Mrs. Lane sighed. "That much we realized. Have you any idea what he could mean by it? We have tried codes, known counter liquors for invisible ink, everything."

Invisible ink? Codes? She lowered the paper so she could better stare at the Lanes, first the couple and then the son. What family dealt in such things?

Thad leaned against the table beside her. "Did he send anything else with you? Some sort of text he uses as a key, perhaps? A book, another letter? Anything?"

Gwyneth frowned. "In all honesty, I can scarcely recall what was in my trunk. So much of the past months has been a fog. But I know Mrs. Wesley emptied it out, and I cannot remember seeing anything in there I did not myself pack."

Her gaze caught on one of the lines. Not on the words, but on their arrangement. The spacing looked off. A word more narrow than the rest. Papa usually had such measured script, all in a careful, elegant flow. And there, on a line near the bottom, was a touch too much space between two words.

Testament to his hurry, perhaps?

"What do you see?" Thad leaned close, peering at the letter with her.

"Just irregularities in his hand." She pointed at the two places.

A low hum sounded in Thad's throat. "Interesting. You notice things I do not. No great surprise from our resident Michelangelo."

The praise warmed her, though ice rushed through her veins in the next moment. She ought not earn such accolades in this way. Trying to find hidden meaning in her own father's words… Such secrets ought not be chasing her, such darkness ought not be lurking. She ought to be fully ensconced in her first Season, basking in the joy of a betrothal to Sir Arthur.

But he had become nothing more than a shadow in her memory.

She touched a finger to where Papa had signed his name. So familiar, those loops and lines. Like his face, his eyes, his laugh. Yet this had outlived him, this iron gall on paper, and had shown his life to be so very different from what she thought it was. In what had he been involved? What secrets had he kept until they killed him? Why had he never told her, even when matters became so dire he must send her away?

"Would you like to keep the letter?" Thad's voice strummed across her nerves. "It does me very little good without knowing how to find its meaning."

For a moment, she considered the offer. Considered what balm it might be to open this up and see his hand.

Considered how that balm would be negated by the nonsensical words. "I thank you, but no. It is meant for you. You ought to keep it. I…I will go look through all my things to make sure he did not include anything that could help us."

And she would. But what she really wanted to do was put those new brushes in her case and run her fingers over the bristles to get to know their shape and structure. Then to pick up her pencil and cure that sheet of paper of its blank state. Her hand flexed in anticipation. Later. As soon as she had kept her promise.

Thad bent down, scooped up the scattered brushes, and picked up her pencil. He held them out to her with an indulgent smile. "Which will it be?"

She reached for the whole set with a small return smile. "Both. After my search."

Rather than relinquishing the brushes, he held them when she grabbed hold. Which, of course, forced her gaze up to his. The irises shone like amber, holding life within them. "You must remember, sweet," he murmured, "that you needn't feel any disillusionment on account of this discovery about your father. Every decision he made, every bit of information he withheld would have been to protect you."

Her eyes burned, so she let her gaze drop again. How odd it was to need such a reminder. And more, to have gotten it from an American spy.

Sixteen

Y ou told her." Arnaud may have put no question in the words, but it pulsed from his gaze and deepened his frown. "You are mad. Bound for Bedlam. She is—"

Thad shushed his friend and sent a glance around the crowded tavern. "I am well aware of who she is, but at this point we have a mutual enemy in her uncle, and that is unquestionably enough—"

"To let her know you are accustomed to dealing with such things, perhaps. *Perhaps.*" Arnaud leaned forward, the lantern on the table sparking fury in his eyes. "But not enough to tell her names that could ruin us. Even our closest comrades know only that you can get information where it needs to go. But you tell *her* what we call ourselves?"

A chorus of raucous laughter came from the far corner, a perfect cover for the conversation that Thad had wanted to have three days earlier. One thing or another had forbidden it, though, and tomorrow Arnaud would be taking the *Demain* into the tributaries to make it available to Barney's flotilla.

Thad sighed and gripped his half-full mug of coffee, if that lofty term could be applied to the ground-filled brew. "I had to, Alain. I had to be honest with her."

With a growl, Arnaud tossed his fork to his plate. A drop of gravy flew through the air and landed on Thad's sleeve. He wiped it off and touched his finger to his tongue. The place apparently served better food than they did coffee.

"Why?" Arnaud demanded in a fierce whisper. "*Why* did you *have* to do so? Other than because you are crackbrained."

Thad sighed and swirled the vile black brew in his cup. "Because the Lord told me to."

Arnaud leaned against the booth's back. "How in blazes am I to argue with you when you claim that?"

"Well, if you wanted to try an unprecedented tactic, you could *not*."

His friend snorted a laugh and folded his arms across his chest. "I try not to argue with the Almighty, but you have made your share of mistakes."

"I know." Because Arnaud seemed to be finished, he pulled the plate toward him and scooted his mug into its place. "But not when I listen to the Spirit guiding me, *mon ami*. And He was. Trust me on that."

"I seem to have no choice as you did not see fit to ask my opinion *before* you told her everything." He muttered a harsh French something and picked up the mug. "Perhaps you have been blinded by her pretty face."

Thad forked a tender piece of roast and shoveled it in. Yes, a far sight better than the beverage. "A pretty face she certainly has, but so do thousands of other young ladies in Maryland. I can appreciate that without letting it blind me."

Arnaud grunted into the mug. Took a drink. He didn't wince—he chewed. Thoughtfully enough to warn Thad to brace himself for whatever was coming next. "I think...I may take Jacques with me on this run."

Thad's arm froze with a forkful of potatoes halfway to his mouth. "You jest."

The darting of Arnaud's gaze said otherwise. "I cannot bear the thought of leaving him with your mother when he has just gotten settled at home again. It would be only for a week. Two at the most."

"Don't be a fool, Alain. We are at war. A primarily *naval* war. You cannot take your son with you."

A brooding look fell over his handsome face, all glowering brows and pursed mouth. "No one made any objections about safety when I mentioned my intentions—"

"For *you*, you barnacle. But a rumbustious four-year-old?" Thad shook his head and convinced the fork to dispense its potatoes in his mouth. "And you call *me* crackbrained."

Arnaud sighed and rested his head on his hand. "I know. But when I said I was going, he started crying, begging me to stay for Independence Day. What am I to do?"

"Put the trip off for another three days."

Another laborious sigh. "It feels as though I have already put it off too long."

"And so three more days will be nothing. Stay, enjoy the holiday with your son, and then leave him with us for a week."

Though Arnaud nodded, he looked woebegone. "And then another fortnight of tantrums when I get back."

An unfortunate truth. Had Thad some magical elixir to set it all to rights…then pirates and British alike would be banished from the seas, all Redcoats from American soil, and the shadows from Gwyneth's eyes.

Arnaud set the mug down with a somehow accusing *thunk*. "What is that look? You have not worn the like since we were fourteen and you were convinced you were in love with Lizzie Farthing."

"Ah, Lizzie Farthing." He grinned and speared another piece of beef. "Had Aaron Pike not stolen her—"

Laughter cut him off. "Then what? She would have waited for you to grow up? With her already nineteen?"

Thad splayed a hand over his chest. "The heart does not consider such trivialities as age."

"Your heart was in no danger from Lizzie, nor has it been in any since." He sobered and stared at Thad for a long moment. "So why this expression now? You have bowed out of all the balls since Miss F—"

"Hampton."

Arnaud rolled his eyes. "Since Miss Hampton arrived. You have hardly seen any other…*non*. Not her. Thad, of all the ill-advised, ill-fated, ill-timed—"

"It is not." He sighed and set the fork softly down. "At least not for becoming acquainted. She is…I am…I have never felt drawn to anyone like this, Alain."

His friend's laugh sounded half angry, half incredulous. He shook his head as he leaned forward onto the table. "Nearly twenty-nine years you have gone without falling in love. And you tumble that way *now*, of all times, with…with a…" He shook his head again. "Of all the young ladies you know. All you have met the world over. The one you *married*, and this is the one who steals your heart? The one who is half daft with grief and who cannot see beyond her canvas when a brush is in her hands?"

Why, years later, did guilt still swamp him? He laid his hands flat against the table surface. "I cared for Peggy. You know I did. But I cannot help this."

Arnaud's head shake seemed sorrowful now. "Sometimes I wonder if, for all your ability to divine what people are thinking and feeling, you really understand matters of the heart. My soul still aches for Marguerite. Every day. Every…single…day."

"I know." The words had to squeeze past a throat gone tight. "And I think…I think Gwyneth is the one the Lord intends for me. It is too soon to know how or why or when, but I…"

"There you go again with the 'God told me to' business." But Arnaud's lips turned up. "You must tread carefully, Thad, or you could ruin it. With all she has been through…"

Wise words indeed. He nodded.

Arnaud tapped the table. "And your own heart needs guarding as well. You must be absolutely certain your motives are what they ought to be, that this is really love and not some imitation that will fall to pieces in another month."

Now he was just trying to rile him. "I am no adolescent to need that particular lecture."

"But in love you are untested." Not giving him time to argue, Arnaud stood. "We had better away. I have my doubts that Mrs. George got Jacques into bed, and you should get home so that Miss…*Hampton* can rest."

Thad pushed to his feet too, but then he sat down again. "Turn your back, quickly. And take one step to your left."

Arnaud obeyed without hesitation, blocking the line of sight between Thad and the door. His posture went tense. "Who is it? Did someone come in?"

"Hmm. Mercer."

"Mercer?" Arnaud sighed and rolled his eyes. "You had me worried."

"Well, I would avoid him if I can. One moment…there, he headed toward the back. Quickly." Thad slid out of the booth and jammed his hat low on his head.

Arnaud fell in beside him as he strode for the door and chuckled. "The only man in all of Baltimore you actively avoid."

"Better avoidance than your habit of snarling until you provoke him to argument."

"Is it?" His chuckle deepened as he pushed open the door onto the balmy evening. "My way seems much more satisfying."

"You may have a point. I…" He halted in the middle of the street when the tingle swept over him. Stopped and listened, though he never knew if it were an audible sound or one in his spirit he ought to be waiting for.

Then it came. *The Masquerade*. He angled toward the waterfront.

Arnaud's questioning gaze was illuminated by the last rays of sun. "Where?"

"My brig."

"Do you need me?"

He didn't think so, not just to pick up a communication from the place in his cabin where Tallmadge's courier always hid them. He shook his head. "I'm going to see if Mr. Bolton has been in touch." After taking a step, he stopped and pivoted toward Arnaud again. "When will you leave?"

A sigh seeped out. "Early on the fifth, I suppose."

"Good. *Bonsoir, mon ami*."

"*Et à toi*. And, Thad? Tread lightly."

He waved him off and followed the slight downward slope of the street to the bay's edge. The faces he passed were all familiar, the usual bored sailors who still populated the harbor for lack of anything else to do. He nodded here, waved there, and called out a greeting when one was required. And soon he had the pleasure of setting his boots upon the boards that signaled home every bit as much as the ones in his house.

Masquerade welcomed him with a gentle bob, seeming to sigh her satisfaction at his coming aboard. He ran a hand along the rail and sighed right back. "Soon, old girl. Soon this blasted war will be over and we shall ride the waves again."

Her answer was a creak that said, "Not soon enough."

"I do agree." As he strode across the deck, he could almost pretend it was a calm day at sea, could almost imagine open water beckoning from all sides.

A minute later he had slipped into his cabin, with its specially chosen furniture all bolted down. The desk he had liberated from a sinking British ship. The weapons cabinet that came from a Mediterranean bazaar. The small strongbox that he had built into the underside of the bed.

He fished the key out of his pocket and crouched down, inserted it into the box, and turned. At the *clank* of the locking mechanism releasing, he swung open the slender door, reached in, and felt the folded paper he had anticipated.

He had long since removed all of his counter liquor and code books back to the house, so there was, sadly, no reason to linger. With a farewell pat to *Masquerade*'s railing a minute later, he disembarked and headed for home.

The sun had slipped fully below the horizon by the time he turned onto his street, the sky now a dark purple dimming to black. The air had scarcely cooled, though, still hanging heavy with humidity.

His lips tugged up. The Redcoats sure to arrive soon to reinforce their fellows wouldn't fare so well in a muggy mid-Atlantic summer, accustomed as they were to the cool climes of England.

Gwyneth was beginning to adjust, thankfully. Her movements had become lighter, her complexion healthier, and her appetite had improved.

His step picked up at the thought of her. Let Arnaud question it all he wanted. Thad knew his own heart.

He also knew his duty, and became aware anew of the missive in his pocket the moment he stepped inside. For now, this business must come first.

The steady cadence of Mother's voice came from the library, and a light burned in the drawing room as well. He eased his study door shut and turned to his desk. After lighting his lamp, he sat and pulled out the letter.

A small, faint A lay in the upper right corner. He read the visible message as a matter of course, but even while doing so pulled out the counter liquor and brush. Uncorked, dipped, tapped, stroked.

Within two minutes, the stain had darkened to near black, and Congressman Tallmadge's script leapt off the page.

President Madison has called for a new division for the protection of Washington, to be peopled from the neighboring counties. Directives will go out to governors in the next several days. Knowing you as I do, you will be tempted to volunteer for this assignment.

Thad grinned. The congressman did indeed know him well. If by chance the British headed first to D.C., he wanted to be there. Wanted to do all he could to rally the city.

Do not, I repeat, do not volunteer.

Thad sighed, swept his hat off his head, and sent it flying toward the leather chair across the room.

I have need of you where you are, Mr. Culper. Come to my office on the fifth or sixth, whenever you can get away. I think you will approve our plans.

Approve them he may in three or four days, but at the moment Thad had the urge to try one of Arnaud's snarls on for size.

He let the irritation stew for a moment, but then a breath of calm whispered over him. They had no proof the British would march to Washington. It would make more strategic sense for them to choose Annapolis or Baltimore. And would he not feel the fool if he went to defend his neighbor city and the enemy advanced on his own?

Tallmadge had experience enough in military things to be trusted with these decisions. He had been, after all, one of General Washington's most trusted officers. So Thad would obey. And he would rub his hands together at the thought of finally leading the Culpers into some offensive action.

Seeing no need to pen a response that would likely not reach him before Thad did anyway, he put his stains and quills into the bottom drawer of his desk. His fingers then paused, hovering over another tome he had slid in with his code books. The leather cover had gone soft and worn over the years, the paper had begun to yellow. His grandfather's script had faded to brown, but Thad had found peace within the prayers copied from his Puritan ancestors, as his mother had before him, and her father before her.

He gripped the precious volume and took it with him as he stood. Perhaps it could impart its peace again to another who so sorely needed it.

He headed for the light in the drawing room, having a feeling Gwyneth was in there and not with his parents. A feeling that was proven correct a moment later when he leaned into the doorway to watch her at the *secretaire*.

Her hand moved in large, bold strokes over the paper, her pencil putting life to the blank page in a way he could watch endlessly. He edged closer to see what picture she created today and ended up leaning on the writing desk with a laugh. "'Tis the *Masquerade*."

The pencil stopped, and Gwyneth smiled up at him in a way that made his stomach knot. "I thought I had better sketch it before I mixed my paints tomorrow. Your parents took me to the harbor today to see it."

He forced his gaze from the Lord's masterpiece of her face to the one underway on the paper. "Your memory astounds me. You captured her. Her details, but more, her soul."

Her laughter trilled like music, light and brilliant. Had he heard her laugh before? Perhaps a measure of it, but never a full chorus like this, one that chased the shadows from her eyes and lit her face.

Oh, he was sunk. No question. Now his life's quest would have to be teasing that laugh from her again and again.

Even when the music tapered off, still it glinted in her Caribbean eyes. "I was unaware a ship had a soul."

"Don't be ridiculous." He took the excuse to lean closer under the guise of tapping a finger to the page—a blank spot on it, so as not to smudge her work. "You are obviously aware, for there you have put it to paper."

She laughed again, though all too soon went serious. "I looked again through my things, Thad. Still I could find nothing from my father."

Seeing the shadow that cast on her face, he nearly wished he had never brought her into this business. But then, *he* hadn't, had he? Her

own family had. Still. He brushed aside one of the red-gold curls from
her cheek—only half of her hair had thus far been pulled loose by her
oblivious fingers—so that he might look squarely into her eyes. "You
needn't keep searching again and again, sweet. There is no need to
revisit it every day."

"But there is." Brows knit, her face followed his retreating hand for
a moment, until she seemed to realize what she was doing. Were it not
for the troubled spark of her gaze, it would have made him smile. "As I
looked, I remembered that each and every time I traveled before Papa,
he tucked a note into my things somewhere. Without fail."

Thad sighed and rested his hand over hers on the *secretaire*. To give
comfort, not to feel the frisson of heat in his fingers. Not at all *that*.
Ahem. "Perhaps Mrs. Wesley found it when unpacking for you and
put it away somewhere."

"That was my thought too, but I cannot find one *anywhere*." She
averted her face, blinking rapidly. "If only I could ask her."

"There are only so many places she could have put such a thing. I
will ask Rosie to help you look. She has been finding whatever I lose
since I was a boy."

That at least earned him another laugh, albeit one that quickly
faded. She sighed and lifted a hand to her neck, stretched, and winced.
She kneaded at the spot where the ivory column met slender shoulders.

"And how long have you been hunched over this desk, sweet? Since
I left?"

"Perhaps." The turn of her lips carried a rare hint of mischief, one
that made his heart squeeze tight.

If only that pain were not still on her face. He motioned toward
her neck. "May I?"

Her expression went blank as her fingers fell back to her lap. "Pardon?"

By way of answer, he raised his hand to her neck and rubbed where
hers had been. "Philly, the silly thing, would always read until she was
stiff and sore and headache ridden, and she would force me to help
her relieve it."

"Oh." The word was not an acknowledgment of the story, but
rather a wonder-filled exclamation that accompanied the tilting of

her head to give him better access. "Oh, that is exactly what I needed." She chuckled. "Aunt Gates would no doubt think this scandalously improper."

No doubt any London matron would. A thought which made him grin. "Aunt Gates, is it? Do we like her?"

Another breathy chuckle. "We do, though she is a bit staid. Very concerned with appearance. She could not possibly realize that her husband…"

Just like that, her neck went so tight and tense he silently cursed himself. Aloud, he clucked his tongue like Rosie would do. "Do relax lest you render my ministrations useless."

She made an effort, though it was largely in vain. "Better?"

"Not a bit. Which means, I suppose, that I shall have to stand here the longer, scandalizing your poor aunt's would-be sensibilities."

There, the tease relaxed her. She loosed a slow exhale, and another pin slipped from her hair, letting a curl fall across his hands.

Thad saw no reason to move the silken curtain. "You look as though you have been sleeping better."

A little hum sounded in Gwyneth's throat. "*More*, anyway. I thought—the night before the Wesleys left, I had no nightmares. I thought a corner had been turned, but…well, they have come back since. So it has been fitful and I awaken often. But I can at least get back to sleep."

"Progress."

Another hum. "Thanks to you, I believe. Sharing my fears…"

And staying home, though he had no intention of pointing out that correlation. Besides, he had given her new fears, new worries and wonders about the father she'd never before had to question. "I am happy to listen whenever you want to share what is plaguing you. I imagine there is more even than that loss. You are away from all the rest of your family. All your friends. And that beau in the suit of armor."

Ah, yet another chime of laughter. "Sir Arthur."

As if he had forgotten. He slid the prayer book onto the edge of the desk so he could put both hands on her shoulders. "Ah, yes. I imagine you miss him too."

"Not enough for it to have been what I thought it was." She reached for the book. "What is this?"

"Puritan prayers, transcribed by my grandfather. I thought they might lend you some peace." He let his lips purse at her observation on her feelings for Sir Arthur. Notwithstanding that he was glad of it, the fact remained that it was the second expression within the hour of how fleeting such things could be. "I imagine he is missing *you* sorely, having not been through the trauma you have."

She ran a finger along the spine of the book and flipped it open. "I cannot think so. We scarcely knew each other, and he would have been put out by my disappearing on him without a word that morning after I promised to speak with Papa. Oh, isn't this lovely. 'If I should suffer need, and go unclothed, and be in poverty, make my heart prize Thy love…'"

"That morning?" His hands paused and rested on her shoulders. "He was there?"

"In the garden. Too far away to have known. Now, I wonder what the author meant by this line about being constrained by His love. I have never thought of the Lord's love as being something to bind or restrict, but I suppose in this sense, it holds us to contentment."

His thumb moved over her neck again, though he neglected to put any force into it. "In the garden, you say. Does Sir Arthur perchance bear a resemblance to Arnaud, but with fairer coloring?"

"I suppose so, at first glance." Her head bent toward her chest. "How did you know?"

"You drew him your first night here." He had thought the figure looked lost to the observer—and what if that were more the case than that she had felt nothing real for him? What if she felt resignation, or even a sense of betrayal, that he had been so close but unable to help her? What if he were still ensconced in her heart, but she was just too struck by grief to realize it? His fingers wove through her curls. "What was it you promised to speak about with your father, Gwyn?"

She said nothing. Just breathed in and then out in a slow, even rhythm.

Thad sighed and crouched down beside her. Her eyes were closed, her fingers limp against the pages. He gathered her curls over one shoulder and then couldn't resist resting his hand against her cheek.

"One of these days, my love," he whispered, easing the book from her hands, "we will finish a conversation."

Seventeen

Arthur looked up when the tin cup plunked onto the table before him, and he smiled at the expressionless lad who had brought it. "Thank you, Scrubs. With this storm raging, I am afraid I am more in need of the ginger than usual."

"Sorry for my tardiness, sir. When the wind kicked up, I had to help secure everything."

"I understand."

In the corner of the cabin, Gates turned a page in his book. "Stop your chattering and let the boy get to work. The breakfast tray spilled when that wave struck. Of course, had you picked it up when you said you would…"

Arthur sipped the ginger water, welcoming the bitter taste that would help settle his stomach, which seemed bent on echoing the roll of every wave. Blast these summer storms. "Pay no heed to his testiness, Scrubs. Mr. Gates does not like being confined to our cabins."

Gates snorted.

Scrubs merely headed for the mess by the table.

Arthur studied his older companion, both amused and bemused at how *his* usually stoic demeanor had given way to such acidity today. He suspected it had less to do with being asked to remain below than it did the captain's words about the delay the weather might cause.

149

He took another sip. "Have you been to America before, Mr. Gates?"

He didn't even bother to look up from his page. "Of course. I have been to nearly all of England's colonies."

Scrubs paused halfway into his reach for a fork they had overlooked on the floor. "You visited before the Revolution then, sir?"

Now Gates looked up with an expression of disdain. "No, my visits have all been in the late eighties and after."

The boy grabbed the fork and tossed it to the tray with a clatter. "Then you did not visit her as a colony, did you?"

The narrowing of Gates's eyes promised a biting retort. Arthur cleared his throat and quickly interjected, "What is it like? I have never been."

The man's gaze remained locked on Scrubs. "Too cold in the north, too hot in the south, and filled with arrogant boors." He slapped his book shut. "What say you to that, boy?"

Scrubs pulled out his ever-present rag and went to work on the floor. "What ought I say, sir? Other than if you think so poorly of the place, it seems odd you would still want to claim it as an off-shoot of Merry Ol' England."

Rage flickered through the elder man's eyes but was quickly tamped down as he stood. "As I said, arrogant boors, the lot of them. Do excuse me, Sir Arthur. I have a matter to discuss with the captain."

"Until later, then." Arthur did his best to hold down his grin until the man had left. "I do believe that was the longest sentence I have ever heard you deliver, Scrubs."

The lad barely glanced up.

Arthur took another sip and considered letting the silence reign... but he had spent too many hours with only quiet Gates for company. "Well, I am glad to finally know your opinion on something."

There was a hitch in Scrubs's movements, but no other response.

Arthur sighed. "I am looking forward to seeing America. I have heard about the beauty of the wilds."

"Is that why you are traveling there? To see the wilds?"

"Nay." His voice came out more quietly than he had intended, so he cleared his throat. "My betrothed is missing and her life is in danger. We think her father sent her to Maryland. It is our hope to find her before his murderer does."

Now Scrubs's motions ceased, and the boy looked up at him with that ageless gaze of his. "Forgive me, sir. I did not realize your purpose was so grave."

"How could you have?" He forced a smile and swirled the bitter drink around in his cup. "I imagine you have seen much of the world already. That is quite a blessing."

Only when the boy's eyes snapped back to blank did Arthur realize compassion had entered them. He attacked the floor again. "Blessing, aye. I am certain my mother and sisters thought just that when their sole provider disappeared."

Sympathy tugged, but what was the use in indulging it? The boy had been a fisherman, as easily snatched away by a storm as a captain seeking a fuller crew. Still… "How far is your home from where we are going in Maryland?"

Another pause in the scrubbing. "Why?"

Why indeed? Why should Arthur worry with one boy separated from his family when so many the world over suffered far worse plights? Scrubs, at least, earned a living aboard Yorrick's vessel, which he could send home to his mother—assuming any pound notes made it through the post. He sighed. "Gates has requested that Yorrick remain at the open port in Annapolis until our business is concluded. Perhaps that would afford you time enough to visit them."

Scrubs snorted. "We could be there a year, sir, and the captain would still never let me out of his sight."

"I would take responsibility for you." The offer slipped out before Arthur could stop his lips. Wisdom called him a fool, but some other part of him whispered that this young man was one of integrity. "Assuming, of course, you gave me your word that you would return to the *Falcon*."

Not meeting his gaze, Scrubs grabbed his rag, stood, and hefted the tray. "I appreciate the offer, Sir Arthur. And I respect the kind of man who would make it." He strode to the door, paused with a hand on the latch, and turned his stoic face toward Arthur. "Which is why I couldn't give you that word."

Arthur grunted as the boy slipped out. No doubt that was for the best. Taking charge of Scrubs would only distract him from his real purpose anyway. Finding Gwyneth must remain his foremost, his *only* priority.

And with Gates's help, surely he could manage it.

⁓

For a long moment Gwyneth stared at the painted face of her father. She gazed into his canvas eyes and willed life into his ever-still lips. "Oh, Papa. What are you trying to tell me?" Were she not aware that some of the paint was still tacky—even a week had been insufficient for it to dry in this damp air—she would have reached out and touched the familiar shoulder.

No comfort was to be found there, though. No wisdom from his mouth or affection from his eyes.

She had never once had to question that he loved her, but as she stared at the face she knew so well, she wondered how well she had really known her sire. And why, when she needed it most, he had left her no words to guide her.

She turned from the painting she'd so carefully carried up to her room last night and studied the rest of the chamber again to try to divine where Mrs. Wesley might have stashed a random piece of paper. Where she herself might have slipped one in a stupor. Where amid her things Papa might have folded one.

She had searched her three books, her trunk, even the spaces under the furniture in case a page had fallen and fluttered there. If only she could ask Mrs. Wesley—if only Rosie had been able to offer some insight—if only Papa had left it somewhere prominent—but no.

She was alone with her questions and her fears. Alone with her future.

A shout of laughter from below made her catch her breath. Perhaps not alone, but how wise was it to become attached to the Lanes? They were on opposite sides of a war.

Though Papa had been the one to send her here.

They were spies.

Though arguably the only ones who could help her evade or out-smart Uncle Gates.

They would not want her here forever.

Though her mind conjured up Thad's voice, his whispered bid that she promise to stay. Had it been a jest? Dare she trust her perception of the gleam in his eyes? Or was he just doing as he always did—saying exactly what he knew she needed to hear, giving what she needed to receive? As he did with absolutely everyone?

And why did her heart twist? Why did it hope she was more to him than that? Why did her feet even now pull her toward the door, toward that laughter? Toward him. Always toward him, it seemed.

Foolishness. She knew it even as she gave in to the tug and exited her room.

The family had already made their way to the breakfast table, and it was young Jack eliciting the laughter. His face liberally smeared with oatmeal, he held a slice of apple in front of his mouth and said, "Look, Grandmama! I have a smile."

Gwyneth couldn't help but put on one of her own, though she meant to keep it aimed at the boy and not to direct it toward Thad. Somehow, though, her gaze swung his way. His was already on her, and it twinkled with good humor.

Mrs. Lane laughed at Jack. "And what a handsome smile it is."

Thad stood and pulled out Gwyneth's usual chair for her. "My lady."

"Oh, I am not a…" She trailed off at his mischievous little grin and slid into her chair. Of course he knew she was no titled lady to deserve such a greeting. American he may be, but he was no fool. "Are you being deliberately gauche, Captain Lane?"

"Never." He scooted the seat in, and his hand rested for a moment on her shoulder.

Jack had flipped the apple slice over and now held it above his lip. "And now I have a moustache!"

It was all Gwyneth could do to swallow past the catch in her throat. Her shoulder felt warm long after Thad regained his own seat.

She could only imagine the scolding Aunt Gates would give her each time he touched her unnecessarily. And given that warm feeling, 'twas a scolding she needed. The Lanes may have accepted her into their family for the time being, but she ought not be getting any ideas about Thad. No matter how bright were his eyes. No matter how compelling was his smile. No matter how her heart trilled at his every touch…or the fact that she felt completely safe when in his company.

The point still remained that when all this was over—the war and her uncle's schemes—she would have no place here.

And that was assuming she lived through it.

Mr. Lane passed her the plate of biscuits, soon followed by the eggs and sausage. Though they no doubt thought they were being discreet, each of the Lanes watched to see how much food she ladled onto her plate. She had already learned that if she didn't choose for herself what they deemed "enough," someone would slip on more when her attention was elsewhere. Except for Rosie, who didn't bother with subtlety and added more overtly.

And because she was beginning to look more like her old self and less like a half-starved, sickly waif from the streets, she could thank them for their efforts.

"Have you plans to paint today, Gwyneth?" Thad's voice came under the next laugh from Jack, quiet and warm.

The desire swelled, moving from mind to heart to hands. In her ears crashed a symphony of waves on the hull of *Masquerade*, the waters gleamed turquoise before her mind's eye, and the sky... She cast a dubious gaze at the window, where dark clouds brewed overhead, and let go the fingers of the muse. "I daresay not today. Even if the rain holds off, the light is not good."

"You are welcome to come with me then." Mrs. Lane set her cup of steaming coffee down, smiling. "I plan to fit in a quick trip to the shops before it rains. Amelia mentioned a pressing need for salt and a few medicinals."

Jack bounced in his chair. "May I come, Grandmama? May I?"

Mrs. Lane leveled a stern gaze on him, though Gwyneth had no trouble detecting the sparkle in her eye. "Only, my darling boy, if you give me your word that you will beg for neither a sweet nor a trinket."

Jack's face scrunched up, but at length he heaved a sigh worthy of a man ten times his age and picked up another apple slice. "All right. I shall still go."

"Gracious of you." The woman lifted her cup again and smiled into it.

Gwyneth slathered some strawberry preserves onto her biscuit. "I shall join you as well, Mrs. Lane, thank you." She darted a glance to Thad, hoping he would volunteer to accompany them. But he said nothing.

Ignoring the vague pulse of disappointment, she focused on her food.

"Bennet darling, will you come too?" Mrs. Lane reached over to wipe the oatmeal from Jack's cheeks.

The elder Mr. Lane scarcely glanced up from the *Baltimore Patriot and Evening Advertiser* before him. "Hmm? Oh, not today, my love. I have some correspondence to which I must respond, and I promised Philly I would read her latest treatise on vacuums."

She grinned. "You have not read it yet? She has some very interesting addendums to Monsieur Pascal's essays confirming Torricelli's theory on why nature does not, in fact, abhor a vacuum."

Mr. Lane grinned right back. "Well, don't spoil it for me."

Strange how the banter made that aching pulse intensify. Forget that she had no idea who Mr. Torricelli was or why nature might be offended by space devoid of air. The thud inside her was not from being outside of *that*, but rather from being outside of *this*. The comfort, the tease, the intimate knowing of another.

She selected a bite of egg with more care than it required. Who was left who knew her so well?

"I pecked into the drawing room at your easel yesterday, Gwyn." Thad sliced off a bite of sausage, his eyes bright. "The *Masquerade* is coming along beautifully. Are you sure you do not want to work more on it today? Father could get clever with lanterns and mirrors and canopies to give you adequate illumination."

The tension eased. A bit. "I thank you. But I am afraid there is no substitute for natural morning light."

He speared the piece of sausage and lifted the fork straight up, motioning with it. "You have painted from dawn to dusk before."

"I made do. But it was no substitute." She reached for a smile, found one, and produced it. "That painting was for me, so if the light and shadows were a bit off, only I would care. This new one is for you to hang on these shamefully bare walls of yours, so it must be perfect."

Something flickered through his eyes when she mentioned light and shadow, but it soon vanished behind his fresh grin. "I suppose so. Since you insist on foisting it upon me."

"Will you come with us, Uncle Thad?"

He turned his smile on Jack. "Not today, my little mate, though I will also be out and about. I had a note that one of my partner ships made it through the blockade, which means I have business to attend."

Business. Gwyneth sank her teeth into the biscuit and tried not to wonder if this business was goods smuggled to port or information.

Most likely both. The bread stuck in her throat. A sip of tea washed it down but did little to erase the feeling of it there.

Jack's eyes went big and bright. "Can I come with you instead?"

Thad seemed to consider it, which she found surprising. What man wanted a child underfoot as he attended his business? But then he set down his fork with obvious contemplation. "I think it would be too dull for you, Jack." At the pout of the boy's lip, he added, "But perhaps you could go with Grandmama now, and then she could walk you down to me. That will give me some time to clear out the requisite legalities, and then we can explore the goods together."

Jack bounced again and looked as though he would have leaped upon his chair and shouted for joy had a warning glance from Mrs. Lane not quelled him. "Thank you, Uncle Thad, thank you!"

Thad went back to his breakfast with a grin.

Gwyneth focused on hers as well, giving only half an ear to the renewed chatter of the little one and the answering laughter of the Lanes.

Having Jack around had no doubt been a balm when Thad lost his babe along with his wife. What a terrible blow that would have been. What, she wondered, had Peggy been like? She took a sip of her tea and tried to remember if she had seen a likeness of her anywhere. Certainly no portraits graced the walls. She had not noted any drawings that could have been of her. Nor so much as a silhouette like she and Mama had done for each other when they had only a lamp and paper for company.

And now that she gave it thought, she had never heard the Lanes speak of Peggy but for when Gwyneth had questioned Philly. *'Tis a topic still quite sore*, she had said about the death of her sister-in-law and niece or nephew. A topic that was therefore avoided.

Odd. She set her teacup down and lifted her fork again. This family did not seem to avoid other difficult subjects. They spoke so freely of their concerns for the war underway, for Captain Arnaud and Jack, for Gwyneth. And, in recent days, even their worries for the responsibilities of what they referred to as the Culper Ring—their groups of intelligencers, as Thad had requested they be called.

The Culper Ring. The name made her shiver as she took a bite of sausage, though she was unsure why. Certainly the words themselves had no great meaning to her. But the fact that they had a group that *needed* a name…

Her fingers tightened around the fork. They seemed such a normal family. Loving and open and…and…knowable. Like Papa had always seemed. Well admired, well respected, trustworthy.

Why must it all be marred by secrets?

"Are you ready, dear?"

Gwyneth blinked away the rumination and realized everyone had finished eating, herself included. She could scarcely recall what anything had tasted like, but only a few scraps remained on her plate. She summoned a smile. "Certainly. I will go fetch my bonnet and reticule."

Minutes later she came back downstairs to find Mrs. Lane and Thad standing on the porch examining the sky.

"I think it will hold off another few hours," he said.

Mrs. Lane nodded. "Excellent. I should like a bit of exercise if that suits you, Gwyneth dear."

"It suits me well, ma'am, thank you." And it would without question suit Jack, who was even then dashing about the lawn outside.

"I had better take a carriage, though, as I daresay I will not beat the weather home. And you two had better not dawdle." Thad's gaze moved to include Gwyneth, and he held out a hand toward her.

She had no reason to put hers in it. None whatsoever. She certainly needed no help walking down the two steps off the porch, and as he would have to repair to the carriage house, he would not be seeing them to the street. But he invited. And before she could control her wayward limbs, she had stepped forward and rested her fingers in his.

Eyes sparkling with mischief and something far warmer she daren't name, he raised her hand to his lips and pressed a kiss to her knuckles. "I shall see you at the *Masquerade*."

Images blurred together in her mind, the words conjuring up a different setting, a different man. Hyde Park before her instead of a Baltimore lawn, Sir Arthur Hart's gaze lingering on her, a short quarter hour after their introduction. *I shall see you at the masquerade.* They had just established they had both accepted the same invitation, and he had requested she save him a dance. Oh, how excited she had been.

She blinked, and the memory faded to a fog. The masquerade had been naught but a crush of bodies, the rooms overcrowded. No real mystery as she had wanted there to be. And though she had danced that reel with Sir Arthur, they had barely exchanged a score of words. It had been nothing. Nothing.

Drawing in a deep breath, she gripped Thad's fingers and gave him a small smile. "You shall indeed." His *Masquerade* was built of solider stuff than expectation. And his face was one that evoked in her something far more than the giddy thrill of Sir Arthur's.

She was no fool, though. Given the way her emotions had been swinging like a pendulum these months, she would not put too much weight on them. Even if they overwhelmed her as she stepped away and followed his mother to intercept Jack. When Mrs. Lane shot her a knowing grin, heat stained Gwyneth's cheeks.

They walked a goodly ways with only Jack's impromptu song about the birds to break the silence. When his serenade lapsed into an enthusiastic hum, Mrs. Lane turned warm green eyes on Gwyneth. "Are you happy with us, my dear? Your grief aside."

A small laugh slipped out. When had she last considered something so transient as happiness? Perhaps, fleetingly, during that bit of the Season. But in general, not since Mama fell ill. And yet…was there anywhere else she would rather be now than with the Lanes? Nay. "I…I suppose I am, as much as I can be at this juncture. Though there is so much to worry over, not the least of which is what I might be bringing upon you by being here."

Mrs. Lane laughed, a beautiful sound as vivacious as her daughter's. "Gwyn, you have brought nothing to our door we did not first invite. You surely realize that."

A truth she couldn't deny, much as she wished she could. She looked from her hostess to Jack and to the city, so young compared to those she knew. And then beyond, to the glimpse of treetops and churning gray sky. What wilds lay that way? Frontiers as yet untouched, filled with dangers unknown? Were the roads between here and Canada safe or wrought with peril? "I do hope the Wesleys write and let me know they are well. To think of them traveling so far without so much as a pass—"

"Ah, you needn't worry about that part." Mrs. Lane looped their arms together and gave her a comforting smile. "Thaddeus gave them his."

Had Jack not been tugging them forward, Gwyneth would have come to a halt. "His...he had a pass? But wh—"

"One never knows." Her smile turning mischievous, the lady patted her arm. "But I can tell you he gave it to them so that the knowledge might bring you peace. Did you know your father gave Bennet and me passes that allowed us to escape the City of New York with our lives during the Revolution?"

Had she known? Nay. Did it surprise her? Yes...no. Given what she knew of them, Gwyneth could infer that such a gift could have caused her father trouble at the time. And Papa had been a firm believer in rules, in honor, in duty.

But he was also a firmer believer in the bonds of love and friendship. She summoned up a smile and hoped it had even a fraction of the light Mrs. Lane's held. "I did not, but I am glad he did if it resulted in your survival."

Mrs. Lane chuckled but then fell solemn. "He was a good man. One of the best I have ever known. One who always did what was right no matter what politics told him was expedient. Men like that are rare in this world."

"And rarer now." The words slipped out before she could stop them and brought a burning to her eyes. "I am sorry."

"We are all sorry." But Mrs. Lane visibly bolstered herself, squaring her shoulders and producing another smile. "Thaddeus tells me he lent you our book of prayers. My father copied them himself from sermons and manuscripts his grandfather left him. I hope they bring you comfort."

A far safer topic. "Oh, they are lovely! And so profound. I have been reading from them daily."

They turned the corner, and the bustle along the street increased tenfold. Chatter filled the air and horses clopped along, while pedestrians hurried this way and that. Mrs. Lane tugged Jack a bit closer to her side. "It has long been one of our family's most beloved tomes. The fact that my son shared it with you…well. There are few he does not call friend, but fewer still he would deem close ones. I am glad to see you are numbered among that elite group."

Gwyneth could only stare at Mrs. Lane and trust the woman to keep her from running headlong into some innocent bystander. "Am I? I must say, ma'am, I had rather thought he would give to anyone whatever he saw they needed."

"But only ever so rarely what will give them true knowledge of *him*."

So his treatment of her was unusual? Something special? Something she still ought to have better sense than to relish. Clearing her throat, Gwyneth did her best to make her smile easy. "It is a blessing to have—and to be—a true friend. Especially now, when I need them so acutely."

"A need that never lessens. And you are welcome with us always, Gwyneth. I hope you know that. Or," she said, her grin back in place, "if you have a desire to go elsewhere, I daresay Thaddeus will be more than happy to ferry you anywhere in the world aboard the *Masquerade*."

How strange a thought, that the world was open to her. There had never been much of a world to her mind beyond the one she knew. But the inspiration that may wait somewhere out there! Scenes waiting to be painted, the unknown waiting to be discovered by her pencil.

They made their way into the busiest part of town, where shops and businesses and taverns kept the streets filled with people, and where the brackish scent of the bay occasionally swept by on the breeze. Where carts and drays were as numerous as barouches and chaises.

Where, from the ambling, bustling crowds, one particular movement caught her eye. She knew, even as the terror choked her, it was not Uncle Gates. Knew, even when the man turned as if he felt her gaze catch on him, that it was the one Thad had called Mr. Mercer and not the monster of her nightmares.

Knew it. Yet she couldn't reason her mind from wanting to flee in the other direction when Nathaniel Mercer smiled and strode their way.

Eighteen

"Miss Hampton. How good to see you again." Mr. Mercer stepped in front of them with that same posture and way of moving that had first alarmed her in the stationer's. "I trust you recovered from your spell?"

His gaze—too warm, too curious—made Gwyneth suppress a shudder and press closer to Mrs. Lane's side.

Her chaperone cleared her throat, nudged Jack into the space between them, and extended a hand toward the newcomer. "I don't believe we have met, sir. I am Mrs. Bennet Lane."

Mr. Mercer took her hand and bowed over it. "Nathaniel Mercer, ma'am. You have no doubt met my mother, who resides in Annapolis. I happened across your son and cousin in town some weeks ago, but I am afraid Miss Hampton had an episode that day. I have thought of you often, miss, hoping you had recovered."

Her stomach went queasy, and no doubt the smile she forced out reflected her distaste for being accused of having episodes. Which implied some sort of habitual event, which she certainly did not have. If one discounted falling asleep randomly after bouts of insomnia, which one certainly should, because...because one *should*.

"Miss Hampton—" Mrs. Lane spoke the name without a hitch,

though Gwyneth had heard her and Thad having a rather heated debate on the wisdom of the falsehood— "has been quite well, thank you, though we had better hurry on our way. The clouds have grown darker still, and I certainly do not want to be responsible for my charge catching her death of cold."

Gwyneth hadn't seen any great change in the heavens, but she noted one in Mrs. Lane's countenance. Her eyes had gone decidedly blank, and her face, while smiling pleasantly, seemed entirely devoid of consideration. As if she had slipped on a mask.

Mr. Mercer breathed a laugh that oozed condescension. "I daresay with as warm as it is, the worst the rain can do is damage your very lovely bonnet. But far be it from me to be responsible for so great a travesty."

How did Mrs. Lane manage to blink in such a way, as if the man had spoken in Greek? Which, come to think of it, the lady likely knew. "Do you take issue with wall hangings, sir?"

Mr. Mercer frowned and then renewed his smile. "I believe you are thinking of a 'tapestry,' Mrs. Lane. A travesty is a grotesque imitation."

Mrs. Lane lifted her nose into the air. "Well, certainly I have seen some poorly woven ones, but there is no need to insult the craftsmen."

Only her bafflement allowed for Gwyneth to hold back a snort of laughter.

Mr. Mercer inclined his head and took a step backward. "Of course not. And I shan't hold you up, as you will be eager to get home before it rains, in any case." His gaze moved to Gwyneth again, and again turned too familiar, too meandering. "My mother will be coming for a visit after my current trip to Virginia. Perhaps your family would like to dine with us one night to welcome her to Baltimore."

Mrs. Lane dismissed him with a flip of her wrist. "Send an invitation round when you have returned, sir. Come, Gwyn dear, we had better hurry or all the best lace will be gone."

Lace? Hardly the staples Amelia had requested, but Gwyneth would play along if it meant escaping this companion. "Of course. Good day to you, Mr. Mercer."

He tipped his hat to them and stepped out of their way. She felt his gaze on her all the way down the street, until Mrs. Lane led her into a dry goods store. Only then did she dare lean closer to her and whisper, "What was that you were doing?"

A sheepish look overtook Mrs. Lane's face. "Ah. An old habit, let us call it. One that seems to reemerge when faced with someone for whom I do not much care. 'Tis how I got through the Revolution as a Patriot in a Loyalist stronghold. When one acts utterly silly, no one ever thinks to look for deeper motives." Her lips bloomed in a smile. "Until my Bennet, that is."

Gwyneth glanced to the door, though Mr. Mercer was thankfully nowhere in sight. "You do not care for him either, then?"

"Even less than I care for his mother, whom I avoid when I can in Annapolis. We will not be accepting any invitations from him."

A chill skittered up her back, and she had to check over her shoulder again to make sure he did not still watch her. People aplenty clipped past, but the only indication she saw of him was the last of the line of roped-together slaves shuffling out of sight. A fresh chill danced after the first. What a despicable man.

Jack snagged her attention with a squeak of distress. His gaze was latched onto the bins of sweets, but he pressed his lips together against his obvious instinct to beg for one. And the resulting confliction had him hopping from foot to foot. Gwyneth exchanged a smile with Mrs. Lane. "May I?"

She winked. "What Grandmama does not see, hmm?" She turned down an aisle and perused the offerings.

One hour and two stores later, with Jack sucking happily on a stick of peppermint candy, Mrs. Lane had found the items her elder daughter had requested. And from the looks of the sky, they had not a minute to spare. Gray clouds had compounded and shoved their way into a low-hanging, roiling mass of black.

Gwyneth couldn't resist a smile at the impending weather. Maryland had far too much sun. 'Twould be a pleasant reprieve to have a day of rolling thunder and cleansing rains. Perhaps she would sit by an open window while the storm rolled through and let the wet breeze caress her. Or if she could escape the watchful eye of Rosie long enough, she might even sneak out to the garden as she did when they were in the country so it could soak her through. She could even—

"Watch out!"

In a chaos of shouts and grunts and shoves, Gwyneth's breath evacuated her lungs as something pressed her to a wall of warm, damp brick. Her fingers still clutched Jack's, but before her was only a jumble of muted browns and blues as at least a dozen men surged by. A few tossed apologies over their shoulders, but none slowed.

She ran a hand over Jack's head to make sure he was well. Given the sticky grin he aimed at her, he scarcely noticed the hubbub, but where had Mrs. Lane gone?

"Gwyneth?" Pain laced the voice.

"Grandmama!" Jack jumped away from the building and must have spotted her. He lunged around the corner, pulling Gwyneth with him.

Mrs. Lane sat in the alley, her face so careful a blank canvas that she must be working hard to maintain it.

"Mrs. Lane!" Gwyneth crouched down beside her. "What happened? Are you injured?"

"I twisted my ankle, I think. Would you…" She paused and let half a wince slip out. "Would you kindly fetch Thad with the carriage?"

Responses vied for a place on her tongue. That she could help her up, a question of how much it hurt, of how she was to find Thad from here. But she knew well that Mrs. Lane would not have asked her to find help unless she needed it. So she would go and waste no time arguing. "Of course. But," she added when the first drops of warm rain hit her forearm, "allow me to at least help you inside."

The woman's hesitation told her clearly how much her ankle must be paining her. To prefer to stay in such an ignominious position rather than to face rising… Gwyneth gripped her hand and prayed the Lord would soothe. "It is only a few steps. You can lean on me. I am stronger than I look."

Jack's eyes filled with tears. "Are you all right, Grandmama? Do you need me to kiss it?"

Even her smile was tight with pain. "My darling little one. I will be right as rain in no time. Could you carry this?"

Jack took the sack, his lip still trembling.

When her gaze swung to Gwyneth, the edge of control frayed. "Are you certain you can support me? The way it is throbbing—"

"Have no fear of that, Mrs. Lane."

A strained smile flitted again. "I think it ought to be 'Winter' at this point."

"Winter." She slipped her arm around her. "On the count of three. We will take it slowly."

They got her to her feet, and Gwyneth served as a crutch for the short but difficult journey to the nearest shop. Jack latched onto her skirt and didn't relinquish it until Winter was seated inside the haberdasher's, her injured ankle upon a footstool, and she invited the boy onto her lap.

Despite the lady's assurances to the little one that she was perfectly well, the truth pulsed from her eyes. "Can you find the waterfront from here, Gwyn?"

"Of course I can." She gave Winter's hand a squeeze, Jack's shoulder a pat, and headed back out into the spitting rain.

Not that she had any rational thought of which way to turn or how to get to the docks from this street. But she didn't need one. She had only to think of Thad and let her feet take her wherever they willed.

❧

The wind whipped whitecaps onto the Chesapeake, turning its waters to a murky, steely gray. Thad signed the last of the requisite documents for transfer of goods from ship to shore as the first drops splashed down from the heavens. Handing the papers to Captain MacKenzie, he fastened his gaze on the ever-darkening clouds. "It is a blessing you arrived last night rather than tonight, Mack."

MacKenzie snorted a chuckle and adjusted the hat over his too-long orange hair. "Methinks it a blessing the clouds had already begun rolling in last night to provide cover. I thought for sure we would have to go the long way round."

"Hmm. Everyone else has had to." Thad planted his hands on his hips, watching as the men loaded the last of the crates into the cart. They would take them the short trip to his warehouse, and he would oversee the sorting and selling. Not his favorite part of the business, but the one that allowed him to have his fun upon the open waters.

"How daft am I that a coming storm makes me want to order my crew aboard the Masquerade and set sail?"

A meaty hand landed with a *thunk* upon Thad's shoulder. "No dafter than the rest of us, though it's glad I am to be in port for a spell. Try as we may to make a menace of ourselves, there be too many British vessels wandering the waves now that Napoleon no longer keeps them busy."

The longing punched, itched, and made Thad's feet want to slide along the planks until he was near enough the Masquerade to climb aboard. His hands yearned for the smooth wood of the wheel or the rough hemp of the ratlines. And to smell naught but the fresh tang of brine and taste sweet sunshine on his lips.

Someday...but not until he knew he would be coming home to a land once more at peace, to a family secure in their homes. And to a pair of eager, waiting arms and smiling blue-green eyes as fathomless as the sea.

He glanced up the street and thought for a moment he had summoned her with his thoughts. Or that he imagined her, running his way with abandon, her bonnet having fallen to her back and a few curls now tumbling free, for what would possess her to actually do such a thing?

But MacKenzie's wide eyes disproved that theory. "Now here comes a bonny lass."

"Indeed." Though where were Mother and Jack? He lifted a hand to get her attention, though she was already on a path straight for him. Odd, since he was at the end of the docks opposite the Masquerade, and she couldn't have known he would be.

Her gaze found him, and her pace increased still more.

His friend lifted fiery brows. "She's *your* bonny lass, is she? Well, then, I shall remove myself and accompany the boys to the warehouse."

Thad nodded, mumbled something about meeting him there later, and started toward Gwyneth. The nearer she drew, the more the twisting of his heart told him it was not simple desire to see him that had sent her running through the streets of town.

Though still, when a gust of wind swept down the avenue and tore another mass of curls loose, he could hardly help sucking in a breath of appreciation. She looked like some sort of mythical character, whimsy and ferocity combined, with that frown upon her brow. Like Miranda, perhaps, from Shakespeare's *Tempest*. So bound to the wind and rain that one could never be sure if she echoed it or it her.

"Thad." She flew over the last few feet, hands extended and worry darkening her eyes.

Her hands he took in his, finding them warm and rain-wet. "What is the matter, sweet?"

"Your mother." She paused to draw in a long breath and tilted her head back so she might look at him. "A group of men rushed by and knocked her down. She has injured her ankle. Can you bring the carriage?"

Mother, hurt? He wove her arm through his and led her toward the vehicle. "Of course. Is it bad?" It must be for Mother to admit to the need for assistance.

"She would not say for Jack's sake, but it must pain her a good deal or she never would have asked me to come for you."

"How well you know her already." He hurried them around a corner and signaled to Henry, who was even then emerging from a warehouse. "Where are she and Jack?"

"Ah." Though her feet didn't slow, her face reflected a pause. "Some...I believe...a haberdasher. The one...that is...I am not sure of the direction."

Thad pulled open the door to the carriage and helped her up. "And how did you find me if you didn't know the way?"

Eyes wide, she sat upon the cushion and untied the ribbon that had kept her bonnet from flying off. Then she shrugged in such a way that made him want to gather her close and laugh.

He settled for a smile as he climbed up behind her and pulled the door tight. "The one beside the stationer's?"

The shake of her head was decisive. No doubt she would have paid close attention had she been near her beloved paper. "No, it was near the chandler's."

"Ah." He opened the window enough to stick his head out into the gusting rain. "Henry, could you take us to Mortimer's Haberdashery? Mother hurt her ankle."

Henry was even then vaulting to his place upon the box. "Sure thing, Captain. Won't take but a few minutes."

Settling back down, he shut out the rain and turned to Gwyneth, who had already managed to repin her hair and put her bonnet back on, much to his dismay. She offered him a tight smile. "Have I met Henry's wife yet? I cannot recall."

"You would, if you had." A breath of amusement slipped its way into the statement.

Gwyneth's brows lifted. "Why is that? Has she three noses?"

"Right on the first try." Had Emmy heard him say so, she would have delivered a sound smack to the back of his head. And had her husband heard him…Henry would only laugh and tell him to say it again when she could hear. Which he would be happy to do, to see that fire of temper leap into her eyes. She had always been as fun to torment as Philly and Amelia.

Gwyneth lifted her eyes to the ceiling and shook her head. Though the gleam soon dimmed to worry. "I do hope your mother isn't too hurt."

He looked down at their interwoven fingers. When had he reached for her hand? Or had she reached for his? Hard to say, given how comfortable her fingers felt around his, as if they belonged so always. "I assume Jack stayed with her?"

She nodded, her gaze falling too to their joined hands before lifting to his face again. "Do you…" Tugging her fingers free, she cleared her throat. "Do you see your nieces and nephews much? Amelia's children, I mean? Obviously not as much as you do Jack, whom you obviously think of in much the same way."

"Much the same, yes." Though not exactly. A complexity he was not about to explain during a five-minute carriage ride. He leaned back and studied her. Did she ask merely to have something about which to talk? Or was she genuinely curious? "But I haven't seen Amelia and Jacob's family nearly so much as I would like since the war began."

Her eyes went unfocused, as if seeing far beyond the carriage wall behind him. "War makes so many things uncertain. Never knowing when or where one may be needed."

Perhaps it was her father's face she saw now, or the image of him striding away in his red coat, bound for France or wherever else he had been sent through the years. Wondering if he would return. Thad cleared his throat. "I was extraordinarily blessed to have parents who never traveled without us for more than a week at a time. And who, even in wartime, stay close."

Her gaze went sharp again, and teasing. "Though the same cannot be said for their son, who, I'm told, has a knack for finding adventure where a sane person would see none."

Philly. He smiled and shook his head. "My sister exaggerates. We are at war, yet I am at home more than ever. A complete reversal of what one would expect from an adventure-seeker."

"Because you have a purpose too important for your leaders to risk your life in battle." A battle which seemed to be waged now across her countenance. Her inborn hatred of what he was, fighting against who she knew him to be; her liking of him pitted against her loyalty to her nation. Then as quickly as the weapons flashed through her eyes, they stilled. And she looked to that place beyond him again. "Do you know what Papa called this war?"

Quite a few words filled Thad's mind to describe it, but he didn't know the general well enough to guess at his choice. "Pointless, perhaps? Vengeful? A meaningless drain on British resources?"

She permitted a brief twitch of her lips and then schooled her features into a pleasant expression. "Foolish." A smile half won its place, and she loosed a long breath. "I had forgotten that, but...he had been quite vocal about it being a drain on the French campaign, with which plenty agreed. But then when Napoleon surrendered and someone said something about it freeing the troops to be sent here... He always had England's best interest at heart, but he thought this war a mistake."

His throat went dry. "He said this in public?"

She nodded.

He gripped the cushion's edge. "And now your uncle has announced they suspect an American spy murdered him, thereby turning against us any voices who would have been swayed toward your father's way of thinking."

For a moment Gwyneth moved her mouth as if about to speak, yet no words emerged. She just stared at him, agape, a million possibilities rampaging through her eyes.

Thad slid over to the place beside her and touched her hand. She sucked in a breath and blinked as she met his gaze. "I never...I never really paused to consider his opinion on it, what with Mama...But looking back now…He wanted this war to be over. He thought it stupid and vain. And Uncle Gates was loudly in favor of it. They debated it often. What Papa said that day, about destroying two nations with his greed…they must have been speaking of the war."

He would have liked to smooth away the furrow in her brow, but he suspected he had a matching one in his own. "What could greed have to do with it?"

Her hand turned over under his, and her fingers found their place around his own. Given the contemplation saturating her face, he had a feeling she had no idea she had made such a move. "I am aware that men aplenty profit from war, but he is well enough positioned. His mother's estates went to him. He had no need to sully himself with trade."

Thad pressed his lips against a smile. "What a relief. A tarnish a man could never live down."

Her snapping gaze came his way, the smile she wore so mischievous he nearly kissed her then and there. "Not in a civilized land."

"Uncivilized, am I? And here I thought my hospitality and civility worthy of the Prince Regent himself."

Her laughter filled the carriage, brightened it, and seemed to bring the sun through the clouds. "Nay, it is far too temperate and well considered."

What was he to do but lift her fingers and kiss them? "I know not how I can suffer such an insult."

Mirth fading to a smile, she shook her head. Her gaze tangled with his. "Thad, when you told me about your…Culpers. When I considered that I was apparently on your side, I knew not how to reconcile that with who I knew Papa to be."

He ran his thumb over her knuckles, a seal upon the kiss. "But?"

"But Papa thought this war a mark against England. He wanted it over and he wanted my uncle stopped. Somehow those two are linked. So whatever I can do, know that I will do it."

For her father, and perhaps also for England. He nodded because in this case it would also be for them, for *his* homeland. A war like this could benefit neither nation. All it could do was wear down both until there was little left worth the fight. "Your assistance I accept most gratefully, my lady."

As Henry pulled the team to a halt, she sent him an arched glance. "Just do not expect me to play at espionage with you, Thaddeus. I will not do it."

"I would never ask it." Not, at least, until she volunteered.

He opened the door, jumped out, and reached up to help her. As his hands circled her waist, a tongue of lightning streaked across the heavens, and a peal of thunder rolled over the city, loud enough to shake the windows.

And Gwyneth, nymph that she was today, looked up at the sky with a smile. Thad put her feet upon the ground and drew her closer than he ought. "You want to play in it, don't you?"

"I have not dared since I was a child, but there is nothing in the world like it."

He chuckled and led her toward Mortimer's. "Come, my Miranda. Let us see to Mother first, and then you can frolic in Prospero's storm."

She took a step away and grinned at him over her shoulder. "You know Shakespeare. Impressive, for an uncivilized savage."

Oh, was she lucky that Jack was even now pulling open the door for them, or he would have…

"Uncle Thad, Grandmama has a stained ankle." Jack tossed himself at Thad's waist with his usual faith that he would be caught.

Thad swept the boy up. "I daresay you mean 'sprained,' matey."

Mother's face bore lines of distress, but her cheeks had good color, and her smile wavered only slightly. "My best guess. It is swelling and throbbing, but the pain has ebbed a great deal already. Your father will wrap it tight for me, and I shall be up and about again in a few days' time."

Thad didn't dare argue, knowing her as well as he did. She would be up and about, even if it required a crutch. He gave Jack's back a pat. "Go to Gwyn for a few minutes. I must carry Grandmama to the carriage."

The fidgety Mr. Mortimer shifted, drawing Thad's attention to where he stood a few feet away. "Need you any assistance, Lane?"

"With the door, if you please. I do appreciate it, Morty." He passed Jack to Gwyneth so he would not be underfoot. As he leaned down to his mother and slid his arms around her back and under her legs, he whispered, "Are you all right, Mum?"

Her arm encircled his neck, and she offered him a reassuring smile. "I did not want to alarm Jack, though it was quite debilitating at first. It still hurts, but it really has gotten better since Gwyn went for you."

"Good." He lifted her and turned toward the door. "Father is going to fret something fierce, you know."

Mother breathed a low chuckle and tightened her grip on him as he started forward. Then she hummed. "No wonder Jack climbs you and your father as if you are trees. You have a lovely vantage point from up here."

Leave it to her to notice such things when injured. "I think so. 'Tis why I decided to grow so tall, after all."

"Wise of you indeed."

Grinning, he maneuvered her carefully out the door, nodded a thanks to Mr. Mortimer, and eased his mother into the carriage door that Henry held open, battling the wind to do so. A few passersby paused to offer assistance, but he assured them he had matters well in hand.

Next he reached for Jack from Gwyneth's arms. She relinquished him with a lopsided smile. "Is there anyone in the whole city of Baltimore with whom you are not acquainted, Thad?"

He settled the boy beside Mother and then pasted a thoughtful look on his face when he turned back to her. "Possibly. Though if so, I don't know who it would be."

"Clever, aren't you." She accepted his proffered hand and settled inside.

Thad turned to Henry. "Sorry about the weather, old man."

"You know I don't mind, Captain." He nodded toward the opening. "'Specially if it's for your saint of a mother. Now get on in so's we can get goin'."

"Aye, aye." He ducked and climbed in, giving himself a mental pat on the back for arranging the seating so that he had no choice but to be beside Gwyneth. Though his smile he aimed at his mother, tapping a hand upon his knee. "Allow me to be your footstool."

It took only a few minutes for them to arrive home, for Thad to help her up to her room, and for Father to begin hovering, insisting she lie still, that she turn her foot just so, that she tell him exactly *how* it hurt, that she conjure up the names of who caused the mishap so he might devise a formula with which to torment them...

Thad shook his head and wandered to the window while Father wound a bandage round Mother's foot and ankle. Gwyneth had said something about seeing that Jack was put down for his nap, and she must have succeeded in record time. For there she was in his backyard, circling around on the swing with her face tipped up to receive the drenching summer rain, her hair a river of burnished gold.

Oh, to be able to join her in the downpour without the fear that doing so would send her running back inside. To give the swing a twirl and hear the laughter sure to echo, to catch it again and threaten not to let go until she gave him a kiss. To chase her around the tree when she playfully escaped him. To catch hold of her, pull her close, and taste the rain upon her lips.

Thunder and turf, he had better go put himself to work. He spun toward the door—and collided with two amused, far too knowing gazes from his parents, who regarded him as if he were a child who had just, finally, learned how to add two and two. He groaned and held up his hands. "Don't look at me like that, prithee."

Mother grasped Father's hand. Probably as much to keep him from fussing with the bandage again as because she was really so moved by the love-struck gleam she must have detected in Thad's eyes. "Come now, Thaddeus. We have been waiting thirty years to look at you like this. Do not deprive us of the joy."

"Humph." He folded his arms over his chest. "Eight-and-twenty. And if you intend to lecture me like Arnaud did—"

"Alain does not approve?" Father frowned and slid one of his hands away from Mother's to smooth down part of the bandage.

"Bennet."

"Sorry." He looked nowhere near sorry, though still plenty curious. "What did he say?"

Thad waved it off and strode toward the door. "He does not trust my judgment in love, that is all."

"Thaddeus." That particular tone of Mother's could, he was sure, halt a stampede of wild mustangs. He stopped with one shoulder through the doorway and looked back at her. She sighed and repositioned her gown over her ankle. "The wound is still fresh for him. Those two years we were mourning him, he was living for the thought of coming home. To get here and find his wife deceased and—"

"I know." All too well.

Mother lifted her brows. "It is understandable that he would preach caution. He does not want to see you hurt."

Thad said nothing in reply. He merely nodded and ducked into the hall. He saw no point in arguing with his mother.

But sometimes, when talk turned to the topic love, he had to wonder if Arnaud really wished him well. Or if he rather thought Thad deserved to be every bit as miserable as he.

Nineteen

Gwyneth jolted upright in bed, her eyes searching the dark for some clue as to what had awakened her. Not a bad dream. Her heart wasn't thudding, and no ferocious images snapped at the back of her mind.

A noise. She had heard a noise, and she heard another outside now. Not a suspicious one though—unless it was such to be whistling when the only light from the window was the pearly gray of predawn. She tossed aside the sheet and scurried to the window overlooking the street. Little light was needed to tell her who was striding down the walk with such cheer. She had yet to see any other man in Baltimore as tall as her Thad.

Thad—not *her* Thad. Heavens. She pressed a hand to her gritty eyes and spun back to her room, lest he look back and catch her watching him. And divine, as he so often did, exactly what she had been thinking.

Bother. Now her heart pounded, and she had no handy nightmare on which to blame it. And certainly no hope of claiming another hour of sleep. That was all right, though. With a lilt to her step, she dressed in her simplest day dress, jabbed a few pins into her hair, and gathered up her art supplies. If she went out to the garden now to set up, she would be ready for the first touch of morning light. She could finish her rendition of the *Masquerade* and then still be available to lend a hand to Winter later. Her ankle was largely healed these ten days after the accident, but stairs still caused her discomfort, and she walked with a limp yet.

Her shoes in hand so she could slip silently down the hall, she tiptoed past Jack's room, the elder Lanes', and down the stairs. Last evening Thad had mused that, as it was mid-July, Captain Arnaud ought to be back any day—an observation he would not have made around Jack had he not been certain of it.

She paused at the back door to slip on her shoes and let herself out into the pleasant morning mist. Warmer than any she had known in England, but still familiar, this fragile veil that hung over the day.

By the time the silver had turned to gold under the rays of the rising sun, Gwyneth had set up her supplies and brought out the nearly finished painting. She had thought it done four days ago, until she realized it had yet to pulse, had yet to breathe. Something was missing.

Some*one*. She had known right away that she would have to add Thad, though she had hesitated to do so. He had seen the truth of her father so quickly in that one. What would he see in this, if she included him?

She blew out a long breath to steady her hands and picked up one of the brushes he had bought her. Perhaps she risked revealing emotions of which she was still unsure, but she had no choice. The *Masquerade* needed her captain at the helm.

And she knew exactly how he must be—as she had sketched him that morning he took her to the stationer's. His feet braced on the pitching deck, spyglass in hand, eyes sparkling with fascination with the world around him. His nose a strong line leading to his lips, quirked in that way of his. One side raised and the other steady. Not quite laughing in the face of the encroaching storm, but showing clearly that his respect for it gave no way to fear.

Finally, that pulsing surrounded her, each thump of light in time to the strokes of her brush. The *Masquerade* danced upon the waves, partially hidden by the froth and the coming tempest, but still bathed in sunlight that lit fire upon the water. So sure of her triumph, because her captain could take her through any storm, against any enemy.

She lifted her brush away from the black it had been headed toward, shook her head. No, no thought of enemies. Not now, not in this painting.

A curl fell into her face, obstructing her view. She shoved it aside and dabbed a bit more brown onto her brush. Just a touch, enough to add that depth, that texture to his hair.

Hers fell again, and again she shoved it aside. If she had to put her paints down to fasten her frustratingly unruly mane...

The mass of it lifted from her back, came away from her face, and cool air caressed her neck. She drew in a happy breath as she felt it twist and coil against her scalp. She reached out to stop his hand from grabbing the brush nearest him. "Not that one, I will need it in a moment. Use the bigger one."

A low rumble of laughter tickled its way across her as he secured the knot of hair with the larger brush and then rested his hand on her shoulder. He circled his thumb across her nape.

She made one more dab, so minuscule it could scarcely be seen, and then paused. Her next stroke must be even more precise, and so she had better wait. Wait for his arm to come around her waist, wait for him to pull her back against his chest, wait for his lips to whisper from her temple to her jaw. Wait for...for...

"Oh!" She fumbled her brush, heat scorched her cheeks. What if he realized the thoughts that had flitted through her mind? And why, *why* had they so flitted? Why would she be waiting for something she had never experienced, never even dreamed of? Certainly never dreamed of. Those would be far sweeter images than the ones that visited her in the night.

She put her brush upon her palette and splayed a hand over her frantic heart. "You were not gone long."

Thad chuckled again as he soothed and frazzled her simultaneously with another sweep of his thumb over her neck. "An hour, which was sufficient for verifying that Alain was home."

Though her cheeks still felt warm, they no longer stung. She risked turning her head, tilting it back to look up at him. He was studying the painting. "Verify?"

His gaze fell upon her face, warm enough to make her cheeks flame anew. He grinned. "I awoke with an intuition and thought to see if it was accurate. Though I daresay Alain, who had only stumbled into bed two hours prior, would have preferred I had waited until noon to investigate."

Her lips couldn't help but mirror his. "I for one am glad I heard you leave. The light is ideal this morning."

"So it would seem," he said with a nod toward the painting. "It is perfect, sweet. I cannot fathom how you manage it. The sun glistening off the water, the mounting clouds on the horizon..." He shook his head, gave her neck an encouraging squeeze, and then stepped away.

Disappointment whispered until she saw him reaching for two steaming mugs on the small table near the door. He handed one to her and raised the other to his lips, his gaze still upon the canvas.

"Thank you." Gwyneth took a sip and found the tea exactly as she preferred. The thought warmed her more than the beverage. Whether he had fixed it or Rosie, either way it was evidence of her welcome.

Thad folded his arms over his chest, his mug still half-raised as he studied the painting. "Is it finished?"

She moved beside him, trying to examine her work as a critic might. "It is hardly perfect. That section of the water there... But mostly finished, yes, except for the figure, which I just began."

"Well." He straightened and lifted his chin. "From what you have thus far, I can tell it is a most dashing figure indeed. You have already perfectly captured your subject's poise and good looks, and the charm he oozes with every—"

"Oh, stop it." Laughing, she gave his arm a shove as she would one of her cousins. "I obviously still have quite a bit of work to do to capture his insufferable arrogance."

His laugh seemed to wind its way through hers, making it richer, deeper, fuller. Even when it faded to a smile, still it echoed within her. He tilted his head to the side. "Over the mantel, do you think?"

Over the mantel—a place of honor. She wrapped her hands around her mug and took another happy sip. "It ought to fit well there."

"Of course, once we start adorning my walls, we must make an honest go of it. The others will look all the barer, so I suppose you had better paint portraits of Mother and Father. And Philly, if you can convince her to keep her nose out of a beaker long enough." He shot her that lopsided grin. "Or perhaps one of her with her nose in the beaker, since it is her natural state."

She attempted a haughty look, but her smile no doubt ruined it. "If you intend to keep me so busy, Mr. Lane, I may have to start charging you a commission."

"We can negotiate terms later." His gaze, as he said it, swept down to her mouth and lingered there.

Which set that frisson of heat skittering over her again. And made her wonder, again, if he had somehow caught a whiff of her thoughts when he first arrived.

Well. She had learned to flirt in the drawing rooms of London. She could manage his lingering gaze in an isolated garden. "Why do I get the feeling your idea of negotiation wouldn't be entirely proper, sir?"

"Me?" Merriment sparked in his eyes. "*You* are the one setting the terms, my lady."

And hers the thoughts not entirely proper. She cleared her throat and turned back to the painting, hoping that if she raised her cup to her mouth again, he would think her flush a result of the hot tea. "But I am a gentlewoman, sir, unaccustomed to such base matters as trade. And certainly I have no idea what the going rate is for a masterpiece in such a savage land as this."

"Careful, Miss Fairchild. Call this land savage often enough, and it may decide to show you how right you are. Though at least you can be sure that I am a gentleman." He sent her a smile that no doubt deepened her cheeks from rose to scarlet. "Most of the time."

Her throat went dry, and the drink she took did nothing to help her. Gracious—she had been bad enough at flirting in the staid and chaperoned London drawing rooms. What was she thinking, attempting it in an isolated garden? She swallowed another gulp of tea and faced forward. "You will need one with Jack too, and his father. And perhaps…" She squeezed her eyes shut, knowing, even as the words formed, that she ought not say them. Especially not *now*. "Perhaps one of Peggy. If you have a likeness of her, or could describe her for me…"

He sighed, but it sounded more resigned than pained. "Perhaps someday, Gwyn. But not for my walls. This was never where she wanted to be."

"What? But…" She turned to him, ready to probe further and make sense of that. He had never said anything to make her think his marriage had been unhappy, but for its ending. Granted, he spoke of Peggy only rarely, even less than Captain Arnaud spoke of his Marguerite.

But Thad's eyes were narrowed, not at her but at the painting. He traced it with his gaze as he had the one of her father, as if following her brush strokes one by one. Then he loosed a surprised breath. "There are no shadows in this one."

Of all the inane—Gwyneth pivoted back to the canvas. "Of course there are. The shadow of the hull on the water, of the sails, and within the clouds. The only one I have not put in yet is yours."

"No, that is not what I mean. Down here." He motioned to the edge. "There are no unexplained ones."

"What in the world are you talking about, Thad?"

"I am talking about—I shall show you." In one smooth movement, he spun toward the door and grabbed her free hand, pulling her along beside him. He tugged her through the door, into the drawing room, and over to the *secretaire* where all her drawings were, along with the painting of Papa that Winter had asked her to move back downstairs.

He released her hand, set his mug down, and strode to the windows. A few stiff tugs opened all the drapes and sent morning light onto her work. Then he was back at her side, pointing. "See? Here. And here, and here." He shuffled from page to page. Then he pulled forward the sketch of Papa's study and tapped a finger to the bottom. "And especially here. Which is the same one you put into the painting. Your uncle's sword, yes? That one I figured out."

She could only blink at the evidence—so clear, yet she scarcely remembered putting it there. She would never have identified it, had anyone asked, as a blade. But obviously it was. The shadow of Uncle Gates's sword, visible where he wasn't. "I did not…"

"But these." He indicated the other shadows. A scalloped edge, darting on and off the paper. "What are these?"

"They are…" She felt like a lazy pupil, unable to solve the simplest equations. Her eyes burned as she shook her head. "I do not know what or why. They are just there. When the images come, they are there in them."

"In all of them." He shuffled the papers again. "Your father's study, the garden, this country scene, your mother. The same shadows in all."

"But not in the *Masquerade*." She set her cup onto a table before she dropped it and rubbed at her temples. "I...I wish I understood. But you saw the blade when I did not. Surely you will make sense of this too. If it even matters."

"It matters." When he framed her face in his hands and tilted it up, his gaze left no room for disagreement. "You have information yet trapped inside you, sweet. Still locked behind the pain and grief. This is how you work it out, through your art. Like the painting of your father."

A shudder coursed through her. Secrets—those things she had always hated when she spotted them surrounding her—were trapped within her own mind, and she couldn't lure them out. She didn't even know they were there until a memory surfaced that ought never have been sunken to begin with.

"What is wrong with me, Thad? I am broken."

He pulled her close so she could press her face into the sandalwood-scented fabric of his shirt, so that she could wrap her arms around him and hold on while the earth rocked beneath her like the sea.

But even while she held on, she was ready to reject whatever assurances he would offer. He would try to tell her she was well, she was fine, there was nothing wrong with her. But there *was*. She knew it. She could feel that fracture within her. That missing piece. Visible only in those displaced shadows.

"Ah, sweet." He sighed, shuddered with her, and rested his cheek on the top of her head. "We are all broken."

The light had turned red-gold as the sun drifted toward the horizon, bathing the clouds in a rainbow and the Arnaud lawn in a soft warmth. Thad relaxed against the weathered wood of the chair he had claimed and smiled when Jack tossed the ball wide with admirable vigor.

Arnaud praised the boy's strength...and heaved a sigh as he ran, yet again, to fetch the toy. Thad hooked his hands behind his head and made sure he looked more relaxed than ever when his friend came huffing back. "So how did the flotilla look, then?"

Arnaud tossed the ball to his son, gently and precisely. "Good catch, Jacques!" He glanced at the sky and then at Thad. "In well enough order, I suppose. Though when one examines the state of things, really examines it, it is a wonder this war has not already ended in our defeat. Have we won any battles whose victory gained us an advantage?"

Thad ran his tongue along the edge of his teeth. "In the Chesapeake? No. But that is not the kind of war being waged, is it?"

Arnaud jumped high to snatch the ball. "Good one!"

The boy grinned, ran in a circle, and then pointed wildly at a bush. "Look, Papa, the fireflies are out! Can we catch them? Can we?"

"An excellent idea. You look over there and I will look over here." Arnaud let the ball fall to the ground and leaned against a tree trunk. "I cannot say *what* kind of war is being waged. We are not a Napoleon, trying to take over the entire world. We are not a rebellious colony that must be subdued. What, then, is their goal? To defend their Canadian territories against us, yes—that I understand. But here? If they are trying to conquer us again—"

"Then they must first weaken us." Thad rubbed his hands over his face. "Divide us against ourselves. Send a portion of us running in fear and let another portion wax into complacency and so forget we are even fighting a war."

"Papa, you are not looking for them!"

Arnaud grinned at his son. "Of course I am, Jacques. There is one right here, and I do not want to startle it." He made a lazy swipe at an even lazier bug and scooped it into his palm. Jack let out a whoop and dashed over to look.

"How do they make their bottoms light up, Papa? I have tried, and mine will not do it."

Thad snorted a laugh. "That sounds like a question for Grandpapa."

"Most assuredly." Arnaud stretched his hand flat to release the insect. "One more minute, *mon fils*, and we must ready for bed."

With the expected groan, Jack took off after another slow wink of yellow light. Arnaud turned back to Thad. "Something else is bothering you, *oui?*"

"Gates." He heaved out a breath and leaned forward, his forearms braced on his knees. "He must have something invested in this war. I cannot think what, not with so little knowledge of him, but it is the only thing that makes sense with all Gwyn has said. Her father's accusation of his greed, his determination to blame Fairchild's death on us Americans."

Arnaud quirked a single brow. "Not just us Americans, Thad. *Us*. The Culpers."

"He does not know who we are."

"We do though, *non?* The only organized American espionage ring."

Thad closed his eyes. "I wish I knew what we were up against."

"That famed intuition of yours will decipher it." Arnaud pushed off the tree and made a waving motion at Jack. "Come, Jacques. Time to go inside."

"Do you want me to go or stay?" Thad asked in an undertone.

Arnaud's sigh spoke of exhaustion. "You had better stay. It being his first night back at home, we both know how this is likely to go."

All too well.

"But, Papa!" From his spot across the lawn, Jack stomped a foot and scrunched up his face. "It is still daytime."

"It is still light out," Arnaud said, the epitome of patience. Thus far. "But the clock says it is bedtime. You know it stays light later in the summer, but we still must go to bed."

Jack's lower lip made its appearance, and he folded his arms across his chest. "No. I want to go back to Uncle Thad's."

"No, you don't." Thad put on a grin. "I would have put you to bed half an hour ago."

With a huff, the boy stomped toward the door.

Arnaud made a show of loosening his shoulders, as if in preparation for a brawl. "If I require reinforcements, I will shout."

"Alain." When his friend paused a step away, Thad sighed and passed a hand over his hair. "Have I made it worse by being always here these last two years?"

For a long moment, Arnaud simply held his gaze, his own a surprisingly calm sea of sienna. Then he gave him a small smile. "It matters not whether it has made it better or worse, Thad. You are my brother in all the ways that matter. You were the steady presence in his life when

I could not be here. You are our family. And so you *will* be here, always. I would never wish it otherwise."

Thad nodded and let him stride after his son. But his gaze remained for a long time where Arnaud had stood. And he wondered. Wondered if it would have been better for this little family had he gone to sea once Arnaud came home, gone away and stayed away until Jack forgot that Thad's house had once been home. That for those six bleak months, Thad had been the only parent he had.

No, Gwyneth was not the only broken one. Perhaps her memory had not yet fought its way back from the fracture that sudden trauma and months of sleep deprivation had caused. But it had only been a few months.

Thad had had four years to deal with his best friend's presumed death and all its consequences, and sometimes he still looked at his life and saw only the fragments that had been left by that news. Shards that would never quite fit perfectly together again, even now that Arnaud was home.

And he would just have to wait and see what kind of mosaic the Lord would make from the pieces.

Twenty

"How about now?"

Gwyneth took a step back and tilted her head, surveying the placement of the frame on both its horizontal and vertical planes. And not—most assuredly *not*—the long, well-muscled arm that held it there. "A pinch to the right and it will be perfect."

"A *pinch?*" Thad sent her a patronizing grin over his shoulder. "Since when is 'pinch' a unit of measure anywhere but in the kitchen? I am my father's son, Gwyn. I need precision. An inch more? Half of one?"

"I don't know." She raised her hand and pressed her fingers together. "This much."

Thad rolled his eyes. "And you pinch your fingers, as if this is salt going into a bowl. Very well." He made a show of raising his pressed fingers and moving the frame that amount.

A smile tickled her mouth, but she held her lips together against it. "No, no, not *your* pinch. Your fingers are too large. My pinch."

The glower he aimed her way was so exaggerated she had to put a hand to her mouth to hold back the laughter. Without taking his eyes from her, he scooted the frame back to the left a wee bit. "Better, my Lady of Exactitude?"

"Much." She batted her lashes and heaped sugar into her smile. "That will do quite nicely, my Lord of Facetiousness."

185

"That would be Mr. Facetiousness, thank you. No pesky titles in my fair land." He had turned back to the wall again, but she heard his smile. With a few quick motions, he picked up the pencil from the mantel and made several faint marks on the wall.

Gwyneth nestled a little deeper into the eastern-style couch directly across from the dormant fireplace. The ottoman, she had learned, was directly from the empire after which it derived its name, brought back on the same nearly catastrophic voyage as the rugs Thad so adored. "Are you certain you do not need my assistance?"

"You ask as you stretch out like a cat ready to nap in the sun."

"One can hardly help but do so on such a comfortable chaise." She stretched a bit more for show. "Still, I would get up if it meant seeing my masterpiece properly hung."

"No need for such a sacrifice, my lady. I daresay I can manage to get it square." Laughter colored his voice, and he sent her a warm look over his shoulder. One that made her infinitely aware of the fact that her stretch had brought her skirts up an inch too far and put her figure on rather prominent display.

She all but leaped to her feet. "So you say, sir. But I have no evidence of that, have I? For all I know, your walls are bare because you have never managed to hang anything straight upon them."

"You have found me out." Ruler in hand, he measured something against the back of the frame, and then held the wooden strip up to the wall and made another mark. "I have proven myself utterly incapable of nudging a frame along its wire until it is straight. 'Tis a curse that plagues me daily."

Gwyneth chuckled and eased across the space between them because…because unless she had a purpose for being elsewhere in a room, she always seemed to end up at his side. A realization that did indeed plague her daily. "I see no other reason for your dreadfully stark walls."

The glance he sent her this time was far too serious for their banter. "I used to have a few decorations. I sent them all to Alain's new house when he escaped the Turks. To help Jack make the transition from my home to his."

Her feet came to an abrupt halt with half the room still between them. She frowned. Was this another fact that had slipped through the cracks in her mind, or had it never been mentioned? "Jack lived here?"

"Hmm." He scratched one more mark. "Before Alain returned home. Which was six months after Jack's mother passed away. Alain had hoped to return from his trip in time for his birth, but instead we got the news of his death. When Jack's mother died too, I was the closest thing he had to family."

A shiver overtook her, despite the evening's heat. That explained much. "You said it was Barbary pirates who captured him?"

"First they left him for dead, and the sole crewman to escape brought back word that he had been killed with the rest. 'Twasn't for another two years that we realized he had survived it, and that when they saw he lived, they sold him into slavery. We had no idea until he returned one day, out of the proverbial blue."

Slavery. Another quake coursed through her. "What horrors he must have faced."

"He has spoken to me of it only once, which was all he could bear." Thad picked up the nail he had waiting on the mantel, and the hammer along with it. With one solid whack, he had driven it in just enough.

Poor Captain Arnaud. Gwyneth forced her feet back into action so that she could lift the painting and put it in his waiting hands. "There you are."

"There I am indeed. And my first love with me." He lowered it until the wire across the frame's backing caught on the nail and then nudged it to the right. "Is she level?"

Gwyneth retreated a few steps to better see. "Tap the left side once more." Latching onto levity again with both hands, she grinned. "Or is 'tap' too imprecise?"

He narrowed his eyes and tapped once upon the frame. "You tell me."

Her breath caught in her throat as she took it in. Her painting, so prettily framed and hung in the center of the wall, where every visitor to the Lane house would see it. See her interpretation of his ship, the sea he so loved, him as fearless captain. Made all the more complete with said fearless captain leaning against the mantel and studying her as she studied her handiwork.

Her fingers tangled together over her abdomen. "Well, look at that. You managed it."

"A feat that will inspire minstrels for years to come." He too took a step away to survey it. "I daresay there is no finer painting in all these United States."

Gwyneth chuckled. "I am afraid that is not saying much for your country."

He turned to face her, brows raised. "Do not disparage your talent, sweet."

She knew well her grin must look impish. "I am not. I am disparaging the rest of the art to be found here. You ought to have heard the things said of you Americans in the London drawing rooms."

"Prithee, what things?" A sparkle in his eye to belie the slope of his brows, he took a step forward.

She inched back. "The ones you might expect. That the land is still untamed and uncultured, and the people in it have no appreciation for refinement."

"Rubbish." The sparkle turned to an outright glint as he swept his gaze down her. "I have great appreciation for refinement."

Had the sun reemerged and blasted her through the window? She felt its heat to her very bones. "Of course you would think so. How would you know better? Given that all Americans are uneducated bumpkins."

"Bumpkins!" He took another step toward her, though if he wanted to look menacing, he would do better to keep the smile from the corners of his mouth. "You are calling me a *bumpkin?*"

She edged back a bit more. "Not I, sir. The *ton* of London. They are the ones who view you all as ignorant—" she had to take a larger step back to counter his stride forward— "uncouth—" she bumped into the leg of the low table— "uncivilized—"

"Uncivilized again, am I?" He caught up to her and reached out to keep her from tumbling backward with his long, strong fingers around her elbows. "Shall I show you uncivilized, Miss Fairchild?"

Yes, please. Thank heavens her breath had escaped her and kept her from uttering such embarrassing words. Not that he gave her time to speak. His hands jerked her close, one sliding around her waist and the other moving to tip up her head.

Her heart galloped when her gaze clashed with his. Amber eyes molten, sparking like a flame tossed by the wind. Terrifying and alluring and invigorating all at once, so intense she had to close her own to take it in. And then his lips were on hers.

Civility indeed had no place in his kiss. 'Twas more the embrace of an adventurer, one who was seeking, hungering, demanding…yet not demanding more than she yearned to give. She wrapped her arms around his neck and surged up onto her toes.

How could something feel both familiar and new? Never had a man kissed her like this—never, in truth, had she wanted one to. Yet as Thad's lips caressed hers, she had the sensation of waking from a dream and finding it real, part misty wonder and part warm reality. And his arms…they felt like home around her.

Her smile took her mouth from his, and she opened her eyes to find Thad smiling too.

His fingers wove through her hair, making her wonder what happened to her pins this time—she had never had such trouble keeping track of them in England. He pressed a gentler, quicker kiss to her lips. "That will teach you what you get for calling me uncivilized."

Laughter bubbled up and spilled forth. "It will indeed, you uncouth, uncivilized brute."

Another brush of lips on lips. "You are an astoundingly slow pupil."

"Perhaps you are a bad teacher." She tightened her arms around his neck. "You ought to try that lesson again."

"Well." One more kiss, feather soft, tempting as a cup of chocolate. "If I must."

He deepened it again, and this time was even more consuming than the first, making her imagine a thousand futures she could have in his arms. Tossing seas and galloping horses, exotic mountains and untamed wilds. Bustling streets and familiar faces, nights by the fire and days side-by-side.

So long as she could feel forever this certainty in her heart, that wherever he was, that was where she should be. As her fingers moved through his hair and onto his cheek, her heart beat in time to his.

A blistering French exclamation from the doorway made them both jump. Her feet firmly on the ground again, Gwyneth's vision blurred from the rush of blood to her face. She leaped away from Thad and pressed her hands to her burning cheeks.

He dragged in a breath and turned leisurely toward the door, where Captain Arnaud stood glowering. "Thunder and turf, Alain. You startled a year off my life."

Gwyneth slid to the side to keep Thad between her and Captain Arnaud, though she wasn't sure why she felt the need to do so.

Arnaud swept his hat from his head and dashed it to the floor. "Is that what you call treading carefully, Thad? Taking matters slowly?"

Gwyneth drew in a long breath. They had spoken of her? Or rather, of Thad's feelings for her? The thought made her insides turn to mush... until she realized that his best friend obviously did not approve. The mush hardened to lead and sank into the pit of her stomach.

Thad's head came up. "Yes, that is exactly what I call it, given how long I have wanted to kiss her and held myself in check."

Her breath caught. How long *had* he wanted to do so? Since she first started imagining it?

Arnaud muttered something too low for Gwyneth to make out, though the intonation was unmistakably French once more. He shook his head. "You are too blind to see the dangers. She is a guest under your roof, yet there you stand taking liberties—"

"Liberties! 'Twas only a kiss, and my parents are directly across the hall. I am hardly—"

"You are." He stooped, scooped up his hat, but then he tossed it down again with even more fury as soon as he straightened. "Blast it, Thad, look at yourself. You have not courted her. You have only known her eight weeks. She is still distraught over her loss, and you swoop in and take advantage."

Ridiculous. He would never... Joke as they may about him being uncivilized, Gwyneth had not a single doubt that he was a gentleman. She slid to her left, willing to risk being within Arnaud's line of sight so that she might see Thad at least in profile. She found a muscle in his jaw ticking.

"Watch yourself, Alain. I have granted you many a jab over the last two years, but I will not suffer another now."

Arnaud loosed a scoffing laugh. "You have *granted* me...? Is that what you call refusing to discuss something?" He strode across the space between them and gave Thad a push that would have sent a smaller man tumbling backward. "It is time you give me answers. Is this how you treated my wife, Thaddeus? How you convinced her to marry you while I was rotting in a louse-infested pit in Istanbul?"

Gwyneth staggered back as if she was the one he had shoved. What could he be talking about? Arnaud had been married to Marguerite. Thad's wife had been Peggy.

Peggy—short for Margaret. Gwyneth tried to blink away the realization, but it still clouded her eyes. Had she not found it amusing that Captain Arnaud called his son Jacques while everyone else used the Anglicized version? Yet she had never once considered he was doing the same with his wife's name.

She felt Thad's gaze on her and refocused her own past the shock. Why did she feel betrayed? He had never lied to her about it, had never said anything to deliberately make her think Marguerite and Peggy were two different women—but he had certainly never explained it, either.

Still, there was no missing the hurt clouding his eyes as he looked again at his friend. "Alain, you had been gone two years. Dead."

Arnaud held out his arms, needing no words to point out the lie.

But Thad shook his head. "*Dead.* Your crewman saw you struck down. You were gone. And you know well what that did to us all."

His friend pivoted away, strode to the fireplace, and braced himself on the mantel. The clouds in her painting suddenly seemed darker, feeding off his inner storm. "Two years would not have been enough for her to grieve me." His tone proved it, so heavy with mourning for his Marguerite that she *must* have felt the same.

Gwyneth's gaze went again to Thad, whose Adam's apple bobbed. "No. Nowhere near. But she was dying, Alain, and the money was gone. What was I to do? Leave her and Jack to starve?"

Arnaud speared him with a sharp glance and a quiver at the corners of his mouth. "You take them food."

"To where?" He lifted his hands and let them fall again. "You know well she sold the house to buy medicine. They had no place to go. Your widow, the son you had never even met, would have been left to the streets."

"My *wife.*" Slashing a hand through the air, Arnaud's nostrils flared. "So you swoop in to play the hero as you must always do. As you are doing now, again, with another grieving woman."

A second blow to her chest. Wishing she had a shawl to clutch around her, Gwyneth stumbled another step to the left.

Thad sent her a helpless look before turning it back to his friend. "It is not the same. Peggy needed someone to care for her. It was a matter of survival—"

"She was carrying your child when she died!"

That accusation ripped through the room like a bolt of lightning, making Gwyneth feel stranded in a tossing, tempest-ridden sea. Having no part in this, not really, yet trapped within it. And she shook her head. *That* was why no one would mention Peggy and the babe. Not because of Thad's grief, but because of Arnaud's.

A grief so very understandable. She took another step away from them. To come back from death, back from slavery, and find that one's wife had died in one's absence...as the wife of one's closest friend. To find that the woman supposedly so ill she could not survive on her own had been with child...

The slight stoop of Thad's shoulders hinted at the weight Arnaud's words brought crushing down on him. "We believed you were not coming back. And we were left with whatever we could make of the pieces that truth brought upon us. She was my wife—"

"She was *my* wife!"

Thad sighed. "Please try to understand. Please. Every day I fell to my knees and prayed for her healing. Prayed the Lord would touch her and make her well. Because the only future I could see was the one that seemed true at the time—that you were dead, that she and Jack were all I had. And so my priority was not to guard *your* feelings. It was to try to forge a sound marriage, one that could grow strong when my prayers were answered. That was the only reality I had, Alain."

A soul-rending cry tore from Arnaud's lips as he flew across the room, heading straight for Thad.

Gwyneth spun away and darted out the door. She understood that Arnaud had long bottled up his feelings over this and they were now erupting. She understood she had been an unintended casualty from an issue too long ignored.

But understanding did nothing to hold together the shards of her heart.

She nearly collided with the elder Lanes, who stood in the hall a few steps from the door. Her face flaming again, she tried to hurry away.

Winter's hand on her arm stayed her. "Gwyneth, I am sorry. You did not realize…and I never paused to consider you wouldn't. I should have explained it to you."

"No, *he* should have." Perhaps not at first, given how sensitive a subject it was, but sometime. Certainly sometime before he took her in his arms and kissed her senseless. A thud came from within the drawing room, all the inspiration she needed to pull her arm free. "Excuse me."

She took a few steps, but Winter shadowed her. "Gwyneth, he— you have a right to be upset. But know that regardless of what Alain says in his anger, your situation now is nothing like Peggy's was. Thaddeus has never looked at any woman the way he does at you."

Maybe that was true, but who was to say it was not because she was more broken, more in need, more in distress than any other damsel he had yet come across? Because she provided more opportunity for him to play hero, as Captain Arnaud had called it?

She needed to get away, to be alone, to close out this whole family and all their noble, terrible truths. And so she headed for the stairs, the one place Winter still moved slowly, and ran up them two at a time. Gaining her room, she slammed the door. And for the first time since her arrival, she turned the key in the lock.

Twenty-One

T had bit back a choice word when his elbow connected with the table's edge on his way to the floor, and he gave Arnaud a foot in the gut to push him away. "Blast it, Alain, that *hurt*."

"*That* hurt?" He scrambled back to his feet, leaving Thad little choice but to jump back to his. "Try being whipped until your back is raw."

Thad rolled his shoulders forward, his arms raised. "I *told* you not to go. Why could you not have listened?"

"You think I have not asked myself that a million times?" He took a swing that Thad ducked. Then he charged him and knocked Thad onto the chair.

He used the momentum to roll Arnaud over him and onto the floor with a thud. "It would all be so different."

"I know!" Fury drenched the words, fury obviously aimed at himself. Not that that stopped him from hooking a foot under the chair and tipping it backward, Thad along with it. "I *know*. But someone had to go, and you refused."

The impact was negligible, just enough to make him want to let loose a few strong words. Words that would be aimed more at the past than the jab of pain. "You are right. It should have been me who went."

Arnaud spat out something in French and lobbed a pillow at Thad's head. "Of all the idiotic things to say! Why? Why should it have been you? Because you could have evaded the pirates? Outsmarted them?"

"Because I had nothing to lose! No one was depending on me." He grabbed the pillow and whipped it at Arnaud's face before pushing up to his feet.

Arnaud sent the cushion flying toward the ottoman. "Are you daft? You have an entire nation depending on you. *You* are the one who knows every blasted man, woman, and child from Florida to Canada. *You* are the one Tallmadge trusts implicitly, who *everyone* trusts implicitly."

"What then, Alain?" Thad spread his arms wide, making himself a target if that was what his friend needed. "What should I have done? Should I have kept my distance and left Peggy and your babe with no help?"

Arnaud spun away and kicked another stray pillow. "Don't be a fool."

"What then? What should I have done?"

"I don't know! Perhaps exactly what you did!" Somehow he made it sound like an accusation, even pivoting around with a pointed finger. "Yes, you should have taken care of them. You should have raised Jacques as your own. Perhaps you even should have married her. But if so, then you should have *loved* her, Thad! She deserved to be loved."

He might as well have hurled grapeshot at him. Thad took a step back, his arms falling limp at his sides. "How?" His voice came out like a rusty hinge. "How could I love her when she was still yours? When *you* were every other word that fell from her lips?"

Arnaud's finger shook.

Edging closer, Thad reached out and gripped his friend's shoulder. "We did what we felt was best. But her heart was yours, was *always* yours."

There had never been room for him. He had known that the day he proposed. And she had apologized for it the day she died. As if it had been something she could help, as if he had not understood. As if he blamed her for it, and for not holding on long enough to give him the family she thought she owed him.

Arnaud drew in a shuddering breath. "Do I apologize for that?"

"No." Thad swallowed. "Just do not begrudge me my chance now. Please."

Arnaud knocked his arm away. "Again with the idiocy. Why do you think I am trying to keep you from making an utter mess with Miss Fairchild?"

"I am not making a mess of anything!" He shoved Arnaud two steps backward. "We were getting along quite well before you came in and exploded like an overcharged cannon."

"Fire and brimstone, Thad, if it were anyone else you would be the first to point it out." He indicated the door. "That girl is not ready for you."

Growling, he shoved his hands into his hair and gripped it, but that did nothing to relieve the pressure building in his head. "Why is it that every man, woman, and child from Florida to Canada trusts me except for *you?*"

Arnaud had drawn closer again and reached out again to push him. "Why is it that you think you are the only one who can ever know what is right, ever *do* it right?"

"Because you cannot even figure out why you are angry! Is it over Gwyneth or Peggy? Because I married your wife or because I didn't love her?" He returned the push, though Arnaud leaned into it and tried to reach his shoulders.

"Boys!"

There had been a day when that tone from his father would have stopped them both cold. And it had, on many occasions, brought an end to a scuffle much like this one. Not today.

Father huffed. "This way of solving your differences may have been understandable when you were ten, but now? How old are you?"

Arnaud rolled his eyes. Only, Thad was sure, because his back was to Father. "Younger, I believe, than you were when your brother last visited, though I recall seeing you with your arm locked around his head."

Father's lips twitched. "Entirely different. Archie and I were not *fighting.* 'Twas all in good fun."

Arnaud changed his position, and they both staggered to the right.

Thad smiled. "I daresay that for this to be termed fighting, we would have to be trying to hurt each other."

They staggered back to the left.

"Hmm." Father leaned into the wall. "You do have a point. But you scared Gwyneth away."

"What?" Thad straightened and absently steadied his friend. Of course he had known Gwyneth left the room. But he had assumed... what? She was outside in the hall? Waiting to wrap her arms around him when he emerged? "Where did she go?"

"Up to her room, behind the locked door." Father jerked his head upward in illustration. "Your mother followed her up to make excuses for you—"

"*Excuses?*"

Father leveled a glare on him. "You ought to have explained the situation well before now, Thaddeus, if you have fallen in love with her. In any case, I was sent in here to try to intervene. As if I were going to come between those flailing limbs."

"See?" Arnaud pulled his waistcoat back into place and turned to face Father. "He is moving too fast and not taking the time for leisurely conversations that allow them to share all this necessary information."

Father tilted his head to the side. "He may have a point, son."

Thad lifted a hand in exasperation. "She may have only been here two months, but I have seen her each and every day. And I *know* this— I know I love her." Seeing the shaking of Arnaud's head, he moved that extended hand toward his sire. "Father, how long had you known Mother before you realized you had fallen in love?"

Father's head moved to the other side. "He does have a point, Alain. I had scarcely even seen her in the two and a half months I had known her, but there was no question where my heart had inclined."

Arnaud folded his arms across his chest. "And then you courted her another nine months before you proposed. Because you had to be sure you really understood each other before you made any commitments."

"And that point is Alain's."

"How is that one his? I kissed her. I did not call the reverend to marry us here and now."

Father opened his mouth, but Arnaud pivoted to Thad again,

outrage in his eyes. "She is living here! Do you think it wise to go around kissing her if you do *not* intend to marry her quickly?"

Father's sigh sounded as blustery as an October day. "I am certain Thad is aware of the delicate balance he must strike."

Arnaud's aristocratic nose went into the air, which gave Thad a sudden understanding of why the peasants in France had hauled all the aristocracy to the guillotine. "I am none too sure. Tell me, sir, what would have happened with you and your wife, do you think, had you *not* taken the time to properly court?"

"Ah." Father's eyes lit, and he lifted a finger into the air. "I have given it thought. I daresay that had we—"

"Alain." Thad slapped his friend's arm. "Asking him to expound on a hypothetical? What were you *thinking?*"

Arnaud snorted. "My mistake. I apologize."

"Insufferable pups. Though I suppose I should be glad you can agree on *something*." Father pushed off from the wall and took a few steps into the room. He measured Thad with his probing gaze and then turned it on Arnaud. "You cannot know how it has pained us to watch the two of you lately. Always you had been like brothers, even before we took you in, Alain."

Arnaud's nose moved back down, past its normal angle and into a humble one. "You know I am grateful for all you did for me. Sending me to school, funding my ventures—"

"I am not asking for thanks." Father drew in a deep breath, his regard making Thad want to wriggle like a recalcitrant schoolboy. "I know how it must have hurt when you returned and discovered what had happened while you were gone. But we all thought you dead, every one of us."

Arnaud shifted from foot to foot.

Father shook his head. "For two years Winter and I have watched, waiting to see if the fissure would be healed or grow into a chasm. Frankly, I am amazed you have gone this long without having it out about Peggy."

Without moving his gaze from Father, Arnaud reached over to punch Thad in the arm. "We spoke of her often enough, but if ever I tried to draw him out on my feelings over him marrying her, he would ignore me."

Rather than hit him back, Thad slid a step away. "Draw me out? Bait me, you mean. And I did not want to fight with you over her."

"Maybe I needed you to. Has that never occurred to you? You, who can always tell what everyone *else* needs?"

"Did it help?" Thad took another step away, his mind screaming that it was time to leave. Time to escape this conversation before he lost his brother yet again—forever this time. "Do you feel better now for having accused me of seducing her, for insinuating I was wrong for marrying her, and then wrong for not loving her as you did?"

Arnaud didn't budge. "You did not avoid the topic because you thought it best for me. You avoided it because *you* did not want to face what you did. Because deep down you felt you betrayed me by marrying her."

He took another step toward the door. "I did not."

"Face it, Thad. You could as easily have sent her and Jacques to your parents, to Amelia, to Philly. Any one of them would have taken them in. But it had to be you. It always has to be you who swoops in to save the day."

He could only shake his head.

"And now you are doing the same thing with Miss Fairchild."

Enough. "You, of all people, should understand that I love her. You, who still love Peggy to the depths of your soul." He ate up the distance to the door and paused at the threshold to face Arnaud again. "The problem is that you don't trust me. You haven't trusted me since you came home."

Not waiting for a response, he ducked his way out of the room and strode down the hall. He grabbed his hat as he charged out into the warm twilight.

His head hurt. His chest ached. And he hadn't even the satisfaction of slamming the door behind him, as Father's foot stopped it. Thad opened his legs to their full length to put space between him and the man who always saw far too much.

"I will run to keep up if I must, son, but it would be the kind thing to spare my aging joints and wait for me."

"If you intend to lecture me, Professor, stay home." But he held up at the gate.

Father approached with that infuriating, knowing smirk that had plagued the family for decades. "Where are we going?"

Thad shrugged and led the way to the street. "Are you going to take his side?"

Father chuckled. "Probably, to you. And then when I talk with him later, I will take yours."

"Ever the devil's advocate."

"Ever the father who wants his children, even the one not born of his flesh, to have no rifts between them."

"'Tisn't a rift." It couldn't be. Rifts were permanent. "'Tis only a... strain."

Father's silence deafened him. And it stretched on and on until they turned the corner and headed, as Thad's feet always did, toward the bay. At which point the elder man finally spoke, so softly that Thad could scarcely hear him over a wagon rattling by. "You may have chosen the sea above the classroom, but I taught you how to examine an argument. Have you done so here? Have you paused to entertain the notion that Alain may be right about your motives with Peggy?"

Thad shouldn't have waited for his father to catch up. "I could not have sent her to Amelia. She had just had the twins and her hands were full. Philly had lost her babe, and Grandmama Caro had just moved to Maryland. You were having troubles at the college—"

"But family has always come first, and Peggy and Jack were family. You know any one of us would have helped."

"Yes, but..." He could hear Arnaud's accusation ringing in his ears, that it must always be *him* that saved the day. But it wasn't that. "I had nothing to put aside. Nothing to juggle. I was the one Lane with no obligations, no family of his own...and I had already been helping so much. Jack...I was his father. The only one he had."

Father sighed and followed him when he turned down a random, shadowed alley. "Your grandfather Hampton once gave your mother an ultimatum. Do you remember the story? She must marry by July or be tossed to the streets. I had been courting her for six months and had yet to break through her wall, and I had no idea she was in such dire straits. She stood there, the night when she had run out of time, and kept that terrible secret to herself. Because she thought if she told me, I would marry her in an instant."

Thad glanced over at the familiar crease in his brow. "You would have."

"Of course I would have, in *half* an instant. But your mother held her tongue because she did not want a marriage of obligation. Which is exactly what your marriage to Peggy was. And while I believe you would have found a steady resting place, the point remains that it is a difficult way to begin a life together. All you two ever had was a beginning."

A beginning haunted by her husband's ghost.

He blinked it away as he shook his head. "You know what plagues me, Father? The questions of what would have happened had the Lord granted her healing. If she were still alive when Alain came home, if he found her married to me..."

Father winced, though surely he had wondered it as well. There wasn't a question in the universe Bennet Lane had not entertained at one point or another. "An ugly possibility."

"Which leads me to a prayer of thanksgiving that God, in His wisdom, spared us that. But that, of course, begs another question."

"Thad." Father paused at the alley's mouth and stayed his son with a hand on his arm. "You cannot think that way. To think He let her die to save you from that awkwardness, that it is therefore your fault she died because of the decision you made to marry her—that way is a twisted path that will lead you straight into the jowls of depression."

He focused his gaze on a crumbling brick in the corner of the building behind his father. "Was it a mistake? Your honest opinion. Should I have married her?"

Father made no rash answer. He let his eyes wander upward as he pursed his lips. Then, after a long moment, he met Thad's gaze again. "It was not a mistake. You provided Jack with a family, a sanctuary. You gave Peggy a feeling of purpose again. She told your mother it was the first time she had had a goal since she lost Alain. To be a good wife, to show Jack what family was meant to be."

That was what he had always told himself. But somehow, with his best friend staring him down, it came off lacking. He let out the breath he had been holding and started forward again. "Maybe. But maybe I should have refused to touch her—"

"That is not how God designed marriage, son. And certainly not how He designed man. Which leads us to Alain's concerns about you and Gwyneth."

Thad groaned and, after a quick glance both directions, crossed to the other side of the street. "He overreacted. I kissed her, yes, but that is all. I will not apologize for it."

"I will settle for you apologizing to her. Not for kissing her, but for kissing her before you explained what has made you the man you are and gave her the chance to reciprocate."

He clenched his jaw and let that simmer as they closed the distance to the next intersection. "How upset was she?"

"She ran away from your mother. What does that tell you?"

That this might have to be a very long walk if he hoped to return and find her calm enough to want to speak with him. He lifted a hand to rub at the sore muscles in his neck. He was getting too old for wrestling matches with Arnaud. "What am I to do? I love her. I love her like I have never loved anyone, like I had begun to think myself incapable of loving."

"Then you rest in the knowledge that a love so deep will not fade, and you give her the opportunity to mourn her father and recover from the trauma of seeing him killed."

The scent of the bay teased Thad's nose, and he caught a glimpse of dark water between the buildings. He knew what waited there—the Chesapeake merchant fleet, stranded in the harbor. And beyond it, over the horizon, the line of British vessels that held them there.

A vise went tight within him; a shiver slithered up his spine. "What if I haven't that much time?"

Father again came to a halt, more abruptly than before. "Why would you say such a thing?"

Thad quickened his pace, his feet pulling like a lodestone toward his ship.

"Thaddeus!" A few pounding footfalls, and Father was at his side again. "What is it?"

"I don't know." But whatever it was, it thrummed through him, setting every nerve ablaze. "It is the same feeling I get out at sea when a storm is coming."

"Your mother insists you are no changeling, but I think you must be to have such a strange intuition. If I could bottle it, I would be the wealthiest man in the nation."

Thad laughed and mentally thanked his father for a reason to do so. "I thought the stories of changelings were that the fairies stole the real children and replaced them with ones who were stupid and oafish."

"There is no need to insult yourself, son. You are odd without question, but not stupid."

He laughed again. Then he stopped as another alleyway loomed before them, stopped a mere second before a figure stepped out. Familiar, but not familiarly clothed. He sucked in a breath. "Mr. Bolton?"

Congressman Tallmadge, dressed like a farmer, emerged from the shadows with a frown. "The Misters Lane. You could not have received my note already."

Father's frown matched his friend's. "We were out for a walk. What brings you to Baltimore, B—John?"

The congressman glanced between them and then nodded toward the Chesapeake. "Walk with me and I will explain as we go." They flanked him as he continued on the path Thad had already set out. "Captain Lane, forgive me for taking liberties, but I sent my men to gather your crew. The moon is new and the night will be dark, thereby safe to slip past the British. Henry assures me he can pilot you safely through the blockade."

Thad's heart pounded nearly as fast as it had when he held Gwyneth in his arms. "You are sending me to sea? *Tonight?*"

"I have little choice." His voice low, Tallmadge looked all around them. "We both know the British fleet is on its way from Europe, and as soon as they arrive, they will decide where in the region to attack. We need to know where they are, how many they are, and when they will be here. We cannot wait for someone else to discover this by chance, Captain. And if you wait any longer, the moon will *not* be new, and you will be forced to go the long way around to avoid detection."

But if he intended to set sail tonight, it would have to be when tide and darkness were both with him. Which would mean that he would have to board his brig within the next few minutes.

He sighed. Tallmadge's point was undeniable. And had it been any other day, Thad would have bounded most gratefully onto *Masquerade*. But today? Tonight? *Now*? He looked past the congressman to his father.

Father stared right back at him. "You said a month ago you wanted action."

"Yes, but Gwyn is already upset with me." Arnaud would understand, but would she? "If I leave without warning..."

"A bit of distance just now may be for the best. I will explain the situation."

Tallmadge's head swung from Thad to Father and back again. "Gwyn? The Gwyn you mentioned when you came to see me last month? Why would she be upset if you leave?"

Thad cleared his throat. He had a feeling that the head of the Culper Ring would not be entirely thrilled to learn that his Samuel Culper III was in love with the daughter of a British general. A murdered British general, whose brother-in-law was set upon the destruction of their country.

Father laughed. "Take one guess, old man."

Tallmadge sighed. "In my day, one waited until the war was over before one turned one's attention to matters of courting."

Father, bless him, nudged his longtime friend with an elbow. "*You* may have. Some of us are quite capable of juggling both concerns at once."

With a shake of his head, the congressman turned with Thad toward the docks. "Tell me you will go. If you do not, I cannot think who to send."

His crew would be but a skeleton. Getting out of the harbor would be dangerous, finding the fleet risky, and getting home again an ordeal.

But his feet itched with excitement and purpose thudded through his veins. "They will head to Bermuda first, I am sure. I can await them there to get the count. Though *Masquerade* will need water and food—"

"I have men loading it even now, enough for the short trip. You will have to purchase more once there, though."

"A good excuse for landing."

And there she was, his first love, bustling with life again after two years asleep in the harbor. Dock workers carried crates and rolled barrels toward and onto her, and the *Masquerade* bobbed joyfully in response. He spotted his crew—the few still alive and not fighting off the Redcoats elsewhere—on the deck, in the lines, on the dock.

Henry jogged their way, his white teeth the only thing on his person that stood out in the quickly falling darkness. "There you are, Captain. I wanted to tell you I talked it over with Emmy, and she knows I be gone longer than usual this time. You gonna need me to lend a hand the whole way."

He slapped a grateful hand to Henry's back, nodded at Tallmadge, and caught Father's gaze. "You will make sure she understands?"

"I will." And he would see everything at home was cared for, Thad knew.

Except he could not promise to bring rest to Gwyneth's spirit, could he? The insomnia might come back. The nightmares might strike again in what minutes of sleep she could find. When he managed to return, it might be to find her hollow and haunted once again, their progress lost.

You must always be the one to swoop in to the rescue.

The tension in his chest throbbed. *Dear Lord...* But what could he pray? "We had better hurry. Farewell, Mr. Bolton. Father—give everyone my love and request their prayers."

Father nodded.

Thad's fingers curled into his palm. *Dear Lord...I commit her to You.*

Twenty-Two

Gwyneth stared out the window into the darkening night, her arms folded over her middle. No light shone now from the heavens other than an early star or two, but a square of illumination fell onto the lawn from a downstairs window. She hadn't lit a lamp in her chamber. Why bother? The shadows draped her, warm and velvety, like a cloak.

A figure turned in from the street, and when he passed through that square of light, she recognized Mr. Lane. Alone, though she had watched him leave with Thad an hour earlier. And walking with a sort of...resignation.

Her throat tightened. Where was his son? Out at some tavern, listening in on rum-loosened tongues, getting a feel for the prevailing state of mind of his neighbors? Or perhaps gone to make amends with Arnaud, who had charged out five minutes after he departed?

Her eyes slid shut, though that scarcely added to the darkness. Why had she not seen it? Not made the connection? And why did it bother her so? She had known he was married before, had known the reasons.

But somehow it changed it to know it was his friend's wife. Not even because of the strangeness that came with Captain Arnaud's return from the dead, but because she *knew* them. Arnaud and Jack.

She saw Thad with them nearly every day, had made comments about Peggy that made it clear she had *not* made the connection—and he had left her with those misunderstandings. Left her in the dark.

She had thought he trusted her. She had thought he wanted to involve her in his life. Was that not why he had told her about his Culper Ring? She had thought he, unlike her father, thought her worthy of the truth, able to handle it, able to *help* with it.

The truth is too much for you. The thought came like a silent whisper in her ear. *Your mind is too weak.*

She spun away from the window, flew to the door, and followed the sound of conversation down to the kitchen. Then she came to a halt at the sight of an unfamiliar woman within.

At once she knew it must be Rosie's Emmy. They had the same fog-gray eyes, the same shape to their faces. But Emmy's skin was as near to Gwyneth's cream as to Rosie's brown, her hair a middling brown rather than black. And her face was even more stunning than Philly's.

No wonder Thad had said she would not forget an encounter with this woman. Her fingers ached for a pencil with which to put her likeness to paper. And her mind filled with questions.

Rosie spotted her lingering in the doorway and waved her in with a smile. "Are we keeping you awake, Miss Gwyn?"

As if she could have slept? Gwyneth returned the smile and shook her head as she eased into the room. The elder Lanes were both there; Winter at the table with a mug before her, and Mr. Lane pulling out a chair for her, his face somber.

"Sit yourself down, and I'll get you some lemonade." Rosie nodded toward the stranger. "I don't believe you have met my Emmy yet."

Her Emmy smiled, which made her even more beautiful. "I've scarcely gotten free of Henry's sister all summer, Mama. Poor thing. But I've heard all about you, Miss Fairchild. And just how smitten Thaddeus is."

Heat surged into her cheeks as she sat. "Call me Gwyneth, please."

Emmy took a sip of water, her gaze not leaving Gwyneth's face. "I meant to visit before now, but with Liza bedridden I have scarcely seen my own home since May, much less anyone else's. Henry has been so worried I would overtax myself." She patted her abdomen, which drew Gwyneth's attention to its rounded state.

An even more perfect picture. She needed a riot of blooms in the background, her standing in the midst of them with her focus downward, one hand on that expectant stomach. Dressed in something filmy and whimsical, with a breeze playing at the hem.

Winter smiled and patted Emmy's arm. "I am glad you will be with us for a while, Emmy, and I know Philly will be ecstatic to learn you are back home."

"Ah." Mr. Lane brightened, leaning around his wife to grin at the young woman. "Will you be staying here with us, Em?"

"Mm-hmm. Henry recommended it while he is away with Thad, and I thought it a fine idea. Better a few weeks with my favorite people than all alone at home."

Gwyneth had gripped the glass of lemonade that Rosie put before her but didn't lift it. At the moment she needed no cool drink—her veins had filled with ice. "Away with Thad?"

For a few *weeks*?

Mr. Lane cleared his throat. "Congressman Tallmadge intercepted us on our walk, my dear. He needed Thad to sail immediately to Bermuda to see how many ships the British are sending here."

Her fingers loosed the glass, slid over the table, and tangled with the fabric of her dress in her lap. "But he left with nothing but a hat—"

"He keeps the basics in his cabin on the *Masquerade*." His smile was tight. "I am not certain why Ben did not give him any more notice than he did, but it was imperative he leave at once."

So he did. Without a word, without an apology, without an explanation after those kisses and then the confrontation with Captain Arnaud…he just left, because some politician told him to. On a mission to spy on her father's friends in the navy. To put his life in the gravest of danger. To possibly never come back.

She pushed away from the table, working hard to keep a smile upon her face. "I imagine if anyone can give the congressman the information he requires, it is your son. Now I am afraid I must beg your indulgence and promise to visit more in the morning. I have a bit of the headache."

Another chair scraped as she turned, and warm fingers touched her arm before she could make it through the doorway. "Gwyneth." Mr. Lane's voice was low, pleading. "He had little choice. Concerned as he was with how this would seem to you—and you were his first thought—'tis a matter of the safety of us all. Having this knowledge could make the difference between—"

"I understand, sir. I grew up in a military home, remember." Though Papa had never left without saying goodbye.

Rosie elbowed Mr. Lane aside. "I'll see after her. You go on and have some of that tea." She guided Gwyneth forward, the untouched glass of lemonade in hand. "You may want this yet."

She didn't want anything. Not lemonade, not company, not soft words from biased parents. She wanted only silence. From the talk, from the thoughts banging around her head like war drums. From the heart that said his name with every pulse. *Thad, Thad, Thad.*

"I could smack that boy," Rosie muttered, leading Gwyneth away from the stairs she'd intended to go back up. "Leaving now after upsetting you. And just when you had started feeling at home here too."

The sentiment eased her, yet it made her tongue jump to his defense. "He is doing what he must, Rosie. I cannot be his only concern." Though when she saw that the housekeeper was leading her toward the drawing room, she dug in her heels. *Thad, Thad, Thad.*

Rosie scolded her with a look. "You think you can avoid the thought of him anywhere in this house? Come on, now." She pulled her inside.

The same lamps were lit that had been two hours earlier, when she and Thad wandered in with her painting. It hung now over the fireplace as it had after their jesting. Thad, on his ship. His first love, he had called it. And back he had gone to her.

Of course he did. His ship is freedom. You are shackles. A burden.

She turned away from the painting. Rosie steered her across the room to her oasis of comfort, the *secretaire* that had been her home more often than not since she arrived. Where pencils were happily scattered and paper always freshly stacked. Where she could block out the rest of the world and make sense of it all through the order of black on white.

She sat, pulled out what she would need, knew just what she would draw—Emmy. Though the vision made her pause. She looked up at Rosie as the woman put her lemonade on the corner of the desk. "Rosie, you have a beautiful daughter."

The stern brow softened, and a rare smile lit her face. "I know. She's the only beautiful thing that came of that life."

"Is she…?" She could think of no delicate way to phrase the question.

But Rosie's eyes reflected no pain, no bitterness as she nodded. "My Uncle Free tried to buy my freedom time and again, but the master would never let him. And you can be sure my opinion was never asked, not about nothing. But he died when Emmy was a little thing, and the mistress was happy to get rid of us quick as she could. When Uncle Free asked me where I wanted to go, and the Lanes invited us to their home—it was the first time anyone ever *asked* me anything. So I told them. And I ain't never stopped telling it like I see it since."

She leaned forward and cupped Gwyneth's chin with strong fingers. "Now listen, child. You fight for what you want, what you need. You fight whatever's against you. Whatever's been making you think you're not safe unless he's here. You *are*. You hear me? We're gonna take care of you while he's gone, and when he comes home—well." She straightened, those gray eyes gleaming like silver. "Then you'll show him it ain't you who can't live without him. It's *him* who can't live without you. Understand?"

Gwyneth understood the words, yes, and the sentiment, and they brought a wave of determination through her. If she wanted this to be her home, if she wanted to make a life with Thad, she must not sit idly by, bemoaning his absence. She must be strong like Rosie. She must… she must…

That whisper still filled her ear. *You are shackles. You are a burden.*

She must find a way…she must be more than…

Thad, Thad, Thad.

"Fight it off, Gwyneth girl. Don't give it purchase. Don't let it win after you've come so far. Fight it off."

Her fingers curled around a pencil, willing it to be an anchor. "How?"

Rosie shook her head. She pulled a sheet of paper forward for Gwyneth and patted her shoulder. "Draw it out. And pray. Pray and pray until the Lord grants your pleas just to quiet you up. And know I'll be praying too."

All Gwyneth could do was nod and then put her pencil to the paper.

But it wasn't Emmy's figure against a backdrop of flowers that took shape. It was Papa's face in front of bookshelves. It was Thad's beside it. And it was strange scalloped shadows she couldn't explain.

Halfway. Captain Yorrick said they were only halfway there, and Arthur felt a keen stab of fear that the ginger would run out before the ocean did. He gripped the rail and took a moment to be grateful for calm seas, a stiff wind in their sails, and a bright noonday sun.

"I look forward to seeing you without that green cast to your skin." Gates took up position at the spot beside him, looking chipper as a lark as he turned his face into the wind.

Which helped with the queasiness, so Arthur followed suit. "I daresay I shall kiss the ground when we land."

Gates chuckled. "Ah, but if we find my niece quickly, we will quickly sail home. We could be back on the *Falcon* within a week of landing."

Funny how one could at once pray for a thing and dread it. "I hope we do, but I may require more than a few days ashore."

Still smiling, Gates braced his forearms against the rail. "My father was a ship's captain before he inherited the earldom from his brother. Perhaps I inherited his sea legs."

"How fortunate for you."

The sarcasm seemed to roll right off him. "I, for one, will be quite happy if we can find Gwyneth and hurry home. Maryland is insufferable this time of year."

Arthur drew in a long, salt-laden breath, and told himself it steadied him. "Did you lose someone in the Revolution?"

The man lifted a brow. "Pardon?"

"It is just that you seem to have such a personal dislike for the Americans."

"One need not to have suffered the plague oneself to hate it." Gates motioned westward. "America's pride is based on nothing but petty rebellion cloaked with words like 'liberty' and 'democracy.' A deceptive disease, Sir Arthur, is the most dangerous kind."

Arthur hummed. He had no great fondness for the Colonies, but he had no great hatred of them either. They were, so far as he could tell, little more than capitalistic tradesmen who had won their independence solely because of the incompetency of the generals running the campaign thirty-five years prior. "I would not go so far as to call them a disease, but I doubt they will ever prove a strong force in the world."

Gates loosed a scoffing laugh. "Nay, never. I have gone several times to keep abreast of their politics, their growth. They are in their very foundation a house divided. If you ask me, it is a kindness to hasten their fall."

Arthur saw no reason to argue. If England could add the United States back to the empire… "I hate to think of Gwyneth there, though, with this war going on. The troops will not know who she is. They will not know to spare her if she is present during a battle."

Gates straightened again. "If the army draws near her location, let us pray she has the opportunity to flee to them. I daresay any of the generals would offer her sanctuary."

Something relaxed inside him, some tension he must have been carrying all along. "Of course they will."

"And as for my dislike being personal—perhaps it never used to be. But I am quite convinced it was an agent of the United States who killed my brother-in-law." Gates straightened his waistcoat as his gaze went steely. "That makes it *quite* personal."

The tension came back tenfold. It was one thing for the man to suspect it, even to bandy it about in the gossip rags. But to say it privately? That spoke of honest concern, not just a theory that supported one's politics. "You really think they have had spies in England?"

"More, I think Fairchild knew who they were and had taken action to stop them, and that is why they killed him. I think he sent whatever information he had found away, quite possibly with Gwyneth."

Arthur had to clamp down on the rising fear and quell it before it could master him. He straightened as well. "Why, then, to America?"

"The least likely of places, Sir Arthur. The least likely of places." With a small smile upon his lips, Gates sauntered away.

Arthur drew in a slow breath through his nose. And took accounts.

One—if they had such trouble divining where Gwyneth had gone, then any American spy would have as well.

Two—if said intelligencer had known Fairchild were on his tail, he would never think the general would use other Americans to protect her.

Three—in only four more weeks, Arthur would be there, would find her, and would take her in his arms. And may God help anyone who stood between them.

Twenty-Three

Thad figured he was either daft or brilliant. As he lowered his spyglass and turned to Henry, he wasn't sure which. All he knew was that if he got out of Bermuda alive and with none of his men impressed, it would be due solely to the Lord. And if he didn't…then may his family remember him for how well he loved them and not for the madness of this endeavor.

The Union Jack snapping in the balmy breeze on his mainmast, meant to give credence to his claim of being a British merchant, did little to put him at ease. Not given the fact that it was surrounded by twenty other identical flags on ships a great deal larger than his, all lined up prettily in Bailey's Bay and filled to bursting with soldiers, marines, and sailors.

Thad heaved a long breath and eased closer to Henry's side. "Did anyone see you coming out here?"

Henry smiled as if it were just another run out of the Chesapeake and lowered one of the sacks of flour he had carried aboard while more Negroes from a second rowboat brought up other supplies. "No one looks twice at a black man laboring like a black man does. Just like no one looked twice at me in that tavern, being as I had a broom in my hand."

Thad wanted to shudder but continued staring out as if unconcerned with anything Henry said. "If Emmy knew I let you go in there, she would skin me alive."

"Then tan your hide and make a pair of boots out of it so she could stomp on you. But Emmy don't need to know." He held out a hand. "You wanna pay me for these supplies, mister?"

Thad folded his arms across his chest. "I appreciate the dedication to your cover, but try again. What did you learn?"

Henry leaned in, as if arguing with him. "Captain Crofton of the *Dictator* been loose tongued enough that everyone knows the ships what arrived here a few days ago be bound to America. But there's some kind of question of who's in charge. See those ships coming in now?"

See them? Thad had done little but worry over them since they had appeared on the horizon. Twenty vessels were already here, poised to descend on his country. Did they really need half a dozen more?

"Word is they carry three Regiments of Foot under the command of a major general who outranks Ross, who came in with the first bunch. They intend to figure it out and meet with Cochrane on the *Tonnant* to plan and organize."

Thad glanced toward the newcomers again. Another hour, maybe two before they would set anchor. Then he had no doubt this major general would come quickly to shore to assert his authority. And that General Ross, whom Thad had already made it a point to identify, would be quick to try to maintain his.

Some things were universal, no matter the color of coat one wore.

"All right. Good work, Henry. When they make port, I shall happen to be ashore to overhear them."

Henry straightened again. "You need me to do any more, you let me know. I gotta go back with those fellas, but I'll sneak onto the *Masquerade* after nightfall."

Thad nodded and strode away, his mind skipping over the sooner meeting in anticipation of the one further off. How was he going to discover what was discussed with Admiral Cochrane? He headed aft to the one spot on the *Masquerade* from which he could catch a glimpse of the vice admiral's flagship. *Tonnant* sat at anchor on the other side of port, looking proud and stately and deserving of her name of "thundering."

Thad closed his eyes against the sea of red jackets milling about on the decks dotting the water. *Father God, guide me along this perilous way. Put my feet upon each step You would have me take, and bar me from any against Your will.* He savored the breath he drew in, heavy with salt and the tang of fish. *God of my end, you know how I love my country, how I want to serve it in this way You have put before me. I believe with a whole heart that You have purpose yet for the United States that can be achieved only through the freedom to which we cling. So help me, God of my fathers, to help her. And bring me safely home again.*

The mere thought of home was enough to bring the images to his mind. Not so much the places, though they served as backdrops. But the people. The farmers and merchants and smithies all laboring to build a legacy for their offspring. The fishermen who could weave a yarn like no other, the trappers who had explored the great unknown to the west, the lawyers who philosophized on what their land could be with the proper guidance. The strangers who could someday be friends.

And his family. Mother and Father, Amelia and Jacob, Philly and Reggie, Arnaud and Jack. And Gwyneth. *Dear Lord, Gwyneth.* More words than that would not come, though his spirit called out still on her behalf as it had so often during the five days since he'd left. How could he give utterance to all that filled him at the thought of her? Hope and fear, love and regret. And that constant, soul-deep prayer that God would wrap her in His arms.

"Captain?"

Blinking his eyes open again, Thad turned from the *Tonnant* and back to the *Masquerade* and the crewman needing his advice. Seeing to such needs filled the hour until the six newly arrived British vessels made their way into port, and then that pull in his feet toward the rowboat told him it was time to go ashore.

Minutes later the wooden vessel bobbed beneath him on the turquoise waters of the bay, and the white sand beckoned from the beach. He had always enjoyed his stops in Bermuda—looking up the cliffs at Mount Wyndham—the Admiralty House—that sat hunkered amid the rocks and tropical trees.

Perhaps he and Gwyneth could sail here some winter after the war was over, warm their toes in the water that matched her eyes, and lounge about on the beaches. It would make a happy wedding trip, if she accepted the proposal he intended to offer.

Assuming she would even speak to him when he got home.

The boat slid onto the sand beside a row of similar small craft, and Thad exchanged a nod with Michaels, his first mate. They both knew the plan.

Of course, they had no sooner angled toward the tavern where General Ross had been taking his dinners than Thad paused, that familiar sensation sweeping up his back. He looked to his left and saw Ross striding along with Vice Admiral Cochrane, their feet pointed up the hill toward Mount Wyndham.

Time to adjust course. He opened his stride, dodging the throngs of red-coated pedestrians choking the streets.

Michaels ran after him. "What're ya doing, Captain? At this rate, you'll catch them!"

"Exactly." He had learned long ago that a man of his height best not try to slink about unseen. When he went information seeking, he did it under the pretense of openness. "Do try to keep up, Mr. Michaels."

His first mate sidestepped a brutish-looking fellow. "You shoulda brought Arnaud with ya. He can actually grasp the fool workings of that brain o' yours."

A chuckle slipped out. "That he does. Unfortunately, neither of us excels at obeying the orders of the other, so we make it a point to stay off each other's vessels. And so, my friend, it falls to you to dog my heels and try to convince me I have gone daft."

Michaels grunted. "I daresay ya know it already."

"Aye. I daresay I do." And if he were going to be mad, he might as well do it wholeheartedly. Jogging up the sloping road, he held up a hand and called out, "Admiral! General!"

"Heaven help us," Michaels muttered under his breath.

The men were already halfway up the incline that curved toward the Admiralty House, looking so deep in conversation that Thad doubted they even noticed his shout. However, one of their aides glanced over his shoulder at him.

Good. He had been noticed, which would make his following them look purposeful and not surreptitious.

The aide held up, his countenance reflecting idle curiosity. "Have you business with the admiral or general, sir?"

"I have." Thad drew even with the man—a lieutenant, given his insignia—and then brushed past. As he spoke, he was careful to maintain the clipped syllables of his English cousins. "I am Captain Thaddeus of the merchant brig *Masquerade*, and I have a profitable proposition to make Cochrane. Or Ross, if he will be taking authority of the forces in America."

"Now see here, Captain." The lieutenant pivoted and then jogged a few steps to keep up. "They are busy men. They cannot be expected to give an ear to every merchant's ideas and concerns."

"Of course not. I only ask them to give an ear to *mine*." He nearly laughed at the incredulity in the lieutenant's small brown eyes.

"I am sorry, sir, but now is not a convenient time for them."

Thad breathed a scoffing laugh. He had only to keep the man talking a while longer. The Admiralty House was just ahead, its verandas giving it an inviting look. "Nonsense. They will be eager to hear my proposition, and it must be now. I have precisely twenty minutes to spare."

"You seem to be missing the point." But the young man looked more baffled than put upon by his obtuseness. "As...*interesting* as I am certain your business is, neither General Ross nor Admiral Cochrane have the attention to spare. They are fully engrossed in the matters of the campaign—"

"Come, man." He slapped the lieutenant's shoulder, friendly but too hard. "You think me an imbecile? My proposition has to do with the campaign!"

The officer frowned, looking dubious and mildly irritated on top of it. Perfect. "Does it now? Prithee, *how?*"

Thad came to an abrupt halt. Cochrane and Ross had reached the steps of Mount Wyndham, and he would give them plenty of time to settle inside. Slamming his hands onto his hips, he glared down at the lieutenant. "You think I intend to share my ideas with you? A lowly aide?"

Ah, there it was, the sizzle of dislike in his eyes. "I am a *lowly* aide because Admiral Cochrane trusts me, sir. He trusts me to keep the charlatans out of his company so he can attend to *important* matters."

"Charlatan?" Blustering with the presumed outrage, Thad reached for the pistol at his hip.

Michaels, thankfully, knew his role well. He jumped to his side and stayed his hand. "Now, Captain." He somehow managed to make his tone both panicked and placating. "Calm down, sir. You remember what happened last time you called out a fella. We haven't been able to step foot in St. Lucia since."

Thad sniffed and made a show of lowering his arm. He wasn't sure if the lieutenant looked more relieved or disappointed.

"There now." Michaels gave his arm a pat and motioned toward their companion. "Why not give this gent an idea of our business so he can present it to them?"

He grunted and pursed his lips. Then let out a gust of breath and leaned toward the lieutenant. "Tobacco."

After a momentary pause, the lieutenant shook his head and walked again toward the house.

Thad took two large steps to put himself beside the officer again. "I am sure they will want to speak with me right away."

The glance he received bordered on weary. "With all due respect, sir, tobacco has nothing to do with the campaign. Now, if you are interested in buying a commission and—"

"A commission? What good would one more soldier do?" Thad waved that idea away. "Better to affect the morale of them all than add one more body to the mix. Though granted, I am a crack shot and a natural-born leader."

'Twas all he could do not to echo the lieutenant's snort of mocking laughter. He could handle a weapon as well as most, but Mother and Amelia both put him to shame.

Which was neither here nor there. "Tobacco, my good man, is as crucial to our soldiers as gin. Provide good tobacco, and you provide an escape from the perils of war for a blissful five minutes at a time. With my suppliers, I can guarantee enough of the finest tobacco for the entire army."

The lieutenant sighed. "The army has tobacco enough, Captain."

"Enough perhaps, but good enough? Do our chaps not deserve the best?"

The veranda loomed a mere stone's throw away, close enough that Thad could get a gauge of it and calculate the best approach to his plan. The stairs were always an option, but trickier to handle. The door, though, if low enough…which it was. With a silent apology to his forehead, he clapped a hand to the officer's shoulder. "I do appreciate your willingness to vouch for me, Lieutenant. I shall be sure to put in a good word for you. Now I shall show myself in."

"No! Sir, you must wait in the receiving room."

Thad bounded up the stairs, onto the wooden decking, and toward the door. And he winced well before allowing his head to make contact with the lintel. The *thwak* of collision brought Michaels rushing up to support him.

The officer didn't hurry in the least.

Thad pressed a hand to his forehead, which protested despite his apology to it. Once the lieutenant passed him, he blinked rapidly, careful to keep his eyes unfocused. "I think…I think I shall await the admiral out here, Lieutenant."

"You do that, sir."

A moment later the door shut behind the blazing red coat. Thad stumbled along the veranda—in case anyone watched—until he rounded a corner. Then he went silent, easing from open window to open window until he heard the voices he sought.

"Ah, there you are, Lieutenant Grey. Who was that who detained you?" Admiral Cochrane's voice. Thad had heard him speaking yesterday in town.

He caught Michaels's gaze and grinned.

The sound of a clearing throat floated through the window. "No one of import, Admiral. I dismissed him."

Ah, so he intended to leave Thad waiting indefinitely. Not the most active offense, but it had a certain charm.

"Very well. Cigar?"

"Ah. No. No, thank you, sir."

Shuffling sounds floated out, and idle chatter. Thad noted everything they said, though none of it struck him as more than gossip. After five minutes or so, he heard the opening of the front door again, and those in the room all seemed to rise.

"General Gosselin, Admiral Codrington, how good to see you again. You remember General Ross, I assume?"

Gosselin. Thad closed his eyes as he slowly ticked down his mental list of officers. That would be major general, and for longer than Ross had owned the title, which meant he was the higher in rank. And Codrington—Rear Admiral Sir Edward Codrington, the captain of the fleet. Esteemed company.

Pleasantries were exchanged but kept brief. Codrington soon cleared his throat. "I thought I had better speak with everyone at once and produce the orders to clarify why we need two major generals in attendance."

Thad could hear the sounds of nervous laughter, the scuffle of paper, the crack of wax seals breaking. "Ah, yes. As I assumed. Gosselin, you will take your force to the Canadian front. Ross, you will lead yours to the Chesapeake, and Cochrane will join you."

"Yes, sir. And what shall we do there? Have we a target?"

"That is for you and Cochrane to decide, along with Cockburn, once you have arrived and had the chance to speak with him. Having been there so long already, he no doubt has an opinion on the most logical places to attack."

Several of them spoke at once, but Thad's ears focused on Cochrane's low words. "Join me on the *Tonnant* this evening, Ross. We will discuss our plan."

Ross's affirmation was all he needed to hear. Silent as ship rats, Thad and Michaels crept away. Around the veranda, down the steps, and back onto the road. Not until they were back in the hubbub of town did either of them speak.

Michaels broke the silence first with a warning cough. "Tell me you don't intend—"

"What was the point in coming otherwise?"

His first mate sighed. "You have the counts. And the destinations."

"The greater destinations, yes. But knowing they will go to the Chesapeake tells us no more than we already guessed. We must learn their target." Thad shook his head, his mind churning.

"How will you...?"

'Twas his turn to sigh. "There is only one option, really. I can hardly sneak aboard."

Michaels muttered a curse. "'Tis a fool plan."

Hoping to lighten his friend's mood, he jabbed him with an elbow. "Thus far your disapproval has been the kiss of good fortune."

And really, how terrible could a nighttime swim in the warm Bermuda waters be? So long as no sharks or mantas had the same idea to eavesdrop on the officers, he would be fine.

Or at the least, the hope got him through the next few hours. He was back aboard the *Masquerade*, in his cabin, when a knock sounded on the door and Henry stepped in. "Michaels told me about your 'fool plan.' Need a second?"

"Bless you." Henry, he knew, could swim like an eel. Dabbing black greasepaint onto the last open inch of his forehead, Thad turned around. "I was hoping you would volunteer."

Henry regarded his darkened skin with raised brows. "You make one ugly black man, Captain."

Thad laughed and smudged the greasepaint over his hands as well. "So long as I am invisible in the night, I can live with being ugly."

"Guess you have some practice."

What choice did he have but to lob a boot at him?

Henry dodged it with a laugh of his own, and then he glanced down at his tan breeches. "I think I oughta put on some darker clothes. And just so you know, if any sharks come calling, *you* get to fight them off."

"Noted." Alone again, he finished concealing any flesh that could be visible over the water, tucked his black shirt into his black breeches, and headed for the door.

He got within a foot of it when a sudden image swamped him. Gwyneth, so vivid he felt he'd slammed into her. Gwyneth, with shadows back in her eyes and a frantic pencil in her hand. Gwyneth, wringing at his heart.

Turning from the exit, he lurched toward his bed and fell to his knees beside it, clasping his hands upon the extra-long mattress.

"Ready, Captain?"

Ready? No. He could not leave, could not budge, could not do anything until this hand had lifted. He shook his head, squeezed his eyes shut, and prayed.

Twenty-Four

The monsters roared and snapped. Gwyneth could hear them, could feel them, and from the corner of her eyes, could see them. But if she turned toward them, they vanished. Like smoke, like vapors. Like life.

She drew in a deep breath as she positioned her hand over the paper again. But she trembled too much and didn't dare to touch the pencil down.

"Help me. Lord, please." The words slipped past parched lips and buzzed about her head. But did they then float through the drawing room ceiling? She looked up, frowned. Not the drawing room, her bedchamber. When had she come up? Or had she never gone down? She was still in her nightdress, and it was dark outside the window.

It always seemed to be dark. A time that had once meant rest and peace. Or had signaled dancing and laughter, and then a sweet fall of exhaustion onto a down-filled bed.

Maybe that had been the illusion, nothing but a dream. Maybe this was reality, this endless tunnel of echoes and locked doors. She could bang upon them for hours and only give herself a headache.

You cannot know, the monsters whispered from their crevices. *You are not strong enough to know. The truth would break you.*

She looked at the corner it had come from, expecting to see the gnashing teeth and yawning mouth. Nothing. Breath heaving, she squeezed her eyes shut. She needed sleep. That was why the monsters had returned, that was all this was. Hallucinations. Waking dreams.

A hand touched her shoulder, and she shrieked.

"Gwyneth child, you said you was going to bed." Rosie. Just Rosie.

She dragged in a breath and shoved her hair from her face. "Did I?"

A *tsk* was the woman's only answer. Steady hands smoothed the tangled hair away and started to braid. Slow, deliberate movements that brought a single notch of order.

There is no order, only chaos. Your father is gone.

Gwyneth shuddered and couldn't stop.

Rosie sighed. "You gotta take better care of yourself, child. You eat the pudding I brought you and then get yourself into bed."

Your father is gone.

She looked at the bed and her stomach cramped. 'Twasn't a soft mattress, nay. 'Twas hard wooden planking covered only in a red-stained rug. Hard. Forbidding. Cold as the grave. "I…can't."

Thad is gone.

The heavens cried out, low and moaning, and a slender tongue of fire shot through the sky. Gwyneth jumped. "What was that?"

Rosie's breath came out and in, slow and steady. "A summer storm over the bay, child. Thunder and lightning. Nothing more."

Thunder and lightning. *Death and destruction, to take him away forever.* Another mocking laugh from the clouds.

Air wouldn't come, her lungs wouldn't fill. A cloud of gray edged out her vision.

"You stay with me, now. Take pity on an old woman, I can't carry you into bed alone if you faint. You hear me?" Rosie gave her a little shake.

She blinked until the fog retreated a bit. "I can't do it again. I can't lose anyone else, I can't. I can't."

Rosie crouched down before her. Somehow her face looked soft and comforting while her eyes snapped with flint. "You haven't lost anyone else, Miss Gwyn."

Thunder roared. *We will devour him whole. We will steal him from you, we will kill him…and we will destroy you.*

"The storm." She choked back a sob. She mustn't cry. Uncle Gates would hear her. He would come. "The storm will take Thad."

Rosie gripped her shoulders and leaned close until her face was all Gwyneth could see. "That storm's here, not in Bermuda with Thaddeus. Do you understand that? It's *our* storm, not his. He's fine and well, and he's out adventuring like he loves to do."

Like he loves more than you. Because you are nothing but a broken glass figure. Shattered. Worthless.

Though she closed her eyes tight, still she could see the sizzling flash of lightning. "He is never coming back."

Warm hands framed her face and bade her listen. "Look at me, child." When she obeyed, she found Rosie's eyes damp. "I don't believe that for a minute. But what if you're right? What if Thaddeus never comes home?"

Gwyneth shook her head, a frantic attempt to keep the words away.

"What would you do then? Waste away until you die too? Let the nightmares taunt you into doing something stupid?"

Another sob tried to bully its way up her throat, but she held it back with a hard swallow.

Rosie shook her head. "You do that, missy, and you let them win."

We've already won.

"They've already won."

The woman snapped upright, her eyes sparking. "Oh, no, they haven't." She reached past Gwyneth to the paper-strewn vanity top and came up with a book. Its worn leather cover looked familiar, but what was it?

"'Blessed Lord, let me climb up near to Thee...'"

The prayer book. Of course. But what good could it do? Perhaps God had listened to those men who had first prayed the words. Perhaps He had let them climb onto His lap. But they had been so very much stronger than she, strong enough to flee persecution and build a new life in this wild land.

And what, beloved, have you done?

She lifted her head and turned it toward Rosie, though *she* had not been the one to whisper those words. Those soft, silent words that filled her heart rather than her ears. That beat back the shadows just a stitch and lifted that foggy veil just an inch.

"'...and love, and long, and plead, and wrestle with Thee, and pant for deliverance from the body of sin, for my heart is wandering and lifeless, and my soul mourns to think it should ever lose sight of its beloved.'"

Mourn, came the hissing breath that clawed up her spine. *Mourn the loss of your beloved. He is gone. They all are. Everyone you loved.*

A shiver overtook her...but then a warmth seeped in. *Am I gone? Am I dead?*

"No." Her lips formed the word, though no breath gave them voice. *No. I* AM.

Yes. He was. She closed her eyes again and watched as another flash of light danced across their shuttered lids.

"'Wrap my life in divine love, and keep me ever desiring Thee...'"

"Oh, God, forgive me." She leaned forward, eased off her stool until the summer-warm floor welcomed her knees. How long since He had been her desire? How long since she sought Him, sought Him and expected to meet Him? "Let me climb up near to Thee."

Rosie settled beside her and rested one comforting hand on her back. "'...always humble and resigned to Thy will, more fixed on Thyself, that I may be more fitted for doing and suffering.'"

Fitted for suffering. Suffer she did, but not for Him. Not for His glory, but for her own misery, and that, it seemed, was a crucial difference. Because the grief that consumed her, while understandable, had kept her fixated on herself, not on Him. She had not been like Papa, who turned ever more to the Lord in the face of mourning. She had been like...a child.

My child. Come unto Me, my laboring and heavy-laden child. I shall give you rest.

"Rest." The word came out on a moan. A yearning, a plea. She stretched a hand along the rug as if she could grasp that promise and pull it close.

The hissing, waking nightmare of a voice came again. *His rest is death. If that is what you seek, then go find it. Join your father, your mother.*

"No." No, no, no. Exhausted as she was, she knew that was no answer. Had she wanted death, she would have screamed when her father fell. She would have let Uncle Gates strike her down then and there. She would have slid into the jowls of the monster on the ship and plunged into the netherworld. But death was not what she sought—simply peace. Rest.

And she had thought she had it. Had thought it in her hand and, more, happiness with it. That all she had to do was make a place for herself here, beside Thad. That if she could but stay in his arms...but he had left. And what if, as Rosie asked, he never came back? How would she survive then? How, for that matter, could she join her life to a ship's captain's and suffer this anew every time he left?

Rosie wove her fingers through Gwyneth's still-outstretched ones. "Where is your rest, Gwyneth child? Was it in your daddy?"

Her muscles went taut across her shoulders, up her neck, down her back. Papa, precious Papa—his death certainly marked the end of her peace. But if it had been in him, then would she not have felt so anxious, so exhausted every time he was away? On each and every campaign? But she hadn't. She worried, certainly, but it had never consumed her. Not like this.

She shook her head, the rug rubbing her forehead.

Rosie smoothed a hand over Gwyneth's hair, so neatly caught back now. "No, your rest can't lie with him. Maybe it seemed so at first, since his loss started you on this journey. But he never stopped being gone, yet you stopped being so restless for a while there. Right?"

She tried to swallow, though her throat felt too dry. "I..." An attempt at a steadying breath sent a tremor through her. "I cannot explain it. I had begun to feel safe—"

"Only when Thaddeus was here. Ain't that right?"

Of course not. That couldn't be, and she opened her mouth to say so. But her tongue tangled around the words, and the realization pounded her like the rain did the pane of her window.

Every time, every *single* time she had slept before he went on this trip had been when he was home. As if attuned to his footsteps, she had awakened the minute he left the house—and often fallen asleep within minutes of his return. Beginning, for some bizarre reason, the very day she arrived.

"That makes no sense." She squeezed Rosie's fingers and wished she could grasp the workings of her mind so easily. "Perhaps now it would, given how much I..."

Rosie chuckled. "Go ahead and say it. How much you love him. We all know you do."

Perhaps she did, and perhaps they all knew it. But such words ought not be spoken so casually. "But at the start, I scarcely knew him. I knew only that..."

She jerked upright and met Rosie's gaze. "I knew only that my father trusted him, and so I trusted him."

Rosie patted her hand. "Makes sense when you think of it like that. Rest can't come unless you put your trust in someone. Problem is, you put yours in a man. And as wonderful a man as he is, he can't always be here, child. He gonna go away now and then. He gonna mess up now and then when he's home. He gonna fail you."

He will fail you always. He will never come home. Why should he come home to you?

She shook her head to clear it of those doubts and called up the image of Thad. Thad, with his selfless heart and intuitive spirit. Thad, who must have altered his entire life to accommodate her needs these last two months. His smile, always so quick to try to tease out hers. His hands, so quick to catch her when she fell. His eyes, speaking those words she wouldn't yet put to voice.

Was trust enough to have made the connection she felt to him? Was it merely that her father had entrusted her to him? It couldn't be. That alone couldn't account for how her feet always found him, for the way he had filled her heart.

Had Papa known, when he sent her here, that she would tumble straight into love? But loving him wasn't enough. Not when his absence sent her back into this abyss.

Rosie tipped up her chin. "Where is your rest, child? In who?"

Nowhere. In no one.

Her lips parted, ready to echo those words so obviously true. Had she anyone to give her such a thing, any place in which to find it...

"Come unto me, all ye that labour and are heavy laden, and I will give you rest."

She heard Him, heard Him call her. Heard it in the silence, in the whisper within, the murmur that pulsed with a light from which the darkness fled. Inch by inch, the next flash of lightning seeming to strike within her.

Blessed Lord, let me climb up near to Thee…

"Oh, dear Jesus." Tears blurred her eyes, and she made no attempt to blink them away. They magnified the truth before her. When the Lord blessed her, she needed to rejoice and praise Him, recognizing that a gift had been given, one so thoroughly undeserved. And when loss came, as it always did, then hers was not to rail, was not to succumb to the dark waves. Hers was to focus her eyes on Him and walk across them. Not just to weather the storm, but to trust Him to still it. To breathe peace into the night.

To be her rest, if she would but go into His arms. His, that would never let her go.

"Did you hear what Emmy was reading this morning?" Rosie urged her up and steadied her when her knees wobbled.

Gwyneth shook her head. Since Thad left, the days had run together like watercolors.

"I didn't figure. You was more focused on your drawing than anything else." She slipped an arm around Gwyneth's waist and led her toward the bed. "She read that part in Mark four where Jesus was asleep in the boat and the storm came up."

Gwyneth stood still while Rosie positioned the pillows against the headboard and pulled back the blankets.

"There, now. You sit and have your pudding right here."

Pudding in bed. Shaking her head, Gwyneth sank onto the mattress and leaned back upon the feather pillows.

Rosie fetched the treat from the tray on her vanity and brought it over. "While she was reading, something jumped out at me that never did before. Now, the disciples, they were right scared of that storm."

A roll of thunder punctuated her words. But it sounded more distant now, muted. Gwyneth spooned up a bite. "They woke Jesus up, frantic. They asked Him if He cared that they were perishing."

"That's right. And do you remember what Jesus did?"

She let the sweet taste of the pudding dissolve on her tongue and then swallowed. "He chided them for their lack of faith and spoke to the storm, commanding it to be still. And it obeyed."

"Close." Rosie grinned and patted her knee. "He rose up and

rebuked the storm first. *Then* He spoke to the men who ought to have had faith enough to know that the Son of God wasn't going to be killed by no random weather. He calmed the storm, child. He calmed the storm *first*, because His friends were scared and asked Him to. He calmed it so that they would be at peace. And *then* He could speak to them of faith."

Calm my storm, Father God. Please Lord, calm my storm. Still my fears. Be my rest. Though she spoke not aloud, she heard her prayer as a cry within her and felt it shudder the very foundations of her being. That shaky, fractured foundation so desperate to be shored up.

You are shattered. Broken.

Yes. She smiled into the hiss as she let her eyes slide closed. She was shattered. Broken. And she was His. She had only to put those pieces into the Potter's hand and let Him make her into a new vessel.

The weight was lifted from her hands as Rosie took the dessert dish, and Gwyneth snuggled between her soft sheets. More, the weight was lifted from her soul, and she climbed up into the lap of the Father who had never been any farther away than a whisper.

Twenty-Five

The sweet sound of sails snapping in the crisp wind brought a smile to Thad's lips. He raised his spyglass and scanned the horizon. As with every other time he had done so since weighing anchor at the break of dawn, he breathed a prayer that those waters would remain clear. That no British ships would follow him out of Bermuda, that no new ones would appear. That he would make the Chesapeake free and clear, and that the Lord would provide a quick way back into the bay.

Home. Home to Gwyneth, who had yet to fade more than a shade from his thoughts since the Lord brought him to his knees last night. To his family—Philly had been heavy on his mind this morning too. And to Tallmadge, who would be eager indeed for the news he carried with him.

"If the wind stays with us, we should make it home in less than a week." Michaels stepped up beside him, his eyes alight. "Though part of me would as soon stay out on open water. There are plenty of British ships begging to be harassed."

Thad chuckled as he slid his spyglass closed. "True as that is, and much as part of me would love to play the menace, we need to get back. This information will be helpful to our military."

Michaels snorted. "Assuming they listen, you mean. A grand assumption, if you ask me."

"They will listen. This time they will." They must. If they didn't…
well, then the entire region would pay for it, as they would for their
months—nay, *years*—of refusal to prepare for the coming attacks.

Because this would be more than another raid. If Cochrane and
Ross gave Cockburn his way, which they had sounded inclined to
do while Thad treaded water by the hull of the *Tonnant* last night,
then Washington City would be the next target. As soon as this newly
arrived fleet made its way from Bermuda, they would plan the attack.

Assuming it took them another week where they were, then a week
to organize in America, that meant two weeks after Thad reached
home with the news to get everyone ready. Two weeks to strengthen
their early warning method of keeping abreast of British activities. Two
weeks to fortify and position troops. To call *up* troops.

A chill swept through him despite the balmy early August breeze.
God of my end, my nation rests in Your hands. Deliver us.

As if in response, a gust of wind blasted by and sped them over
another wave.

"I'm going to check my charts." Thad gave Michaels a pat on the
shoulder and strode toward his cabin. Henry was already inside, his
gaze not on the navigation charts but on the map of the Eastern Sea-
board. "Plotting where to bury your treasure?"

His friend offered him a wide grin. "Oh, I buried that long ago."
He turned back to the map and tapped the area along the Patuxent.
"The system Smith set up under Barney ought to work well enough if
we fortify it."

"I have been thinking the same thing." They had a reliable enough
way of conveying information on the British movements. Cannons
and guns were fired by one town as soon as the enemy came near,
and tracking that from village to village gave the next one advance
warning of their coming. And for more specific information, they had
mounted couriers to take messages from one observation station to
the next.

Thad had assisted in the construction of it months ago. He would
put all the members on alert as soon as he got home, especially in the
areas between the British's current location and the capital city. As
soon as the enemy moved that way, messages would begin to fly.

But as Michaels had wondered, would the politicians listen?

Thad shook his head. "I am not surprised they are considering Cockburn's plan, yet I cannot quite believe they would do it. Tactically, it makes no sense. Winning Washington will accomplish them nothing in terms of position."

Henry tilted his head to the side. "Ain't you the one who said this war isn't about gaining strategic positions?"

"Too true. 'Tis about destroying American morale—nothing more and nothing less. Dividing us. And they think destroying our capital will defeat our spirits."

Henry's lips twitched into another grin. "More the fools, them."

Thad smiled back. "They have obviously not heard that their similar attack on the city of Hampton has become a rallying cry."

"Still." Henry nodded toward the map again. "Best to try to head them off and keep them away from the cities and townsfolk."

No doubt the generals would have the same thought and would seek to meet them well outside the city. "Let us hope we have the strength to do so. Unfortunately, the newspaper articles that have convinced Cockburn we are weak enough to make this a viable plan are not mistaken."

"There's still time to strengthen."

But enough? "Let us hope so." Just as he would have to hope that there would be time enough to strengthen the foundations of his own house. To resolve the issues with Arnaud. With Gwyneth. To convince them both that they hadn't the leisure to indulge in bitterness. Not when Washington was a target and Baltimore could easily be the next.

Thad could feel it, the coming wave of war. Feel it mounting on the horizon like a hurricane. They would all have to batten down the hatches of their defenses and of their lives because there would be no avoiding the thick of things. Not if they intended to hold on to their liberties. Even if that meant a certain risk to their lives.

Gwyneth's face filled his vision again, and he shut his eyes to better see it. Was she well? Sleepless again? Would he return to that shadowed shell, one filled with anger with him instead of the horror of her loss? That need that hit him last night, that had kept him praying for two solid hours...

"She's all right." Henry gripped his arm and gave him a tiny shake.

"You felt the peace last night like I did after we prayed. You wait and see. My Emmy's there, and you know well she can set the world to rights with one bat of her pretty eyes."

Laughter brought Thad's eyes open again. "I don't doubt it. Still, I worry for her. Does that ever stop?"

Henry gave him a look that labeled him an idiot. "What do you think?"

Thad sighed and pulled out his navigation charts. He thought he had a whole host of worries that would be waiting for him when he got home, none of which were ever likely to fade. So he had best see about getting them home safely and quickly. And keep his heart inclined toward prayer.

"He said *what?*"

Gwyneth pressed her lips together, but still she couldn't hold back the smile. And why should she? Dabbing her brush in the sepia, she added depth onto Emmy's countenance and then glanced up at her model again. "That you had three noses."

From behind her, Philly laughed in that full, lively way of hers. "Oh, Emmy, you should see the look on your face. Paint her like *that*, Gwyn."

Emmy repositioned her hand on her rounded abdomen and made an unsuccessful attempt to school her features. Though the outrage had faded, now it was a grin that marred the peaceful expression Gwyneth had put to canvas. "He has never forgiven me for besting him in that footrace when we were children, that is all."

"No, more for your refusal of a rematch after he grew a foot in eleven months." Laughter colored Philly's voice, though a moment later she set her cup down with a clatter, and her "Oh, dear" sounded anything but amused.

Emmy abandoned her carefully set pose and rushed to her friend. Gwyneth put her brush down and spun too, to find that Philly had put her head in her hands and was drawing in a series of deep but shaky breaths. "Are you ill, Philly?"

The woman waved off Gwyneth's question, nearly smacking Emmy in the face as she did so. "It will pass. Give me a moment."

Emmy eased down beside her with drawn brows. "What is it? You are never ill but for when…are you…?"

Gwyneth looked from one of them to the other, feeling out of the circle. And then dreadfully naive when Emmy's meaning struck and heat flooded her cheeks. Not that she had any reason to feel embarrassed by a married woman being with child. Especially when the couple obviously wanted a babe so much and had been so long denied one.

Philly whimpered, though it sounded more an emotional response than a physical one. "I am not certain. I think perhaps, but…perhaps not. I almost hope not, much as I hope so. I am…I am so very afraid."

That was something Gwyneth could well understand. Setting her paints down, she moved to Philly's other side and slid an arm around her. She was hardly an expert on this, with no wisdom to offer or intelligent questions to ask, but she could sit beside her, and she could pray peace upon her. She could be a friend.

Emmy smoothed a hand over Philly's hair with all the warm familiarity of a sister. "I know how hard this has been on you, Phil. I do. And for sure and certain, the Lord never promises His children will have no pain. But He *does* promise He will see us through it. Each and every time."

"I know." But Philly kept her hands over her face. "He has, and I know He will. But I still…I was beginning to think I would never again— I am afraid to hope. Because if I hope and am disappointed, it will hurt so much more than if I do not let myself expect anything."

"Would it?" When both women looked over at her, Gwyneth shrugged, surprised at herself for speaking. "It seems to me that if one does not hope, one does not really have faith. Fear…fear is natural. But Jesus offers to take us beyond that if we keep our eyes trained on Him. Does He not?"

Emmy winked at her and patted Philly's shoulder. "You listen to the girl. Mama and I have filled her full to bursting with Scripture and prayers this last week and a half, haven't we, Gwyn?"

"You have." And in the past six days, since that night when she had heard the whispers of the Lord, clarity had begun to return. Those verses and prayers had filled her mind as she went about her daily tasks. The monsters still lurked; she could sense them. But they daren't come close, not so long as she remembered those promises of peace and held them tight to her heart.

Philly rubbed at her eyes. "I need to speak to Reggie about my suspicions. I haven't yet, being not quite certain, but he should know. Whatever comes, we can weather it together."

"That's a good idea, and you should speak with your mama too. She always knows what to say when I'm anxious. Besides." Emmy smiled that stunning smile of hers, directing it to Gwyneth over Philly's bent head. "We probably oughtn't talk too much about such things in the presence of a young thing like Gwyn."

Philly managed a partial smile of her own and eased back up. "She is not so young. I was married by her age, as was Amelia. And I daresay she will be in the near future too, given the way my brother has been looking at her."

"Humph." With a superior sniff, Emmy lifted her chin and folded her arms over her bulge. "After hearing how he insulted me, I'm not sure Thaddeus deserves a pretty little thing like our Gwyn. Three noses…"

Chuckling, Gwyneth looked up at the sky to gauge the angle of the sun. The ideal morning light had shifted, and so she might as well pack up her oils and brushes and finish the painting tomorrow. Emmy would be happy to sit for her again, she knew. Not that Gwyneth really needed a model before her, but it had been pleasant, these past five mornings, to chat and get to know each other while she put color to canvas. An easy, beautiful time. No heavy-handed muse breathing down her neck and forcing oddities into her work, no burning to paint anything but the image before her.

To make a friend. To learn more about the Lanes, what it had been like to grow up in their house. To hear about how so many frowned upon Emmy because of her mixed blood, but how love had finally found her when Thad decided to take to the seas and so had met Henry, who had come home with him one night, seen Emmy, and fallen head over heels.

The paths of their lives could be so unpredictable, so seemingly random, but always the Lord led them where they needed to be. And He had led Gwyneth here. Right here, at this point in time. Chased away by horror, yet ending up surrounded by friends.

Philly stood slowly and came to Gwyneth's side to look at the canvas. "Nearly done and so very breathtaking. What will you do with this one?"

Gwyneth swished her brushes around in a jar of turpentine. "I am not certain. Give it either to Henry or Rosie, though I have not decided who should have it. Or perhaps I shall let them fight for it."

Emmy laughed and gathered up the lacy shawl that had slid from her arms to the ground while she modeled. "That could be sporting."

Reaching for a jar of paint and its lid, Philly sent Gwyneth an almost hesitant look, which was strange for her. "Gwyn...if you mind my teasing about you and Thad, you have only to say so."

She could not resist the twitch of her lips. "And you will do what—stop? I find that very hard to believe, having seen this family interact for several months now."

Philly grinned too. "Well, I wouldn't stop teasing *him*, but the last thing I want to do is scare *you* off with it."

Scaring her off—a valid concern not all that long ago, but at this point? She wanted to be nowhere else. The thought of Uncle Gates finding her here still lit a fuse of panic, but she would give that, too, to God, and trust His leading.

Gwyneth screwed a lid back on another pot. "You needn't fear that, Philly. I have no intention of going anywhere, certainly not before that brother of yours returns and answers a few questions about why he didn't see fit to tell me about Peggy yet thought to kiss me senseless."

Philly's eyes lit with mischief. "Senseless, you say?"

"Phillippa!" Emmy's tone was admonishing yet ended on a laugh. "Don't pry."

"Why ever not? 'Tis a matter of scientific investigation." Still grinning, she leaned close. "Have you not ever wondered why one man's kiss can leave us cold and another make us melt like wax?"

Emmy slapped at her friend with the end of the shawl. "And when have you conducted *that* experiment?"

"Not since I met Reggie, I assure you. Or, well—he was the final installment of said experiment. Which, granted, did not have enough data to be thorough." She closed up another color of paint, that light still glinting in her eyes. "It is an intriguing phenomena, though. And one of chemistry, which we all know is my area of expertise."

Gwyneth slid the paints into their box and angled a saucy grin at her friend. "Were your brother here, I imagine he would say that his library rug contests your claims of expertise."

"That was entirely his fault, startling us like he did." Philly added another jar to the lot and then sighed. "I think I shall go find Mama. And Gwyn?"

"Hmm?"

Philly leaned over and gathered her close. "I hope you keep him, so we might keep you." With those whispered words, she turned and bustled her way into the house.

Gwyneth glanced at Emmy, who smiled and followed her friend inside at a more sedate pace. For her part, she finished storing her supplies, carried everything in, and headed toward the kitchen with a light step. As soon as she entered the warm room, she snagged her apron from its hook and clapped her hands together.

"What will you teach me today, Rosie?"

The housekeeper looked up from the sink with the same frown she'd given her every other day she had asked the question—as if that would deter her. "I'm baking bread today, and you will just be in the way. Get on out of here and go make a picture."

Instead, Gwyneth laughed and moved over to the counter, where two bowls were already sitting. "What kind of bread?"

"Nothing special. Just regular ol' wheat. You don't need to be gumming up those smooth hands of yours with the dough, now."

Gwyneth tied the apron strings over her white day dress. "Nonsense. Though perhaps I ought to wash the paint from them first, hmm?"

Rosie made a disapproving noise, but she stepped aside to give the younger woman access to the wash water. "Don't know why you got it into your head you had to learn how to cook. Ain't that why I'm here?"

"And what about when you go to visit Emmy for a few days after she has her baby? Who will cook then?"

"Mrs. Lane can manage—"

"And so should I be able to." She sent a warm smile toward her companion. "Can you not see, Rosie, how important that is? When I was in England, had I sullied my hands in the kitchen, it would have meant my family was poor. It would have meant no chance of a good match."

Rosie huffed. "Well-off girls don't cook here neither, Gwyneth."

"But here, in this family, they *can*. I can learn how to help when help is needed. I can be *useful*." More than just a pretty miss, taught more than how to play the pianoforte or embroider. She could do something that, in times of need, could lift a burden for someone.

As Gwyneth had known she would, Rosie sighed and handed her an old towel for her hands. "The most important lesson in bread making is knowing the dough—whether it's too dry or too wet, which ain't never the same day to day. The air has an awful lot to do with it, and the dough don't rise a hoot on a dry, cold day. You'll have to learn where to put it to rise in the wintertime so's it gets enough heat from the stove but not so much it starts crusting up too soon."

Gwyneth dried her hands and prepared to absorb all she could. She mixed, she kneaded, she added flour, she punched, and she nodded when Rosie indicated it was elastic enough, noting the consistency. Then she covered her beautiful ball of dough in its bowl and smiled at the victory.

A knock sounded on the front door, and both she and Rosie looked down at their messy hands.

"I got it, Mama," Emmy called from out the hall. Her footsteps sounded, and a moment later they heard the squeak of the door opening.

"Good morning." A male voice echoed their way, familiar enough to make Gwyneth want to run for the closet. Apparently Nathaniel Mercer was back from his trip to Virginia. "Is Mrs. Lane or Miss Hampton in?"

Another set of footsteps, this one the sure, measured step of Winter. "I am in, sir, but I regret that Miss Hampton is otherwise engaged this morning."

And planned to be every morning, and any other time he might drop by.

There was a softer exchange that Gwyneth could not make out, and then the soft pad of Emmy's steps toward the kitchen. Gwyneth moved to meet her as she entered the room, curious about her new friend's reaction to the man.

His voice came her way again, too soft at first for her to catch over the other noises of the house, though as soon as she halted, she could make it out again. "...lovely young woman, and breeding too. If you feel the need to sell, she would fetch a high price, and I would be happy to—"

"You overstep yourself, Mr. Mercer." Winter's voice was as frigid as her name. "Emmy is no slave, nor is her mother. We *have* no slaves in the Lane family, as it is an abominable institution. Now I will wish you good day."

Emmy looked positively smug, even making a little kicking motion as if to boot the man out the door.

Mercer cleared his throat. "I do apologize. I only thought—"

"I know what you thought, and I wished you good day. Now *good day*. And I thank you not to darken these doors again."

Oh, Gwyneth could kiss that woman, and she would have run out to the hall to do so the moment the door slammed shut had she not been aware of the flour and dough still caking her hands.

Emmy shook her head. "Never in my life have I more wanted to spit in the face of a man. And oh, but does it make me miss my Henry. I hope they come home soon."

"Soon." Saying the word lit a lamp inside and warmed the oil of Gwyneth's being until it spread all through her, as Thad's kiss had done. "I think it *will* be soon, Emmy. I think they are close."

"Do you?" Emmy's voice was hopeful and just relieved enough to indicate she trusted her word.

Odd, really. But no odder than the surety she felt as she nodded. "I am certain of it."

Emmy grinned at her mother and nodded toward Gwyneth. "I think Thaddeus really has met his match."

Gwyneth indulged in her own little smile as she cleaned the dough from her hands. He had indeed. In ways he had probably yet to realize.

Twenty-Six

Thad slipped through the shadows beside Henry, tamping down the urge to look over his shoulder. The British ship that had come so close while they were running the blockade had certainly not followed them into port, so he needn't worry. He need only praise the Lord for those beautiful clouds covering the moon, and for an able pilot who could steer them into the bay on the darkest of nights.

A pilot who now yawned long and gustily. "Think anyone will be up?"

"At two in the morning? Doubtful." Which was fine. He wanted only to slip inside, change out of his salt-encrusted shirt, and sleep so that he could be up early enough to ride to Washington and share what he had learned with Tallmadge.

All right, so that wasn't all he wanted. But much as he longed to gather Gwyneth into his arms, he hoped she was sleeping soundly. If she had been wracked by insomnia again because of his twelve-day absence—his stomach clenched at the thought.

They cut through the alley, strode silently along the street, and went around the back of Thad's home. Henry angled toward the carriage house and the rooms above it with a lifted hand. Thad nodded his goodnight and headed for the kitchen door. He'd slipped inside and shut it behind him before he realized a lamp was lit upon the table, though surely it had glowed through the windows. Thunder and turf, but he was tired.

"There you are."

Her voice didn't exactly startle him, but it brought his pulse back up to the rate it had taken when that British vessel had drifted so close she would have spotted the *Masquerade* had her watchman not been asleep at his post. "What are you doing up, sweet?"

Gwyneth stepped into the lamplight. She smiled, and while there were shadows under her eyes, they were too faint to indicate any-thing but being up late tonight, not for nearly a fortnight. She was still dressed in a pale day gown, the only indication of the hour the fact that her hair was in a braid down her back.

"I was waiting for you." Her voice was soft but clear as she spoke, and steadier than it had been in those first weeks of sleepless torment. And then she glided toward him, not stopping until her arms were about him. His closed around her with such relief that he wasn't sure he would ever be able to convince them to release her again. She pressed her cheek against his chest and let out a long breath. "I tried to retire at a reasonable hour, but I couldn't shake the feeling you would be home tonight."

And she had greeted him with an embrace rather than a slap across his face. Good news indeed. He tightened his hold on her as he ran a hand up her back and under her braid. "I feared you hated me by now."

She chuckled and tilted her head back when he so urged. "How could I ever hate you?" Yet when the weary yearning of his heart had his head dipping, she pulled away from his arms altogether, a light of mischief glinting in her eyes. "Though there will be no more of that for a while."

He nearly groaned. May have, in fact. "Why in thunder not?"

Another light laugh spilled from her throat, so beautiful even if devastating. "Because you are going to court me properly before you kiss me again. Are you hungry?"

"No." Then she moved past him, and he caught a whiff of bread. "Yes. And how am I to court you properly? Shall I call on you in the drawing room at a set hour?"

She indicated a chair at the table with the same brusque command

Rosie or Mother would have used. Which was terrifying enough that he sat without protest. "That sounds reasonable. But the most important thing is that you have the blessing of my guardians."

He grunted and leaned on his hand while she did something over at the darkened counter. "I *am* your guardian."

"I should think not, or your romantic intentions would be highly questionable." She turned back to him with a plate in hand and slid it onto the table before him. "You are my host. Your parents are my guardians."

Butter-slathered bread, cheese, a cluster of grapes. After ship fare, it looked like heaven and smelled even better. "I suppose I ought to be glad you will not insist upon the blessing of your father's brothers or some such."

"Papa did not send me to them, did he?" She moved behind him and rested her hands on his shoulders. "Having not heard his will, I cannot be sure who my legal guardian is now, but he entrusted me to your parents."

He may have argued that he had entrusted her to *him*, just to tease, but her thumb slid up his neck and then down again, rubbing at the tension stored there. All he could do was swallow his first bite of bread and grasp vainly at coherent thought.

"Is the bread good? I made it myself."

"You—what?" He would have turned to stare at her, had he not been loath to disturb her gentle ministrations. "Rosie *let* you?"

"She taught me." Her haughty tone dissolved into another chuckle. "Under protest, but I won the debate by pointing out that I want to be useful."

She had won a debate with Rosie. Surely she was a young woman unmatched by any other the world over. He took another bite of bread, though his chewing felt slow. "It is delicious."

"Well, be sure you praise Rosie tomorrow on her skills as a teacher so that she lets me back in for my next lesson." Her hands rubbed at the sore spot where neck met shoulders. "How was your trip? Did you discover what the congressman needed?"

One corner of his mouth tugged up. "Ought I be concerned that a British general's daughter is trying to pry information from me?"

"Perhaps, were I the daughter of a different general, one who actually thought us enemies. Who did not just want this war to be over, as it never should have begun at all. Besides, were I to contact any of them, they would no doubt try to force me away from here. And we cannot have that." He felt her lips press against the top of his head.

"None of that, now. There will be no more kissing until you court me properly." He popped a grape into his mouth and then let his hand merely rest on the table, as it felt too heavy to lift again.

Gwyneth breathed a laugh and rested her head on his for a moment. "I missed you, Thad. I was so afraid you would never come home and that it would destroy me."

"Ah, sweet." Though it felt leaden, he lifted his hand and rested it over hers on his shoulder. "I was afraid too. That I would come home and find you but an echo again. But you are not. You seem..." Something. Something good. Something strong.

She spoke again, but it was too soft. Her voice seemed to billow around him like a spring breeze. Light and darkness merged into a shimmering twilight, one where time slowed and vision skipped ahead of itself. He floated there for a while, though he could not have said how long. A second, an hour, it hardly mattered.

Until the touch of her lips on his jolted him back to alertness. He blinked his eyes open and found her an inch away, smiling at him. "Wake up, Sleeping Beauty. I cannot carry you to your bed as you have done for me."

He caught her hand before she could retreat any farther. "Gwyn, I...I love you."

Her eyes gleamed with emotion and lamplight as her hand settled on his cheek, making him aware of the days it had been since a razor last touched it. "Then why did you not tell me the truth, Thad? About Peggy and Alain and Jack?"

"Because..." His eyes closed again, though it wasn't the cloud of sleep that filled them. "Because I did not want you to see how I betrayed my brother."

"You did not. You thought him dead. You could not have known otherwise."

"I should have. Alain was right. I sense so many things...I should have sensed *that*. But I didn't, and I ended up hurting him in a way..." Unable to find the right words, he shook his head.

Her thumb stroked over his cheekbone. "You are a good man, Thaddeus Lane, but you are not God, and you cannot know everything. You cannot *do* everything, but only what He allows. Do not blame yourself for that."

She kissed his forehead, straightened, stepped away. "You need to rest. Then in the morning you can go to Washington City as I have no doubt you need to do, and when you return, we can pack a picnic and take a promenade or a ride somewhere. So long as we are back before dark. I have very protective guardians, you know."

He smiled as she retreated toward the door. Smiled and knew to the depths of his soul that *this* was the Gwyneth who had been waiting these past two months to break free. "Confidence becomes you, sweet."

The lamplight caught her smile in the moment before she disappeared into the hall. "Goodnight, beloved. Sleep well."

He would. How could he not? She called him beloved.

"Another fortnight, you say?" Arthur stood beside Captain Yorrick and Gates. His legs, if not his stomach, were steady on deck. He didn't know whether to rejoice or despair at the pronouncement of two more weeks at sea. It fit the projected arrival after the series of storms knocked them off course, but he had rather hoped they could make up some of the lost time.

But it seemed that time, once lost, could never be regained. He dared not consider what that might mean regarding Gwyneth. What had she been doing since she left in April? Had she thought of him as often as she consumed his thoughts? Even half as often would suffice.

Yorrick nodded and turned a bit to include Arthur in the conversation. "If the weather remains with us from here, yes. We will sail directly to Annapolis."

Annapolis. He already had the direction memorized, courtesy of that letter from Mr. Lane that had been in the book on chemistry. As soon as his feet were on solid ground, he would ask someone where he might find King George Street. He would run to the dwelling if it was nearby, rent a horse if too far, and knock upon their door before the sun set upon his arrival. Explain that Gwyneth was his betrothed—

"Why do I get the feeling you are already in the Colonies and well ahead of yourself?" Gates offered him a tight smile. "I assure you we will find her quickly, Sir Arthur, but you had best start preparing yourself now for a reasoned approach. We will go first to an inn, rent rooms, and bathe. Take a hot meal. All of which I am sure you agree is a wise course."

He swallowed and bent his knees a bit as the ship rolled over a swell. He had to grant the man's point. When he arrived to claim his bride-to-be, he had best be clean and pressed. "Of course you are right, Mr. Gates."

Yorrick's grin was about twenty degrees warmer than Gates's had been. "No one faults you for your eagerness, lad. Though wisdom would also dictate you brace yourself for a longer search than you obviously anticipate. Even if she is with this family, it is quite possible they are no longer in Annapolis. When I was last there, a great many of the residents had already fled the city upon our arrival."

The *Falcon* headed into a trough, and his heart went with it. What if she were not there? Then where would they look?

Worse, what if the Lanes had not been there when Gwyneth and the Wesleys arrived? What would they have done? Had Fairchild sent them with ample coin to keep them? Would an American town be safe for a British trio with no local host? What if they had been robbed of what the general *had* provided?

"And now I have caused you to worry. My apologies. That was not my intent."

Gates waved off the captain's words. "You oughtn't apologize for logic, sir. Your point is valid. And if the Lanes are no longer there, we will simply ask a neighbor where they have gone. I have a few acquaintances I can call upon to help us find her."

Acquaintances. Arthur had no trouble cataloging what that might mean. Gates worked in the Home Office, which meant that Gates's "acquaintances" were likely men he had recruited to feed him intelligence. Men loyal to England—or at least to the silver they could provide—who would have taken note of anything they deemed of interest. Which he hoped included said trio of British subjects.

He nodded and, when movement to his right caught his eye, turned to Yorrick. "Captain, when we land, I would like to request that Scrubs be allowed to come ashore and act as my valet. He has been a great help to me."

Gates narrowed his eyes and the captain pursed his lips. 'Twas clear as day that neither thought it a request tempered with wisdom. It likely wasn't, given that the boy had all but admitted he would take off the first chance he got.

Perhaps he would. And perhaps it would allow him to make his way home and see his mother again, and the sisters he had mentioned. Perhaps doing so would allow that family, who no doubt thought Scrubs lost to them forever, to have a measure of peace Arthur so sorely needed himself right now as he searched for his betrothed.

And perhaps, once that was satisfied, the boy would come back. Assuming, of course, they could even get permission for him to put his foot to shore.

He kept his countenance clear and schooled while Yorrick studied him. At length the old man blinked and relaxed. "I will consider your request, Sir Arthur, though I make no promises."

Arthur could ask no more than that. And he wouldn't mention it to Scrubs at all unless he secured a positive answer. Though he suspected that even if they got one, the boy wouldn't thank him for interfering.

So be it. He would do the right thing anyway.

⚬✐⚬

Gwyneth pressed her lips against a grin as Thad made a show of cocking his head this way and that, studying the nearly finished painting of Emmy with a series of hums. The show, of course, was for the benefit of Emmy and Henry.

At length he shook his head. "You got it all wrong, sweet. Only one nose on her face—"

"You watch yourself, Thaddeus Lane." Emmy narrowed her eyes, but there was no disguising the pure contentment in them as she stood close to her husband's side.

"No evil glinting in her eyes—"

"You be nice or I'll slip something into your food. I have done it before and I will do it again."

Thad laughed and turned to Gwyneth. No doubt her question shone from her eyes. "Dye. I walked around with black teeth for a full day."

"Wish I had seen that," Henry said, slipping an arm around his wife. His eyes remained fixed on the painting. "It's beautiful, Miss Gwyn. The most beautiful painting I ever saw."

"Not that our humble Emmy can possibly compare to the beauty and majesty of the *Masquerade*..." When Emmy drew her hand back as if to slap him, he laughed again and leaned over to plant a brotherly kiss on her forehead. "Glad you are back in town, Em. And the painting is breathtaking."

Emmy's perfect smile unfurled, and she looked to Gwyn. "Are you certain you do not need me to sit again as you finish?"

"Quite certain. You go on home and get settled."

The couple needed no further encouragement, and after a round of farewells, Gwyneth turned back to Thad and found him studying not the bright and whimsical scene with Emmy but the sketches strewn over the *secretaire*. The ones she had drawn before that night she would forever look upon as a pivot.

He traced a finger over the unexplainable scalloped shadow and then tapped the blurred figure in the background. "Sir Lancelot?"

A chuckle slipped out as she took her place next to him, wishing she dared to weave her fingers through his in the light of day. She wondered at how she had been audacious enough to act as she had when he got home last night. "Arthur. As you well know."

He grunted and flipped through a few other papers. "He is in quite a few of them."

Gwyneth lifted a shoulder in half a shrug. "I suppose part of me blamed him for being so near yet not helping, even if logic says he could not have had any way of knowing what was happening inside the house."

"Hmm." He let the pages settle. "Do you think he is searching for you?"

"No." At the glance he sent her, she held out her hands, palms up. "We scarcely knew each other."

"Well enough, apparently."

"Not really." At the look still churning in his eyes, she grinned. "You are not jealous of him, are you, Captain Lane?"

His brows went up. "Me? Jealous of some London dandy?" He folded his arms over his chest. "I most certainly am. He ought to have known better than to make advances toward the woman I love. Even if I didn't know her yet."

Another chuckle and a tingling wash of joy at that phrase. *The woman I love.* She held out a hand. "You needn't be jealous."

His fingers engulfed hers, and he raised her knuckles to his lips. Lingered far too long over them, though she made no objections. And oh, the way his eyes gleamed for her. "No?"

"No." The word came out as little more than a breath. And if he could have such an effect on her just by kissing her hand…tamping down another smile, she pulled her fingers from his and took a step away. "Hadn't you better be on your way, Mr. Culper? I daresay your congressman is eager for your report."

"Not home but seven hours, and already she is giving me the boot." His lips turned up, and he turned toward the door. "Have that picnic ready this evening, sweet. I have already obtained your guardians' permission to take you out for a carriage ride after I return from Washington."

"I will be waiting, sir." With a tripping heart and a ready smile.

He winked as he ducked his way out, greeting his mother in the hallway. Winter entered the drawing room a second later, holding an envelope out toward Gwyneth. "This just came for you, dear."

Gwyneth's smile pulled down into a frown. A letter for her? Here? She took the folded white paper, not recognizing the handwriting. After breaking the seal and opening it, she looked first to the signature.

"Mr. Wesley." Her gaze flew back to the top of the brief letter, and her heart both eased and went tight somehow. "They made it safely to his cousin and are searching for a ship home."

No mention of forgiveness, of prayers, of anything warm. Just quick, cool words. An update to an acquaintance. She lowered the page and dragged a long breath into her lungs. They would go home, and they would tell Uncle Gates where she was.

And what if, she now wondered as her gaze drifted to the desk, Sir Arthur was searching for her too? What if that old life that seemed so far away found her? When all she wanted to do was stay lost.

Twenty-Seven

The rhythmic clopping of the two trotting horses filled the silence that fell after Thad finished telling Arnaud all he had learned in Bermuda. When he had arrived at his friend's house, Jack had greeted him with his usual enthusiasm, eliminating the need for any awkwardness. And as they set out for Washington, it had been so easy to fall into talk of safe things. Like war.

Now, though, they had exhausted the topic, which brought back all the things still echoing in his mind from that argument before he left. He cast a glance at Arnaud, trying to twist his tongue around something pleasant. Or profound. Or even just lacking in stupidity.

His friend cast him an amused glance, half a smile on his face. "I imagine you noted the change in your lady love in about ten seconds, *oui?*"

Not sure if Gwyneth was a safe topic or not, Thad nodded. "Though we have not yet spoken of the reason behind the shift."

A chuckle rumbled forth, blending with the clop of hooves. "From what I could gather when we dropped by last week, it came of her arriving at the startling realization that her savior was not here—" he jerked a thumb toward Thad— "but there." He turned his thumb upward.

The words were the same old bitterness that had been lurking these last two years, but the tone—the tone was light, free of resentment. Or perhaps that was wishful thinking. Thad eased back in his saddle. "That would explain it. I cannot say how glad I was to see such confidence in her eyes, such light. And you will be happy to know that she demanded a proper courtship." He hoped.

Arnaud's smile doubled into a real, full one. "Good. That is all I wanted to see, Thad. A bit of care and caution to temper the emotion."

He sounded sincere. Because at the root of it, theirs was a friendship more like a brotherhood, one chosen and not given by chance. Thad drew in a long breath. "I told her I loved her."

"Oh?" Arnaud quirked a brow and gripped the reins tighter when his horse sidestepped a rut in the road. "What did *she* say?"

Thad felt the beginnings of a smile in the corners of his mouth as he remembered the surety in her eyes, that surety that said she would not cling to whatever she could find, not anymore. She would demand instead what she deserved. "She asked why, then, I had not explained our situation to her sooner."

Though he could have, Arnaud did not ask what his response had been or chime in with anything snide. He simply nodded and looked ahead, where the first buildings of Washington City were in view.

"Alain, I...forgive me. Please. You are right. It always felt like a betrayal to me, but I could not admit to any other options. I don't know, now, if my reasons at the time were right or not, but I know that I would undo anything that hurt you if I could. You are my brother."

"As you are mine." Arnaud looked his way again, those brooding Bourbon looks deep with contemplation. "I am sorry as well for never realizing how hard it would have been with my ghost between you. But we cannot undo any part of our past, Thad. And we needn't. We need only to forge ahead with wisdom and humility."

Thad's chest tightened as he considered anew all the Lord had given them...and then perceived anew the cloud of war on the horizon. "How right you are. And how ill we can afford any chasms between us now, with the future so uncertain."

"'Tisn't uncertain. The British are coming, and they will do anything they can to break us. We knew all along that would mean more than raids on the farms nearest the waterways."

"If only those in Washington had listened to us before now."

Arnaud shared his opinion of the politicians and then speared Thad with an uncompromising regard. "I know I needn't ask, but I will anyway. If anything happens to me in these battles knocking upon our door, you must take Jacques in again and raise him as your own."

Idiot man. "You were right. You needn't ask."

The glare turned to a grin. "And if anything happens to you, shall I marry Gwyneth in your stead?"

What could he do in answer but sweep off his hat and reach over to smack him with it? They laughed together, but it soon faded away, and Thad sighed. "You must see she is safe from her uncle. He will find her. Sooner or later, he will find her, and when he realizes she saw what she did… If I am killed in the war, you must promise to protect her."

Arnaud nodded, solemn and somehow looking all the more noble with that fatalistic shadow in his eyes. "And if we both die, then your parents will have their hands quite full, *n'est-ce pas?*"

"May God forbid it."

"I pray He shall."

They said no more, given that they were near enough Washington now that they were no longer alone on the road. In silence they made their way to Tallmadge's office. In silence they waited for his secretary to show them in.

Arnaud stood before a framed painting of Tallmadge's home, staring at it for a solid two minutes before opening his mouth. "Do you ever miss Connecticut, Thad?"

He looked at the painting and called to mind the house he had grown up in. "Parts of it, and the idyllic childhood we passed there in New Haven. But I am content to call Baltimore my home."

"And so I trust you will be ready to defend her."

Thad stood at the familiar voice that came from Tallmadge's office door. Senator Samuel Smith was one of the few politicians Tallmadge trusted enough to work with on matters of intelligence—and he was also the general who had been given charge of Baltimore's defenses. "General, how good to see you."

Tallmadge appeared behind Smith's shoulder and waved Thad and Arnaud in. "I didn't dare hope you would be home already. Sam and I were discussing how to implement some of our ideas."

The general stepped aside to let them enter. "We will need to call upon your resources, to be sure. Arnaud, good to see you again."

Thad sat down in his usual chair as his friend responded in kind. Tallmadge perched on the edge of his desk. "Your trip was a success?"

He filled them in on the numbers he had observed, the fact that with their addition, the British's Chesapeake fleet would swell to fifty ships. And finally Cochrane and Ross's inclination to allow Cockburn his way in regard to attacking Washington.

Smith nodded throughout. "Not as many as we feared, honestly. And no surprise as to their target."

Thad leaned forward. "Can Washington be readied, do you think?"

Tallmadge snorted. "With Secretary Jones stymieing our efforts at every turn and General Winder being always undermined by him? I have my doubts, though we will pray Winder overcomes political resistance. But if by chance the British succeed, if Washington falls, we must have our next step planned out."

Thad nodded even as his pulse kicked up. The plan they had already discussed as a possibility. "Lure them to Baltimore."

"Which will be ready for them." Smith folded his arms as he made the pronouncement, his steel-gray hair and firm jaw daring anyone to argue. "The mayor backs my plan entirely, and I am ready to enact it at a moment's notice. We will rally every man, slave and free, and put him to work. We will fortify, we will dig trenches, we will drill. Every day, round the clock, the masters beside their servants."

"And we will not let them know we are doing it." Tallmadge picked up a piece of paper and handed it to Thad. "These are the messages you are to plant, Mr. Culper."

He read them quickly, though they but provided details to what they had already decided. An article for the paper to falsely report that Baltimore was dreadfully unprepared. And other, slier messages to send by word of mouth reporting the Potomac force as weak and in trouble.

"I have a few messengers in mind, and I am well acquainted with the editor at the *Patriot*. But sirs, they have their intelligencers too. The generals and admirals were talking of them in Bermuda. We must tread carefully." With the thought that every step they took could make it to the ears of Cockburn, Cochrane, Ross.

And then over the sea to Gates.

"I know. Trust me, I know." Tallmadge stood and paced to the window, his hands clasped behind his back. "But our best defense against their scouts is what you already do for us—know everyone, watch everyone. And somehow convince the populace that *they* are our last, best line of defense."

Thad agreed, and he and Arnaud took their leave a few minutes later. But once they were outside the city again, surrounded by naught but chirping birds and open land, his friend looked over at him and asked the question weighing on Thad's mind too.

"How, exactly, are we to convince the populace of this?"

The question that had been plaguing them since this blasted war broke out. How to move a languid people? How to unify a nation divided on so many issues? How to overcome a generation's worth of lassitude when two years of war had not accomplished it already?

Only one way came to mind. "Remember Hampton."

Arnaud sighed. "But we cannot *wish*, cannot *plan* for another such violent, cruel attack. We cannot *hope* that Washington will be the next Hampton."

"No. But we can be ready with the battle cry if our first defenses fail." He urged Electra to go a little faster, eager to be home. To let all these matters simmer in the back of his mind and focus the fore of it on his evening with Gwyneth. "That is our best hope, Alain. That though their goal may be to crush our spirits, they have never understood them well enough to do so. The harder they hit us, the more we awake to fight. The stronger they press, the more we lash back."

Arnaud grinned. "*Vive l'esprit américain.*"

Long live the American spirit indeed. And may the British never comprehend it.

They rode in companionable silence for a while and then spoke of lighter things. Of Jack's exploits during Thad's absence, of Emmy's return from Henry's sister's. Of the latest letter from Amelia, in which she shared that her husband had joined up with Hagerstown's First Maryland Cavalry regiment, which they expected to be called to Washington's defense.

There it was again, that shadow of the war.

By the time they parted ways at the corner of Thad's street, his mind screamed for respite. Something to still the swirl of British army red and naval blue behind his eyes, the images of ships and flocks of soldiers.

He led Electra round to the carriage house and stabled, brushed, and fed her. Then he headed inside, half expecting to find Gwyneth in the garden finishing her painting despite the afternoon slant to the sun.

Mother was instead the first one he saw, and from the look in her eyes, she had been waiting for him. She greeted him with a finger on her lips and a motion for him to follow. Too curious to disobey even had he been so inclined, he tiptoed behind her up the stairs and into his parents' chamber.

"What is it?" he asked in a whisper when she shut the door behind them.

She smiled and turned to her vanity. "I want to give you something. For Gwyneth, when the time is right."

Thad swallowed as she lifted the lid to her box of jewelry. She never wore much—the occasional necklace, and the ring Father had given her to mark their engagement. What could she possibly be willing to part with?

His brows furrowed when she pulled out a necklace she had always reserved for the most special of occasions. A delicate strand of gold with three pearls upon it. Mother withdrew it with an almost reverent care, placing the pearls in her palm. "Do you remember the story of this necklace?"

Apparently he should, but he had not even seen it in years, and why would a boy pay any heed to tales of such girlish things? He shook his head. "Only that it was your mother's."

"The necklace itself, yes. The pearls came from a strand my grandparents had given me. I was wearing it the night Grandfather had me beaten and tossed to the streets. The night that could have been my end, had God not led me to Viney."

Viney he remembered—the pure-hearted prostitute who had saved Mother's life, and who had later harbored Father when he was out spying on Benedict Arnold. "I recall that part of the tale."

Mother nodded and touched a finger to one of the pearls. "I gave her the necklace so that she could sell the pearls and have enough money to live on until the consumption took her home. When your Father later met her, she gave him what remained of them—these three." She looked up now and caught Thad's gaze. "That was the day he proposed, the day we realized our causes were not so different. The day he learned of the Culpers. And so this has always, in my mind, been a Culper necklace more than just a family one. It ought to go to you and Gwyneth."

Though part of him wanted to insist she keep it, the greater part recognized that this, too, was part of the mantle his parents had passed to him. A symbol of how beauty rested in a thing's purpose. How God's path could be found in the most unlikely of places.

His fingers closed around the gift when she held it out. "I know it will mean as much to her as it does to me. When should I...?"

Mother smiled, rested her palm against his cheek, and shook her head. "That, my darling boy, is for you to decide. But whenever you choose, know you have our blessing. We suspected as soon as she arrived that you two would be well suited. And so you are."

"Is *that* what Father— Oh, I will never hear the end of this. For the rest of our lives, he will be crowing about how he knew from the start that we were meant for each other. He will try to claim it as some scientific deduction."

She chuckled, patted his cheek, and stepped away. "And you will smile, pull your beloved close, and let him crow."

"If I must." He smiled now, pulled his mother close, and gave her a squeeze. "Thank you."

"You are so very welcome, darling one. So very welcome."

They exited together, Thad slipping into his own chamber long enough to deposit the necklace in a box with his cufflinks. Mother waited in the hall, and they moved together toward the stairs. Her face had gone serious. "The war will reach us soon?"

Perhaps some men would have tried to protect their matrons from that truth. His probably knew it before he did. "Within a fortnight, I would say."

"And you will be out drilling under Smith's command soon, digging trenches and what have you. When they come, you will be in Fort McHenry."

Somehow hearing her state it so definitely... "Assuming that Tallmadge and Smith do not assign me elsewhere."

They reached the ground floor, and Mother stayed him with a hand on his arm. Her gaze was intent, insistent. "I cannot shake the feeling that while you must take a careful, well-considered course, you ought not dawdle upon it. 'Tisn't a time to leave things undone. Too much is at stake, and too many stakes are easily lost in war."

Of what exactly was she speaking? Culper business or personal? Or some combination of the two? He would have asked, but voices came from down the hall, Father's and Gwyneth's and Philly's. Mother made a quick motion. She took one hand from her mouth downward and touched it to her opposite fist.

Promise.

He could do nothing but nod as he tucked her hand into the crook of his arm. And wonder for what the Lord was steeling him.

Gwyneth crowded around the map with the others, her heart racing in a strange sort of excitement. Captain Arnaud had dubbed himself the general of this campaign, the irony of which made them all smile. Of their assorted family members, from young Jack to arthritic Grandmama Caro, he, with his generous scowls, was the least likely to order them all out to spread cheer.

Hence, she suspected, why he had volunteered. Now he struck the city map with a rod, indicating the quadrant nearest Thad's house. "Grandmama and Bennet will take this section here. Urge everyone downtown that you can or, failing that, over to the Washington road. Winter, you and Rosie will pick up here and work your way westward. Philly and Reggie, get everyone out of the shops and into the streets. Gwyneth, you will be with me—"

"Try it, General, and you will have a mutiny on your hands." Thad delivered the line with a somber face, but amusement gleamed in his eyes.

The same reflected in Captain Arnaud's. "A general does not have a mutiny, you salty dog. Those only happen at sea."

"Then we shall call you Admiral instead. But Gwyn is with me, as you well know."

Arnaud loosed an overdone sigh. "Fine. Upstart sailor. As punishment, the two of you are in charge of making sure the band is in order and nearby on the streets. And who will go with me then?" He made a show of looking around as his son all but danced upon his chair, so high did he try to raise his hand. "No one? No one wants to go with me to the docks?"

"Papa! Me!"

Gwyneth laughed with the others as Arnaud exclaimed as if he had not seen the boy and then scooped him up. And she made no objection when Thad laced his fingers through hers. He had done so frequently the past two weeks, first at any excuse, then at fabricated ones, and finally without even that pretense.

She shot him a warm smile in reward.

"All right then, soldiers, you all know your orders. This is the most serious campaign you will likely ever undertake, and I expect you to treat it with dignity and respect."

Jack giggled and wrapped an arm around his father's neck. "Papa, it is a *parade*."

"Exactly, my little corporal." He tweaked the boy's nose. "A parade to send off our boys to Washington in such a fashion that they know they take us all with them. To mark the twenty-first of August as a day to remember."

And there was the regret that colored the joy. They were sending their neighbors off to their possible deaths—deaths at the hands of Gwyneth's countrymen. Some of whom she undoubtedly knew firsthand, who had likely served under her father. Possibly with whom she had danced at a ball earlier that spring.

What a terrible thing was this war.

As the group broke up, Thad kissed her knuckles—another move that had become so common yet still sent such a thrill through her. "Are you certain you want to join us in this, my love? We all understand that you are—"

"Thad, please." She squeezed his fingers and pulled him out the door behind his grandmother. "I am English, and I will always love England, but that does not mean I cannot see her mistakes for what they are. And it certainly does not mean I want to see this country crushed when it deserves the chance to thrive."

"Just making certain." A smile saturated his tone, though she didn't look back to see it. Not until they stepped outside into the wet blanket of scorching heat.

"Oh, heavens. I do not envy the men their march to Washington." Already, after a mere handful of seconds in the sun, perspiration dotted her brow. Or perhaps it was merely the humidity finding a surface to which to cling.

Thad pulled her away from the others and off toward where the musicians had been told to gather. "They have been in this heat all summer. They will be fine. 'Tis the chaps in red you ought to be concerned about on that count."

Poor fellows. According to what Thad learned and then shared with the rest of them, the six thousand men who had arrived so recently had not fared well on their march. No doubt they were out of condition from the voyage, weeks and months of inactivity, and then to be forced into this suffocating climate after being accustomed to the cooler European air…no wonder all the reports of men collapsing. "I do not wish the nation crushed, but I certainly do not wish my countrymen such an arduous time of breathing."

Thad was not so conflicted, if the impish grin on his face were any indication. "It seems to me that it is another valuable military lesson. Just as Napoleon learned not to wage war in Russia in winter, so the British ought to learn to stay out of the Atlantic states in the summer."

"They were here before."

"And look how well that turned out for them."

How was she to resist a breath of laughter and a shake of her head? Gwyneth pulled her fingers free of his, but only so that she could tuck her hand into the crook of his arm, the easier to walk beside him. The levity had little choice but to fade as she considered again *why* all these men were slogging through the ninety-five degrees that felt well over a hundred with the humidity.

Cochrane had approved Cockburn's plan. Her father's friends had set a course for Washington City.

She dabbed at the sweat from her brow with her handkerchief, though she knew even as she did so it was a vain attempt.

A gaggle of women approached, all looking to be in their thirties, all with parasols to block the vicious sun. Thad called out a greeting, spouting out all seven names without a hesitation, though Gwyneth had never seen a one of them in her two and a half months in Baltimore. And she and Thad had been out together nearly every day the past two weeks, walking or driving or shopping or attending services at church.

The ladies obviously knew him too, and they took in Gwyneth with a knowing glance and satisfied grins. As if they had all been waiting for the day when Thaddeus Lane became someone's beau.

Perhaps they had.

"I do hope you are only headed home to drop off your packages, ladies. Our boys in the Fifth Maryland Infantry are headed to Washington City in an hour's time, and we are sending them off with enthusiasm."

"Oh!" One of the ladies grabbed the hand of another. "That must be what the musicians were doing. Of course we will be there."

Another of the women dabbed at her eyes. "Yes, of course. My brother is in the Fifth."

"Then Washington is in good hands." Thad bowed to them and pulled Gwyneth onward.

It took them half an hour to cover their assigned distance, not because they had to go far, but because Thad stopped to talk with each person they saw. Issuing an invitation here, a bit of encouragement there, speaking, as he always did, to each one's need.

More often than not, she merely watched and listened. And she wondered how she had been so lucky as to capture the heart of this man. Gwyneth knew so many authoritative men—generals and admirals, politicians and lords—but true leaders she could count on one hand.

Thad was one of them, and of a sort she had never really seen before. He was not the ship that cut through the waves, he was not the captain at its helm, he was not the general plotting strategy at a desk in his cabin. He was the current in the water. Propelling, driving, pulling. He was a man capable of directing the leaders. Of influencing the masses. Of steering whole cities at a time.

And he was hers.

"Thad?"

"Hmm?" He lifted a hand to the band's conductor, who indicated with a nod and a smile that all was set with the group of musicians clustered around him with their instruments.

"You know those hand gestures your family makes to communicate silently?" It had taken her too long to pick up on the fact that they were, in fact, a form of speech, but once her mind was cleared of exhaustion, it had been obvious.

Thad glanced down at her with a smile. "'Tis sign language, sweet. My grandfather and Rosie's uncle, Freeman, developed it to communicate with my great-grandmother, who was deaf. It's based upon a few systems from Europe."

She hoped to meet this Freeman someday. And, for that matter, Thad's grandpapa. "Would you teach it to me?"

"Of course." His eyes glowed, obviously pleased she had asked. His hand covered her fingers on his arm. "I would be delighted. We all would."

"Could we begin now?"

He glanced to the band and then the gathering crowd, seeming to indicate the situation as a whole with that one simple move of his eyes. "*Now?*"

"Just one phrase." Careful to keep her face pleasant but otherwise neutral, she blinked up at him in the same way that had always made her parents sigh and give in.

Thad sighed and gave in. "Very well. One phrase."

She could scarcely tamp down the beginnings of a smile. "How do you say 'I love you'?"

His every muscle seemed to freeze for a moment, with not so much as a twitch or a tic to betray his thoughts other than the emotion swirling through his eyes. Then the slight flare of his nostrils as he drew in a breath. "Gwyn."

Oh, how her lips ached to grin. "Do you not know that one?"

He pulled her an inch closer to his side. "I know it," he said, his voice low. "I am merely wondering why you want to."

Gwyneth lifted her chin and did her best to imitate Aunt Gates's haughty way of tilting it. "Because there are some things a young lady does not say aloud in public, sir."

"I see." Amusement joined into the amalgam of other sweet feelings dancing through his gaze. He loosed her arm and turned toward her. "It is a rather simple one." He pointed to his chest, crossed both arms over it as if embracing himself, and then pointed to her.

The smile finally won her lips, though softer than she had thought it might come out. "I will never tire of your saying that to me, Captain Lane. Now let me see if I have it right." She mirrored his movements, slowly and deliberately.

His smile was as soft to behold as hers felt. He took her hands and held them tight. "And why, my sweet, do you choose to say such things to me now, when we are in a crowd of our neighbors and I can do nothing about it?"

"Because in a crowd of your neighbors is where you are at your best. But have no fear. It will be just as true later, when we are out of the crowd."

Grinning, he tucked her hand back into its spot around his elbow. And the band struck up a song.

Twenty-Eight

The faint thunder of distant cannons invaded his perception as Arthur walked up Church Street with Gates on one side and Scrubs a few steps behind. Happy as his feet—and stomach—were to be on solid ground again, he had a difficult time focusing on the city of Annapolis around him with that familiar echo in the air.

"How far away is it, do you think?" Scrubs spoke in an even tone, but the fact that he spoke at all said volumes.

Gates looked to him. Arthur shrugged. "As faint as it is, it must be at least twenty miles away, I would say. Perhaps as much as thirty, depending on how sound carries here. Not too close."

But it made his hand reach for the sword no longer fastened to his side. For the Brown Bess no longer slung over his shoulder. It made his ears strain for the next command from his superior officer. It made the scar throb in his leg.

"It sounds like it is from the direction of Washington City."

Arthur would have to take Scrubs's word on that one, having never had cause to learn much by way of American geography. "Their capital, is it not? Perhaps we have made progress, then."

Gates turned on him with an exasperated sigh. "Do watch your tongue, Hart, will you? And your very way of speaking. If we hope to discover information from the locals, we ought not shout from the rooftops that we are British."

Yet again, Gates managed to make him feel the dunce with the aid of a few curt sentences. "My apologies, sir. I haven't your experience with the covert."

"You could at least use common sense. Boy—what is your real name?"

Scrubs looked from Gates to Arthur, his silence pulsing with reticence. But at Gates's continued stare, he swallowed and said, "Willis, sir."

Arthur was about to ask if that was his given name or family, but his companion apparently did not care. "You will act as our guide and mouthpiece. And rest assured that while I may not be as familiar with the area as you, I will know if you are lying about anything, and the penalty for such will be severe. Are we clear?"

"As ice."

No, the boy had certainly not thanked Arthur for getting him off the *Falcon*. And his tone at that last burned of resentment, in fact. Arthur wiped away the sweat beading on his brow. "'Tis hot as blazes."

"I told you it would be." Gates pointed up ahead, past the rows of buildings, many with windows still bricked over to avoid the old window tax, toward the one at the apex of the road, up upon the hill. "The Maryland Inn is there. When we rent our rooms, Willis will tell the proprietor we are from his area in Virginia. Try to imitate his speech or, if you cannot, say nothing."

Arthur opted for a nod. He longed again for his weapons, a uniform, and a battle plan. Far better that than this underhanded nonsense.

But it was for Gwyneth, so he would do whatever he must. Gwyneth, who he prayed was safely within this very town. Which, given its size, would mean no more than a mile away even now. A bath, a meal, and he could be with her.

Another whisper of a boom echoed through the air. Arthur looked around to try to gauge the townsfolk's reactions but found none to study. Odd for this time of day, surely. Perhaps Yorrick's prediction was true and most of them had fled. Or perhaps the distant sound of war had scared them all indoors.

They hiked in silence up the hill, the slope of which would have seemed gentle had he not been two months aboard a vessel that afforded him little exercise, and had the very fires of Hades not been trying to devour them even now. By the time they reached the inn, Arthur was silently cursing himself for not taking better care of his condition on the *Falcon*. He ought to have anticipated this and found a way to drill in his cabin. Close quarters was no excuse for sloth. Although he had hardly felt up to exercise, what with the constant motion of the ship churning his stomach.

The door to the inn stood open, as if the meager air moving up the street would do anything to cool the interior. They moved inside, Gates having waved Scrubs into the lead, but to no purpose. No one stood behind the desk, nor was anyone anywhere within sight. Gates tapped the bell, but a full minute of waiting produced no results.

Another muted blast of a cannon.

Gates spun for the door again. "Come, this is foolishness. Annapolis has few enough residents that all know each other. We will simply ask someone."

Arthur and Scrubs followed him back out, where he looked around and chose a house seemingly at random, marched up to it, and knocked upon the door. A door which remained firmly closed. Though after another round of knocking, and an increasing frown upon Gates's brow, a neighboring door opened and a well-dressed woman of middling age stepped out.

"Good day, there. Are you looking for Mrs. Mercer?"

They all turned to the woman, Mr. Gates presenting a smile far brighter than his usual one. "Is she in, do you know?" Gone was the clipped, upper class London accent from his voice. In its place was one a bit slower, of a different cadence. More like Scrubs's.

"She is not." The woman's curls danced at her temples when she shook her head. "And she will not be back any time soon. With all these threats of encroaching battles, she has gone to Baltimore to weather the war there with her son."

"Ah." Gates nodded and hooked a hand in the pocket of his waistcoat. "A wise decision, from the sound of it. And how is her son? I have not seen him in years."

Arthur shifted his weight from one foot to the other. As much as he appreciated Gates's smooth handling, of what import was any of this? He needed to ask after the Lanes. After Gwyneth.

The woman's face went from friendly to merely polite. "Well enough, last I heard. Would you like me to tell her you gentlemen called when she returns?"

"That will not be necessary. We will be making our way to Baltimore ourselves." He turned back toward the street and then to the neighbor again, as if a new thought just occurred to him. "If I might have one more moment of your time, madam, are you acquainted with the Lanes? Bennet Lane, a professor at St. John's College, and his wife, Winter?"

Now the woman's eyes lit up, and her smile returned bright and cheerful. "Of course I am. Everyone is. Oh, but they too are gone to Baltimore to be with Philly and Thad until the college resumes its classes after the war. No point in staying here, they said."

Arthur's fingers curled into his palm, but he kept his face from so much as twitching. If only he could keep his heart from sinking so easily.

Gates sighed. "Again, logical if disappointing. Did they have a young lady traveling with them, do you know?"

"A young lady?" Her face went blank. "No, they have had no guests for a year or more."

The sharp teeth of fear bit down, dug in, threatened to tear away Arthur's careful control. That the Lanes were gone was no more than a disappointment, one easily dealt with. But Gwyneth was not with them?

Had they been wrong? Had Fairchild not sent her here after all? Or had she arrived after the Lanes left? Which would mean that even now she could be alone somewhere, unguarded but for her aging servants. Where? Here, in Annapolis? Or had she followed them to Baltimore?

Gates was uttering his thanks and leading them back toward the street. His gaze latched hold of Arthur. "What do you think? The day is young yet. Shall we rent horses and head to Baltimore?"

For once Arthur got to look at Gates as if he were the idiot. And he put to voice the facts coalescing into a list in his mind. "No. First we check the inns and rented houses in Annapolis to be sure Gwyneth and the Wesleys did not decide to wait here for her father. Then we find our commanders in the area to ascertain where this action is taking place, where they are marching next, and how we can best stay out of their way and still make the trip in safety. Then, and only then, do we head to Baltimore."

Gates seemed to ponder that advice for a long moment, and then he nodded and held out a hand toward the Maryland Inn. "Back we go to await the proprietor. We will settle in and afterward begin our search."

On the night of August 24, pacing the rooftop widow's walk long after darkness had fallen, her arms wrapped around her middle, Gwyneth figured no one would accuse her of unreasonable insomnia. They were all there with her, keeping watch for familiar figures on the street. Their eyes were all cast toward the southwestern horizon, where the orange glow had grown from a suspicion to a terrible certainty.

Something big was ablaze. And the only thing in that direction that could put up such a glow from this distance was Washington City.

Winter rubbed a hand over Jack's back, though he had been asleep on her lap for hours now. "I should put him to bed. We should all go to bed. We can help no one by being exhausted come daybreak."

Yet she made no move to rise from the single chair they had brought up, and no one else acknowledged her statement. Just as they hadn't the last time she had made it, an hour earlier.

The heat had dulled, but not by much. Even at midnight it hung heavy as a drape over them and thrummed with a sizzle that seemed to denote a storm was on its way. Perhaps if it hurried, it would put out the fire.

"I sure wish they would come home." Rosie rubbed her hands over her arms as if she were cold. She leaned on the rail next to Gwyneth, her eyes locked on that eerie, flickering orange glow. "Knowing them, they are out there helping folks secure their belongings, never giving any mind to the fact that we all be waiting to hear what happened."

"Of course they are." Gwyneth expected nothing less of either Thad or Arnaud. She hadn't been surprised when they lit out at midday. They promised they wouldn't get near the battle itself—they had *promised*, so she tried to take solace in that—but they had been gone twelve hours, and now Washington was burning.

Congressman Tallmadge had come by at dinnertime, long enough to let them know that their forces had fallen back from the battle at Bladensburg, outside Washington, in disarray. Thad had been helping organize the removal of all of the most precious American documents from Washington, and Arnaud had been tasked with warning the first lady away from the White House. Tallmadge had assured them that the president and cabinet were all evacuated, and he had insinuated that their men would return to them soon.

That was six hours ago, and still no familiar silhouettes.

Gwyneth drew in a long breath. "I have a confession, Rosie."

The woman looked her way. "Make it a good one, child. I'm in sore need of a distraction."

She chuckled. Perhaps it was halfhearted, but she would take any ounce of amusement she could find today. "I thought I had fully conquered the insomnia while Thad was in Bermuda, but I have been sleeping even better in the fortnight since he returned."

Rosie made a dismissive sound. "Lands, girl, that's one sorry confession. We all sleep better when he's home. Leastways, I do. Comes of caring for someone and from knowing they care for you."

Care for. A mild way of putting the joy that saturated every inch of her being when she was with him, that spun over her nerves when he took her hand, that twirled in her stomach when he smiled at her. And the ache that took its place now, when he was not only away from her, but somewhere out there where danger scorched the sky.

A hot wind blew over her face. Was it her imagination, or did it smell of smoke?

Eventually, they moved their vigil inside. Winter put Jack to bed, Rosie made coffee and tea, and they pulled out the remains of a cake. Gwyneth had no appetite, no more than the Lanes or Rosie. She turned her slice into crumbles on her plate and forced a bite past her lips now and then.

At some point she gave in when Mr. Lane urged her to the sofa. She even closed her eyes.

And she jerked awake in a panic when a noise pulled her from the silence of sleep. A panic that flipped to excitement in one accelerated beat of her heart when she realized the noise was Mr. Lane declaring, "They're here!"

Gwyneth shook the cobwebs from her mind, stumbled to her feet, and charged toward the door. She collided directly into a solid chest. Arnaud's, given the height of it and the accompanying chuckle.

"Whoa, there. I believe you meant to throw yourself into the arms behind me." He grinned as he delivered her into Thad's embrace.

She was laughing as she wrapped her arms around him and nestled in. Dawn, she saw when her face turned toward the window, had crept upon them. "You must be exhausted."

"A bit. We hunkered down for a few hours when the drizzle started and stole an hour or two of rest." His hands buried themselves in her hair, his lips pressed to the top of her head. "Sorry to worry you all. We thought we would have until morning to clear Washington of the last stragglers and of anything of import, but the British arrived before dusk and set about burning every public building."

Winter shook her head. "We saw the glow. Tell me you were not still in the city when they arrived."

"Not for long." Arnaud smiled, but it was too weary and worn to look as confident as he must have intended. "Then we headed to the surrounding farms. The army seemed bent on destroying anything they could touch, and most of the farmers were happy to help by destroying first anything the British might try to take."

Mr. Lane pinched the bridge of his nose. "Is there a count yet on how many dead and wounded? Tallmadge did not know when he stopped by last evening."

She felt Thad shake his head, and his voice came as a rumble in the chest under her ear. "The retreat was too disorderly. Everyone was eager to protect their own homes. All I know for certain is that Barney was injured and taken prisoner. I expect they will parole him, but it was a hard blow."

Gwyneth closed her eyes. Papa never spoke of the details of war, not when she was near. In this moment, she almost wished he had, so that she might be steeled against it. "You still think they will come here next?"

"I have no doubt. Already we heard a rumor of Annapolis being their next target, but I know misdirection when I hear it. Annapolis has nothing to draw them. Baltimore, though—Baltimore is the center of commerce. If they can cripple us, it may mean the end of the war."

She tilted her head back and looked up into the face she had come to know so well, treasure so fully. "What if you cannot rouse the people? If they are too disheartened by Washington—"

"Oh, sweet." He grinned and stroked a thumb over her cheek. "Washington is not to us what London is to your countrymen. The location means nothing. Our government can operate as well from a tavern or a plantation. Its destruction is like throwing water on a cat. It will not disable us. It will make us spitting mad."

He obviously knew his neighbors better than she, but it seemed strange. And if strange to her, who had been living among them for months, how strange indeed it would seem to the British generals and admirals planning out their strategy.

Her arms tightened around him. "And when they come, you will not be content to run about taking people to safety or scouting their position, will you? You will fight." And he was no general like Papa, who could avoid the front lines so that he might command others to them. Thad would go wherever he was told and do whatever must be done, no matter the danger to himself.

The familiar teeth of fear nipped at her and made her heart squeeze tight. She could lose him. In a matter of days, she could lose him, and it was not fair. She had scarcely had him. Could only by audacity call him her own, not by rights. With tears flooding her eyes, she drew in a long breath. *I give him to You, my Lord and my God. I put him in the palm of Your hand. And I will climb up into Your lap and wait out the storm there, trusting You to...trusting that...just trusting.*

"Gwyn." The warm tone drew her gaze to his face again, where his eyes burned as fiercely as Washington must have in the night. He cupped her cheek. "Will you marry me?"

Her arms slid away, but only so she could settle her hands on his chest, where the reassuring, quick *thump-thump* of his heart could touch them. "Yes."

He didn't smile. "Before they come?"

"Yes."

"Today?"

"Yes." This time it came out on a laugh, part joy and part desperation. *Yes*, let it be soon, let it be now, this very minute. Let God join them together so that no man could tear them asunder.

Now he smiled, in a quiet sort of way, and looked to the others in the room. "If anyone has any objections, speak now or else get to work."

Rosie was the first to jump into action. "A wedding dinner with only twelve hours' notice? I had better get Emmy to help me. We have that ham, a mess of potatoes still, and those greens. Emmy can make the cake." She paused beside them, the sparkle in her eyes belying the matter-of-fact words. Her hands settled, one on each of their arms, and gave a little squeeze. Then she bustled from the room.

"Alain?"

Arnaud was glancing around the chamber as if taking its measure. "How many do you think we can fit in here? Ah, no matter." He grinned and sank into a chair. "I will invite all of Baltimore and let them fight out who can witness the nuptials. Although I will give them time to rise first."

"And I will find Reverend Gruber." Mr. Lane approached with a warm smile and reached for her hands. "Gwyneth, my dear. You know we welcome you most happily to our family. And I believe, with everything within me, that your father would approve of this."

She nodded, those tears stinging again. "I know he would."

Winter looked to be fighting off tears of her own. "We ought to find you a wedding gown. And send for Philly, who will never forgive us if we exclude her. Oh, how I wish there was time for Amelia to come, but she will understand."

"She will indeed." Thad took her hands from his father, winked, and pulled her toward the door. "Just as I am sure you all understand when I beg you to excuse us for a moment."

A laugh stuck in her throat as he tugged her into the hall before they could object, down it and around the corner until they were out of sight, and then he lifted her enough to set her feet upon the bottom step of the stairwell, evening out their heights. "There," he said. "Now the important part."

"Thad, I—"

His lips silenced her, caressing hers with a warm urgency, a patient need. Once, twice, a third glorious time, and then he mumbled, "Were you saying something?"

She looped her arms around his neck and kissed him when he waited a second too long for her liking. "I cannot think what."

He took the kiss deeper, and she held on as her knees went liquid, let herself get lost for a moment in the rush of sensation. Was it some facet of chemistry that did this to her, as Philly suggested? Some magic? Or was it, as it felt it must be, a knitting of their souls?

"Oh." She pulled away, though not by much. A fraction of an inch, enough to fit in a smile. "I was going to say I love you."

Thad grinned before feathering a kiss over her cheek and down to her jaw. "A good thing to say. I ought to say the same." From jaw to lips. "In one moment."

The moment stretched, crystallized, and only ended when Winter cleared her throat and stepped up beside Gwyneth on the stair. "We have much to do, and there will be time enough for that after the vows are exchanged," she said, a smile in her voice.

Gwyneth smiled too and loosed her arms from their happy home around his neck. And hoped, prayed his mother was right. That there would be time enough.

Winter looped her arm through Gwyneth's. "Come, my dear. We will go through your dresses, and— Where are you going, Thaddeus?"

He was already halfway up the stairs. "I have something to give her, if you recall."

"Ah. Yes, he does."

They took a more leisurely approach up the staircase, arriving at the top as Thad emerged from his bedchamber. Which, Gwyneth realized with a dry throat, would be hers tonight as well. A thought which might have terrified her had Thad's smile not filled her so completely with joy.

"Here we are." In his hands he held a delicate chain of gold with three pearls upon it. Even as she admired the simple beauty of the necklace, he reached to fasten it around her neck. "I realize pearls are not the traditional engagement gift, but these have a story I'm sure Mother will share in a few minutes. And since I do not know if I will be able to get a ring in time—"

"Of course you will have a ring," Winter said.

Thad grinned and kept his gaze on Gwyneth, as if his mother were not even there. "I mean, I will have a ring."

"My mother's."

"'Twas my grandmother's." The clasp secure, he dropped his hands and leaned down to kiss her cheek. "But I am afraid not much else will be what you likely envisioned for your wedding, and the honeymoon trip will have to wait. When the war is over, though, my love, I will take you anywhere in the world you please."

Gwyneth grasped his hands and cherished the feel of the cool pearls against her skin. "Perhaps I once daydreamed with my friends of orange blossoms and wedding trips to Paris and Rome, but all I ever really wanted was what I have right here. The kind of love I saw in my parents, with the promise of forever they taught me was paramount."

He leaned down and brushed a single, soft, eternal kiss upon her lips. "I love you, Gwyneth. More than life itself."

A moment later he was bounding down the stairs, leaving her in a haze of bliss to veil the frightening night just passed. She looked to Winter. "I fear I am dreaming."

"No time for that today." With a smile, Thad's mother took her hand and pulled her into Gwyneth's room. "Show me your best things. I daresay your gowns are more in ton than anything Philly or I could offer, though we would be happy to lend you anything you might need."

As she pulled out dress after dress, each and every one she had packed, Gwyneth felt a bittersweet stirring in her heart. Mama ought to have been with her on her wedding day. Papa ought to be below with the gentlemen. The Wesleys, at least, should have been fluttering about, the mister trying to be useful and the missus with her constant "Now, love" this and "Here, love" that.

But they were not, none of them, and some by choice. All her ties to England seemed to have drifted away like smoke on the wind. How blessed she was that the Lord had put her in another family just as loving, just as true to Him, just as much her own.

Philly joined them within the hour, Emmy not long after, and, given the constant stream of visitors she heard downstairs, Arnaud had been busily spreading the word. All the exclamations that floated up the stairs sounded joyful and, perhaps, edged with desperation. The fierce clinging to life and hope in the face of destruction.

Around midday, Rosie poked her head into the room, where they were all mending gowns and adding bits of lace. "Gwyneth, Mrs. Lane, Reverend Gruber arrived and would like to talk to you."

Though she had been sitting in a pew in Reverend Gruber's church every Sunday for months now, nerves still jumped and twitched in Gwyneth's stomach at that. The good reverend, like everyone else outside the family, knew her as Miss Hampton. That would have to be rectified before he officiated the wedding. If he would even agree to do so.

"I showed him to the study. Mrs. Rhodes and her girls are at work decorating everything else."

"Come, dear." With a calming smile, Winter took her hand and led her down.

The minister waited within. Thad was there too, which helped the knots unravel. As did the warm smile Reverend Gruber gave her.

"My dear Miss Hampton. Many congratulations. I cannot say how glad I am to have learned that you and our Captain Lane have decided to wed."

She let him take her hand and returned his smile, but she glanced to Thad. "Thank you, Reverend. But there is one thing…"

"Ah." Thad chuckled and tucked an arm around her waist. "Quite right. Her last name is actually Fairchild, sir. Gwyneth is the daughter of the British general."

When the minister's face went pale, Gwyneth feared the worst. That he would refuse to marry them, that he would storm out announcing to one and all that she was the enemy. Then the man shook his head. "The one who was murdered? I read about it in the papers. How very terrible for you."

She relaxed against Thad's arm. "It has been, yes."

"And given that, you can see why we thought it best to introduce her as a distant cousin. Though certainly we do not want to use the wrong name in the vows."

Reverend Gruber waved that off. "First names will suffice in the ceremony, and I will enter it in the register correctly, but as no one will really look at it, you needn't worry. But, my dear, you haven't reached your majority, have you?"

"Nay, sir. I am nineteen."

He pressed his lips together, turning kind blue eyes from her to Winter. "Who, then, is her legal guardian?"

Winter merely shrugged as Thad hummed. Gwyneth shook her head. "I do not actually know. Both of my parents have passed now, and I was not present for the reading of the will...someone in England, I suppose. I have a whole host of uncles. But the Lanes have taken on the role here. They are the ones to whom my father entrusted me when he realized he was in some danger."

His gray brows pulled down, Gruber thought about that for a few moments and then nodded. "That is good enough for me. No one in this country will much care, and I daresay by the time your uncles may object, it will be too much ancient history for them to make an inquiry."

Not to mention that Papa's brother the earl, the one most likely to be her guardian, would by no means want to invite the scandal such an objection would bring. Gwyneth loosed her pent-up breath and looked up at her beloved.

Within a few more hours, they would be man and wife.

A rumble of thunder roared through, so loud it shook the glass in its panes. The reverend started and then looked toward the window and the angry black clouds clustering over the bay. "I do hope neither of you is superstitious about rain on wedding days."

Thad, bless him, grinned. "A rain that will help extinguish the fires smoldering in Washington can be only a blessing on our union, my friend."

Gwyneth held tight to his side and watched the roiling cloud bank move in. *Dear Lord, let it be so.*

Twenty-Nine

Smoke drifted thick through the air, black and roiling, burning Arthur's nose as he looked around at the collection of buildings that had once been whole but were now little more than rubble. Though from the looks of it, Washington City had not been much to begin with. *This* was the capital, the heart of a nation? He shook his head and nudged his mount to the right. "You are certain Baltimore is safe?"

His friend and former superior smiled and pulled his horse to a halt. "As safe as any town could be to you when burgeoning with panicked Americans. You really think Fairchild's daughter may be there?"

Arthur shot a glance to Gates. Though he trusted General Ross with his very life and had fought directly under him in the past, it had not been his decision to share their reason for seeking information on Baltimore, and he was still unsure as to why Gates had done so. But the man looked as unflappable as ever, so Arthur shrugged. "If she is in this country, it is the most likely place to find her."

Ross nodded and scanned a row of smoldering buildings. "Cochrane and Cockburn and I have yet to discuss our next point of attack, but Baltimore is the likely target. We have received word that the Potomac is grossly unprotected, and their own newspapers are reporting the sad state of their defenses. But you will have several days to get in and out before we would march in that direction. We—"

An enormous *boom* cut him off, and Ross muttered a curse as he spurred his horse in its direction. Arthur signaled Gates and Scrubs to keep up as he followed the general outside city limits, heading toward the fort at what they had recently learned was Greenleaf Point. All along the way they heard exhausted soldiers asking in a panic if the fighting had resumed, but Ross made them no reply.

"General!" A colonel galloped their way, his face smudged with soot and one cuff singed.

Ross pulled up. "What is it, Calcott?"

"The gunpowder you instructed us to destroy…the well must not have had enough water to cover the barrels we tossed down it…someone threw in a cigar stub…" He paused to take a breath. "A score are dead or wounded, sir."

As if howling in protest of the tragedy, the wind screamed over them. Thunder roared and a crack of light split the air, momentarily blinding Arthur. The lightning hit a tree nearby that creaked and groaned and crashed its way to the ground across the road.

Their horses reared, whinnied, and tried to turn and flee. Arthur glanced at Scrubs, who surveyed the coming fury with what looked like a satisfied smile, and Gates, who eyed the churning clouds with far more sobriety.

"I think," Gates said, loudly to be heard over the wind, "that we are not going anywhere today. We had better find shelter."

With huge drops of rain pelting his shoulders, Arthur had no recourse but to agree.

Music nearly drowned out the din from the storm, but occasionally a deluge of rain would overpower the fiddle and whistle, or a rumble of thunder would shake the whole house. In those moments Thad had glanced out the window at the tree limbs littering the street and the debris gusting by and whispered a prayer for safety and protection for their homes. Then he had spun Gwyneth into his arms again for another dance.

His wife. He had been smiling so much this afternoon that he would likely strain a cheek muscle, but it couldn't be helped. The woman who owned his heart had agreed to marry him and pledged herself to him before as much of Baltimore as could squeeze into his house, and she was even now watching him from across the room with joyful eyes.

When he had married Peggy, it had been a quiet, somber affair. Just his family and one of her friends, a private ceremony, a small supper. This was more like her wedding to Arnaud had been. What a wedding *ought* to be. Pure, unbridled hope with no ghosts haunting it.

Arnaud stepped up beside him now, slapping a hand to his back. "Did General Smith grant you time off for a honeymoon?"

From his other side, Smith snorted. "If only we could afford such leisure. He may stay at home with his beautiful bride as long as this storm rages, but once it is gone, we have much work to do."

"I know." Still Thad grinned. His next days and weeks might be filled with drilling, digging, and fortifying, but he would come home each evening to Gwyneth. Able to take her in his arms whenever he pleased. To hold her and be held.

"I have special work for you two." Smith turned to face them, his countenance empty of anything but casual well wishing. "You must drill with everyone else, of course, but rather than dig, I need you to organize support from the local businessmen. We need, above all, capital. The state has little to give us, so go to the bankers, the merchants, and anyone else with sterling to spare. With Washington in ruins, I expect an outcry that will bring volunteers here in droves. We need farmers and bakers willing to feed them. Townsfolk to house them. Our every effort, our every focus must be on readying this city for the British arrival."

Thad felt a soft touch on his back, and Gwyneth slipped under his arm, resting against his side. "We can all help with that, sir. Encouraging the people to share what they have with those who will be flooding the city. Thad's mother was saying how we would do our part while the men are drilling by organizing food and shelter. And, of course, Rosie intends to have our kitchen working at its capacity."

"How fortunate she taught you to cook." Thad grinned at his bride and gave her a squeeze. She looked beautiful in her best dress, with her hair so carefully arranged, but he had to be honest. 'Twas that light of beneficence in her eyes, the determination to help others, that made her radiant.

And the way she looked up at him with that expectant warmth didn't hurt either.

"Your assistance will be much appreciated, Mrs. Lane. If all greet our efforts with such enthusiasm, then Baltimore will soon be a bastion of safety." The general smiled as he bowed slightly at the waist. "Allow me to say that Thaddeus has found himself a jewel of a wife, with a spirit as lovely as her countenance."

"Thank you, General." Her cheeks flushed a perfect pink at the compliment.

Arnaud caught Thad's gaze and winked, nodding at the window. "It looks as though we are in a lull. I had best get Jack home before the next round hits."

Thad made no argument, especially when the majority of his friends and neighbors followed suit. Within fifteen minutes the house was empty of all but those who had offered to help clean up. He knew Mother and Philly would be stealing Gwyneth away any moment to help her take the pins from her hair and change out of her dress, and his pulse thudded. But he would steal her himself for a moment first. While the others were saying their farewells to the mayor and his wife, Thad tugged her into his study and shut the door behind them.

She laughed as he swept her into his arms. "Why, Mr. Lane. There are still neighbors who needed a goodbye."

"They will understand, Mrs. Lane." He kissed her soundly, as he had been wanting to do all afternoon, until a gust of wind tore by with such force that it sounded as though the window might be pushed from its frame.

Gwyneth held tight to him, her face toward the shuddering glass. "Are your summers always so stormy?"

"Some years are worse than others. It seems that the higher the heat, the more we see. And, of course, hurricanes strike us occasionally, though not as often as in the southern states. Perhaps this is the edge of one." He stroked a hand down her back and then up again to where her hair so often tumbled down, though today none had dared escape Mother and Philly's careful arrangement. "Not exactly the sunshine you likely envisioned for your wedding day, hmm?"

"Stop it." She pulled his head down to place the caress of a kiss upon his lips. "I would have it no other way. I married *you*, which is all that matters. In God's time, according to His plan. And if He feels we need a storm to sweep us into our life together, then so be it."

That was his Miranda, straight from *The Tempest*. Though when a bolt of lightning hit somewhere nearby, the crack deafening, she jumped and all but melted into him. Apparently even Miranda had a limit to what she appreciated in a storm. "You were saying?"

Chuckling, she tilted her head back to look at him. "So it is a bit fiercer than to what I am accustomed. I still cannot regret it, especially since with all the havoc it is wreaking on the trees, it will slow the army's progress if they intend to march this direction."

"How very true."

"And if I am a trifle unsettled by it, I have no doubt I will still sleep better tonight than I have in years. In your arms." A blush stained her cheeks, but she held his gaze, absolute trust and love and expectation in her Caribbean eyes.

He could hardly resist trying to tease out an even brighter blush. "You think I intend to let you sleep, do you?"

Indeed the pink deepened, but she grinned. "I daresay you shall have to at some point, my love. You were out all night and have a full day of work ahead of you tomorrow."

Was it only this morning he had ridden home with Arnaud after verifying the defeat at Bladensburg, the destruction of Washington? Only this morning he had asked her to be his for all time? He touched the pearls resting just beneath her collarbone. "I cannot know what the future holds, sweet, but know this. Whether we have five days or fifty years as man and wife, I promise you will never, for even a moment, regret marrying me. You are the most amazing blessing the Lord has ever sent me, and I will cherish you always."

She caught his hand and gripped it. And though moisture gleamed in her eyes, the turn of her lips was brave. "And I you. May it be fifty years and beyond, Thad. Only a lifetime would be enough."

He could promise her devotion for the rest of his life, but he could only pray that would outlast the war.

Gwyneth stretched, blinked open her eyes to the soft light of early morning, and decided that if there were a more pleasant way to awake than to a kiss from one's beloved, she had certainly never discovered it. She smiled at Thad, who sat beside her, already dressed.

And beautifully so. She reached out to smooth a hand over the braid of his blue jacket. "My, look at you. I had no idea I so appreciated a man in uniform." Yesterday they had been out from dawn to dusk, clearing away storm damage. This morning, though, he must drill with all the other men of Baltimore, and apparently they all insisted on looking the part.

Chuckling, he took her hand and kissed it. "Loath as I was to wake you, I did not want to leave without telling you goodbye. Do you still want to meet me after my drills to canvas businesses for donations?"

"Of course. Ten o'clock?"

"At the bank on Lexington Street, yes." He brushed away a curl that had escaped her braid, leaned down, and kissed her again.

Yes, this was the way a day ought to begin. She wrapped her arms around him and held fast, even though she knew he must be away in a matter of minutes. They might as well make those minutes count.

When he pulled away, it was with a groan. "Blast this war for taking me from you for even a few hours. When it is all over, sweet, we are taking a trip. One where we can laze the day away in each other's arms if we so please, and go out only when we feel the desire."

A happy thought, but not their reality yet. She smiled and kissed him once more. "I shall hold you to that. And now I will shoo you out the door before you are late for reveille."

He stroked his thumb over her cheek and then stood. "Can I get you anything before I leave? A cup of tea?"

"You haven't the time for that." She smiled and scooted up to a sitting position, fluffing her pillow behind her. "Though if you would hand me my Bible, I would appreciate it."

He looked around his—their—chamber, which had yet to be put to rights after they transferred all her belongings into it. "And that would be...?"

"Still in my trunk, I think. I had no time to read yesterday. No doubt on the bottom, so I can get it. You should—"

"No bother, sweet. You stay right where you are." One stride brought him to her trunk, the soft morning light catching on the lid as he raised it. He dug through, tossing her dressing gown at her and earning a laugh when it landed on her head. She pulled her arms through the light fabric as he continued to sift through her things. "There we are." Yet he frowned.

Gwyneth lifted her brows when he merely set the tome upon the floor and bent down to examine the outside of her trunk, one hand still within it. "What is it?"

Rather than answer her, he tipped the thing backward a few inches and ran his hand along the underside. Dropping it back to the floor, he turned to her. "Do you realize this has a false bottom? There must be a compartment under the main one, though there are certainly no drawers."

"A hidden compartment? But..." Her eyes went wide as Mrs. Wesley's words drifted back to her. *Our trunks have a hidden drawer for to keep it. You've no worries, love.* "Oh, I am a dunce! Mrs. Wesley mentioned that their trunks had such a thing, but I never even thought to look for one in mine. Perhaps that is where Papa put a letter to me."

And had the Wesleys not left before she thought to even wonder about a letter, they surely could have reminded her of that.

Thad glanced at the trunk again and then at the clock. "I would help you with it, but—"

"I know." She tossed aside the bedclothes and hopped out, too excited now for lounging. "You must hurry, Thad. I will see if I can get it, and if not, you can help me after evening drills. It has waited this long."

"I suppose so." He drew her close, kissed her once more, and then headed for the door. "Ten o'clock at the bank." Pausing with a crooked grin, he made the sign for *I love you.*

She repeated the gesture. Wished, as he hovered one moment longer, that every instant could be as sweet. Then he straightened out his smile and slipped through the door.

It clicked shut behind him, and Gwyneth turned slowly toward her trunk. Anticipation gnawed at her stomach at the thought that somewhere in the bottom of it could rest words written in her father's hand. Something to help them make sense of Uncle Gates's role in this war, of what he had intended Thad to do other than keep her safe.

But she had gone through the trunk time and again. It had sat empty for months, but for a few art supplies, and when she got those out she had never once noticed anything unusual in the bottom. No latches or catches or hinges. How, then, was she to discover the secrets it held, short of breaking the thing open? And she couldn't do that either, lest such violence injure whatever might wait within.

She would be reasonable and go about this logically. Still, her hands shook as she picked up her Bible from the floor. The familiar leather under her fingers spoke reassurance into her heart. This would be her first step—spending time with the Lord and asking for His guidance. She settled back on the bed and opened the book to where she had left off two days before, in the fifth chapter of Ephesians. Hard as it was to keep her mind focused, she read and reread until the words penetrated.

Ye were sometimes darkness, but now are ye light in the Lord: walk as children of light...See then that ye walk circumspectly, not as fools, but as wise, redeeming the time, because the days are evil.

Her eyes slid closed. Oh, how long she had been in darkness, living with it always a veil over her eyes. Clouding her memory and making a mystery of what ought to be clear. Fear, always fear at her heels. But her Lord and Savior had made a light of her. He reflected His own brilliance off the mirror of her being, and now she need only point herself where He wanted her to shine.

And that last bit—these days were certainly evil. War and hatred, vengeance and greed at every turn. Did the Lord really expect them to redeem the times? What a humbling thought. That the redemption of an entire generation rested on those who were faithful to Him. That without them, there would be no redemption.

"Help me, my Lord and my God," she whispered into the still morning. "Help me to walk circumspectly, to be wise. To be in this world what You want me to be. And help me, please, to find my father's wisdom."

Her first step was to dress, her next to find places in Thad's wardrobe for all of her belongings. He had made space for her, but there had been no time yesterday to fill them. Now she straightened and arranged, trying to make her things at home without displacing his. That done, she turned to the trunk.

She ran her hands all along the exterior, the interior, the bottom and sides. Nothing. She tried poking and prodding each piece of metal to no avail. She turned it this way and that, tried the key at half and quarter turns, and stood up with a huff, glad that Rosie chose that moment to call her down to breakfast. The elder Lanes had already left for the day to do what they could in the city, so she stewed over her solitary meal, Rosie too busy in the kitchen to join her.

Soon she stood in their room again, staring at the confounding thing. 'Twas not some complicated device, merely a wooden box. Why did it refuse to give up its secrets? Nothing but strips of wood, metal fastenings, and the brocade lining meant to protect her...

"Ah!" She fell to her knees and jabbed a thumbnail under one of the tacks holding the lining in place, then another and another until the bottom section was free. Lifting it out, a smile touched her lips at the circular hole it revealed, just large enough to fit a fingertip in. Which was all she needed to do to tug up on the plank of wood and remove it too.

Almost afraid to look inside lest she find nothing but empty space, Gwyneth paused, closed her eyes, and drew in a long breath. And then she prayed, yet again, that the Lord would help them find the truth they so desperately needed.

When she opened her eyes and looked down, her breath caught. Not empty. And not, as she had feared too, filled with nothing but more coin. To be sure, there was a bag that matched the ones Mrs. Wesley had thrust into her hands that terrible day at the end of June, but her attention was snagged by the unfolded paper resting on the top of other, bound stacks.

Her hand shook as she reached for it, tears blurring her vision at that elegant, quick hand she knew so well. She had to blink and blink again before the ink stopped waving through her tears.

My Dearest Gwyn,

I haven't much time, but I had to leave you with something, some quick note. One just to say that I love you so very much. That your mother and I prayed so long and so hard for a child, and that you were our all, our everything, the perfect answer to that yearning of our hearts. That without her you are my whole world. All that matters.

No doubt you are reading this and wondering why it sounds like such a final goodbye. Perhaps, my dear one, because I fear it is so. I fear the evil away from which I am sending you will catch up with me before I can join you. And if it happens that way, so much will be called into question. But please, I beg you, trust me. Trust my loyalty, my heart, and most of all my devotion to our family. Trust that all I have done is for you, and for the future you deserve to have.

Forever your
Papa

Gwyneth swiped at her eyes, but new tears took the place of that which she wiped away. Fumbling for her handkerchief, she shook her head. Dear Papa. He had known her uncle would kill him. And she had stood there that last morning with him wondering if he had gone mad, questioning his decisions and insisting that anything that took her away from him could not be right.

She drew in a shaky breath and looked down at the letter again, her gaze falling now on the postscript at the bottom.

P.S. Please see that the two packets marked T.L. are delivered directly into the hands of Thaddeus Lane or, if he is unreachable, his parents. The one marked G.F. is for you.

She set the single page down and picked up the packet with her initials. Fingering the twine, she stared at that sheet of paper with nothing but G.F. upon it. Gwyneth Fairchild. A name she had scarcely used since coming here, but for in this house. Not for shame of him, but to protect her and his memory from whatever evil pursued them. A name she no longer even carried. Could Papa have anticipated when he scratched out that *F* that it would someday be an *L*? That she would be, by the time she read it, Gwyneth Lane?

Sniffling, she pulled loose the bow and removed the twine, setting it and the cover sheet aside. And then she frowned. The first piece of paper was no letter, no document, just a drawing she had done two years ago while he was still in France, right after Mama had fallen ill. She had asked Gwyneth to draw her something whimsical, a scene viewed through a keyhole. But the scene had been cut out and lay there separately, leaving only the drawing of the wood grain and lock intact.

Her brows pulled together. Why would Mama cut it out so? Carefully, yes, but still. Had she been planning some clever way of displaying it? No—she had sent it to Papa, Gwyneth remembered now. That was why she had asked for it. For it to be a reminder to him that if he peeked ahead, he would see a view of something other than the war in Europe, one with children dancing in gardens and Mama sitting there watching.

She flipped it over and saw that Papa had written a date upon the back, along with a second one, two weeks after the first. Odd.

The rest of the stack was equally baffling. Letters to Mama he had written over the years, but none from her to him—wouldn't those have been the ones he kept? More of Gwyneth's drawings, most of them intact but a few others with sections cut out and dates upon the back. A copy of his will, which she hadn't the heart or clarity of mind to read through right then.

Shaking her head, she put that stack down and picked up the two for Thad. She would take them down to his desk in his study. But when she pushed to her feet, the top bundle slid, the twine gave way, and she let out a small scream as she envisioned the entire stack flying free. Grabbing at it, she managed to keep all but the first two sheets in order.

Those two leaves went fluttering, the second one catching a draft from the open window and dancing before her for a moment, light winking at her through another cutout. She caught it up, tempted to frown at yet another sheet with an open design in the center of it. But the writing scratched on this one made her breath catch.

Master mask. Copy to T.L. following letter of Jan. 12

Letter of January…gasping, she bounced to her feet and flew down the stairs, her aim Thad's study. This, she knew, was where he kept the letter from her father. The one dated the twelfth of January. He had told her that any time she wanted to read it again, she had only to ask and he would unlock…

"Blast." She tried the drawers of his desk, but all were secured. And the chime of the clock on the mantel made her spin around with wide eyes. How had two hours flown by already? She was late for her rendezvous with him; she certainly hadn't the time to search for a key. Which he likely carried on his person anyway, knowing him.

Well, then. She would find her husband first and then they could solve this puzzle together. The mask still in hand, she turned on silent slippers and left the study to go down the hall and out the door.

And straight into the arms never meant to hold her, with the mocking smile of her worst enemy right behind.

Thirty

"G wyneth! My darling." Arthur pulled her tight against him, not caring that they were on a public street with her uncle and Scrubs as an audience. The relief, the utter joy that pounded through him overcame any other thoughts.

Until he realized, when she pulled free, that she was as stiff as a saber, and her wide eyes were latched, unblinking, upon her uncle.

Gates brushed him aside and embraced her next, though she looked just as unyielding in his arms. Shock, perhaps? That would explain the glaze over her eyes. "My darling girl. You cannot know how good it is to see you safe and well. We feared the worst."

"You..." She must indeed be shocked, the way her words seemed to have escaped her. She swallowed, shook her head, and stepped away, her gaze flicking to Scrubs before going back to Arthur. "What are you doing here?"

Caution cast the slightest shadow on Arthur's joy. He reached for her hands, but she took another step back. She had a crumpled piece of paper in her grip, and her face had gone so pale...

Well, she certainly hadn't known they were looking for her and had likely given up on anyone searching her out. Arthur smiled and let his hands fall to his sides. "We have been seeking endlessly for you, my love."

"We?" Those luminous eyes stared at him in utter disbelief.

Understandable. So far as she was aware, he scarcely knew her uncle. "Indeed. After—oh. My darling, we have bad news." He looked over to Gates.

The man's expression was softer than he had ever seen it as he reached out and clasped her arm. "About your father."

She swallowed and tried again to pull away, but Gates held fast to her fisted hand, the one with the paper in it. "I know." Her voice quaked a bit but was otherwise strong. "The news made it here eventually."

How Arthur ached to draw her near again, to assure her that despite probably thinking herself abandoned, they had never, for one moment, given up on finding her. "I am so sorry. We looked everywhere for you, all over England and the Continent. Your uncle and I pooled our resources, and when I told him a lad at the docks had spotted you—"

"You?" A host of emotions flew through her eyes, too fleet of foot for him to follow. When they came to a rest, her face had gone blank again. She shook her head. "I don't understand. Why would you go to such trouble?"

He breathed a laugh and reached halfway for her again before stopping himself. She was too surprised to respond. He must give her a few minutes to believe her eyes and let her move toward him next. "Why would I not? You are my betrothed. I would turn over the earth itself to find you."

"Betrothed?" Her eyes went wide. "Sir Arthur, I…I am not."

"But of course you are." Wishing he had made this trip alone, he edged closer so he could pitch his voice down. There was no hope Gates would not hear, of course, but perhaps the boy behind him would at least not catch it. "I asked you to marry me, and you said yes."

Gone was the blank look, and he almost wished it back when pity took its place. "I am so sorry. It never occurred to me you would think that after I left as I did. My father—"

"Did not give his blessing. I assumed as much, but that hardly changes the fact that you had accepted."

"Of course it would." Her attention shifted, and she snatched at the paper Gates had just taken from her hands. "Uncle!"

"What is this?" He looked over the mangled sheet with little interest. "Rubbish you were throwing out?"

Arthur swore his heart stopped beating. What did she mean, that of course it would change things? She was his betrothed. She was *his*. He had come halfway around the world to find her.

But she paid him no mind at all, reaching instead for the paper again. Gated stepped away and unfolded it, grunting at the bizarre shape upon it. "Where did you get this, Gwyneth dear?"

'Twas as if someone doused her in ice water. She went utterly still and stood up straighter. "I found it amid my things. I haven't any idea what it is."

"Your father must have slipped it in by mistake. Something we use on occasion, nothing for you to worry yourself over." He proceeded to rip it once, twice, thrice and again until he had only a pile of pieces that he then tossed into the brisk wind.

Arthur felt himself dangerously close to fracturing as surely, especially when she lurched after those shreds with the excitement she had sorely lacked when he had lurched for her.

Gates caught her round the waist with a laugh. "Darling child, do not fuss so. I realize you would cherish anything from your father, but that was worthless, I assure you. And surely he sent other mementos with you?"

She shook now as she wrenched away from him. "A letter assuring me he loved me and a few drawings I had done for him over the years. That is all, and you just destroyed some of it."

Gates snapped straight, back to the cool man Arthur had come to know. "Enough, Gwyneth. You will have no shortage of things from your father once we are safely home. Now go pack your things. Quickly, we have no time to lose."

"No."

"Pardon?"

"You heard me, Uncle. I am not going anywhere."

Arthur stepped forward, trying to tell himself that whether she still wanted him or not, her safety was the most important thing, and so they must get her away posthaste. Thinking, really, that if he could just have a few moments with her, now or later, he could tell her how he loved her and convince her that she wanted to honor the bond they had made. That whatever these Americans had filled her mind with, it was wrong. "Gwyneth, please. You are not safe here. We must get you home to England."

She clutched her middle again, looking as though she might be ill. "Please go. I am sorry you came all this way searching for me because I am not leaving. I am—"

"Playing the fool is what you are." Gates grabbed one of her wrists and gave her a brisk tug toward the street. "Now come. If you will not go in and get your things like a reasonable child, then you will come away with nothing, but come you will."

"I will *not*!" She struggled against him, pulling, slapping at his arm, even trying to kick him in the shin. Which, when he sidestepped her, nearly sent her tumbling. Arthur jumped in without having any plan but to help, whatever that might mean. First to keep her from hitting the ground, but she certainly didn't thank him for catching her. Nay, she elbowed him in the stomach and stomped upon his toes.

Scrubs, blast the boy, just stood there with his hands shoved in his pockets and that stoic look upon his face. "I don't think she wants to go, gents. Not that such a thing ever seems to stop you British."

Gwyneth kicked at her uncle again, her eyes wild as she tossed her head around. Arthur knew, when she sucked in a breath, that she would scream and likely bring half of Baltimore down upon them.

"Thad!"

The name struck some chord, but Arthur hadn't time to consider why before someone shoved him aside. He caught a blur of blue and white that focused into a man of incredible height bounding past. Somewhere in his mind it crystallized that this must be Thaddeus Lane, whose house they were in front of, even as said man slammed a fist into Gates's face.

For a second, as Arthur righted himself, he had to fight back a smile. Until, that is, Gwyneth wrapped her arms around the man. Not to restrain him, but to bury her face against the crossed straps of his uniform.

Gates staggered back, a curse spilling from his lips. He wobbled a bit, a hand to his face, and then he shook his head and pulled out his sidearm.

The American had his pistol out and leveled at Gates's heart before the elder man had his halfway raised. Arthur could see only his profile, but that was enough to reveal the man's pulsing jaw.

Gates cursed again. "Put your weapon down, man. I am her uncle."

Mr. Lane didn't relax so much as a degree. "And I am her husband."

"Her *what?*" Arthur had been reaching for the pistol Ross had lent him, figuring to show the Yank they outnumbered him, but at that he froze. He turned to a block of ice until a long-dormant fire ignited in the pit of his stomach and melted away his control, leaving him pulsing with raw fury. Surely the gaze he turned on Gwyneth shot sparks. "Your *husband?*"

If possible, she moved even closer to the man's side. "Yes."

"By thunder!" Not since Europe had his vision blurred like this, had he felt each beat of his heart with excruciating clarity. "You mean to tell me I spent the last four months chasing a faithless—"

"Now see here—"

"Stop, Thad. Please." Gwyneth rested her hand on the man's chest. "He has a right to his anger. Sir Arthur, it never once occurred to me that you would look for me so long. We were little more than acquaintances."

The fire burned hotter, and his fingers twitched over the borrowed weapon at his side. "You could not have been here more than three months. What in blazes made you think it wise to marry him?"

Her cheeks flushed, though the glint in her eyes said it was not from embarrassment. "I knew you half that long—"

"And *we* would have enjoyed a lengthy betrothal as we became better acquainted." Arthur spun away, grasping for the reins of his temper as he tried to focus on the facts, but they all blurred together in a maelstrom of betrayal. He pivoted back to them, shaking his head. "You have disgraced your family and dishonored your father. Did you consider that amid whatever rubbish with which this Yankee has filled your mind? You married an *American*. An American *soldier*. One fighting against the very men your father once commanded!"

Her face remained clear, but her fingers curled around the white strap across Thad's chest. "I married a good man. One I love with all my heart."

"This is absurd." Gates stepped forward, his pistol still at the ready.

"I am certain that after we have the chance to enjoy a reasonable discussion, you will regret this hasty decision, but we haven't the time to debate it now. We must get you to safety. Surely even Mr. Lane can see the wisdom of that."

Mr. Lane urged Gwyneth behind him and adjusted his grip on his sidearm. From the glint in his eyes as he glared at Gates, Arthur had to wonder what the man might have done had the lady not been present. "She is not going anywhere with you."

Gates put on that small, patronizing smile. "I have only her best interest at heart, and I will do whatever it takes to see her safely out of this city and country in that interest."

Lane glanced from Gates to Arthur to Scrubs as if taking their measure, his narrowed eyes going wide when they landed on the boy. "Will?"

Arthur turned in time to see Scrubs swallow. His hands were fisted at his side. "How are they?"

Gwyneth must have asked a question of Lane, who said, "Reggie's cousin, the one who was impressed." Looking again at Scrubs, he said, "We thought never to see you again. Your mother is fine, as are your sisters. Reggie has seen to it."

Scrubs's nod was barely perceptible. "Thank him for me, Thad. Please."

On another day, the coincidence might have seemed too much. This other, smaller betrayal might have pierced—that Scrubs had obviously known who Thaddeus Lane was since the first mention of him two days ago in Annapolis but had said nothing. Just now, though, it was no more than a bee sting in the face of a cannonball.

Arthur turned toward his horse before the thunder of blood burning through his veins could consume him anymore. "We are finished here, Gates. Leave her to her fate. Scrubs, come. Now." He withdrew his pistol to punctuate the command, lest the boy get any ideas of staying. No longer was he in any mood to indulge the lad in dreams of freedom.

He sensed Gates's hesitation, but the man muttered something to his niece—or perhaps her *husband*—and followed, as did Scrubs. Followed him onto their mounts, down the street, and around the corner. But where Arthur would have turned left to head out of the city, Gates signaled him to the right.

Thinking the older man wanted to scout out the town for Ross while they were there, Arthur made no argument. If he opened his mouth now, he might spew fire. Best to clamp his lips shut and trot along, taking note of all he saw.

People were bustling about, nearly all the men in uniform, with scads of women bearing armfuls of food and all headed the same direction. Combined with the fortifications they had noted outside the city when they finally got around all the downed trees across the roads, it painted a picture of people doing all they could to prepare for a coming attack.

Not exactly what Ross had said they could expect. There was no panic, no disheartening from the destruction of their capital. Perhaps, as he heard someone else suggest, they would do better to march next to Annapolis.

When Gates stopped before a large house and dismounted, Arthur realized he had led them away from the businesses and port area into a section of the city filled only with similar elegant residences, the sign on the post reading *Lexington Street*. "Gates?"

"Keep your mouth shut, Hart. And, Willis, if you so much as fall a step behind between now and when we regain the camp, you will receive a bullet in your retreating back."

Arthur dismounted, not so much as looking at Scrubs. He merely followed Gates to the door and stood there while he knocked upon it.

A Negro woman answered, and Gates didn't bother with a smile. "Are the Mercers in?"

Mercer. Where had he…? Annapolis. The house he had assumed Gates had chosen by accident. That had belonged to a Mrs. Mercer. Obviously, a family he knew, and well enough to find both their homes with ease.

The woman nodded, stepped aside to let them in, and led them into a receiving room. Arthur looked around, noting the expensive furnishings, all unquestionably imported from Europe. Whoever this Mercer was, he was doing well for himself.

Minutes later footsteps sounded in the hall, and Arthur turned to find a young man probably around his own age standing in the doorway. He wore a finely tailored suit of clothes bordering on dandy and a deep frown.

"Father? What are you doing here? We agreed I would handle—"

"Not now, Nathan. I need you to tell me everything you know about Thaddeus Lane."

All Arthur could do was sink uninvited into a chair and wonder if anything left in the world was what it seemed.

By the time Thad had slammed the door and led Gwyneth into the drawing room, the shaking had come upon her so badly that he had to scoop her up to get her the last few feet to the couch. "Oh, sweet." He settled onto the cushions with her in his lap, holding her tight. "He is gone. You are well. Everything is all right."

She shook her head against him, drawing in a deep breath obviously meant to restore her control. And when that failed, then another. "No. He was here. He was right outside, and I did nothing. I just stood there."

"'Tisn't what it looked like from where I stood." He hugged her even tighter and let his eyes close. Let it all flash through his mind again. The empty walk in front of the bank at ten o'clock, that unshakable feeling he must hurry home to find her, and then seeing her fighting against two grown men. A shudder overtook him too. "The struggle was only over your leaving with them? Gates did not seem to know you knew what he had done?"

She shook her head as she curled her fingers into the fabric of his jacket. "They assumed I didn't even know Papa was dead. I said the news had reached us, which is true enough. Though I—"

"You did exactly right." Had she made an accusation, no doubt Gates would have had that pistol aimed at her head in half a second, and he would not have hesitated to shoot her. Thad knew that down to his very core, otherwise he never would have let the man walk away— but he could not risk Gwyneth's life. There would be another chance to apprehend her uncle.

"No. I did not." Steadier now, she sat up enough to look him in the eye. "I figured out the trunk, and Papa has much in there for you. The top sheets came loose, and there was a mask, a cutout shape to go over that letter he sent you. It had a note on it indicating he had sent you a duplicate that must never have made it to you. I had it in my hand, Thad, and Uncle took it. He ripped it to shreds and then tossed it to the wind."

His heart lurched. A mask. Of course. He ought to have known. Not that knowing would have helped him without the actual one in hand. And not that any of it mattered in the face of his wife's distress. He cupped her cheek and soothed the pad of his thumb over it. "But there is other information he included? We needn't worry about one mask then."

She shook her head, trailing the pointer finger of her right hand over his chest in a dip, a curve, an angle. "The rest will likely make no sense without the instructions. I know how my father did things. He would not send anything, even hidden, that could be easily understood by anyone to come across it. The key is in that letter, I know it. But without the mask…"

Her finger returned to its original position and then began trailing along again. In the same pattern. Thad glanced down at her hand and then up to her clouded eyes. And he nearly cried out "Eureka!" as Father was wont to do in his laboratory. Standing with her in his arms, he grinned. "I don't think we are without it at all, sweet."

"Pardon?"

Why waste time on words? He merely carried her to her *secretaire*, set her carefully down on the chair, pulled a blank sheet of paper in front of her, and put a pencil in that twitching hand. "Draw."

"Draw? Thad this is hardly the time." But her fingers closed around the pencil. And how could it then do anything but what that shrouded part of her mind told it? A sweep, a curve, a sharp angle.

He leaned over to watch her, planting a kiss upon her head. "That is my girl. You know what it looked like. You never need more than a glance to duplicate something. Let it come."

She looked down at her hand with a wide-eyed gaze. As he watched, realization dawned. And if for a moment he feared that conscious thought would make her freeze, he needn't have worried. That light of recognition caused only a pause, and then she bent over the paper and increased her speed. Within seconds she had drawn a complete mask, and even the slightly off-center rectangle around it that must indicate the size of the paper. It looked right to him, the same size as the letter in his desk.

"I need a blade."

He pulled out his knife and set it beside her. "I will fetch the letter."
He ran out, ducking through the door and down the hall to his study. It
took him only seconds to grab the key from its place on the lintel and
insert it in the drawer, to pull out the letter from Fairchild, and then to
retrace his steps. By the time he arrived at Gwyneth's elbow, she was
putting his knife back down.

He handed her the letter and she put it behind the mask. And
together they read.

I know

I can trust you

to do what is right with

this bit of news.

I have always been against

this war but now I have

disturbing

information about my

Julienne's brother

Gates

and his son

there in America.

They are stealing

seized

goods from your north

bound for England

selling them and using

funds to purchase

slaves

"Good heavens." Thad shook his head while she flipped the letter over and reapplied the mask. Before they continued reading, he

said, "They are using the war to fund the slave trade. Stealing from the North to sell to the South."

"And stealing from England too." She rested her head in her hand, her breath coming out tremulously. "With a son. He and Aunt Gates have never had children, which means he...he has an American son. One in the slave trade."

Her thoughts galloped across her face, her question obvious. Thad shook his head. "It couldn't be him. Mercer may not be our favorite person, but—"

"When I first saw him, I thought he was Uncle Gates. Not because they looked so much alike, but because of the way he moved, his demeanor. Something about him." Her gaze went vulnerable. "Tell me it is impossible, Thad. Tell me you know his father, and he is the very image of him."

Would that he could. "From what I have gleaned, they moved to Maryland from one of the Carolinas when Mercer was very small. I did not meet him until I moved to Baltimore. His mother is a widow." Or, if Gwyneth's suspicions were right, she merely claimed to be.

She forced out a shaky smile. "Well. I imagine Papa knew this son's name and will mention it somewhere."

At that cue, they kept reading. About Fairchild's fear of the lengths Gates would go to for his greed, fear that Gwyneth was in danger. That the general would be sending his daughter to Thad with all his evidence of Gates's crime, and that it began in a code using as key the book Ben had sent him.

"What book?" He straightened, looking around as if the answer would be written upon the walls. He could ask his father, of course, and no doubt he would remember without a single hesitation—books being top priority, after all. But who knew when he and Mother would be home?

Gwyneth shuffled through the papers on her desk, the stack of drawings that had grown so deep. She went all the way to the bottom, to that first one she had drawn her first night here, of her father's study with its lines of shelves.

Her breath came out in a startled huff, and she tapped that strange shadow at the bottom, the one with the scalloped edge. The edge that now looked so familiar. "It is the mask. I must have seen it, must have known...oh." Her eyes slid shut as her fingers fisted. "The night before Papa told me I must go. It was out on his desk, and we heard Uncle come in. He put it away so very quickly, when usually he had not bothered with such things around Uncle Gates. A book had been out too. This one." Her finger moved to the drawn shelf and tapped a tome that looked to be sitting an inch farther out than the others.

Thad breathed a laugh as he read the French title. "Of course it is. What *but* Lavoisier would my father ever send to his dear friend? One moment." He dashed out to his library cum laboratory and quickly located the volume of *Méthode de Nomenclature Chimique* that Father had made certain he had on his shelves. When he spotted a second, identical-if-well-worn copy on the table, he grabbed that one too.

When he returned, Gwyneth was not in her chair, though he heard her step on the stair. She came in with her arms laden with paper, of which he happily relieved her, though the sheer mass made him shake his head. "Thunder and turf, let us hope it is not *all* encoded, or we will not get through it for years to come."

"Papa was an orderly sort. He likely put the most important things on top." She pulled out the first page, which was filled with numbers rather than letters. From the expression on her face, Gwyneth's father had certainly not given her the lessons in cryptology Thad's father had given him. "Can you make sense of this?"

"Not at a glance, but it is a simple methodology." He tapped the first combination of numbers. "The first number is for the page, the second for the line, the third for the word on the line."

"And when there is a fourth number?"

"The letter in the word, which he would use to spell out words not in the book, such as names." He sighed. "Of course, this will be in French."

She angled a grin up at him. "Do not tell me that cows you, my love. I have heard you speaking French with Arnaud."

"Very little." He leaned over and kissed the tip of her nose. "We will leave that part to you, who can no doubt translate French to English in your sleep."

She smiled and rested her hand on the Lavoisier. "Should we start now or head out to the banks as planned?"

"The banks will be there in an hour or two. We have waited long enough to know your father's mind. You work from the top down, and I will work from the bottom up."

It was tedious business, full of flipping and counting and note taking, especially laborious any time Fairchild had had to spell out a word. But with two of them at work, they made good progress. Once the entire sheet had been deciphered into French, Thad scooted their page to Gwyneth. "If you would, my darling."

Though she flashed him a smile, anxiousness tinged it. "Certainly." With a deep breath, she scanned ahead and then began. "'I pray you are in receipt of my letter and the mask you need to unravel its message about my wife's brother's schemes. I send this information to you, good sir, because I know the legacy your parents would have passed to you, and I know too the esteem in which you are held by all who know you. Most of all, I know you seek first and foremost the will of the Lord. I believe this war to be one of vengeance rather than justice, and though I have done all I can here, Gates's influence runs too deep. Yet his motives for continuing the war are pure avarice and malice.'"

She paused, swallowed, and shook her head before continuing. "'If you are reading this letter, it is because my daughter has safely arrived at your home. I pray you, look after her and keep her out of the clutches of her uncle, who would destroy her and any other of my family who gets in his way. I know in my heart you will fast become friends and have a feeling more could easily develop between you. If so, know you have my blessing. If not, dismiss this as the rambling of a desperate old man who only wants his precious child to be safe and happy.'"

Thad rested his hands on her shoulders and gave them a long, gentle squeeze. He could not fathom how the man had suspected what would happen when he scarcely knew Thad except through his parents' letters. But how wonderful that he had.

Gwyneth cleared her throat and swiped at her cheeks. "'I have also sent with Gwyneth a copy of my will, wherein you will find that your parents have been named as her guardians, unless Gates has passed away before they can come for her, in which case my elder brother would receive the guardianship. I have left instructions with my solicitors in England that they are not to read that section of the will unless Gwyneth is present, so if she is with you, then my family is still unaware of this stipulation. I trust you can imagine why I would make it.'"

Her eyes fell to the final few lines. "And here he says that the rest of the evidence will either use the corresponding masks or a dictionary which he sent to your father a year ago as a key."

He circled his thumb over the base of her neck and let a loose tendril curl around it. "Good. Not so much spelling out will be required."

But he already knew what the information in the documents would tell him—that he had to stop Gates. Stop the war, stop the crime. And pray, with all his being, that the Lord would heal the nation this man would rend asunder.

Thirty-One

Arthur stared into the fire long after the camp behind him settled into silence. He watched each dancing flame, each pop of spark. And he wondered which tiny ember might land upon him next and set him off like a keg of gunpowder. That was what his Uncle Hart had called him, was it not? Volatile. Dangerous.

No. His hand fisted against his leg, and he tamped that lid back down, if a keg he was.

You are not brave, his uncle had declared the very day he was knighted. *You are simply a fool whose irresponsible behavior happened to save a few lives this time. But such folly must cease, Arthur, if you are to be my heir.*

He had never liked the viscount. Not as a lad, and certainly not when the man cast a shadow on what ought to have been his proudest moment. Not when he insisted Arthur sell his commission and stay in England to familiarize himself with the estates, though all he had wanted, once healed from his wound, was to rejoin his comrades. But duty was ingrained too deep. Staying was a necessity, not an option. Though still he had tried to argue the point of his folly.

And still his uncle's reply was burned into his mind. *Face the facts, boy.*

Face the facts.

One—he had charged into a situation with a reckless abandon.

Two—it was nothing but good-fortune that turned the tide in his favor and won him accolade rather than death and dishonor.

Three—his happy acceptance into society had been more due to his cousin's death and his presumed inheritance of a title than his own earning of a knighthood.

Four—he had apparently charged in without reason yet again when it came to Gwyneth.

He was a fool. A fool who had chased an illusion halfway around the world and now would face the consequences for it. *Those* were the facts.

"Have you finished brooding yet?" Gates's voice came quiet as a ghost, his form but a shadow as he settled beside Arthur on the log.

He shot the man a glare.

Gates deflected it with the arch of a single brow. "I have given you two days. Now remember yourself and move on. This petulance does not become you."

Petulance? Arthur's fingers dug into the cloth of his breeches. "How very generous of you to 'give me' two days, sir, while you have been off visiting with your *son*."

Gates's low laugh sounded menacing in the heavy night air. "You will judge me? Judge me for doing what all men do when they are strapped to a cold, unfeeling wife?"

Arthur kept his gaze on the dancing fire. If he were to describe either of the Gateses as cold and unfeeling, it would not have been the missus. "I will judge you, sir, for your hypocrisy. You, who say you despise all Americans, yet—"

"I never said they did not have their purposes, just that they ought not be governing themselves. But my son is not the one with whom you take issue. 'Tis my niece who has you so riled."

"Because she is no more constant than you!" He clamped his lips shut, grateful he had at least had the wherewithal to make his accusation quiet, if ill-advised. Frustrated and angry as he might be, these days in camp had proven that Gates was held in a rather fearful respect. Those great men, the men to whom Arthur had been trained to listen above all, listened in turn to *him*.

Gates's chuckle grated on his every nerve. "She is nineteen, Sir Arthur. An impressionable young woman with a brain filled with nothing but images of pretty things. Is it so shocking that her head was turned when she was without proper guardianship?"

Arthur kept his mouth sealed tight.

Gates leaned forward, as if seeking the heat from the fire, though the night had scarcely cooled to livable. "Your anger is understandable, but do not give up so easily. She will soon realize her error."

"And what will it matter if she does? She is married." Married! To think of her in the arms of that man, to see her looking at Thaddeus Lane as she ought to have been looking at him…

"Again, I would remind you that she is *nineteen*. Not one-and-twenty. She can make no such decisions on her own. That marriage is not legal and can easily be annulled as soon as we can wrest her free of them." His gaze now bore into Arthur. "The question is, are you going to fight for her or roll over and let them kick you like a mutt?"

Arthur sprang to his feet and strode away, out of the circle of firelight and into the towering shadows of trees. Seething, storming, stewing. And wishing, wishing he could let go the reins of his temper and rage. Wishing he could be every inch as irresponsible as his uncle had accused him of being. That he could do something stupid with no thought as to the consequences.

That he could—what? Fight for her? Why should he? Why should he want to? She wasn't worth it.

"If you will give up so easily, then you are no more constant than you accuse her of being." Gates's voice came somewhere from the shroud of trees, from somewhere in the enclosing darkness. "She was vulnerable, alone, and obviously grieving after the news reached her. Lane took advantage. Will you hold that against her?"

A hot wind gusted through the trees, shook their leaves, and set his nerves thrumming. Into his mind came the image of her eyes, so large and limpid. Gazing at him in modest adoration. Those perfect rosebud lips that he had longed to kiss from the first moment he saw her. All his friends had been as struck by her beauty as he. All had vied for her dances, for an excuse to put a hand on her waist. But he had been the one at whom she had batted those lashes and given her smiles. He had been the one with the hope of winning her. *Had* won her.

"She is yours." Gates's voice had moved, coming from the side now rather than behind, though his footfalls had been silent on the carpet of pine needles under them. "She gave her promise, and as her guardian now, that is the one I approve. Forgive her for her foolishness, Hart, and take her back. Take what is yours. We both know you want her still."

He turned away from the murmur that made it sound so base and shook his head. Beautiful as she was, as much as he longed to take her in his arms, his motive had not been only bound up in that, had it? He had been drawn to more than her face, more than her figure. He had...he had...

He hadn't even known her. He still didn't know her. He had simply been enamored with her pleasing disposition, been thrilled at the sound of her voice, and, yes, been so very attracted to her. He had wanted her to be his, wanted everyone to see that he had won the most beautiful young lady in London. He wanted the right to hold her. To kiss her.

The viscount had been right. He had chosen his bride not in the interest of the Hart line but in the interest of his bed.

Fire burned his throat, but he swallowed it back. Why should it shame him? If he had not chosen her because of her beauty, he would have chosen someone for her name or her dowry. Lust, either way. Lust for prestige, for money, or for a person herself. It was, it seemed, the only reasons to wed. Who was to say one was any baser than another?

And which of those things had influenced Lane? Was it the Fairchild wealth he sought, or merely the allure of Gwyneth herself?

"You have a noble heart, Arthur. A good heart." Gates's voice came from the other side now, though Arthur had not sensed his movement. "Surely you see how she must have been hurting. Surely you see that she is a victim to her own grief, and to the vile maneuvering of a villain who would use it against her. We must free her from him. We must save her."

Arthur turned, trying to locate Gates in the darkness. But it was too thick, impenetrable. Not so much as a shaft of moonlight softened it. "How? You saw how fiercely he claimed her, and according to your son, his parents are staying there. I daresay after we tipped our hand that they will not let her out of their sights. She will not be left alone."

"When Baltimore is under attack, confusion will ensue. And her militiaman husband will be at his post in Fort McHenry, too far away to help. His parents can be handled easily enough."

Was it hope that sparked inside him? Not quite. Hope was not so dark nor so determined. "But you know as well as I that those reports about the city's unpreparedness are mistaken. We ought to advise the admiralty against attacking. We ought—"

"We ought to advise they plan an attack from the water, toward Fort McHenry. We ought to recommend they destroy that bastion and kill all within it." How could Gates's voice be both hard and smooth? "We ought to encourage them to burn this center of commerce as they did the center of government, so that the Americans can fight no more. And when they are crushed, we can take what is ours and go home."

Arthur swallowed as he turned toward the sound of rustling to his left. The man advised an entire campaign built around personal agenda. War to fuel their own purposes. "We ought to tell them what we observed. That the Americans are stronger than our leaders think."

A scoffing laugh sounded, but from the right. "Tell them that and they will choose the easier target of Annapolis. Nay. They can handle those quickly built fortifications with no worries."

Could they? "The men are tired from all the fighting in Europe, and this heat has stripped their defenses still more."

"They are trained members of the most elite military in all the world. The Americans will pose no more a threat at Baltimore than they have anywhere else, especially after our men have rested for a week or two while the roads are cleared of trees and the fleet has moved into position."

A moment's consideration made him nod, though Gates wouldn't see it in the dark. But he was right. The motley collections of farmers could do little more to defend themselves than brandish their hoes and mound up piles of dirt. British rockets and cannons would win the day.

And when that day came, they would seize their chance. Free Gwyneth of the Lanes while her husband—if he could legally be called that—was being blown to bits along with Fort McHenry.

When that day came, she would, at last, be his.

"Amazing." Gwyneth looked out at the long line of wagons loaded with produce and at the farmers who wore smiles upon their faces and determination in their eyes. And then to Winter, who surveyed the sight before them with a satisfied sigh. "All it took to convince them to come to the city was the assurance that their horses and wagons would not be confiscated?"

Her mother-in-law nodded and looped their arms together to keep them moving toward the makeshift hospital. They each carried a basket full of rolled bandages and what medicinals they could spare. And they were only two of many women about the same business.

"It had apparently been the only thing keeping them on their farms. Thad was right."

At that, Gwyneth had to chuckle. "I imagine they are all eager to get a fair price for their vegetables anyway." Because they all knew if they did not before the British army marched through, then their choices would be to burn it all before it could be confiscated or hand it over in exchange for their lives.

It was, had always been, the way wars were waged. And yet not at all the way the Americans were running this one. She spotted a baker up on a cart loaded with breads, heading toward one of the temporary barracks dotting the landscape. A man down the street led a group of officers into his home with the words, "Welcome" and "As long as you need" drifting to her on the wind. Everywhere, all over the city, normal business had ceased. Every effort, every person was focused on preparing for the attack they all knew was coming. The two-week lull since the burning of Washington had not seen any spirits flagging. Nay, it seemed instead that each day was viewed as a blessing and a cause for redoubled activity.

"Mrs. Lane!"

They both turned to the voice and then exchanged a smile. Gwyneth had expected it to take months before she was accustomed to answering to her new name, but with as often as people called it in the last fortnight...

A young man rushed their way with a beaming smile. His gaze was on Gwyneth, though it included Winter too. "I spoke with my father last night, and he approved our contribution to the cause. Does that bring the total above the half-million mark?"

A little thrill moved through Gwyneth. When Thad had told her that the plan to pay for the fortifications rested on contributions and loans from both banks and private businesses, she had to admit to skepticism, but the people of Maryland had risen to the task. "It does, Mr. Jones, and well beyond. I do believe that will bring us to more than six hundred thousand dollars."

Mr. Jones did an impromptu jig as he laughed. "He will be pleased beyond measure. I am headed to the bank now to draft the cheque. Good day to you, Mrs. Lane. And Mrs. Lane." He reeled his way past them. "And good day to you too, Mr. Mercer."

Gwyneth froze, willing it to be some other, *any* other Mr. Mercer. Knowing, even before the expression that stole over Winter's face when she glanced behind them, that it would not be. She started forward, hoping he was merely passing down the side street and would pay them no heed.

Yet she was not at all surprised when that too-familiar figure matched his pace to hers. "Mrs. Lane."

Gwyneth gripped her basket tighter. "I believe you mean 'cousin.'" The documents Papa had sent said as much, and so much else besides. All the details of the slave trade that Uncle Gates had set up with the help of this baseborn son of his, first in foreign waters, stealing Africans from their own shores, and later, when that trade was made illegal, within the borders of the United States.

Mercer gave a small smile. "An odd discovery, was it not? Here I had resigned myself to never meeting any of my father's family. How very fortuitous that I would stumble across a first cousin in my own city."

Her back went stiff as her step picked up still more. "I daresay my Aunt Gates would not find it so."

Winter's hand found her wrist and gave it an encouraging pat.

Mercer breathed a laugh. "I suppose you did not realize your uncle was a bit of a rake, hmm?"

A rake. That would imply that Mr. Mercer's poor mother was not his only indiscretion. And why, knowing all she did about him, did that fact still make disappointment weep through her? "I did not. But I know he is a murderer."

He didn't stumble, didn't so much as falter in his stride. He merely lifted a single brow at her in the very way Uncle Gates did. "Do you now?"

She raised her chin and turned the corner with Winter, who sent her a questioning gaze. But what did it matter if she told Mercer now that she knew? The worst he could do was tell Uncle Gates, and the worst *he* could do was come for her again, which they all knew he would do anyway. He would know very well, no matter what she had said, that if Papa had sent a mask with her, he would have sent more. And he would stop at nothing to get it back, to stop them from revealing his crimes to both the American and British governments.

So she tilted her head Mercer's way, their gazes clashing. "I watched him kill my father."

His expression softened, reflecting not shock or horror, but sympathy. "That must have been difficult for you."

Her feet sprouted roots and brought her to a quick halt, forcing the others to stop with her or pass her by. "That is all you have to say?"

His face naught but a blank canvas now, he held his hands out. "What else would you like me to say? That I am surprised? I cannot. I watched him kill the man everyone thought was *my* father when I was but four, when Mercer had the misfortune to at last return from a prolonged expedition during one of Gates's visits."

She nearly reached out to touch his hand to give him comfort. She might have, had it been anyone but him. "I am so sorry."

"Why?" He met her quiet statement with a shrug. "'Tisn't as if I had ever even met my mother's husband."

"Even so. To see such violence at such a tender age—"

"I am my father's son. There was never any doubt about that. It had no great effect."

How she wanted to doubt that. Yet she didn't know if she could, given the calm acceptance in his eyes. Were some people born without compassion? Without that basic respect for life? If so, perhaps they could pass it down to their children. "None at all?"

"Well." Now he smiled again, actually smiled. "It did certainly convince me that I ought not cross my father."

She drew in a long, contemplative breath. "Is that why you take part in his schemes? For fear of him? Is that why you trade human beings as if they are cattle?"

He sent an amused glance to Winter. "Is she always so quick to make excuses for people? I cannot decide if such naïveté is charming or pitiable." The infuriating man chuckled as he looked back to Gwyneth. "I do it for the money, cousin. Gauche as that may sound to a London gentlewoman, sterling really does make the world go round."

"And what of your country?" Winter shifted, her tone regal. "Do you care nothing for it? Will you not help defend your home?"

His spine snapped even straighter, his hands clasped behind his back. "Of course I do, madam. But America's future rests in a strong economy built on agriculture and trade, which can only be achieved through cheap labor. I am supplying a need that will grow this nation, and must, in fact, lead another slave train south, out of harm's way, in the morning."

Gwyneth raised her chin. "Your father believes and plans for this trade of yours to do the opposite. To widen the chasm between North and South so that even if America wins this war, they will fracture and crumble internally."

"Hmm." He made no other reply to that, but she recognized the glint in his eyes, having seen it often enough in Uncle Gates's. Calculation. Then he nodded and took a step back the way they had come. "I will not hold you up any longer, ladies. But, cousin?"

Why had she suggested he call her that? "What?"

His smile now shone with genuine warmth—the last thing she had expected to see from him. "Know that I wish you well. I wish you all happiness with your husband."

"You do?"

"Of course." He bowed and backed away another step. "You are, after all, a full third of my family. That carries a great deal of weight with me."

Gwyneth shifted the basket of bandages again and shook her head. What an unsettling thought.

Thirty-Two

Thad tensed, held his breath, and listened. All of Baltimore must have held its breath with him, for the next signal came and seemed to echo through the streets, through the church without hindrance. His fingers tightened around Gwyneth's where he held them on the pew between them.

The British were coming. They had been waiting for days for the word to spread from gun to gun, from cannon to cannon, from town to town. And there it was, echoing over them on a Sunday, of all times, when they were all at worship.

From the pulpit Reverend Gruber eased shut his Bible and waited for the final signal shot. After its report faded, silence held for a moment. Then the minister lifted a hand. "Let us pray."

A shuffling as Bibles closed, as heads bowed. Gruber cleared his throat. "Father God, we ask every week that You will go with us as we leave these hallowed walls and head back into the world. We ask it especially today, when so many of our men must now leave this place and go to one of imminent danger." He cleared his throat again. "The Lord bless King George, convert him…and take him to heaven, as we want no more of him!"

For the only time in Thad's memory, laughter joined the chorus of "Amens," and the congregation all but surged to their feet.

Thad rose more slowly, his gaze on Gwyneth's precious face. She wore her features in a brave arrangement, lips turned in a fearless smile, eyes shining with pride. But he had felt the way her arms clung a little tighter to him each morning when he left to drill. The very same way his did to her. Because they both knew that each new day could be the one in which those signal shots rang out. They both knew each night might be their last.

She pressed to his side now, her eyes absent the tempest they so often showed but luminous. "We had better hurry home."

He nodded and then nodded again at his parents, waiting behind Gwyneth for him to lead the way from the pew.

Already the streets outside were teeming. Families in their Sunday best spilled from every direction, all in a rush. The men Thad knew to be designated couriers tore by on horseback. And from somewhere in the distance, the drums took up their cadence, calling the men to arms.

His blood pulsed in time to each beat. By the time they reached home, it seemed the world must pulse with it too. Each footfall, each galloping horse. The creak of each of his floorboards, the click of their bedroom door.

Until Gwyneth's arms came around him. Then the noise faded, and there was only her. "Oh, sweet." He held her close, closer still, until he could be sure that his nose would remember her scent even when gun smoke burned it. Until he could be sure his ears would remember the sound of her breathing even when deafened by cannon fire. Until he could be sure her vision would fill his eyes even when horror rose before him. "I love you."

"I love you." Her fingers trailed up his cheek, into his hair, urging down his head.

How many times had he kissed her now, in their three weeks of marriage? Too many to count, but not nearly enough. Never enough. Yet none of them had felt like this. Filled not so much with passion as with prayer. Not so much with desperation as with dedication. Their lips touched, held, caressed, and filled him with a strange sort of peace when she lowered back down from her toes. A kind that made him wonder how he would have had the strength to go to his rendezvous point for his rations and ammunition if she were not there, were not his wife, had not given him that very kiss.

"Gwyn—"

"Hush." Her eyes were still closed, her arm still resting against his chest. "I am giving you over to the hands of our Father."

"Ah, well. I certainly do not want to interrupt that."

She moved her lips in silent words. Then she fixed her gaze on him and rubbed a hand over his heart. "He will bring you home, safe and well. I know it."

He had no desire to argue, especially now, with the peace eclipsing the dread that had filled him for days. Reaching for her hand, he nodded. "I had better change into my uniform."

"I know." She moved aside to let him, watched him draw out the dark blue jacket he so carefully brushed clean every night, the brilliant white straps that would crisscross his chest, the matching breeches and tall black boots she herself had polished twelve hours before. He heard the whoosh of the down-filled mattress as she sat upon it. "Darling?"

"Hmm?" He shrugged out of his best jacket, the one he had worn for their wedding.

"I think I am with child."

He paused with one foot raised to remove his shoe and then hopped around so he might look at her. He told the bubble of joy threatening to burst through him to be reasonable. "You cannot possibly know that so soon."

Her grin said otherwise. "I know I cannot be certain, but there is logical hope for it, and more besides. I had a dream last night that I was."

The bubble nearly choked him. It made him want to laugh and shout. He lowered his foot before he fell. "We both know dreams are most often only—"

"I choose to believe, Thaddeus." Her smile was sure, bright, and her eyes sparkling with mischief. Daring him to argue.

As if he wanted to. He strode unevenly to the bed and scooped her up, spinning her around. "Then I choose to believe with you."

Laughing, she slapped him on the shoulder—after, that is, a longer, more exuberant kiss. "Put me down before you trip and finish getting dressed."

"Aye, aye, Captain." He planted her back onto the bed with another kiss and made quick work of changing. "Promise me you and my parents will do exactly as we planned. You will stay here and keep the house locked tight. If by chance you must evacuate, we will meet up at the inn in Randallstown."

"I know. We will. And you…" She hesitated and then sighed. "You have sent the information to the congressman about my uncle?"

He nodded, flexing the hand that had cramped after so much writing. "He will see it reaches the authorities it needs to. No matter the outcome of this battle, sweet, justice will find him. Thanks to your father."

"And to you."

He shrugged and put his hat atop his head. Part of him had wanted to keep the evidence against Gates to himself, to see firsthand that justice would be done. But that whisper in his spirit had chastised him for his pride, and he had handed it over to Arnaud to deliver to Tallmadge yesterday.

From the street below he heard a familiar shout. "Jack and Alain are here. I believe we have a few apples left yet, which ought to help you keep the little rapscallion in good spirits."

"We will be fine, and Emmy and Philly will likely come tomorrow."

"Good." They joined hands and moved together back down the stairs. They stopped in front of the open doors, where Jack had brought his usual chaos of squeals and laughter.

What was left but goodbye? But he couldn't say that. Simply couldn't. So when she came into his arms again, he tipped up her chin and borrowed the little one's tactic of lightness. "Do try and get some sleep while I am gone, will you?"

Her smile would surely carry him through the battle and home again. "I will—so that I might dream of you."

Minutes later the other farewells had been said, final kisses bestowed, and he and Arnaud walked together toward their rendezvous point. Steadily but not exactly quickly.

"Not running ahead of me today?" Despite the light words, Arnaud's tone was flat and heavy.

"No. I intend to stay by your side until we are making this return trip together in a day or two." Thad tried for a smile, tried to cling to that cloud of peace that had existed with Gwyneth. But it went dark and stormy again.

He looked to his dearest friend, hoping to find light in his gaze. But Arnaud wore a glower even more pronounced than usual. "You feel it too?"

Blast. "Something is going wrong."

"The battle?"

Was it? He could not tell. And no matter how much prayer he gave it, the only impressions to come from the Lord were that he was to continue on the set course. "I do not know."

"Well." Arnaud dragged in a deep breath and squared his shoulders. "I suppose we do not need to know. We need only to act as we ought. And pray without ceasing."

The drums beat out their amen.

⚬⚬⚬

Gwyneth flinched again at the sound of an exploding shell and the rumble beneath her feet, fumbled, again, the bread dough she was shaping into rolls, and then huffed in exasperation with herself. Shoving an annoying curl from her face with the back of her hand, she looked over to Rosie. Small consolation as it was, the woman jumped just as high as she did with each blast. "It has been six hours."

"With a shot every five minutes." Rosie shook her head and stirred the pot of stew simmering on the stove. "As long as I live I will never forget the thirteenth of September in eighteen fourteen. And the memories will not be fond."

From the table filled with drying noodles, Winter sighed her agreement. "I keep telling myself that as long as they continue shelling the fort, that means it has not fallen. And yet still I wish it would *stop*." She squeezed her eyes shut and balled her fists against the table. "Why could they not be stationed somewhere else? Anywhere else?"

Gwyneth shuddered. She had wondered the same from the

moment Bennet had returned from his scouting trip into town with the news that it was Fort McHenry being bombarded by the British fleet. But she had felt such surety that her Thad would come home, he and Arnaud both. She must cling to that. She must trust. Must choose, as she had said to Thad about her beautiful dream of a pink-cheeked baby, to believe.

And must pray the Lord didn't take her shaking hands as doubt.

She managed to form the final roll and tuck it into its pan, drape a damp cloth over it and set it aside to rise a second time. No sooner had she turned back toward the table than the door burst open, Emmy leaping through the opening with wild eyes.

The kitchen went silent long enough for a score of terrible possibilities to run through Gwyneth's mind. Then Emmy turned to Winter. "It's Philly."

Winter straightened her spine, yet her shoulders sagged. "The baby?"

Emmy nodded as she palmed away the tears clinging to her cheeks. "She's frightened something awful. Wants her daddy and you to come, Miss Winter."

"Of course." Winter spun toward the hall but then stopped, her gaze tracking upward to where Jack was, inexplicably, napping in his bed.

Gwyneth shooed her onward. "Rosie and I will stay here with Jack. You two go with Emmy."

Wasting no time on arguments, Winter nodded and ran down the hall, calling for her husband as she went. Gwyneth moved to Emmy and grasped her hand. "Assure her we will be praying. Is it—is she sure?"

Emmy shrugged and sniffled. "'Tisn't quite like the other times, I don't think. But I daresay that has made it even worse for her, not knowing what is going on. You know how those Lanes like to *know*."

The laugh that spilled forth felt at once misplaced and an immense relief. "They do at that."

A moment later Winter and Bennet charged in together, and then the trio hurried out the door with a flurry of farewells and bids for prayer.

Rosie's hands landed on her shoulders and propelled her toward the hallway. "Nothing more to do in here, child. But if you've a mind, you could read to us."

"A fine idea. Let me fetch the prayer book and my Bible." She checked on Jack while she was upstairs and smiled at the way his arm dangled off the bed, at the parting of his lips and the rhythmic rise and fall of his chest.

Another boom shuddered over them, causing Gwyneth to jump again, but the boy slept on. She shook her head and left him to his peaceful dreams, praying her own of the other night had indeed been a promise from the Lord. That come spring, she and Thad would welcome a babe into the world. Certainly it was too soon to know, to do anything more than wonder, but she would hope and believe. And if she were proven wrong, well then. She would take it instead as a promise of the future, which would require her husband returning to her.

Rosie awaited her in the drawing room, some mending already out on her lap, and Gwyneth settled in with all the calm she could muster. For the next two hours she read, pausing only a few seconds at each blast upon the fort.

Jack's cry of "Grandmama?" came at the exact moment a knock shook the front door.

Gwyneth rose even as Rosie did. "Would you fetch Jack? I daresay it is a neighbor, perhaps one with news."

Rosie nodded and headed for the stairs while Gwyneth walked to the front door. She paused when she spotted the musket resting beside it. Thad had left strict instructions, so she picked it up before wrenching the door open. Another shell struck, but this time she didn't so much as flinch. This time, it seemed somehow fitting.

At the sight of the handsome man on the porch, her fingers whitened around the gun she gripped so hard. Darting a frantic gaze beyond him, she didn't spot her uncle anywhere. And she didn't know if that was cause for relief or alarm. "What are you doing here?"

Sir Arthur doffed his hat and bowed, his somber face giving her no answers. "Our ship departs on tomorrow's tide. Am I not permitted a farewell?"

"Of course. Farewell, Sir Arthur." She swung the door shut.

It caught on the boot he had wedged in the frame, and his sigh sounded exasperated. "Really, Gwyneth, do I not deserve a mere five-minute audience?" He pushed the door open again and stuck his face in, looking, now, more like the man who had caught her eye on that first turn through Hyde Park, with his golden curls falling over his forehead and that boyish grin in place.

But that didn't change that it was the wrong grin, the wrong man for the here and now. She didn't go so far as to point the weapon at his chest, but she raised it enough to make certain he saw it. "'Tisn't a good time, sir."

"'Tis the only time I have. Please, Gwyneth. I want to give you a letter I found. From your mother to your father."

The thought of something in her mother's hand…but she shook her head and leaned on the door. Not enough to hurt him, but to make her point. "How would you have such a thing?"

"It was in your father's study. I found it when I was looking for some clue as to where you might be."

He had rummaged through Papa's things, in Papa's study? Now she pressed harder on the door. "Then hand it to me and be on your way."

"Please." The word barely made it past his clenched teeth, and his eyes reflected pain. His attempt at a smile looked more like a grimace. "Much as it offends my pride to have to ask for it outright, I need to rest for a few minutes. I have ridden at a breakneck pace through a rather treacherous twenty miles, and my old injury has flared up. I need a soft seat for just a few minutes so I might stretch it out. And a glass of water. I beg you."

She considered telling him to help himself to a porch step, but when he tried and failed at controlling a wince, compassion won out. With a heavy sigh, she lowered the musket and opened the door. "Five minutes, and I will tell you now that I am not alone."

"Of course you are not." He limped his way in, and she shut the door quietly behind him. Turned, jumped, and cursed her own stupidity when he tugged the gun away from her. She made a lunge for it, but the pistol in his hands stopped her cold. "You have here still the slave woman and the boy. I suggest you tell her to take him to the kitchen for a snack, my dear."

Tears stung her eyes when she considered the *or what* of the situation. Never would she have thought Sir Arthur capable of harming a woman or a child, but the dark glint in his eyes shouted that she knew him very little. *Dear Lord, protect us. Protect Rosie and Jack, and protect me. If Thad learns of this…*

Her heart ached. She nodded when he waved the pistol at the ceiling and went to the base of the stairs. "Rosie, would you take Jack to the kitchen for a few minutes?"

"I sure will," the woman called back, sounding that particular kind of happy that Jack always brought.

"Good. Now, a private audience, if you please."

She gave him a wide berth as she passed him, keeping her hands fisted in the fabric of her dress lest he see her trembling, and led him toward the drawing room. "Where is my uncle?"

"He will be along shortly." Cold metal touched her neck and then trailed down to her shoulder, sending a shiver the rest of the way down her spine. "You are looking lovelier than ever, Gwyneth. I hadn't the chance to say so the other week."

She stepped away from the gun barrel once she was inside the drawing room and closed the door behind them so Jack wouldn't wander in. And she prayed her eyes shot fire enough to burn him. "It must be the glow of love."

With the Lane musket slung over his shoulder by its strap, Sir Arthur grunted and held out a piece of paper. When she lifted her brows, he waved it. "The letter. I did not fabricate it, and I have no use for it. I took it for the sole purpose of giving it to you. I thought… I thought you would appreciate something your mother had written."

His tone softened with that last part, but she had no intention of falling for that again. She snatched the letter from his hand without drawing any closer than she had to and nearly choked on a sob at Mama's flowery, beautiful script. Hardly caring where Sir Arthur went, she moved to the chair at her *secretaire* and sank onto it as she flipped the page open. *Mon amour…*

"You see?" His voice came from just behind her, quiet and imploring. "My thought was only for you. For finding you and keeping you safe."

No doubt it had been, and for that she was truly sorry. But still. She read through the letter, blinking back tears. And then she narrowed her eyes. The date. And the gap between *notre* and *fille…*

"You cannot know how I feared. Finding your father was terrible enough—"

"You found him?" That brought her gaze up and around.

He was looking at the ground as he nodded. "I feared you were next. I feared his murderer would be looking for you."

"He was." Hands strangely steady now, she opened the drawer and pulled out the keyhole drawing she had done for Mama. She set it down upon the letter. "And you brought him directly to me."

Thirty-Three

Arthur frowned and gripped his pistol tighter, but her words still made no sense. "Pardon?"

She didn't even look at him. Her focus remained on whatever she was doing with that letter, smoothing down the drawing overtop it. "Uncle Gates killed my father. I saw him do it. I was outside the study." Finally she turned her eyes on him, and he wished she hadn't. They were too bright, too intense. "Papa sent me here to escape him, and you brought him directly to my door."

"Balderdash." Much as he didn't like Gates, he couldn't believe the man murdered his own brother-in-law. Couldn't. Because if it were true...nay, he wouldn't even consider it. "It was an American spy who did it."

When did she learn to give a look like that, one that said in a mere second that he was either a liar or a fool? "My uncle's theory, I presume?"

Rather than need to answer, he peered over her shoulder at the letter. And frowned again. "What have you done there?"

"What my father did when Mama first sent it to him, I think. The dates match." She adjusted the drawing slightly, so that the keyhole cut from the drawing revealed only certain words from the letter.

He moved to the side a step so that he could see both her profile and the page. So that he could watch her wash pale as she read, and then read himself to learn why. And mutter a curse. Both at the words and the tears that slipped onto her cheeks.

Gwyneth shook her head, sending a red-gold curl bouncing. "I suppose I had hoped that this never touched her, that she never realized what her brother had done, but it would seem she was the one who saw it first."

It. That Gates was a criminal. One who had funded his son's slave trade with goods siphoned from the spoils of war. Odd. Arthur had no trouble believing this part and found it changed very little his opinion of the man.

He shrugged and slid over to the window when commotion from the street came through on the breeze. Perhaps Gates had caught up with Scrubs and was returning. "I fail to see why your uncle's behavior is so reprehensible. He is hardly the first man to take excess for himself and turn a profit from it. Rather ingenious, really."

"Would you have done it?"

A different question entirely. "No, but…" What was that the people on the street were saying?

"…from my brother himself. Ross is dead, and the British on land are in confusion."

The news shook Arthur far more than the next blast of a shell against the fort walls. Ross, dead? "No."

Gwyneth sighed. "Perhaps there is hope for you yet, then."

"What?" He snapped his head her way and realized she was still talking about her uncle. "Darling, it is best if you realize now that the world is an ugly place. Trying to fight it will bring you nothing but trouble."

"Trying to fight it is our only choice. If we do not, then the times will be beyond redemption."

"Perhaps they already are." He strode to the door when he heard childish laughter from the hall, but the slave and child walked by without pausing. Good. "Our only recourse is to look after ourselves."

"How very sad that you think so."

"I have never seen evidence to indicate otherwise." He rushed to her side when he saw she had drawn out a sheet of paper. "What do you think you are doing?"

She blinked up at him in a way so very similar to the demure way that had won his heart, yet now it was colored with condescension. "I am going to draw to calm my nerves. Is that acceptable, sir?"

If that was *all* she did… "I am watching you. If you try to write a note—"

"Saying what? I have no idea what you are planning."

And he intended to keep it that way. Folding his arms across his chest, he leaned against the side of her desk to keep a close eye on her drawing.

Gwyneth didn't so much as glance up at him. She just pulled out a pencil and started scratching lines onto the page. "If you want evidence of mankind's potential, you should have seen this city the past few weeks. All normal business came to a halt and every citizen was working together in unity. I have never seen the like. Master and slave in the trenches beside one another, rich and poor rolling bandages side by side, every baker and cook making as much as they could to take to the soldiers, families opening up their homes to house those newly arrived—it was inspiring."

"It was self-serving. They knew they must work together for even a chance of survival."

"When is that *not* true? When would we *not* benefit more from harmony? Yet so rarely do people choose it. Too often they prefer to terrorize their neighbors, to kidnap and steal and kill." She shot him a glare.

He squelched the urge to hide his pistol. Perhaps this plan of Gates's had chafed, this need for duplicity and trickery, but Arthur had not been able to come up with a better way to free her of the Americans' influence. "Things will look different to you once you are home and away from these people. You will see then that we are only trying to protect you and return you to where you belong."

"I *am* where I belong. With my husband."

That word again. He gripped the gun tighter. "He is not your husband. You married him illegally, without the signature of your guardian. No court of law would uphold the vows."

With a few quick strokes of her pencil, her own face appeared on the paper with a wistful, resigned expression upon it. How did she do that so effortlessly? "First of all, it would never *go* to court and is perfectly legitimate in the eyes of God, which is what matters. Secondly, his parents were in fact my legal guardians. Papa sent a copy of his will with me. I could fetch it if you like."

He breathed a laugh. "You are not leaving my sight, my darling, until we are on the *Falcon* and on our way home."

She paused and looked up at him. "Sir Arthur, you are the most sought-after bachelor in London. You could have your pick of beautiful, wealthy young ladies. Why in the world are you set on claiming one who is already wed to another? You do not love me; we both know you do not. You were enamored, and you felt a need to protect me. I appreciate that. But—"

Quick footsteps interrupted her seconds before the door opened and Gates slipped in, his breath still short. "I could not find him."

"Never mind him, then." Arthur straightened, silently wishing Scrubs Godspeed to wherever he intended to go.

"Yorrick will not be pleased."

"He can steal himself another Colonist to scrub his decks." He paced to the window again when another blast came from the fort. "We had better hurry. The Lanes could be back soon, and fighting may spread to the city. 'Twill be a difficult enough trip to Annapolis as it is."

Gates pulled his pistol out as well. "I will take her up to pack a bag. You—"

"I am not going with you." She said it so calmly, as if that alone would make it so. All the while scratching furiously with her pencil. Unable to resist, Arthur came back over to watch the progression of the drawing. Another couple was in it now, looking like the ones he had watched leave the house hours earlier—the Lanes.

Her uncle looked none too amused as he strode to her side and jerked her chin up. "Get up. Go pack. *Now.*"

Rebellion burned so bright in her features that Arthur began to understand what had fueled this collection of farmers and merchants toward uprising forty years earlier. "Or what, Uncle? Will you kill me? Your niece, your own flesh and blood?"

Before Arthur could do more than open his mouth with a warning, Gates had pulled his hand away. Fearing he would slap her, Arthur stood ready to leap to her aid, but no. He only gripped her hair and pulled her head back. No doubt with more force than he ought to have, but she made nary a whimper.

"I would never hurt you, Gwyneth." The words, spoken in a low pulse, were a strange combination with the fury in his eyes. "But I will kill each and every one of these ignorant Americans who have turned you against us. And I will begin with the Negro and child in the kitchen."

The flare of her nostrils was the only indicator of her emotion for many seconds. Until at last she closed her eyes and a tear slipped from her lashes. "Don't hurt them. Please."

Would he? Arthur wanted to think not. He wanted to think it as much a bluff as his own threats had been. But in that moment, he was none too sure.

Gates released her abruptly. "Get up and go pack your things. You will bring home every single thing you brought with you, and I mean *every* single thing."

She turned back to the paper and made a few more quick lines. "I cannot. I do not have it all anymore. I had to spend some of the coin—"

He cut her off with a blistering expletive. "I do not give a fig about the money, you stupid girl!"

The new lines turned into a wagon, one with strange apparatuses within. Roughly drawn, but precise. Then she dropped the pencil and stood. "Very well. If I have your word that you will not hurt them."

He didn't so much as blink. "If you behave yourself. If not, I promise I *will*."

Her burning gaze moved to Arthur. "Can I at least leave my husband that drawing, or will you take that from him too?"

Arthur glanced down again at the sketch. A whimsical image of herself, the man's parents with satchels in hand, a wagon. Hardly a farewell love letter, but if that was what she wanted to leave with him... He shrugged. "Have it your way."

⚜

Thad looked over the wall at the ships in the harbor, waiting for the next flash, the next boom, the next shell to fall upon them. His musket rested along with Arnaud's and Reggie's, its thirty-six rounds untouched. For far too long, the fort's massive guns had been as silent as their personal weapons, their major unwilling—wisely—to waste ammunition while the British vessels remained out of range.

Still. Inactivity pulled the tension taut.

Arnaud toed the unexploded ordinance that had landed a few hours earlier. Across it was scrawled, in black grease paint, *A present from the King of England.* "If we cannot do something soon—"

Another round came screaming toward them. Thad dove for cover, pulling Reggie and Arnaud with him. The walls at their back shook, dust went flying, and the groan of metal came a second before one of the 24-pounders crashed from its place to the ground.

Screams of agony filled the air.

Thad sprang to his feet, but Major Armistead charged forward before he could get to the area littered with men. "We need to evacuate the wounded! And remount this gun, quickly."

Lending his shoulder to the remounting effort, Thad kept an eye out for Arnaud and Reggie to return from transporting the injured. When Arnaud returned, he did so with shaking head. "Two dead. Clemms and Clagett."

"God rest their souls." Thad looked past him to Reggie and a young man. His eyes went wide. "Will! What are you doing here?"

Willis sidestepped another soldier and hurried to Thad's side. "I gave Gates and Hart the slip in the confusion coming into Baltimore."

His blood ran cold. "Baltimore?"

The lad's mouth set in a tight line, and he nodded.

"We have ships pulling within range again, Major!"

Armistead ran to the wall. "Bomb ships—they must have thought they did serious damage with that last one. Ready the guns, boys!"

A cheer went up from the men. Thad gripped Will's shoulder. "Tell me what they are planning."

The boy's Adam's apple bobbed. "To take your wife. Take her back to London while you are here and unable to protect her."

Thunder and turf. He dropped his hand and fisted it, but then he told himself to calm down. "She is with my parents. They will keep her safe."

"They left." He darted a glance toward Reggie. "That mulatto friend of Philly's came, and they all tore off toward her house."

Reggie's face went whiter than a sail. "The baby."

Willis shrugged. "I heard nothing. I just saw them leave, and then I took off myself. You need to get to her, Thad, fast."

"Ready!" Armistead shouted. "Fire!"

Their guns blazed and roared. Thad ran to the major. "Sir, I—"

"Lane, good. I am worried about our powder magazine. 'Tis nothing more than a brick shed. One lucky shot, and this whole place could go up."

He swallowed. "Sir, my wife is in danger—"

"All our wives are in danger if we do not repel these ships." The harried man met his gaze, new lines in his face and the weight of the city visible on his shoulders. "Distribute the barrels of gunpowder around the fort. Take all the men you need."

Thad turned away, aware of the many sets of eyes on him, waiting for his word. Aware of the men feeding the next rounds into the guns, of the shouts reporting where they had hit. Aware that if he disobeyed, it would undermine the fragile unity they had so carefully crafted.

To whom do you answer?

He heard the whisper in that corner of his spirit where the Lord always spoke. Heard it and felt a thrill. "You, Lord," he murmured under his breath. "Tell me to go. Tell me to save her."

But instead he felt that hand upon him, holding him in place. *Am I not able?*

The next round blasted from the guns and shook them. Shook him. Of course the Lord was able. He was able to protect the fort, the country, these men he called brothers and neighbors. He was able to repel the British.

Arnaud stepped in front of him, his brows, as always, drawn. "Thad?"

"We need to empty the magazine and distribute the gunpowder." The words came out strained, clipped.

His friend stepped nearer. "What about Gwyneth?"

Lord, what about Gwyneth?

A rumble of thunder crept across the sky. *Am I not able? Must it be you?*

He squeezed his eyes shut. *Lord, please, don't ask this of me. Ask me to do anything, to say anything, to go anywhere, but not to do nothing while my beloved needs me.*

Lightning flashed in the distance, a flicker compared to the muzzle flash from the British guns. *I knew her before she was in her mother's womb. I loved her before her lips could form My name. I called her beloved, just as I called you.*

"Thad?"

He couldn't speak, afraid that if he tried, he would choke on his words. But he strode toward the magazine. And he saw Gwyneth's eyes, frantic and terrified. *God!*

A return blast from the bomb ships, another quake through the fort's foundation. *Can you love her more than I? Can your hand save her better than the one that formed you?*

He lifted his hand to the door of the magazine. It trembled. "Will, Reggie, give me a hand. Alain, gather a few more men."

The room was large and dim, but he knew Armistead was right—the single layer of bricks between the shells and the three hundred barrels of gunpowder provided no real protection. He grasped the nearest one and rolled it out the door. *He has come for her, Lord. He has come and I am helpless.*

Reggie, his jaw ticking and worry in his eyes that went well beyond the screech of an incoming shell, took the barrel from him. *Philly.* Thad whispered a prayer for her as he caught his brother-in-law's gaze. "Reg?"

He swallowed. "There is nothing I can do there that I cannot do here. I will pray."

Thad released the barrel to him and turned back inside. *I know You can keep her safe, Lord. Keep us all safe. But I also know You do not always choose to. Like Peggy, like Alain for those terrible years. And I...I cannot bear if Your will is to take her from me. Please. Let me help.*

He rolled another barrel out. And the clouds must have parted, for a shaft of light angled through...the roof? He moved further in, to where the sun reflected off something metallic. Something long and shell shaped and taunting in its presence. "Ordinance." Panic pounced until he realized that if it were going to explode, it would have done so long ago.

The entire fort, all these men, could have—rightly *should have*—been destroyed already. The major's concerns ought to have been proven right in a fiery explosion.

But the Lord had preserved them.

You do not wrestle against flesh and blood, but against principalities, against powers, against the rulers of the darkness of this world. So how do you fight them?

Amid barrels of gunpowder and that one terrifying shell, he dropped to his knees. "I know You have it all in hand, Father God. I do. Us here, Gwyneth, Philly. But it is so difficult to practice what I believe. To give it all to You when I want so much to act."

Footsteps gathered outside. "We are ready, Thad."

'Twas as if the Lord chuckled in his ear. *Then act, my child. Where you have been placed. Do what you have been called to do. And trust Me.*

He touched a hand to the enormous shell and then rose. Much as he wished he could, he could not claim any unnatural peace. His heart still strained toward home, toward Gwyneth. The shot still whistled overhead, the noise still filled him till he feared he might burst.

But he rolled another barrel out, and he whispered a prayer.

When darkness fell and torrents of rain came, he hunkered down with his brothers and recited a prayer.

When the night refused to end and the British refused to halt their shelling, he led the men in the hymns that joined the deafening thunder as a prayer.

And when at last dawn broke and silence descended, he stood with the men again to see what was left of Fort McHenry. His gaze went up as morning light broke through the storm clouds, and he saw their flag fluttering in the wind.

They had survived. The fort still stood strong. They had made it. As Gwyneth had said they would. But what of her? He would come home, but where would she be?

"Look! Look!" Arnaud actually smiled as he peered out over the wall. "They are retreating!"

And into his spirit came the word for which he had been waiting all these long, sleepless hours.

Go.

Thad burst into his house, his heart out-galloping any speed Electra could ever achieve. "Gwyn? Gwyneth!"

But it was Mother who surged from the hall, tears in her eyes and everyone else close behind her. Everyone but the one he so desperately needed to see. "She is gone, Thaddeus. We just returned from Philly's. We were afraid to leave during the night. Rosie said Gates was here, that he took her. He threatened to kill Jack if she left the kitchen until morning."

"Where?" He spun to Rosie, whose red-rimmed eyes gleamed with apology.

She shook her head. "I don't know. I don't know. But he said he had men outside who would kill us if we went for help. I wanted to help her, but I had Jack—"

"You did the right thing." The only thing she could have done. He strode to her and planted a kiss on her cheek. Then put his arms around his mother. "We will find her. How is Philly?"

"There is hope, I think. 'Twas the fear that broke her, not pain as with the other times. Thaddeus, I am so sorry. We should not have left Gwyn."

"Had you not, they may not have stopped with the *threat* of violence." He pulled away and looked to Father. "Did she leave anything behind? Any clue?"

Father held out a sheet of paper with her familiar touch upon it.

His gaze devoured it line by line, curve by curve. Gwyneth's figure, her expression full of love and pleading and yet peace. And then his parents, ready to leave. Their wagon behind them with Father's laboratory equipment. As if...

As if they were going home.

"That's my girl." Pivoting on his heel, he flew back out the door.

Father ran after him. "Where are you going?"

His lips turned up as he sprinted toward the stable and Electra. "Annapolis."

Thirty-Four

Gwyneth blinked awake, amazed she had slept at all. She was lying on a couch in the parlor of Mrs. Mercer's Annapolis home, the same one she had fallen onto when they had finally made it here last night, drenched and shivering and exhausted from the harrowing journey over battlefield and through storm. She sat up and stretched, expecting sore muscles, a headache, something to tell of her night's travails.

All in all, she felt quite well.

A claim it didn't look like Uncle Gates or Sir Arthur could boast. The younger man sat hunched over in a chair, head on his hand in what seemed a fitful sleep. Her uncle stood at the window, his eyes ringed in shadows. When she stirred, he snapped around to face her.

"Are you feeling more reasonable this morning, niece?"

She smiled. Largely because she knew it would irritate him. "I am feeling quite reasonable indeed, Uncle. Because I have every confidence that Baltimore would have survived the night quite well, that Thad will come for me, and that justice will be done."

"Justice." He narrowed his eyes. "You sound like your father. Always so concerned with some heavenly justice."

"Thank you."

He looked fit to snarl as he strode her way, grabbed her by the arm, and yanked her to her feet. "Open your trunk. I believe your father packed something in there meant for me."

"No, I do not believe he did." She went where he shoved but sat upon the trunk rather than opening it.

His hand flashed and caught her across the cheek. "I said *open it*."

Sir Arthur jerked up, his eyes still bleary. "See here, what is all this?"

"Sit back down, Hart. 'Tis a family matter."

Instead, his hand settled at his side, where his pistol rested. "Did you strike her?"

"It doesn't matter." She spoke, not to Sir Arthur, but to her uncle. "I can open this trunk and take out every article of clothing and every drawing and letter. I can unpin the cloth and remove the false bottom. I can spill each coin upon the floor. But you will not find what you seek. All the evidence my father compiled against you is gone."

Granite overtook his features one by one. "What do you mean, *gone?*"

Was that what his face had looked like when he asked the same question of Papa? Had the hatred, the violence spewed so hot from his eyes? Had that been the moment when her father knew he would never join her?

Yet he had done the noble thing, the right thing. He had sacrificed himself to give her a chance to get away and to bring all that evidence with her so that someone else might achieve what he could not. So that someone might stop the monster before it devoured them all.

She drew in a breath far calmer than she had expected. "Just that. It is out of my hands and on its way to those who can put a stop to what you are doing before you destroy two nations in the name of avarice. The authorities here as well as those in London. The game, as they say, is up."

A cry tore through the room, guttural and animalistic. Light flashed on something metallic as he drew the blade from its sheath, the same blade she had seen him draw in the study five long months ago. And now that she was closer, she could see it was not just any sword, was not one he had brought with him that day.

It was Papa's.

She blinked away the tears. "You killed him with his *own* sword? And then you stole it?"

A wicked smile touched the corner of his lips. "I didn't have to steal it, you idiot girl. I merely had to ask Lord Fairchild after the funeral if I might keep it for you." He held it out so that the tip touched her chest. Right under the three pearls of her necklace. What was it Thad and Winter had said about them?

That they were a symbol for how God's path could be found in the most unlikely of places.

She could think of no less likely a place than this. *God of my end, You have brought us back to the beginning. Your will be done.*

"You were there." Her uncle shook his head, a low, menacing chuckle in his throat. "I wondered, when Sir Arthur said you tore from the house as you did. And you are too much your father's daughter to be bargained with. So I am very sorry, my dear. Very sorry indeed. But I have no choice."

Gwyneth gripped the trunk and closed her eyes. She could pray nothing but *Father!*

A shot, and then another shattered the single pulse of silence, so shocking that she jumped and slid and landed in a heap on the floor. Her breath came in gasping heaves, her hands did a quick investigation of her limbs, but she felt no pain. No injury. Which meant— She scrambled up enough to glimpse her uncle on the floor and then sat again.

She had had enough of violence. This was a sight she had no desire to behold. But from here she could see the smoke coming from both the end of Sir Arthur's pistol and, in the doorway, Mr. Mercer's.

Arthur glanced to the newcomer. "I thought you were fleeing to Virginia."

Mercer tucked his gun back into his belt and advanced into the room. Heading straight for Gwyneth, he pulled her up. "Are you well, cousin?"

She may not have been, had he not made a point of blocking her view. But she nodded.

He offered a tight smile. "I had a feeling my father would not take you peaceably back to England. And I had a feeling, too, that you and

Thad would have already contacted the authorities. I plan to flee farther away than Virginia and had to stop here first."

Arthur lowered his arm but didn't put the pistol away. "Then I suggest you hurry."

"And leave my cousin with you? I think not. I'll see her safely back to her husband first."

Gwyneth wrapped her arms around her middle. Unlikely paths, indeed. Who would have thought that Mercer, of all people, would end up her champion?

Though from the way Arthur's face crumpled, he was no threat. Not anymore. "I am sorry." It came out no more than a whisper. "I never meant— He swore you would not be harmed, that taking you home was best, and I...I ought to have known better. I will submit myself to your authorities here."

Gwyneth loosed a long breath. "Go home, Arthur."

He shook his head and rubbed at a temple. "I assisted in kidnapping you."

True. And yet he had done so believing she had been mistreated and had come to begin with in fear for her life. Then he had been rewarded with her scorn. She shook her head. "You came here to save me. And you *did* save me, just now. Please. Go home. Live your life and be happy. As I am."

"Gwyn?" Thad's voice came in a muffled shout from the street outside. Seeking and eager and so very precious.

Gwyneth took a step forward, but Mr. Mercer stopped her with a raised hand. "Allow me." He disappeared into the hallway.

She looked to Arthur once more. "I say it again, sir—go."

Though he hesitated, at length he gave a nod. "I wish you all happiness, Gwyneth. If you are certain it is to be found here—"

There was commotion at the front door, Mercer's voice, and Thad's in a low threat. She smiled and moved toward the door. "Thad!"

A moment later she was in his arms, and his hands were running over her hair, her shoulders, as if checking for injury. His eyes, when she tipped her head back to look into them, were ablaze. "Are you well? If they so much as..." he halted as he glanced over her shoulder at where her uncle lay. "Gwyn."

"I am fine, darling." She held him tight, praying her smile conveyed the truth of that. "Sir Arthur and Mr. Mercer both intervened when Uncle Gates's intentions became clear."

He angled her toward the door. Then he paused and regarded first Sir Arthur and then Mr. Mercer. "There are no words to thank you."

"Letting me leave will be thanks enough." Her cousin took a step away but halted and sighed. "I thought it was only about the money. Even so, you will say I ought not have done business as I did. But know that I never intended to harm my country. Whatever else you believe about me, believe that."

Thad, his arm now snug around Gwyneth's waist, made no response for a long moment. "You were feeding him information. All these years you provided him exactly what he needed to undermine us. And now you think to tell me you meant no harm?"

Mercer shook his head. "Call me a fool if you like. I did not realize— He was my father. I thought his interest simply that. Interest. In my life, my world, my business. I did not...perhaps I should have seen his hatred for us. If I had, I would have sealed my lips. I certainly would not have let him use me to divide my own nation."

Thad measured him, staring at him as if peeling away the layers until he could see his motives, see his heart. She felt it when her husband relaxed. "I suppose you proved your loyalties just now. I will not stop you from leaving, but that is all you will get from me. If you linger, I will not intervene with the authorities."

Mercer cleared his throat and motioned behind them. "I'll take her trunk out first, shall I? So you needn't go over there."

Gwyneth slid to the side, out of the way, smiling when Sir Arthur stepped nearer.

His hand extended but then fell to his side. "Mr. Lane, I...I too must beg your forgiveness. I would never have harmed her, but I could not accept— My thoughts concerning you were not gracious."

Thad, in typical form, snorted a laugh. "If we are apologizing for thoughts, then I must beg forgiveness of you as well. I confess I had a few sour ones from the very first mention of your name."

"Unfortunately, mine were followed by actions." His head hanging low, Sir Arthur drew in a deep breath. "Gwy—Mrs. Lane said I ought to leave as planned. But at your word I will submit myself to your authorities."

"My authorities will be busy enough, I think." With a glance over his shoulder, Thad urged her to follow Mr. Mercer out the door. "I will explain this to them in simplified terms. You should listen to my wife."

Gwyneth paused to see his response to that. Sir Arthur's face looked tormented. "Are you certain?"

"Certain that I would have done much the same to find her and bring her home, yes. Sir Arthur." Thad shifted in that way he had, the one she had learned accompanied his intuitions. "There is more than what you think. To life, to love. More within you than for what you give yourself credit."

One corner of Sir Arthur's lips moved up. He put his hat on, slowly and with more care than it called for. "I suppose we shall see, sir. Good day. Best wishes."

"Godspeed." Gwyneth stepped aside so he could pass and then wove her fingers through Thad's. "I suppose we had better call for those authorities."

"Sorry, sweet. I know you want to get home."

"So I do." She wrapped her arms around him again and let her eyes slide shut. "And now I am."

Home, exactly where she wanted to be. In the arms of her beloved.

Epilogue

December 20, 1860
Forty-six years later

T had waited until the dancing was boisterous enough that no one would notice as he slipped away. Not far, not as far as he would have liked. Just into Jack's library, right beside the ballroom. Where the music was just enough muted, where the lights were just enough dimmed. Where the world was just enough away. He moved over to the window that looked out on a skiff of fresh-fallen snow.

And he sighed.

He heard the sound of Gwyn's slippers on the rug behind him, which brought a smile as it always did. Still, he sighed again as her arms slipped around his waist.

"What are you doing in here, my love? Marietta will want to dance with her granddad on her wedding day."

His arms settled into their habitual place around her. "I know. I needed a few minutes."

"You knew it was coming." Her hand rubbed a circle on his back, but it couldn't bring much comfort. Not yet. Not when the fracture was so new.

"I know. I had hoped, I had prayed...but there is no way around it now, sweet. Other states will follow South Carolina. The South will all have seceded in a matter of months. War is coming again."

Now she was the one who sighed. "We are too old for all of this."

"Speak for yourself, woman. I'm as spry as ever." He straightened his spine in proof and decided *not* to look around for a chair to perch on. Instead, he tilted her face up with a finger under her chin and studied it in the moonlight. There were wrinkles now, to be sure. Each one earned from years of living well, loving always. And the same beautiful smile. The same fathomless Caribbean eyes. "You are lovelier than ever, Mrs. Lane."

"And you more handsome, but that is not my point, as well you know." She lifted up on her toes and pulled him down enough to brush a quiet kiss over his lips. "I know you. I know you will rouse the Culpers from their slumber. But you cannot be the one out scouting anymore, riding thither and yon to meet with anyone who might have information. Your place is where the congressman's once was. Behind a desk."

Blasted things, desks. "I know. But the question of who else to bring in…"

They turned together back to the door that she had left cracked open to the ballroom. Thad looked out to see all the most treasured people in his world. Jack, dancing with their Julie and smiling down at her in the same way he had since she was born when he was five—with total adoration. He could ask more of Jack, but he already had his place in the Ring and in the navy besides. Out on the waves that Thad so rarely ventured onto anymore. Each of their boys had his place too, doing what they could.

"Are you certain you need anyone else?"

"I am certain." He pressed a kiss to the top of her head. "We have a different kind of enemy this time around, sweet, one that will stretch our resources to the breaking point."

"What kind?" Worry saturated her tone, and her fingers twitched against him. When they got home, she would head straight for her ever-faithful *secretaire* and its fresh stacks of paper.

Thad watched the colorful twirl of dancers, hooped skirts swishing and swaying as his nieces and daughters and granddaughters, his neighbors and friends all celebrated with them. His gaze fell on Marietta. The youngest of Jack and Julie's children, and the most exasperating.

The one with the most potential yet with the most determination to ignore it. Perhaps that was why she was his favorite.

She was more beautiful than she ought to be in her white silk, with her scarlet curls arranged just so. And that too-practiced smile aimed, now, at her new husband's brother.

He sighed. "Hez's intuition was right. A secret society is operating for the South and placed all through the country, all with a Southern agenda." He had yet to voice their name, afraid he might be wrong. But the invisible ink had revealed it to him just that morning, minutes before he read in the papers that South Carolina had seceded.

The Knights of the Golden Circle.

Gwyn shook her head. Not, he knew, in denial. But in a wish that it wasn't so. "And you think to undermine them?"

"I cannot think how else to reunite our country but to quiet those who sow division."

"How will we find them, Thad?"

His gaze followed Mari as her groom swept her up in a dance. As Lucien Hughes, too handsome, too charming, laughed with his precious granddaughter. Thad's fingers curled into his palm. "I think, sweet, that they just found us."

Discussion Questions

1. When Gwyneth witnesses the horrors of the first chapter, she responds by obeying her father but at the cost of her mental and physical health. How would you have reacted? Would you have fled as he commanded or stayed and sought justice?

2. Thad has an intuition, an attuning to the Spirit, that often leads him to the place he needs to go at a specific time. Have you ever known anyone who seems to do this? Have you ever heard the whisper of the Spirit leading you in this way?

3. Who is your favorite character and why?

4. Family plays an important role for the characters in *Whispers from the Shadows*, both in how they support us and how they can hinder us. Which aspects best encompass your own family experiences?

5. Gwyneth works through the trauma of her father's murder by drawing and painting. What do you do to deal with stressors? What did you think of her method?

6. Thad tells Gwyneth that "we are all broken." In what way is that true of each of the characters? How is it true for you?

7. Do you think Thad did the right thing in marrying Peggy? Why or why not?

8. Rosie helps Gwyneth see that she has put her trust and found her rest in a fallible man rather than our infallible God. Have you ever relied too much on a person? Who, and in what way? What was the outcome?

9. Sir Arthur's decisions take him from a would-be hero to a villain's accomplice throughout the book. How are you left feeling about him? How did your opinions change over the course of the book? What do you think of Mercer's opposite change?

10. The salvation of the United States came when an entire city rallied together, unified, and stood firm against their enemy, though in the years prior they had been languid and more concerned with their individual goods than the nation's. How does that parallel the country today? What can we learn from them?

Author's Note

When I first researched the Culper Ring, America's original and most trusted spy ring, I was intrigued not only by the tight-knit, secretive group who survived because they were all friends and family, but also by the possibility of their secret continuation after the Revolution. When I read that Benjamin Tallmadge, the head of the ring during the War of Independence, was a congressman during the War of 1812, the wheels in my head began spinning. How could the man who organized intelligence during the Revolution *not* have a hand in it when war was declared again?

History records that most of America's intelligence gathering during this second war with England was courtesy of the privateer fleet that wreaked havoc upon the British vessels. Whenever they saw something of interest, they got word back to Washington. Yet again, a network of friends...and so I had to ask, "What if they were organized by the Culpers?" I needed a hero capable of gathering information from sailors far and wide, and so the personable Thaddeus Lane was created.

Where in *Ring of Secrets* the featured tool of espionage was invisible ink, I was excited to add into this story the cutout paper called either a "mask" or "grille." The British were actually using this method as early as the Revolution, but Americans hadn't yet gotten their hands on it. I just loved, though, how this visual tool wove seamlessly into my visually inclined heroine, who was already subconsciously hiding messages in her artwork. Such fun!

I once again drew on the Puritan prayers from *Valley of Vision: A*

Collection of Puritan Prayers and Devotions compiled by Arthur Bennett, which are the ones supposedly copied from a text by Grandfather Reeves.

My primary research book for this one was *The Battle for Baltimore 1814* by Joseph A. Whitehorne, in which he combined traditional with original research to paint a picture of the little-known war in the Chesapeake region. I was dumbfounded by how the politicians in Washington all but ignored the advancing British for two years; I cackled in delight (being from Maryland and West Virginia) at how the hot, humid summer did more to repel the soldiers weary from Europe than the troops did; and I was touched to the core when Baltimore won their pivotal battle by doing what the nation had been unable to do for the two years prior—put politics and daily life aside, and unite with a single focus.

The British admiralty really did decide to attack Baltimore because of misinformation about the preparedness of the city, including a newspaper article in the Baltimore paper that grossly understated their efforts—how could that *not* have been intentional? Combined with that, the British had a basic misunderstanding of the American spirit. They thought our signals were signs of panic and that they could defeat us by burning our capital, never considering it would make everyone spitting mad and, for the first time, united.

My descriptions of the bombardment of Fort McHenry are taken from firsthand accounts, including the unexploded ordinance that landed in the ammunition magazine. Mere hours in, Cochrane knew he had made a mistake, one made all the more clear when Ross was killed in the land battle. Disheartened and exhausted, the British soon withdrew from the Chesapeake and, after the American victory at New Orleans, from the country early in 1815.

But even in its early days, America had a growing rift between slaveholding and non-slaveholding states, one observed from its very founding. I made sure to plant the seeds of concern in *Whispers from the Shadows* because the next adventure of the Culpers is going to put them in a position they never anticipated—smack between the Knights of the Golden Circle, who reportedly buried Confederate gold, and a Pinkerton investigator determined to infiltrate them.

Can you see me rubbing my hands together in delight?

About the Author

Roseanna M. White grew up in the mountains of West Virginia, the beauty of which inspired her to begin writing as soon as she learned to pair subjects with verbs. She spent her middle and high school days penning novels in class, and her love of books took her to a school renowned for them. After graduating from St. John's College in Annapolis, Maryland, she and her husband moved back to the Maryland side of the same mountains they equate with home. Roseanna is the author of two biblical novels as well as several American historical romances. She is the senior reviewer at the Christian Review of Books, which she and her husband founded, the senior editor at WhiteFire Publishing, and a member of ACFW, HisWriters, and Colonial American Christian Writers.

Roseanna loves little more than talking to her readers! You can reach her at: roseanna@roseannawhite.com

Be sure to visit her blog at www.RoseannaMWhite.blogspot.com and her website at www.RoseannaMWhite.com, where you can sign up for her newsletter to receive news about upcoming books.

Love Has No Place in a World of Spies

1779—Winter Reeves is an aristocratic American Patriot forced to hide her heart amid the British Loyalists of the city of New York. She has learned to keep her ears open so she can pass information on British movements to Robbie Townsend, her childhood friend, and his spy ring. If she's caught, she will be executed for espionage, but she prays the Lord's protection will sustain her, and Robbie has taught her the tools of the trade—the wonders of invisible ink, secret drop locations and, most importantly, a good cover.

Bennet Lane returns to New York from his Yale professorship with one goal: to find General Washington's spy hidden among the ranks of the city's elite. Searching for a wife was supposed to be nothing more than a convenient cover story for his mission, but when he meets Winter, with her too-intelligent eyes in her too-blank face, he finds a mystery that can't be ignored.

Both are determined to prevail at any cost...and each is committed to a separate cause. Will God lead them to a shared destiny or lives lived apart?